MEGIDDO

MEGIDDO

Derek Kartun

CENTURY

LONDON MELBOURNE AUCKLAND JOHANNESBURG

For Theodora

First published in Great Britain in 1987 by
Century Hutchinson Ltd
Brookmount House, 62–65 Chandos Place
London WC2N 4NW

Century Hutchinson South Africa (Pty) Ltd
PO Box 337, Bergvlei, 2012 South Africa

Century Hutchinson Australia Pty Ltd
PO Box 496, 16–22 Church Street, Hawthorn
Victoria 3122, Australia

Century Hutchinson New Zealand Ltd
PO Box 40–086, Glenfield, Auckland 10
New Zealand

ISBN 0 7126 1407 9

Printed in Great Britain by
Redwood Burn Limited, Trowbridge, Wiltshire

Chapter 1

The autoroute du Nord runs dead straight south south-west past Charles de Gaulle airport and down towards Paris, curving westward as it passes the corner of the old airport at Le Bourget. Thence it slices its way through the industrial suburb of St Denis, turning due south for the run into Paris at the Porte de la Chapelle. From the interchange at Le Blanc-Mesnil which gathers in the traffic from Le Bourget to the gates of Paris is nine kilometres. Here you can observe if you wish some of the fiercest driving to be found anywhere in Europe as the taxis from the airports jostle for advantage with the long-haul traffic from the Channel ports and the industrial north.

The man standing on the bridge which carries local traffic over the autoroute at Le Blanc-Mesnil had been there for over two hours, and now it was close to five in the afternoon and the intense heat of the June day had not lessened since noon. The man wore a loose jacket over workman's denims. He had not moved at all from his position, leaning on the parapet, facing south, his eyes fixed on the slip road taking the south-bound traffic from Le Bourget up on to the motorway. On the parapet before him was a Japanese transceiver, the short aerial extended, the power switched on. Beneath him, the traffic thundered down towards Paris, and now the rush-hour exodus in the opposite direction had started. Neither the fumes and racket from below nor the blazing heat from above appeared to bother the man. He was dark and squat. He could be from anywhere in North Africa or the Middle East. In fact he was from nowhere. His

1

parents had lived in Hebron and had fled. He had been stateless in a camp in Syria for the whole of his twenty-two years. He called himself a Palestinian but he had no country.

The cars were tailing back along the slip road, waiting their chance to infiltrate the stream from further north. The Paris Air Show was in its third day at Le Bourget. Every few moments a car would accelerate out of the slip road and join the race towards Paris. This was the process which held the attention of the man on the bridge.

At six minutes past five the transceiver crackled into life and the man lifted it to his ear.

'The car has been called on the loudspeaker system. Over.'

The man flicked the switch on the control panel.

'Message received. Over.'

Four minutes later, just before five ten, the voice came in again. The language was Arabic.

'They're in the car now – the three of them and the French official. The outriders are in position – two riding ahead as before. Officials are talking to the driver . . . Now they're off. Exit from the airport parking area is clear. Only intermittent traffic on the road beyond. Over.'

The switch was flicked back.

'Message received. Calling Ahmed. Come in.'

There was a pause, then a lighter voice.

'Ahmed here. What's the news?'

'Did you pick up all that from the airport? Over.'

'No. Distance too great.'

'The car has just left Le Bourget with two motorcycle outriders. The same as the outward journey this morning. They'll be caught in a tailback here. It may be a few minutes before I signal they're on the motorway.'

But the police outriders had decided to jump the queue on the slip road, leading the official limousine on to the verge and up to the edge of the autoroute, their sirens screaming, white crash helmets and gauntlets gleaming in the sun.

'Ahmed, they're about to join the main road. Do you hear me? Over.'

'I hear you.'

'Remember, seven kilometres to the boys. Probable speed a hundred, giving just over four minutes. Now they've joined

2

the traffic and they're off, travelling towards you. Time five thirteen and forty seconds. Over.'

'Message received.'

The transceivers had been modified to shift the signals away from the wavelengths used by the traffic police along the motorway and by the gendarmerie in the area. Despite the precaution, a radio ham idly twiddling the knobs of his set in a modest apartment half a kilometre to the west had heard the exchange between the airport and the man on the bridge and thought it odd. But understanding no Arabic, what he had to say to the police later proved of no value whatever.

The man on the bridge closed down his transceiver and sauntered to the far side where he had chained a motorbike. He made off in the direction of Drancy and the eastern suburbs of Paris. His job was done for the day. He was looking forward to a beer.

The big Citroën had bullet-proof glass and the side panels had been reinforced with sheets of 5-mm steel plate. It was not an adequately armoured vehicle: the bonnet had no protection and nor had the roof. But during the Air Show, with its heavy demands on security, it was all that the transport division of the Ministry of the Interior had been willing to provide. There were six potentates of one complexion or another in Paris on that day and the ministry's four fully armoured cars had been allocated elsewhere by the police, leaving the Israeli deputy minister of defence to make do with the token improvements to the Citroën. The Israeli embassy had been told that it was safe against automatic fire though it was not.

He sat now in the back of the car, on the left behind the driver. His name was General Mordechai Giron. Next to him sat Professor Gideon Avigad, Israel's foremost aircraft designer and technical director of Israel Aircraft Industries. On the professor's right was a young attaché from the Israeli embassy named Harel who was also doing duty as a body-guard. He carried a pistol in a shoulder holster. In front, next to the driver from the ministry pool, sat a lieutenant from the protocol department of the French Ministry of Defence. His job was to tend to the minor needs of the

3

visitors and get them safely back to the embassy and ultimately to their El Al flight on the following day. France was
interested in selling military aircraft to Israel. The lieutenant
was pleasantly conscious of the importance of his role in the
scheme of things. And exceeding the speed limit under the
protection of police sirens was not unpleasant. He was not
yet twenty-four and such things still appealed.

After turning due south in the heart of St Denis, the autoroute sinks below ground level, running through a built-up
area in a kind of gully carved down the middle of a wide
boulevard. At ground level local streets are carried across on
bridges. On one of these, the Avenue de Pressence, stood
the man Ahmed. He too was dressed as a workman. His
transceiver was slung round his neck, the mike just below
his mouth. On the next bridge, carrying the Rue du Landy,
two men similarly equipped were waiting. An unmarked
delivery van was drawn up by the kerb in the centre of the
bridge, the sliding door open. There was a third man at the
wheel.

The Groupe Anti-Terroriste attached to the presidency had
asked the police for special measures during the Air Show,
including patrols along the motorway and police lookouts
on the bridges. The Préfecture had obliged on the first two
days but, unaccountably, had redeployed the men on the
third day, leaving the bridges unguarded. No amount of
investigative journalism or official inquiries succeeded, after
the event, in tracing the source of the changes in the police
order of the day. 'Was there a certain police complicity?'
asked *Le Figaro* in the eliptical style favoured in such
instances by the French press. The question was to remain
unanswered.

Immediately after receiving the message from the north,
Ahmed turned to face south towards the two men on the
next bridge some 200 metres away.

'Car is on the motorway, travelling south. No traffic hold-
ups that we can see. Two outriders. Should reach you at
eighteen minutes past, maybe a bit before. Over.'

'Message received.'

'Good luck. I'll call you up when they come into view.
Remember, that gives you about ten seconds. Then I'll signal

4

again as they pass under me. That's just over six seconds from you. Maybe five if they're moving faster. Got it? Over.'

'Got it.'

'Good luck.'

He was hoping the transceiver looked like a radio. No one paid any attention. In the canyon below him the roar of the traffic descending on Paris was deafening. The northward-bound lanes were almost as busy now.

The radio ham over to the west had lost interest in the guttural dialogue and had closed down.

There was no shade on the bridge. Ahmed was dripping with sweat, consumed by thirst and desperate to go to the lavatory. Commando life seemed to him like one prolonged discomfort with precious little excitement to compensate for the hours of boredom and waiting. He would have preferred to be with the boys on the next bridge but the decision had been taken: two guns only. They'd chosen the best marksmen. Hitting a car coming towards you at a hundred or more, even with a couple of 9-mm Rexims, and hitting it both above and below the windscreen in order to get past the toughened glass, would take steady nerve, high-grade marksmanship and a hell of a lot of luck. Getting away afterwards should be dead easy. There were special arrangements. So they had been told.

Three of the scheduled four minutes had passed. Ahmed kept his gaze on the endless stream of cars racing towards him. Three lanes, all full. Some weaving from lane to lane as cars overtook the twenty-tonners. He was listening now for the howl of the motorcycle sirens.

'Don't rely on hearing them,' he'd been told in the briefing that morning. 'They may switch off, so use your eyes. And keep your voice steady. The boys have to stay calm, so don't try to excite them.'

He felt his own heart racing. Something over half a minute to go. Why couldn't he hear them? Maybe they weren't using their sirens after all. A bit surprising; the motorcycle cops loved blasting their way through the traffic. The unholy din was part of it.

At twenty seconds he thought he could hear the wailing in the distance, out of sight up the autoroute. Or was it a plane taking off from one of the airports? No, it was police sirens. It looked as though their calculations were sound: a hundred an hour, just over four minutes' driving on the motorway.

He flicked the switch on the transceiver. 'Siren heard. Not in sight yet. Hold it . . . I can see 'em. They're travelling in the fast lane. Repeat, the fast lane. Looks like ten metres between the bikes and the car. Traffic getting out of their way. They're nearly on me . . . say four seconds . . . *now!*'

He hadn't been able to keep the excitement out of his voice as the cops and official car swept under him and on towards the Landy bridge. But he'd got the timing right. And now he'd hear the Rexims.

Resisting the urge to stay and watch, he turned towards the eastern side of the bridge. As he did so, the chattering sound from the two sub-machine guns reached him, immediately followed by screaming brakes and the repeated crunch of metal and echoing thuds as speeding cars piled into each other and bounced against the concrete retaining walls.

General Giron had been talking quietly in Hebrew to the professor. He couldn't be sure that the French lieutenant did not understand the language.

'I thought Dassault Breguet were interesting. But I don't think they'll look at a licensing deal. They made it pretty clear, they want to sell airframes.'

'I liked the specification of the Jaguar.'

'That's a matter for you. But if we do a deal, it has to be French. That's political. You can forget that British plane.'

They were approaching the Avenue de Pressence bridge and neither of them had any reason to notice the man leaning on the parapet and watching the traffic. Then they were under the bridge and racing the 200 metres towards the bridge at the Rue du Landy.

The lieutenant had turned round to speak to his distinguished guests.

'It was an interesting show, gentlemen?'

'Very.'

'Is there anything we can do for you this evening?'

*

6

The thing had been nicely calculated. On hearing Ahmed's 'I can see 'em', the two men had crossed the narrow pavement to the van. One had reached in and lifted out the two guns. Each was loosely covered in brown paper. As Ahmed shouted 'Now!' they had calmly moved back to the parapet, pulling the paper off as they went. For a couple of seconds they were standing in a Paris street, each with a Swiss Rexim-Favor 9-mm sub-machine gun, oblivious to passers-by – the street customs of Beirut come briefly to the French capital. Then the short barrels of the guns were poked over the parapet, diagonally down towards the traffic below.

It took the official car two seconds to come within the gunsights. There would be no more than a tenth of a second of firing time before the angle spoiled. In that time the car would have travelled 2.7 metres. One of the men would aim at the windscreen and top of the car, the other at the bonnet. At the guns' firing rate of 600 rounds per minute, each of them reckoned to get five rounds into the car in the allotted firing time as they dipped the guns to keep the speeding car in their sights. Each gun had twenty rounds in its box magazine. There was no room at all for error.

'One good, steady burst will be worth more than a botched effort at keeping the vehicle in firing range for a longer time,' the armourer had said. 'If you get ten rounds into the car between you you're bound to hit one of the bastards. The crash will probably do for the rest of them anyway.'

The boys had grumbled about the unfamiliar weapons, with their solid wooden butts making them conspicuous. 'They're Swiss and they're accurate and they don't jam,' the armourer said. 'The Russian crap spreads bullets all over the landscape. We've modified the flip sights from a hundred metres to forty. Unless your hands are shaking like a couple of women you can't miss the target.'

The guns had reached Paris in the Libyan bag a couple of weeks earlier.

The lieutenant in the front of the car was not destined to get a reply to his offer of official assistance that evening. Six bullets hit the car at the moment he finished his sentence. The aim had been good. In the back seat, the young attaché Harel was killed outright as a bullet smashed through his temple into the brain and lodged in the sphenoid bone at the base of the skull.

Next to him Professor Avigad was hit in the chest, the bullet piercing the subclavian artery and lodging in the spine. He was to die an hour later in intensive care at the Hôpital Claude Bernard. The other three occupants of the car were untouched by the firing, but one shot hit the windscreen, which crazed over as the driver lost control of the steering and slammed his foot down on the brake. The car went into a sideways skid and veered to the right into the path of a Mercedes travelling at over a hundred and thirty. In the crash that followed and which involved eleven vehicles in all, the driver and the lieutenant were flung against the windscreen and suffered severe head and face injuries. Neither had been wearing a seat belt. The minister was thrust forward and sideways, hitting his head against the doorframe and breaking his neck. It was a commando operation of absolute elegance and efficiency.

The two men on the bridge flung their weapons into the van, piling in after them. The man at the wheel then pulled away from the kerb and, following instructions, drove at normal traffic speed westwards along the Rue du Landy towards the river. After 300 metres or so the van turned left into a side street and the three men got out. One of them was carrying the guns under his arm. They got into a grey Renault and calmly drove off, turning south into Paris at the busy Porte de Clichy. From there it was only ten minutes' drive to the safe house, which was not a house but a bleak apartment over a Halal butcher's shop, the proprietor of which was an eminently respectable citizen unacquainted with guns. And now they would be heroes. They were grinning foolishly at each other like a bunch of truants from school. One of them was cursing the fact that he had soiled himself. It was nerves. Always after an action it was like this. Later there would be plenty of drinking. Alcohol had been banned for the past forty-eight hours. With luck there would be women too.

At ten that night a letter was delivered to the offices of the

AFP news agency in the Place de la Bourse. It was addressed to the news editor:

The action today on the autoroute du Nord was carried out in the name of the oppressed peoples of Palestine as a reminder to the Zionists and their equally criminal French associates that we will not allow our demands to be ignored. The criminal General Giron and his accomplice Avigad are in France to buy light bombers. They are interested in the Mirage IIIE and the Jaguar. They saw models of British Aerospace and looked at American equipment. All this we know. Also that discussions with Pelletier of the Jewish criminal Dassault organization lasted for one hour. We pose the question: why do the Zionists want bombers? Why do they express interest in the *range* of bombers? Is not the so-called state of Israel only 450 kms in length? On whom do they wish to drop their bombs? And what bombs? Atomic bombs?

We have punished these war criminals in the name of Islam and the Arab revolution. We will punish more of them. And we have carried out our action in France as a warning to their French collaborators. The loss of French lives today must be taken as a token of our determination. More will be lost.

Long live the Arab revolution!
Chatila

The text of the message went out on the AFP wire at ten fifteen, followed by a piece from the foreign desk speculating about the threat of further action against the French and drawing the attention of editors to the fact that a group calling itself Chatila had killed the Israeli ambassador to West Germany in Bonn at the end of April. Apart from which, nothing whatever was known about them.

Chapter 2

The meeting was not going well. In part, the intractable subject matter was to blame; in part, it was the poor chemistry engendered by the personalities of the three men seated round a low table bearing bottles of mineral water, glasses of the finest crystal and ashtrays loaded with cigarette butts. The convenor of the meeting, one Vallat, chef de cabinet to the President of the Republic, sat upright in a Louis XV armchair, a man of daunting formality, frigid and seemingly without anything as fallible as an emotion. It was said in the offices of the Elysée that no one had ever seen him smile until the occasion when, sorely tried by British prime ministerial nagging, the president had remarked that whereas the time had been when large parts of the map had been coloured red to denote British imperial might, the extensive red on the map nowadays denoted something very different and perhaps the prime minister might consider taking this unfortunate fact into account. Vallat had smiled briefly and had not been seen to smile again.

His devotion to the interests of his master the president was equalled only by his sense of loyalty to that most potent and bewitching of mistresses, La France. To work with him was like fondling a hedgehog.

To Vallat's left sat Colonel Duparc, appointed head of the Groupe Anti-Terroriste by the president himself, who had been acting on what turned out to be misleading information. The colonel would prove to be a man of infinite personal vanity and deep incompetence.

To the right of Vallat sat Georges Wavre, head of the

DST,* his great bulk scarcely contained in his chair, his many chins sunk down into the creases of his shirt collar, perspiration beading on the top of his head. He detested these meetings at the Presidency as much for their content as for their form, which was quite inadequate for a man of his build. The chairs were too fragile and the ashtray on the table was to be reached only with difficulty. Now he was stubbing out the latest in an unbroken procession of cigarettes, having lit a fresh one from its end.

It was three days since the outrage on the autoroute du Nord, which was the meeting's subject matter. The proceedings had barely gone beyond the initial formalities and already the going was getting rough.

'The president sees it primarily as an attack on French security,' Vallat said. 'He is demanding swift action.'

'Presidents in my experience always demand swift action.' Wavre grunted the words through a cloud of smoke.

'I repeat, monsieur, swift action.'

'Then why is the prefect of police not at the meeting? He knows more about all this than we do.'

'My men, on the other hand,' Colonel Duparc said, 'are fully engaged.'

'The president determined the composition of the meeting. Your men may be fully engaged but the president has had no results of the engagement reported to him.'

'Can we hear what has been achieved so far?' Wavre said.

'We found their safe house in the Rue des Moines. The police interrogated the neighbours and made a list of the contents. My service obtained a copy. Here.' Duparc handed over two sheets of paper. Wavre glanced at the crudely typed report.

'The descriptions are useless without physical identification. Too vague.' He read on. 'We learn here that they ate bratwurst, pils, Coca-Cola and halva. It doesn't take us very far. Also, there's nothing about prints. No serious forensic

---

*Direction de la Sécurité du Territoire, the French counter-intelligence service, roughly equivalent to the British MI5 and the US FBI. The DST heads to the minister of the interior and its writ does not extend beyond the soil of France.

work.' He looked up at Vallat. The growl was scarcely audible. 'Tell me, is it also the view of the president that the police have no interest in finding these people?'

Vallat nodded, expressionless.

'Or even – ' Wavre was not allowed to finish the question.

'The president's instructions are that the DST is to take charge of the investigation, with particular reference to the threats of further action against France.'

'Are we investigating the curious behaviour of the police while we're about it?'

'We are not.'

'And the withdrawal of the patrols along the motorway; are we not interested in that?'

Vallat shook his head.

'Who tipped off the police about the gang's safe house?'

'There was a police informer living opposite. The comings and goings made him suspicious so he told the local cops. They reported it.'

'And all those details in the terrorists' message to AFP?'

'We checked that,' Duparc said. 'A Libyan delegation had been talking to Dassault on the same day. The information probably came from them.'

'Anything from the frontier police?'

'Nothing useful. You can check directly, of course.'

'You will realize,' Vallat said sourly, 'that press reports of Israeli indignation are, for once, an underestimation. Fury would be a more accurate description. Their prime minister has been abrasive. Substantial contracts are at risk.'

There was a pause. 'I don't want it,' Wavre said. 'We're overburdened just now. Do you know there are forty-seven new diplomatic arrivals from the Eastern bloc since January? My men are fully stretched and anyway credits are running out.'

'I am instructed to talk to the minister about further credits if they are needed. As for whether you want it or not, my instructions are clear: the DST is to take charge of the task of neutralizing the Chatila group, whoever they are. And Duparc here is to provide extra resources as required.'

Wavre looked quizzically at the colonel. 'I will need,' he

said, 'more effective co-operation than you saw fit to provide in the Ben Afri case.'

'I have nothing with which to reproach myself in that regard.'

Colonel Duparc was what Alfred Baum, Wavre's deputy, described as a verbalizer. 'He will talk,' he said of the colonel, 'but he will not perform. For him, the word is the event. Also, he is bone stupid. And jealous.' It was Baum who would have to deal with Duparc, Wavre reflected. And even Baum would get nothing out of him.

Later, down the street at the DST headquarters in the Rue des Saussaies, Wavre sat gloomily in his charmless and barren office, gazing steadily at the figure of Alfred Baum seated on the far side of his desk. The two men had shared the meagre information from Vallat's meeting, commiserating with each other over the high-handed methods of the president and the impossibility of ever getting on top of the department's work load.

'You will have to take this one yourself, Alfred,' Wavre said. 'It is rotten with politics. A no-win situation.'

'Allembeau could do it.'

'Yourself.'

'I have the East German business.'

'I am not interested for the present in the East Germans.'

'I thought you would say that.'

'Give the East Germans to Allembeau. He speaks the language. Also, he hates all Germans. It qualifies him.'

Alfred Baum managed to sigh with the whole of his considerable bulk. Like Wavre, he was a heavily built man. It was said in the department that between them they weighed as much as a fair-sized horse. But whereas Wavre's style was gruff and deeply pessimistic, there was invariably a touch of humour in Baum's shrewd eyes, set deep behind bushy brows. It surprised those who knew him that an exterior so redolent of good living and a kind of Gallic bonhomie could harbour such an acute intelligence allied to a persistence which his hard-pressed staff regarded as obsessional.

Also, Baum was an acknowledged expert on, and profound lover of, cats. 'You can learn from a good cat,' he had been

13

heard to say. What it was that could be learned from a cat he did not choose to reveal. It could have been patience.

'What will you do, Alfred?' Wavre asked. He did not expect an answer of any genuine relevance, but he liked to ask the question whenever Baum was about to embark on a new *affaire*. It confirmed in an acceptable way that he, after all, was the boss. Having run this flag up the yardarm he was content that the enemy should be engaged without further intervention from him.

'I have no idea.' It was Baum's invariable reply. The familiar ritual was being played out between them. 'I will talk to Ben Tov. We also have contacts of an ethnic type here in Paris. It may throw something up. I don't know.'

'Do we know anything of this Chatila group?'

Baum shrugged. It could be taken as a negative.

'Your friend Ben Tov will tell us something?'

A nod. Then a long silence. The two men looked at each other.

'*Ah, merde alors!*' Baum said as he heaved himself out of the chair and made for the door, passing on the way the statutory portrait of the President of the Republic, looking for swift action. He was still muttering gentle imprecations as he reached his own equally charmless office on the floor below. He had been telling Georges Wavre less than the truth – something he did not like doing. But heads of departments had to be protected from the political risks attaching to accurate knowledge of what their departments were up to.

In fact, Shayeh Ben Tov had been the one to call Alfred Baum. At home in Versailles the telephone had interrupted his dinner on the evening of the shooting. It was his colleague Commander Allembeau.

'Your friend asks you to call him.'

'Thanks.'

That was all. The troublesome procedure had been worked out between them some months earlier when Baum had finally established that some obscure service of the French intelligence community had a tap on his phone. It suited him to take no action in order not to drive these unknown persons to more ingenious methods. Allembeau he trusted unreservedly; him and Wavre. With everyone else he was cautious.

'I must go out,' he told his wife.

'Finish the cassoulet. It took me a long time.'

'And delicious it is, too. But I have to phone. Keep it warm for me.'

Madame Baum, whose honeymoon had been interrupted by the office after only two days, had long since adjusted herself to the exigencies of the case. She shrugged, smiled, removed the plate and placed it in the oven.

'Be quick.'

'I shall rush back to you and your delicious cassoulet.'

'And I shall be waiting for you.'

They liked to exchange gallantries in this fashion.

In the phone booth of one of the nearby cafés that he used for the purpose, Baum dialled ten digits. As the call felt its way through the international exchanges to the Israeli capital, he swung the door of the booth back and forth, trying to get some air into the cabin. But the proximity of the badly plumbed toilet made the exercise counter-productive.

'Yes?' The voice was clipped, impatient in the Israeli mode.

'Foreign friend here.'

'Shalom.' If shalom could be made to sound more like a complaint than a greeting, this voice could achieve such a feat.

'You wanted me.'

'This wretched business this afternoon. I have had a report. Why the hell wasn't the car properly armoured? We had a promise from your people at Foreign Affairs?'

'There are people here who follow alternative policies.'

'And where were the police?'

'I don't know.'

'But a member of our government, for God's sake! And Professor Avigad who is a *truly* useful person. They'll shoot me at dawn.'

'I'm sorry.'

'No one says it's the fault of your department.'

'We played no part in it. I'm sorry.'

'Will you meet me tomorrow?'

'Of course.'

'Where we met last time. If we meet in France everyone will know it within twenty-four hours. I can be at the other place by three.'

'So can I.'

'Oh, and a favour, please. Bring me some Riclés, will you? My wife is waging another war on my smoking habits. Shalom.'

'Shalom.'

Upstairs at the bar Baum paid for the call and six small round boxes of aniseed pastilles which he slipped into a pocket. On the way back to his apartment through the hot streets he kept his mind on the cassoulet and the cheese to follow. There would be time and to spare for other matters tomorrow.

Later he told Allembeau on the phone that the East German business would take him to Vienna on the early plane in the morning. He spent a few moments giving, for the benefit of anyone who might still be awake on the listening desk, a fictional but persuasive account of what he might achieve there in the endless struggle against the troublesome intelligence services of the DDR.

Chapter 3

The apartment where they met was in a turning off the Neulinggasse. It was leased from the landlord by a Frau Schwartz who worked in the box office at the Opera. The rent was met each quarter by a gentleman friend on the understanding that discreet meetings might be held there from time to time. Frau Schwartz, who was in love with the gentleman and frequently short of money, was happy with the arrangement and understood intuitively that it would end abruptly were she to tell anyone about it. Perhaps they were business meetings of a dubious type.

And here it should be explained that Shayeh Ben Tov was head of Arab Affairs at the Mossad* and that the Mossad had enjoyed close and affectionate relations with the DST since the heady days when French policy had been vigorously, even a shade unwisely, pro-Israeli. Those days may have gone for ever but institutions and those who man them sometimes cling to outmoded positions, old loyalties, even old friends. So it was between Alfred Baum and Ben Tov, forty-six-year-old native-born Israeli from Nahariya in Israel's far north, hard man, heavy smoker trying to break the habit, a lover of France but barred from visiting that country by the security rules of his own department.

Frau Schwartz being at her work, the two men had the depressing apartment, loaded with polished oak and swathed in velvet, to themselves. Ben Tov had turned on the radio and kept it on throughout their conversation. He had taken

*The Central Institute for Intelligence and Special Missions.

17

the six boxes of Riclés without offering to pay for them, though he had snapped '*merci*'. He had not thanked Baum for flying over 800 kilometres and back to meet him. He knew Baum would not have come unless he thought the meeting might be fruitful for both of them.

'Today in Jerusalem,' he said, 'the Memuneh* will be having his testicles chewed off by the prime minister, the minister of defence, the secretary to the cabinet, and I daresay his wife and family. Not to mention the media.'

'And will all this anger spill over on to you?'

Ben Tov made a gesture of contempt, dismissal.

'I am not interested in these political tantrums. One question only interests me at present: why was that car not fully armoured? Why were we misled on that point? Who in Paris is helping our enemies with these provocations? And why were there no police on the bridge?'

'Your questions are rhetorical?'

'Of course. If you knew you would have told me already.'

A slow smile spread over Baum's chubby features. 'Don't be absurd. I do not reveal state secrets.'

'You do not know.'

'I do not know. Nor is my department involved. On that you have my word.'

'Who will conduct the investigation?'

'The police, ably assisted by the president's Groupe Anti-Terroriste. A formidable combination.'

'That may not frighten Chatila but it certainly frightens me.' He helped himself to a pastille and did not smile. 'We must work together on this, you and I, my dear Alfred.'

'But what can I do?'

Ben Tov did not answer. He rose from his chair, stepped to the window and looked gloomily out over the grey slate roofs of Vienna towards the elegant dome of the Karlskirche. Then, without turning to face Baum: 'I have a man in Chatila. High up. He must be protected. That is why we cannot abort their plans. We knew they would try against the minister, though I personally think they had a greater interest in the professor, being sophisticated people with a

*The head of the Mossad

clear sense of purpose. Anyway, we knew. Our man said an attack with automatic weapons, between Paris and Le Bourget.'

He started pacing back and forth on the parquet, his steps sounding heavily.

'I simply dared not act openly on it. I did what I could, short as I say of aborting the thing, which could have exposed our man. He is already suspected as a result of my stupidity. They targeted our ambassador in Athens last year and we took precautions. Because they have good security only our man and two others knew the plan of action. He thinks Hanif suspects him and is likely to lay a trap. So now I have to choose: do I keep him there or act on his information?'

'We have a dossier on Professor Hanif.'

'He runs Chatila,' Ben Tov said.

'I know.' Baum paused. 'Your minister of defence and a key scientist in the balance against an agent.' His voice rose scarcely above a murmur. 'And you chose the agent?' It was a delicate moment. 'None of my business, of course.'

'Do you imagine,' Ben Tov snapped, 'that I would accept that equation if there were not other considerations?' Again a silence. The heavy footsteps echoed in the room and rattled the ill-fitting windows. Behind them, Lehar in a reach-me-down medley on the radio. Baum immobile, a portly sphinx, on a sofa upholstered in a vulgar brocade.

'If I regard my man as more important than a minister – any minister – it is because this group Chatila is not like other terrorist groups. The Bonn attack, this thing in Paris, they would be ultimate objectives, great triumphs, for Black September or any of the other hit squads. But for Chatila, I tell you, they are a mere diversion, a smokescreen.'

'Some smoke,' Baum said, almost to himself.

'Everything, my friend, is relative. In peacetime a single violent death is newsworthy. In wartime it's nothing – a bore. Who counts the dead any longer in Beirut? I tell you, Alfred, what these people aim at could give us nostalgia for the days when we only lost one minister at a time.' He paused, expected Baum to demand an explanation. But there was only silence from the sofa at the end of the room. 'Or so I believe,' he added. Then: 'God help me, I may of course

19

be wrong.' It was the point at which, had he been a Catholic, he would have crossed himself.

'Do you want to tell me why you have to take such risks?'

'I have not even told the Memuneh.'

'Do you have to carry such burdens on your own?'

'You talk like my wife. I didn't come to Vienna to listen to my wife.'

Israelis, Baum said to himself, are prickly, like cacti. Didn't Sabra, the term for the native-born, mean something of the kind? 'You must be hell to work with, Shayeh.'

'So they tell me.'

'And how much longer do you intend to live with this dilemma of yours?'

'No longer. It is not to be endured. The pressure on my agent must now be relieved and your help is needed. I have a plan.'

'I repeat, what can I do?'

Standing once more at the window, this time with his back to the city in whose doss houses the drifter who later called himself Hitler had nursed his savage resentments and peopled his fantasies with predatory Jews with hooked noses, Ben Tov told Alfred Baum what he could do and why. 'You will see,' he concluded, 'that all this will be in the interests of France, indeed of everyone else, and not only of my country.'

Baum nodded and said nothing. There was no expression on his face and his eyes were halfclosed. A forefinger tapped on his knee, roughly in time with the polka coming from the radio. 'Also,' Ben Tov was saying, 'you will find yourself in much the same situation as I: unable to bring your colleagues into your confidence because a leak, any leak, can alert these people.'

'Quite.'

A tapped telephone. An armoured automobile which is not armoured. Police patrols shifted on the third day. And a report on a safe house which would have failed any student at the police college. No doubt Ben Tov had his problems too, though they were more likely to be political; the petty jealousies, the paranoia, the tribal excesses of Israeli politics some forty years into the life of the state. Growing pains, national adolescence? Or something endemic in the strip of fertile coastal land – the deadly dangerous highway between the Near East and North Africa – which had been fought over and soaked in blood for 2000 years and more?

'They are the only truly frightening opponents we have ever had,' Ben Tov was saying. 'Habash, the Salamehs, Nidal even – they are nothing when compared with Professor Hanif. Not because he is more intelligent, though he is that. No, it is because Hanif, unlike the others, *has thought this thing through*.' He beat his fist into his palm with each word. 'You don't destroy states by shooting ambassadors, blowing up school buses. You destroy states very simply: by physically destroying them. It is the only way it can be done. Everything else, as you French say, *c'est du cinéma*. Hanif is that most dangerous of political animals, a man who has read history. His discipline is archaeology. All those shards and broken pediments will have given a man of his type an utter contempt for what exists *now*. These dentists and civil engineers turned politicians who run the PLO and its terrorist offshoots – they will kill, certainly, but within a context.' He was pacing back and forth again, hands in his trouser pockets, head sunk low, the steadiness of his voice a kind of counterpoint to the jovial noises from the radio. 'That context is simple: they want to capture our cities and have something to use, to enjoy, for their pains. With Hanif I believe it is different. He is the only true destroyer we confront. I doubt whether he regards a hundred years as more than a moment of time. For him, Jerusalem, Nazareth, Jaffa in ashes would be a matter of indifference, since he has no plans to live there or govern from there or do anything more constructive than drive us out. Another Tamburlaine.'

He paused, like an actor preparing to deliver his exit line. 'These damned pills you brought are disgusting. Give me a cigarette.'

Chapter 4

The villa stood amid cypresses and eucalyptus in one of
the best residential streets of the Syrian capital. It was less
substantial than its neighbours but substantial enough. It
had been built in the fifties for a socially mobile grain
merchant from the south who had moved into the heroin
trade and, hence, into an altogether more imposing establishment. Now there was only one incongruous fact associated
with this respectable bourgeois residence: at the gate stood
two languid youths in worn and frayed denims, khaki shirts
and desert boots. Each had an automatic rifle slung across
his chest, with bandolier slanting diagonally and grenades
dangling at his belt. They were relaxed but they had the alert
and shifting gaze of street fighters.

A taxi drew up fifty yards away and an overweight man
alighted, passed over some money and started to walk
towards the villa. He carried his bulk awkwardly in the
afternoon sun, hitching his army fatigues up around his belly
as he moved. When he reached the entrance gate to the villa's
garden he nodded to the youths, exchanged a brief greeting,
and passed through as one of the young men held the gate
open. It closed behind him with a metallic crash and his
footsteps could be heard crunching the gravel within.

'Anyone else?' The young man asked the question as if he
had no interest in the answer.

'Essat will come,' his companion said. 'We're to stop any
others.'

'Is the old man in there then?'

'It's none of your business, is it?'

There was a brief grin. 'Suppose not.'

The man they called Essat, riding a moped, had approached the villa from the same direction as the big man's taxi and had parked and chained his machine a few yards away. Now he strode vigorously towards the gate and stopped to crack a joke with one of the guards. He was maybe thirty or less, a good-looking, athletic young man with a mop of dark curly hair and the macho moustache much favoured by the Palestinian fighters. His unzipped bomber jacket failed to hide the heavy pistol at his belt.

When he had gone through the gate and his footsteps on the gravel had ended at the villa's steps, the youngsters outside settled back in the shade of the nearest tree.

This was at about the time Shayeh Ben Tov was telling Alfred Baum in Vienna exactly what it was that he wanted him to do.

'You will please give us your report,' Professor Hanif was saying. He looked at the big man, who went by the name of Saad Hayek, sitting uncomfortably on a low stool, his fat legs extended awkwardly. He had not shaved since the day before and he looked exhausted, the small eyes bloodshot, the sparse greying hair straggling forward over his forehead. He had looked very different the previous evening at passport control at Charles de Gaulle airport as the cop had glanced at the mug shot in the Egyptian passport and up at the well-dressed Egyptian businessman with his briefcase and plastic bag of off-duty stuff. Shahid Ansari, merchant. The cop had stamped the passport, slapped it back on to the ledge and waved Mr Ansari through with the flick of a finger, bored out of his mind. This morning Saad had taken an onward flight in Geneva. He had arrived in Damascus, gone to his room, changed into more comfortable gear and come straight to Hanif's, according to instructions. He usually did not shave for some days after an action. He had never asked himself why.

'It went well,' he said. 'We had the necessary co-operation. The boys were OK. But they had to get out of the apartment.'

'Why?'

'Someone must have thought it odd, the sudden to-and-fro, seeing so many of them. I suppose they reported it. But it was OK – we got a tip-off.'

'And without the tip-off?'

The big man shrugged. 'Trouble, I suppose.' He paused and fidgeted on the stool. 'I think it was chance. There's always the odd nosy-parker to be reckoned with.'

'I am not a great believer in chance when it favours the other side. We don't call it chance when something favours us. We say good planning has enabled us to take advantage of opportunities. What do you say to that?'

'I accept that. But the boys did well. They hit the target.' He looked uncomfortable.

'What do you say to that?' Hanif had turned his head slightly and now looked steadily at the younger man, Essat. The gaze was direct and difficult to deal with.

The man who called himself Essat reached into a pocket for cigarettes, thought better of it, tried to return the stare and only partly succeeded.

'Yes, well, I suppose the Paris police have their stool pigeons perching all over the quarters where Arabs live. It could happen – one department not aware of what another department's up to.'

'I disagree.'

Essat shrugged. He longed for a cigarette. The other man shifted again on his stool. The silence was broken by the sound of typewriter keys from a room above.

'We will take note of this matter.' It looked as if Professor Hanif had decided to store in his mind what he seemed to regard as a breach of security. He turned again to Saad.

'You will return to Paris tomorrow. Make new security arrangements for crossing the frontiers. Rasmia has my instructions.'

'A change of plans, then?'

'Let us say a tightening of the time-scale. Also, I have decided that Rome is to be right away.' He turned back to Essat. 'You will go with Rasmia. She will organize your passports. She is upstairs. Go to her now.'

'Very good, chief. What will it be in Rome?'

'You will learn in good time. Rasmia is waiting for you.'

As the young man got to his feet, the professor raised a

hand to stop his companion doing likewise. 'I want a further word with you. Stay there.'

The big man settled back on his stool as the younger man left the room, closing the door carefully behind him. But instead of mounting the stairs to the upper floor, he turned down a short corridor, entered the toilet and locked himself in. Then he took from an inner pocket of his denims a miniaturized transistor receiver the size of a twenty-pack. As he switched it on, voices could be heard on the pre-selected frequency. He held the receiver against his ear, keeping the volume low.

'I come back to the Athens business. Only the four of us knew.' It was the professor's voice from the neighbouring room. 'You had not yet briefed the commando.'

'Of course not. You had forbidden it.'

'Very well, so how does it come about that whereas the ambassador had for the past year always left his home for the embassy between eight and eight thirty, he suddenly becomes eccentric in his timing: nine, seven thirty, eight forty-five?'

'I do not know.'

'And suddenly, too, he has a new driver. A different type of man altogether. The other wore glasses. This one does not. It might indicate that he is a better shot.'

'It might.'

'So I repeat: only four of us knew. I do not gossip. In our four years I have not known you to gossip. So who is it to be?'

'I do not think Rasmia talks to anyone. A very silent girl. And she has no friends.'

'But there appears to have been a leak. And now we lose our safe house in Paris.'

'You think?'

'I think we are not secure. I have said it before.'

'I never talk — never. I swear.'

'And Essat?'

'I have to say it: there is something . . . not right.'

'What?'

'I do not know what it is. An eagerness?'

'We are all eager in the cause.'

25

'He is inquisitive.'

'You yourself ask questions.'

There was a brief silence, the radio picking up background as something was moved on the desk. The man called Essat was suddenly aware of the painful beating of his heart and the dull drumming of blood in his ears.

'All I can say, chief, is that I have this hunch.'

'What are you saying, indiscretion?'

'Perhaps more. It would not astonish me.'

Another pause. He suddenly realized that he could not hold the receiver steady against his ear. The trembling of his hand could not be controlled.

'This mission you are sending him on . . .'

'I know what I am doing.'

'Of course.'

'Also, your own mission to France is not entirely as I described it. I want you to establish a contact there for me. A Major Savary at the DGSE* and through him a man named Tavernet.'

'Does that mean . . . ?'

'I will tell you what is required before you go.'

'Very good, chief.'

'And don't write the names down. You will have a chance to memorize them.'

'Yes, chief.'

'I will only tell you this. Your mission is part of a plan which I consider decisive in our struggle. It is the one action which can change the map of Palestine. You will speak to no one.'

'Very good.'

'My precautions in all this are necessary because the French DST is in the pocket of the Zionists and they must not know of your presence in Paris. You will therefore act as if you were on hostile territory despite the fact that we have good friends there. That is all.'

The eavesdropper switched off the receiver, slipped it back into his pocket, flushed the toilet and made for the stairs.

*Direction Générale de la Sécurité Extérieure. Corresponds to the British MI6 and the US CIA.

He was halfway up to the first floor as the door of the professor's room was opening below.

The girl was from Armenia, where Turks, Greeks and others have mingled their blood over the centuries to produce arresting physical types and an implacable national sentiment, the stronger for its very ethnic impurities. She had come at eighteen to study at the American University in Beirut armed with her beauty, a high intelligence and that almost savage nationalism that is both the hope and the curse of beleaguered minorities. Contact in Beirut with students from Palestine, Syria and Iran inflamed with nationalist and revolutionary anger had widened her sympathies from the fate of her own people, with their age-old quarrel with Turks and Russians, to that of all such peoples. Her subjects, archaeology and ancient history, had underpinned her politics – had given her an intellectual framework within which her passion could flourish, find a form, a justification and a direction. Her mentor and hero had been Professor Javed Hanif, professor of archaeology at the university. She had become what she herself called a revolutionary, what the Turks called a seditious nationalist, the Russians a bourgeois nationalist, and the Israelis an Arab terrorist, though she was no Arab. She had taken the *nom de guerre* of Rasmia Burnawi, and when, after the massacre in the Chatila camp in 1982 the professor had told her that the time had come to put aside her books and master instead the mechanism of the Kalashnikov, she had followed him to Damascus, had taken part in commandos and had made the Palestinian cause her own cause. The theory of the indivisibility of the national liberation movements had that symmetry, logic, transcendent beauty of form that all absolutists seek, and eventually find in the muzzles of their guns. Put another way, it was the domino theory: defeat American imperialism here and it will be weakened there. Smash America's ally the Israeli and her ally the Turk is thereby weakened. A bomb in Londonderry is echoed by the grenade tossed at the Israeli ambassador's car in Bonn. This was the logic. It had all the seductive appeal of the universal, unifying system.

27

She had not been deterred by the shift in Palestinian strategy in the early eighties from international terror to political action. The armed struggles of the sixties and seventies, the professor had told her, had served their purpose but were essentially the achievements of an immature movement – sporadic, ill-coordinated and at the mercy of certain psychopathic personalities among the leaders. The Munich games, Lod, Athens airport, the killing of Wasfi Tell in the Sheraton lobby in Cairo, which had started it all – none of these heroics could any longer serve as a model. The martyrs – Abu Youssef, Kamel Adwan, the Salamehs and many more – were there to inspire the young men of the commandos. But the commandos themselves, with their operations in Europe and the Middle East, were an anachronism, though the young men were not to know as much. Israel would not be eliminated by blowing its ambassadors to bits, any more than it could be by rhetoric at the United Nations. He told her these things though he told them to no one else, because he sensed in her a kindred spirit, steeled in hatred and fortified by courage, and because he intended to make of her his chosen, closest associate. This is what he would talk to her about as they met in the cafés of West Beirut to which he used to take her late in the evenings. And she, mesmerized by the soft, hypnotic, commanding voice, would accept his apocalyptic version of history and accept, at the same time, his increasing dominance over her.

What then? she ventured to ask. If political action could serve no purpose and the gun could not win back the Palestinian lands, what then? What was the Chatila group – a charade? It was no charade; the time would come, he said, when she had proven herself, that he would be able to show her how Chatila would do what the PLO and Black September had failed to do. She must have faith in him, he said. Chatila's armed actions would continue: his young men would not stay with him unless he let them loose from time to time. But the true purpose of Chatila lay elsewhere.

Now she sat at a typewriter on a battered desk in a bedroom which had been converted to serve as an office. There were grey metal filing cabinets, piles of books and pamphlets on the floor, and in a corner a table with an ancient duplicating machine. Against a wall bearing posters depicting Arab heroes and Israeli grotesques embraced by Uncle Sam and John Bull stood a squat safe, painted dark green. A wooden crate with Czech markings stood unopened against a further wall.

'You and I are to travel,' Essat said.

'I know. I am preparing the money and the passports.'

'The boss told you, then?'

'The professor told me last night. We will travel next week – to Rome.'

'You know more than I know.'

'It is possible.'

'What can I do?'

'Nothing until I give you your passport. It will be Iraqi. I will have the same.'

'You're a smart girl.'

'I am comrade Rasmia. It has nothing to do with smart girls.'

'Sorry.'

At that moment there was a call from below. 'Rasmia, a minute please.' It was Professor Hanif's voice. The girl left the desk and went out to the landing. Essat took the few paces needed to reach the safe and crouched in front of it. He could hear Rasmia's voice as she answered the professor from the landing.

A brass plate had been welded to the centre of the safe's door. Essat strained to decipher the text and numerals embossed on it:

Coffre-fort Dejazet   Société Anonyme
14 Rue Feydeau
And beneath that:
Modèle Azure
No. A773810

He was back in his original position, trying to imprint the details, and particularly the number, on his mind as Rasmia returned to her desk.

'So, that's it, then,' he said lamely.

'That's it.'

She turned back to the papers on the desk before her,

29

allowing her heavy black hair to fall forward over her shoulders, hiding the oval of her face.

'Goodbye,' he said. 'I will come to see you again tomorrow.'

'It won't be necessary. I will contact you in the usual way.'

He left the room, descended the stairs and walked past the door of the professor's study. He could hear voices within. Then he went out to the street, unchained his moped and made off towards the centre of the city. As he went, he glanced carefully behind him and at one point doubled back for a short distance. Satisfied with the outcome of these manoeuvres, he continued across the city and into the area of the soukhs and so on to the great Omayyad mosque. Here he chained his moped and made his way across the courtyard, the pigeons rising lazily before him and settling again as he passed. At the entrance to the huge edifice he abandoned his shoes and edged into the coolness of the dim interior. There was the usual bustle of visitors, students pacing to and fro as they tried to memorize their lessons, children in awed crocodiles headed by their teachers, and the worshippers, mostly gathered in an untidy group around the mihrab in the centre. Leaning against the massive pillars were others like him, who had come in out of the sun to rest awhile, no thought of prayer in their heads.

He sauntered slowly towards the busiest end, that which is nearest to the soukh al Hamidieh. Here, merchants were hurrying through, taking a short cut between al Hamidieh and the gold merchants' soukh. Children and old men stood around with nothing to do. Some sat on the ground, leaning half asleep against the walls, or squatted in twos or threes, chatting. From time to time the mosque attendant would shake a sleeping figure, enjoining respect for the holy place. Where voices were raised angrily in some domestic dispute he would hiss at the disputants and shoo them away. Essat watched as the attendant – an old man in a faded galabiyeh, barefoot, unshaven and exuding fussy irritation – worked his way round towards him until he reached a group of children whose laughter appeared to strike him as inappropriately shrill.

30

'There is no longer any respect,' Essat said as the man passed.

'That is so.'

He stopped for a moment, close to Essat but looking away from him.

'You will radio tonight without fail,' Essat said. 'Listen carefully.'

'I am listening. Keep your voice down.'

'The fat one, Saad Hayek, is to return to Paris at once to fix up a contact. Now, note the name: he is to see a Major Savary of the DGSE to be put in touch with a man named Tavernet. The professor wants a meeting with Tavernet. Now I will repeat the names.'

He did so. The old man appeared not to be listening.

'Did you get the names – Savary, Tavernet?'

'I got them.'

'The professor has talked of a decisive action which will change the map of Palestine. Those are his words. They must be reported verbatim, right?'

'A decisive action which will change the map of Palestine.'

'Also I am to leave for Rome with the girl. There will be an action but I do not know what it is.'

The old man was eyeing a group of youths who were jostling each other. Essat took a slip of paper from his pocket. On it were written the details of the safe, including the number.

'I shall drop this paper on the floor and you will pick it up in a moment. It gives some names and a number. Transmit them, please. They will be understood.'

He creased the paper in his hand and dropped it behind him.

'Is that all?'

'There is more, and this is very important. I overheard the professor and Saad Hayek talking. I am suspected. Hayek is convinced I am not what I seem. You will say I believe the situation is very dangerous for me. Something must be done. I await instructions.'

The old man nodded briefly.

'That is all. I will be here each day at the al-maghreb. It is the safest arrangement: I am known as a religious man.

31

If I do not come on two successive days you will inform Centre.'

'Very well.'

The old man shuffled past Essat and shook his head as he retrieved the paper, cursing the untidiness of worshippers. Then he moved off towards the noisy group of youngsters. Essat walked slowly over to the mihrab as the muezzin sounded, and there he delivered himself ostentatiously to prayer, invoking the blessing of Allah: there is no God but God and Mohammed is the Prophet of God . . .

Chapter 5

The Committee for Security and Foreign Affairs is the highest committee of the Israeli government, ranking immediately below the cabinet itself. It has permanent members, of which the most important are the prime minister and ministers of defence and foreign affairs, the heads of the Mossad, the Shin Beth and Military Intelligence, and the secretary to the cabinet. Others are called in as required. The committee meets when the prime minister so decides. It discusses the ultimate issues – war and peace and the security of the state. Some of its decisions are referred to cabinet for approval. Some are too sensitive.

The Shin Beth is the Israeli equivalent of the American FBI or British MI5. Its remit is internal security. The Mossad is responsible for Israel's external intelligence and contacts with certain friendly governments abroad. This is its avowed responsibility. Unavowed is the armed struggle against the hostile states and groupings with which Israel is surrounded. The Mossad at times has spent its main energies on covert operations, with or without the participation of Israel's regular forces. At times it has pursued its war by other means: the traditional techniques of espionage, the running of agents in post, the infiltration of hostile Arab organizations, the gathering of information from the services of friendly countries or, in certain cases, from the friendly services of unfriendly countries.

The Mossad has four avowed departments and a number which are not admitted to. The four are the Evaluation

33

Department, Special Operations, Co-ordination with Foreign Services, and Arab Affairs.

At the urgent request of the Memuneh, the head of the Mossad, the secretary to the cabinet had convened a meeting of the Committee for Security and Foreign Affairs for midday. Whereas the committee would usually meet at the prime minister's office or in the Ministry of Defence, on this occasion it was convened for good and sufficient reasons in the cabinet room in the basement of the Knesset, the Israeli parliament. This was because a cabinet meeting was scheduled there for one thirty and, earlier, a delegation from the US Senate had to be cajoled, charmed and on certain matters misled, over coffee on the first floor at eleven. It had been difficult to persuade the prime minister – an excessively irritable man who had never come to terms with the fact that outside events might intrude on the arrangements already enshrined in his diary – that the meeting was urgent enough to merit squeezing it in in this unseemly fashion. The cabinet secretary had not had an easy time of it.

'I have arranged for you to attend,' the Memuneh had told Shayeh Ben Tov. 'The old man is bound to tell us we're talking rot and I don't see why he shouldn't tell you to your face.'

'It isn't rot.'

'Have I said it is?'

When the prime minister bustled into the room, resentful and impatient, the others were already assembled round the long polished table. They rose politely as he crossed the floor to his chair at the table head, and sat again as he himself sat down. Then he glared morosely round at his colleagues. He had not had an easy time with the Americans. He turned to the cabinet secretary, seated at his right hand. 'What is all this, Uri?'

'The Memuneh will report, prime minister.'

'The Paris business?'

'In a sense, yes.'

'What does that mean? Paris, yes or no?'

'Not *about* Paris, but related to Paris.'

The prime minister grunted. 'Paris comes up in cabinet. It

34

has aspects which concern our trade people. I do not propose to cover the same ground twice.'

'No, prime minister.'

'So what has the Memuneh got to tell us?'

The Memuneh's predecessor had had a certain flamboyance about him, inherited from his days as a tank commander. His temperament and what he had learned at the Tank School in the Judean Hills had overflowed into his management style and thence into the operations of the Mossad. Whereas such a style lent itself well enough to the kind of covert operations much favoured by the Arab Affairs section, it none the less had a down side. He had lost more agents than was deemed reasonable and his teams had hit more than their quota of innocent persons. Such cases of mistaken identity or untidy marksmanship had become embarrassing to the government, who had moved this ebullient character sideways into the general staff, replacing him by an infinitely cautious administrator from the army's planning office. Once the new incumbent had got his feet under his desk at the Mossad's office – and he was very much a desk man – he had developed a thesis which came to be known as The Idea. He had distilled this thesis of his down, in an elegant example of reductionism, to two words only: plausible deniability (or so his colleagues thought: in fact he had stolen the phrase from that centre of the lexicographer's art, the CIA). But plausible deniability was a neat enough phrase and soon became a way of life. The Mossad was always to conduct itself in such a fashion that whatever it did that could not be defended under the harsh light of publicity should be deniable, and that the denial should be plausible: plausible deniability. Neat, but tending to produce a certain constipation in a department which was created in order to take unavowable risks. The Idea was unpopular. Ben Tov was not the least of its critics.

Now the Memuneh adjusted his rimless spectacles on his nose, ran a hand over the top of his head as if there were hair there to be flattened, coughed, fidgeted in his seat and peered carefully at a single sheet of paper before him. On the paper, in neurotically tidy handwriting, were four words, one beneath the other, numbered from 1 to 4.

'We have reliable information that the extremist Arab group Chatila which is supported by the Syrians and operates out of Damascus is about to make contact with a person in the DGSE in Paris. We have grounds for believing that a major action against Israel is being planned with the co-operation of certain French elements. This Chatila group is in our opinion the most irreconcilable and also the most efficient of the terrorist groupings. They have claimed the Paris outrage, as you will know, and also Bonn.'

'So why are you bringing this to the committee?' The prime minister was going to be difficult.

'Chatila talks of a decisive action. The phrase "change the map of Palestine" has been reported to us. We must consider such words in the light of earlier reports that the man Hanif who leads Chatila has close links with Gadafi.' The Memuneh paused. 'I put it to the committee: Is not a link with Libya and a claim to change the map a sinister combination?'

'Is that all?'

'Such a juxtaposition seems to us to merit careful appraisal.'

'So please don't waste our time: appraise.' The prime minister was going to be impossible.

'Ben Tov here will give our view, prime minister.'

'We will not minute this,' the prime minister said. The secretary to the cabinet, who had been taking notes, laid his ballpoint next to his notepad.

'We have a man within group Chatila,' Ben Tov said. He had regarded the slaughter at the Chatila and Sabra refugee camps in 1982 as shining examples of the political stupidity of the army. The morality of the government's handling of the thing had not appealed to him either. He announced the name of the group now with a certain grim satisfaction. No one's expression changed. He went on. 'We now have to take exceptional action to preserve this man's cover, and indeed his life, since we have no intention of withdrawing him. If these people are going to develop ambitions which stretch to some decisive action against us in co-operation with Gadafi we must at all costs maintain our surveillance.

36

This is, for the moment, our prime concern. There are others.'

He had the prime minister's attention. He paused, playing upon it.

'What others?'

'We have all seen the paper produced jointly by Army Intelligence and our own services on the progress of the work at the Libyan nuclear facility at Tukrah. The latest update sets eight to twelve months for delivery of a Libyan weapon. This committee's appreciation, I believe, is that Gadafi will not use such a weapon. But he may be willing for someone else to do so. Chatila could well be such an agent for the Libyans. Or again, Chatila may have independent ambitions, centred on some French source. That is our second consideration.'

'How many of these considerations of yours are there?'

'There are four, prime minister.'

'So?'

'We respectfully suggest that the time has come when the Americans might be prevailed upon to issue a suitable warning to Gadafi.'

The prime minister turned to the foreign secretary. 'You heard what this man said?'

'I heard. We will take it under consideration.'

'Is such a course feasible?'

'Feasible, yes. Productive, I am doubtful. The best way to persuade Gadafi to drop a bomb is to advise him against dropping a bomb. And there is a better way than best. That is to threaten him. But I will take it under consideration.'

There was little enough love lost between the prime minister and his foreign secretary. 'I will want a paper by tomorrow morning. A brief paper, Chaim. Not one of your endless on-the-one-hand-on-the-other-hand papers.'

A number of discreet smiles appeared briefly round the table.

'Very well. But there are aspects. The Americans lack finesse in such matters.'

'And where is finesse bought nowadays?'

'The British?'

'A way to kill Gadafi. He would die laughing.'

A polite titter from the others.

'We have the Tukrah problem under study in the joint committee,' the secretary to the cabinet said. 'The feeling at defence is that the main result of an American initiative would be improved air defences at Tukrah. It would not suit us.'

The prime minister turned to Ben Tov. 'And the fourth consideration?'

'The fourth consideration is that we wish to invoke some help from our friends in Paris. It is delicate. I do not want to elaborate on the matter here.'

'There are risks?'

'There are risks.'

'And what if an error is committed? The Mossad is famous for error, if I may say so.'

'It will be deniable,' the Memuneh said.

'Plausibly,' Ben Tov said under his breath. 'The Idea.'

'I do not wish to know. On the other hand, if there is any sign of political repercussions in Paris I am to be informed forthwith. Is that clear?'

'Perfectly clear, prime minister.'

'And I do not want any Frenchmen killed.'

'Of course not, prime minister.' The Memuneh coughed, paused, then continued. 'We have to consider that if Chatila are seeking a nuclear weapon they will also be seeking a method of delivery. Unless, that is, they already have one.'

'And on that you have nothing?'

The Memuneh adjusted his spectacles again and seemed to be seeking an answer to the question on his sheet of paper. Finding none, he shook his head. 'We have nothing at present. It is evident that the matter has the very highest priority in our office.'

The prime minister grunted and turned to the cabinet secretary.

'We will pursue this in committee. Keep it on our agendas, Uri. So what else do you have?'

'We have the matter of the French aircraft shipments to Iraq.'

'What about the French shipments to Iraq?'

38

The prime minister had not said the Mossad was talking rot.

'The bind,' Ben Tov said as they walked back to their car, 'is a classic one. We have a choice: do we try to stop these people now or do we watch them? By any normal standards, the risks in either case are unacceptable. If we attempt to stop them we are very likely to fail, and thereby accelerate their plans by having warned them that hanging around will be dangerous. We may eliminate certain people like the man Saad Hayek or even the Frenchman Tavernet. Even this Major Savary. Professor Javed Hanif is, for the moment, beyond our reach and I know of no way to get to him. But whoever we eliminate can perfectly well be replaced. If they have the backing of Gadafi he will know more Tavernets or he will get his own bomb. Furthermore, we will almost certainly have blown my man. And even further, I will not have uncovered their plans. And for me, that is the crux. I could get a team into France to take care of Hayek and even the Frenchmen, despite the PM's sensitivity about the French, but Hanif would draw the right conclusions at once, and if we lose my man we lose our only source. Nor will I deliver that young man into the hands of the General Intelligence Directorate in Damascus, which is where they'd send him for interrogation. Their methods are well documented.'

'On the other hand, if you do not act but merely keep watch you will be running equally unacceptable risks. If your appreciation of the situation is correct we are not playing with fire but with annihilation.'

'That,' Ben Tov said, 'is the bind I am talking about.'

The Memuneh climbed into the car and Ben Tov followed him. On the short drive to the Mossad office they sat in gloomy silence. Later, the Memuneh asked: 'What do you want to do?'

'I want to watch.'

'What about your man?'

'There I want to act. He is already under suspicion.'

'How will you act?'

'I do not know how. But no doubt I will think of something. I do not intend to lose an agent.'

39

In fact, it was insubordination, this issuing of short, sharp announcements of intentions but never of plans. The Memuneh found Ben Tov uncontrollable, as others had found him uncontrollable in the army and later during an unsuccessful stint in the Ministry of the Interior. There his nickname had been the Toe Crusher from his propensity to tread on other people's toes as he stamped his way through the bureaucracy. At Arab Affairs he was worshipped by his agents and loathed by his staff, since he was devoted in his harsh and undemonstrative way to the former and systematically hostile to the latter on some principle which he never explained to himself, let alone to his victims. But he was a man of powerful intelligence overlaid upon a foundation of deep mistrust of the motives and intentions of others. His lack of respect for his colleagues was only matched by his careful respect for his opponents, and if this was illogical, so much the worse for logic. The distortions of his personality were ideally suited to his work.

Now he returned to his office, unlocked a drawer in his desk, and stared morosely at the decoded message from Damascus. He took a pen and a pad and wrote furiously for several minutes, referring twice to the message. Then he called his secretary.

'This is to be encoded at once. Then have a messenger take it to Harun at Foreign Affairs for the Paris bag in the morning. Listen to me, Rosa: there are to be no encoding mistakes, right?'

'Right.'

'It is not to be delivered by mistake to the Ministry of Religious Affairs, right?'

'Right.'

'It is to go to Paris and not to Valparaiso, right?'

'Right.'

He sighed. 'With God's help it will happen.'

He sat on a bench in the Sherman Garden, contemplating without much joy the Arp sculpture which was its focal point. It was abstract, provided no nourishment for the soul and no perceptions which could help him in the kind of ethical/philosophical dilemmas which were woven tightly

40

into his job. Someone, he reflected, had spent a lot of money
on the three slightly undulating pillars of stone. Might they
not have done better to ask brother Arp to do them a man
scratching his head with a puzzled look on his face? That
was something a lot of people could identify with. But three
bent columns? He shrugged, glanced around in a manner
which had become second nature to him, wondering idly
why a man in dungarees was still sitting on a bench a few
yards away and why a red-haired girl with a book was
looking at him from time to time instead of concentrating
on her reading. These were the kind of thoughts which never
left him when he found himself in public places. 'I am paranoid,' he told his wife. 'I am suspicious of everyone.'

'Of me?'

'Why not?'

He looked in the direction of Rehov Agron. He assumed
Walters would be coming from the American consulate. Or
maybe his tradecraft had improved and he'd taken a roundabout route. A good man, but sloppy. One day he'd walk
into big trouble in his nonchalant way.

The girl had closed her book and rising from her bench
had started walking towards him. She was swinging her hips
in an aggressive sexual statement as she passed him. She was
taller than he was. A pity. She hadn't even glanced at him
as she passed. He was beginning to develop illusions where
women were concerned. Was that what they meant by middle
age?

The man in dungarees had left too. Paranoia? Or the
obsessive caution of the profession.

'You're crazy, you know,' his wife said.

'I know. But do I need you to tell me?'

Beneath the edgy repartee they understood each other well
enough.

In the event Walters came into sight from the direction of
the Ratisbonne Convent, a rangy man in rather untidy
clothes, looking about him in apparent surprise through
pebble spectacles, a bird-like forward thrust to his head
which had developed from years of peering myopically at
the world. He sat on Ben Tov's bench.

'Hi.'

41

'Shalom.'

'That's a great piece of sculpture.'

'You think so?'

'Yeah. The tension between the three elements. The upward thrust – phallic but somehow feminine too. Great.'

'Glad you like it. We are eclectic in Jerusalem. Something for all tastes.'

'I love this city, you know.'

'Good, good.'

'What is it, the Haifa affair?'

'No. It goes like this. I want something to be said to Gadafi. It has to be unofficial yet not unofficial. Above all, convincing.'

Walters looked at Ben Tov. The thick glasses made it impossible to discern his expression. 'What I like about you,' he said evenly, 'is your ability to think up impossible assignments.'

'I know, I know. I hate it myself.'

'I think you'd better explain a little. If you can, that is.'

'I can explain certain things, not everything. I am talking to you as a professional friend – on a personal yet professional basis. What I am saying is unauthorized and if you help me, that too must be unauthorized. I can only say it is in the deepest interests of Israel.'

'And the USA?'

'Also.'

'That is something you'll have to let me judge.'

'Of course.'

Ben Tov looked around him, took in two nursemaids talking together over their prams, an old gentleman in a skull cap, deep in the day's edition of *Ha'aretz*, some children shouting to no purpose. He took a pack of cheap cigarettes from his pocket, offered one and lit one for himself. He was smoking again.

'On the question of Tukrah,' he said, 'it has been suggested that the State Department might issue a warning to Gadafi. Our people are considering it but I think they will decide against. The idea has been provoked by evidence we have that Gadafi might supply a weapon to a certain terrorist group. Those are the bare bones.'

'Which group?'

'Never mind. Too many people know already.'

'So what do you want said to Gadafi?'

'I can't stand that damned sculpture of yours,' Ben Tov said suddenly. 'Let's stroll down to the Hechal Shlomo. We will talk on the way. Then I might even go in and pray a little, especially if you refuse.'

Later, after leaving Walters, he did not go to the synagogue to pray. Instead, he walked on to Abarbanel Street nearby and let himself into a squat white house set back behind a row of cedars. There he settled down at the telephone, dialled a Paris number and spoke briefly. Then he sat for ten minutes slumped before the phone, deep in thought. When the phone rang he stirred himself, picked it up and spent the next five minutes talking to Alfred Baum in his serviceable French. As he put the instrument back in its cradle he grunted. It was meant to express satisfaction, doubt and great weariness in roughly equal proportions.

The doubt gnawed at him. He had decided to embark on a course of action, to embark on it alone and therefore without support at higher levels should it turn into a disaster, and to run great risks in so doing. He was having to balance the life of his agent against other lives, doubtless of greater value to certain other people but not to him nor, he believed, to the common good.

'Who am I,' he asked himself, 'to be playing at God in all this?'

He who sets himself up . . . He thought there was something pretty harsh about people like him somewhere in the bible. He was no scholar, couldn't remember the quotation, didn't want to . . .

Any fool, he thought, can find the ethical flaws in all this. Moral philosophers are ten a penny. But someone has to bite on the bullet – save this life, sacrifice that one, run this lousy risk to avert that lousier possibility.

He grunted again as he got to his feet and made for the door. It would be Paris over again and possibly worse.

He would issue his instructions and no one in Jerusalem, on the committee or off it, need be asked to share his burden of doubt.

43

Chapter 6

Rasmia and Javed Hanif had become lovers when she moved with him to Damascus, though long before that he had approached her and had been rejected. That was in their Beirut days. There he had been a target for all the more westernized girls in the student body, and the more hopeful ladies of the faculty. The roots of his sexual charisma were obvious enough: the single-minded fanaticism of a man who appeared to have no interest whatever in women and treated them with even greater contempt than he directed at men, used them readily, hardly ever smiled, had no small talk, no politenesses. One day he had broken off from a lengthy monologue on the cultural achievements of the Arabs in their long occupation of the Iberian peninsula. They were together in one of their regular meeting places, had eaten and were sipping thick black coffee.

'We will become lovers, you and I,' he said. 'You are an interesting woman. What do you say?'

He asked the question as if he were quite indifferent to her answer, expecting her to agree and confident he could overcome her reluctance if she did not.

Her hand was on the table but he made no effort to take it in his. He looked into her eyes in the way he looked at everyone, always directly in the eyes. There was no change at all in his expression. It was neither a suggestion nor a request, but a command, undiluted by the shadow of doubt.

But she had refused. She no longer remembered whether she had found refusal difficult, or even whether she found him attractive. But an instinct told her he was dangerous to

44

her peace of mind. And so she had first said she wanted time to decide: then some months later, when he put the question again, that she could not reconcile herself to an affair with a man old enough to be her father. He had shown more patience than she had expected, and for their last year in Beirut had not mentioned the subject. Then, unexpectedly to him, she had acquiesced when they moved to the house in Damascus, and submissively she had started to share his bed.

Hanif did not know why refusal had become acceptance, and because he had no interest in the emotions of others he did not speculate on what she might feel for him. She was an undemonstrative lover, available when he wanted her and seemingly without emotional or sexual needs of her own. He had decided that she was a passionless girl, that her sexual passivity was the mirror image of her silent, withdrawn personality. He did not fully understand her, and this he put down to what he came to see as her emotional inadequacy. That he had failed to awaken her emotions and that maybe someone else could do so did not enter into his calculations. He was not a man with any strong need for women, nor was he interested in his partner's satisfaction. He would come to her room from time to time or call her to his and they would make love, he self-absorbed as if the process were therapeutic and little more, she always obedient yet passive.

He had come to her after midnight and had woken her, but he sat on the edge of her bed and made no effort to join her. She slept naked, and now she sat up against her pillows, her mane of sleek black hair falling forward and obscuring her hard little breasts, save for a brown nipple which had thrust its way through the strands.

'I am tired. Do you want to make love?'

'No. I want to talk.'

'Can't we talk in the morning? I'm half asleep.'

'Then wake yourself up and listen. As you know, I have doubts about Essat.'

'You have told me.'

'That is why I'm sending you with him.'

'I understood as much.'

45

'He is a brilliant leader of men. Very effective in staff work. I would not want to make a mistake.'

She shrugged. 'We cannot afford to take risks with the security of the group.'

'Of course not,' he said impatiently. 'You do not need to teach me simple things of that kind. I want you to understand your assignment fully. You are to watch him during the trip.'

'Of course.'

'He is not to know it. Not under any circumstances.'

She tossed her head impatiently.

'I am giving him an assignment which I believe he will feel unable to carry out if he is working for the other side. At the very least he will have to tip them off.'

'What assignment?'

'He will be told when he gets to Rome. You will meet Khaled and he will have the details.'

'But you can surely tell me?'

'Khaled will have the details.'

She tossed her head again, displeased.

'If he is against us he will try to communicate with his controllers. It will be that kind of assignment. You are to watch and report on any contacts, phone calls, anything he may try. Is that clear?'

'It is clear. But you must leave enough time between the briefing and the date of the operation for him to make contact and receive his orders.'

'I am not a fool. I am leaving just enough time for him to do so, but only by taking risks.'

She said nothing, pulled the sheet up to cover her breasts. He was watching her pensively, as one would watch an experiment.

'Drop the sheet.'

'I thought you didn't want to. Wasn't this a business call?'

'I have changed my mind. Come here.'

He seized the edge of the sheet and pulled it down below her waist as she moved obediently towards him.

Rasmia and Essat travelled the following day to Rome, changing planes at Athens and arriving on an Alitalia flight, two young Iraqis on their first visit to Europe. Itinerary, for those who might ask: Rome, Florence, Venice, and maybe Switzerland too if the money lasted. They went to a seedy hotel in the Via Turati near the railway station and from there Rasmia made a phone call.

'Khaled will be here in an hour. He will take us to eat and will give us our instructions.'

'Think I'll stretch out and maybe sleep a bit until he comes. Wake me.'

Before leaving Damascus he had had one more conversation at the mosque, had given the old man his destination and arrival time. He did not know whether friends had spotted them at the air terminal: he had seen no one but did not doubt that they would be in touch. At the hotel they had booked into adjoining rooms. Bathroom and an evil-smelling toilet were at the end of a dismal corridor. Everything was chipped, fly-blown, stained and peeling. Permeating it all was the smell of stale cooking and dry rot. The hotel appeared to be frequented exclusively by Arabs without money.

Once in his room, he pushed home the bolt on the door. Then he spent ten minutes going over the room. Lying flat under the bed and running his fingers along the inside of the frame, he finally found the bug, which had been neatly secured by means of a couple of tacks and an elastic band. If anyone were listening he hoped the sound of his approaching finger had not alerted them. He wondered how they'd fixed it up ahead of his arrival. Why didn't he know they had contacts here? Or was he so mistrusted now that the local commando had been told?

He hauled himself from under the bed, dusted himself down and set about stowing his few belongings in an ancient cupboard. Then he stretched himself on the lumpy bed, which squeaked in protest, and hands clasped behind his head he reviewed his situation and wondered when the friends would manifest themselves.

It was about an hour later that Rasmia called to him through the thin wall between their rooms. He called back, got up from the bed, put on his shoes and made his way out to the dim corridor and down the stairs. On the landing below, the door of a room stood open. Inside he saw the

47

figure of a man lying fully clothed on the bed, his head wreathed in cigar smoke, his feet propped on the foot board. From an invisible radio came the mournful wailing of an Arabic song. He caught a glimpse of the man's face, sallow, unshaven, with uninterested eyes staring dully out at the landing. Very briefly they looked at each other and Essat thought the eyelids flickered for a moment. Then he was past the open door and on his way to the ground floor.

Rasmia was already in the narrow hallway, talking quietly to a tall youth with glasses. Essat greeted him.

'How do you like being stationed in Rome, then?'

'Well enough.'

'How long is it – a year since we were together in Paris?'

'About that.'

'Still the student? What was it, international law?'

'It was.'

'And now?'

'Now, never mind.'

The young man who called himself Khaled was reticent. Did that indicate . . . ?

They made their way to a trattoria a couple of blocks away. Khaled nodded to the proprietor lounging fatly behind his bar and wiping glasses on a bedraggled cloth, and received a '*Ciao*, Ahmed' in return. They chose a table in a far corner, ordered food and wine and sat in silence until the meal arrived and the Italian had returned to the bar.

'So what is it to be?' Essat asked.

'There is to be an action against the Zionists here in Rome the day after tomorrow. As you know, the boys came in a couple of days ago. You are to help with the lookout work and to collect the weapons and pass them on. It's the usual drill: the action group is not to know the origin of the weapons.'

'Where are they?'

He handed over a piece of paper with a name and address pencilled on it. Rasmia extended her hand quickly and took it.

'They came a few days ago in the Libyan bag. This fellow's a driver at their embassy. A safe man. The professor didn't want me to do the transfer: he says he won't have a head of station directly involved in an action.'

'What kind of weapons?' Rasmia asked the question. 'Do we need to take bags?'

'A couple of automatics – Kalash's maybe – and a pouch of grenades. They'll be in some sort of sports bag. Tennis, golf, I don't know. Anyway, this fellow's expecting you tonight, when we leave here.'

'And the handover?'

'At ten fifteen you're to be in the station concourse. Stand outside the main bookstall. A girl with a red scarf will approach you when she sees the bag. She'll ask the time and you'll tell her it will soon be nine. Then you'll follow her at a distance and hand over the bag wherever she stops and waits for you. Understood?'

'Understood.'

'Any questions?'

'The action, what is it?'

'Didn't the professor tell you?'

'Not this time. I suppose he had his reasons.'

'I can tell you this much. The El Al flight crews stay at the Hotel Commendatore in the Via Nazionale. The crew of the daily flight which arrives from Tel Aviv at 16.30 usually reaches the hotel between 18.30 and 19.00 hours. They have been known to arrive outside these times, but that's unusual. You are to station yourselves at a suitable point on the Piazza della Republica and signal to our boys when you see the El Al minibus approaching up the Via Terme.'

He took a street map out of his pocket and spread it, partly open, on the table. 'This is where you stand, on the north side, here. You'll have a view of the approaching traffic. The El Al bus is painted white. It's a Mercedes. You'll have to be careful not to make a mistake because once you've signalled, the boys won't waste time checking. They'll hit the next white Mercedes minibus they see.'

'How do we signal?'

'You'll lift a rolled newspaper and the comrade across the Piazza from you will pick up the signal and pass it on. OK?'

'OK.'

'Then you leave the rest to the action squad. They know what they have to do.'

'And afterwards?'

'Afterwards you catch the evening flight out to Istanbul. I'll have the tickets tomorrow. I'll leave them for you at the hotel and we won't meet again.'

As they waited for coffee Essat got to his feet and made for the toilet at the far end of the room.

'I must go, too,' Khaled said, and followed him out.

Essat locked himself in a booth, tore off a piece of toilet paper, wrote rapidly on it with a pencil that he took from a pocket, cursing the poor results, screwed the paper into a ball and put it in a pocket. Then he flushed the bowl and came out. Khaled was at the urinal. Nothing was said.

They finished their meal in virtual silence and split up outside the restaurant. They did not shake hands. Khaled made his way to a bus stop and the other two walked back towards the station. It was just after 9.15 p.m.

'I'll collect the guns,' Essat said. 'We don't need to attract attention by both going.'

'We'll both go.'

'Why?'

'I prefer it.'

'Please yourself.'

They took a cab from the rank at the station and directed the driver to the right street but the wrong number. Then they walked for the few minutes needed to reach the correct address. It was a block of modest flats. Khaled's slip of paper gave No. 34. They mounted to the third floor, found the door and rang the bell, taking care to stand within the view afforded by the peephole in the centre of the door. After a moment a man's voice sounded from the far side of the door. 'Yes?'

'We're from Khaled.'

The door was opened by a youngish man in slacks and shirtsleeves. He smelt of alcohol and strong tobacco.

'Come in.' He closed the door behind them. 'Wait here.' He disappeared into a room leading off the cramped hall and reappeared a moment later carrying a canvas tennis bag.

50

'Here. They're knocked down. You know how to assemble them?'

Rasmia nodded.

'There's everything there, including the ammunition. Here, take it and get out quick. If you have trouble, you don't give this address, right?'

'Right.'

'You know the deal the top people did. We help but if anyone says so, we deny it and we help no more, right?'

'Right.'

Essat took the heavy bag and followed Rasmia out of the flat and down the stairs. They met no one, picked up a taxi nearby and returned to the station. It was just after ten. The crowd in the concourse had thinned down but there was movement whenever a train pulled in. They took up a position close to the bookstall, Essat with the bag on the ground between his legs. They said nothing to each other.

Where were the friends? Essat reckoned they had not been followed but he couldn't be sure. If there was a tail it was a neat professional job, well up to Ben Tov's standards. Looking around, he could see no likely candidate. A group of young people, probably Scandinavians of some kind, chatted a few yards away. One of the girls, a handsome amazon, well built, glanced at him from time to time. Probably a mild sexual interest; that kind of girl, he'd found, often went for wiry Mediterranean men; liked to have their soft white flesh maltreated by muscular brown limbs with plenty of black hair on them. Some kind of ethnic turn-on, he imagined. Jockeys would probably suit them best; hard, ruthless little men grown strong from thrashing at their mounts on the straight. At the bookstall a few travellers leafed through magazines listlessly. A middle-aged woman with a holdall was pulling paperbacks out of the rack and replacing them. Looking for a sixteenth-century bodice-ripper? Essat shrugged, turned to Rasmia to say something and thought better of it. When the hell would someone show themselves? Caution was fine but this was becoming ridiculous. He looked at his watch. It was eleven minutes past ten. Their contact would show up soon. The sooner he got rid of the guns the better.

51

'What time is it?' Rasmia seemed reluctant to talk to him at all. He told her.

The Scandinavians were drifting away and the big girl glanced at him over her shoulder and half smiled. He smiled back. It was sex after all. No one else looked promising. A train had just pulled in and disgorged a few exhausted-looking travellers into the concourse. If a friend was here, why was there no sign – a nod from the distance perhaps, or someone bumping into him and muttering a word in Hebrew? Maybe they didn't have anyone tailing him after all. There'd be some kind of message for him back at the hotel. A note in his room, perhaps. Or he'd have to try a phone call somehow, though God alone knew how that was to be done. Now the Scandinavians had disappeared.

'Excuse me, can you change a ten-thousand-lire note? I need to telephone.'

It was the middle-aged woman who had been searching for a novel. She was a nondescript creature with wispy hair untidily caught in a bun, her body wrapped in a shapeless grey coat. Her Italian carried a thick accent. She was holding a banknote towards Rasmia.

'Sorry, I've no change.'

The woman turned away from Rasmia, waved the bank-note towards him. For a moment she was facing him, Rasmia to her left. She made an unmistakable sign with her eyes, raising her eyebrows as if to say, 'What do we do?'

Essat made no sign that he had noticed her expression: Rasmia was watching him. He shook his head: '*Niente*'. The woman shrugged, turned away, approached an Italian who was choosing a magazine. Then she turned, watching Essat.

Rasmia's gaze moved from Essat to scan the concourse. He turned half away from her, his right hand in his pocket. He felt the ball of paper where he'd written the bare facts of the action, the name of the hotel, and the single word: Instructions.

His hand came out of his pocket. He was holding the paper ball. Was the woman still watching him? Thank God, she was. He dropped the ball on the ground with a flick which rolled it a short way towards her. A sign with the eyes: she had seen it. Contact made. Rasmia had seen nothing.

52

It was ten fifteen. A dark girl in jeans and a black leather jacket walked slowly towards them across the open space. Suddenly, as she approached she unzipped the jacket, revealing a red woollen scarf which had been concealed beneath it.

'What time is it?'

Rasmia went through the motion of looking at her watch.

'Nine o'clock.'

'Thanks.'

The girl walked away slowly. After she had gone twenty yards they started to follow. The friend had moved towards the spot where they had been standing. Now she was bending down, perhaps to adjust a shoelace. The ball of paper lay near her foot. As he turned away Essat saw her hand go out . . .

In a tunnel at the far end of the concourse the girl stopped. As they came level with her Essat put the tennis bag carefully on the ground. The girl picked it up and walked quickly away. Nothing was said. There was no greeting, not even a glance of understanding – nothing. Then they returned to the hotel.

He noticed as they mounted the creaking stairs to their rooms that the bedroom door on the second floor was still open, music still wailing and crackling out of the radio. The man was sitting on the bed and looked up with the same listless gaze as they passed to the floor above, where they said goodnight curtly to each other.

Someone had been through his things, which was what he had expected. He wondered idly what they thought they might find. Then he prepared for bed, stretched between the grubby sheets, hoping without much conviction that there would be no bed bugs. Next door he could hear Rasmia moving about, and then the creaking of her bed and the click of the light. Every time she moved he heard the ancient bed protest. A very beautiful girl, he reflected. A hard, nervous body where the Scandinavian in the station had been soft and yielding. He thought about her. But how could you derive pleasure, let alone give any, where an iron mask of indifference came between you? Impossible; a pity. There was all that romantic stuff about proud spirits humbled, indifference melted down into lust and passion, turbulent emotions let loose by means of who knew what erotic skills – all of it rubbish. The girl was a cold fish and Hanif was welcome to her. Meanwhile, his life and other lives were in danger and he was lusting, if only he would admit it, for this driven creature turning in her bed on the other side of the flimsy wall. But thinking about her had also given him an idea. He leant over the edge of the bed and felt gingerly for the mike. It was still there. He wondered how sensitive it was and decided it could probably use a little co-operation from him. He lay on his back and slowly began to produce regular snores which he hoped the mike could pick up. It was curiously tiring work and he reckoned he'd give it fifteen minutes or so. It was nearly that long before he heard a loose board creak suddenly in the corridor outside his room and then a single tap on Rasmia's door before the board creaked again, followed by what he took to be a footstep on the stairs. He cursed his own fake snoring which was preventing him hearing more.

The springs of Rasmia's bed produced a metallic sound and then he caught her footsteps across the floor. A moment later the bolt on her door clicked back and the loose floorboard outside his room delivered its familiar sound as she trod on it. Then came her footstep on the stairs. He wondered if he dare stop his ridiculous snoring, go to the landing and see where she had gone. Why not? Why shouldn't he pay a visit to the filthy toilet at the end of the corridor? He got up, switched on the light and stepped out into the corridor. From the floor below came the eternal Arab song, but muffled now through the closed door of the bedroom. In case he was somehow still overheard, Essat went into the toilet, waited a moment, flushed the bowl and returned down the dim corridor. There appeared to be no change from the floor below. Perhaps Rasmia was down there, conferring with Khaled about him. Maybe the unkempt man with the liking for sentimental songs from the Maghreb was one of Hanif's agents, though it would be surprising. As Chatila's chief of staff Essat was supposed to know them all. But then again, Hanif was more than likely to have a shadow network that only he would know about. It accorded with his acutely developed sense of caution.

The door of the room below opened and Essat tiptoed back to his room, carefully stepping over the loose floorboard. By the time the bolt on Rasmia's door clicked back into place he was lying on his bed, emitting sighs and grunts in what he took to be a fair imitation of broken sleep. Sleep itself evaded him.

Chapter 7

The ringing of the telephone snatched Ben Tov from an unsatisfactory state of half-sleep in which he had been dreaming in disturbing and unremembered snatches. It was after midnight and his wife was still reading by the light of her bedside lamp.

'For all the peace we get at night you might as well have been a doctor and made my father happy.'

He was reaching for the phone, fumbling in his drowsy state. 'I'd have earned a better living too.'

He leant on his elbow, brought the phone to his ear.

'Yes.' There was no sleep left in his voice. He listened, then: 'Is contact easy? Difficult, you say. Dangerous for him . . . sure, sure. Listen, my dear Eva, you will have to give me time, which means another call tomorrow. But I beg of you, caution . . . *caution*. There is no more precious life to us, you understand.' He paused while Eva, in Rome, answered him. Then: 'Fine, fine, I have every faith. Why did I send you if I never had faith? So, you will call me in the morning. I need until ten your time. Yes, call me at the other number. I'll be there, waiting your call . . . You are right, you should have arranged a further contact, but never mind. You couldn't. And be careful; the girl will remember you. So next time you must look different – you or Moishe, I leave it to you. Shalom.'

He replaced the receiver but did not move.

'Rome?' his wife asked without looking up from her book.

He nodded. 'Solomon I am not,' he said, 'but Solomon is what I have to be here.'

'Let someone else make the hard decisions for a change. Sometimes I think you'd elbow God himself aside.'

'This time it has to be God or me. And if I know anything about God, he'll duck it and leave me to make the mistakes. God keeps his nose clean.'

'And the Memuneh?'

'That klutz!' He would slip into Yiddish where there was no better word in Hebrew. Yiddish was good for contempt, for put-downs and definitive character assassination. He drew his small but accurately-aimed vocabulary of Yiddish insults and expletives from his father-in-law, who had arrived in Haifa in the summer of 1948 with a wife at his side and a one-year-old child in his arms as the machine guns chattered on the heights of Galilee, had thrust the baby into his wife's arms as his feet touched the dock and had knelt and kissed the rough concrete, stood up and seized his daughter back and marched forward into what was to be the State of Israel, muttering prayers in Hebrew and declarations of joy, astonishment and wild impatience in Yiddish, and had ever since resisted abandoning the Yiddish for the Hebrew in his daily life. When the baby grew up and married someone who turned out to be little better than a policeman, and a godless policeman without even a uniform, he had finally shrugged and retreated into a joshing, teasing relationship with his son-in-law which had a generous admixture of deep but unavowed affection in it. It was from him that Shayeh Ben Tov, the Sabra, had absorbed a little of the spirit and folk wisdom of the Diaspora Jew, though grudgingly. To him, the native-born were the only true Israelis. The proposition drove his father-in-law to picturesque and loquacious despair.

'I was in Treblinka three years. No one can talk to me!'

'That was over forty years ago, *shver*. You live in the past.'

'When did the Temple fall, tell me that?'

'Two thousand years ago.'

'And they still talk about it. So? Leave me alone!' And he would mutter obscure curses from Bialystock or Riga. 'A policeman yet, and he tries to tell me. You should come to *shul* and learn respect.' It always ended lamely with a vain call back to the strict observances of his forefathers.

57

'To you, everyone is a klutz,' his wife said now.

'Listen, for this decision courage is needed. Does the Memuneh have courage? Ha! Also, political understanding is needed. And love for another person. And a sense of history, destiny even. These are things he never heard of.'

'And your committee?'

'Who heard of a committee with courage, let alone love?'

'So you'll consult no one?'

'Not even you.'

'It's arrogance. It will end badly.' She returned to her book, knowing there was nothing she could say that would have the slightest effect on him. In any case, he only ever told her bits and pieces about his work – more than his oath of secrecy allowed but always less than she needed in order to argue with him. Before switching her light out she touched his shoulder. 'Don't be so hard on yourself,' she said. 'Share a little.'

He was already asleep.

When Eva's call came through from Rome next morning, Ben Tov's instructions were delivered with irritation, as if Eva were herself to blame in some way. 'My instructions to our friend,' he said, 'are to operate strictly according to the orders he is receiving from his associates. Is that clear?'

'Perfectly clear, but . . .'

'There is no but, Eva. Have you understood me?'

'Of course.'

'Good. So you will contact him, tell him what I have said, and then you and Moishe will cease to be interested in the matter. Is that also clear?'

'Of course.'

There was a pause. Then Ben Tov said, 'You will assume that I shall warn El Al direct, right?'

'I already assumed that.'

He almost barked at her. 'Correct. You can tell our friend that too.'

Then he hung up, let himself out of the house in Abarbanel Street, and walked slowly towards the Mossad office. Anyone sufficiently interested in the passing of the wiry, greying figure strolling along the pavements, his head sunk on to his

58

chest and his hands clasped behind his back, would have assumed some minor official with time to spare and no constructive way to fill it. Save that he looked angry.

Later, he gave his daily report to the Memuneh, in that person's meticulously tidy office.

'What about your man in the Chatila group?' the Memuneh asked eventually.

'Nothing,' Ben Tov said.

'Are you in touch with him?'

'Intermittently.'

'Where is he?'

'As far as we know he is in Damascus as usual, where else?'

'Still in danger?'

'Still in danger.'

It was all he was prepared to say. He made no attempt to carry conviction, and the Memuneh, who was dull and timorous but no fool, was not convinced that he was hearing either the full story or even a truthful segment of the full story. But he knew no way to learn more.

'We must not have political repercussions from what you are doing in this matter,' he said.

Ben Tov took his time over replying, searching first for cigarettes in an inside pocket, then finding a Riclés box instead.

'How, political repercussions?' His face expressed surprise at such a question but only the mildest curiosity.

'How, I do not know. But there is plenty of room for political trouble. I do not want to have to go apologizing to the prime minister.'

'I imagine not,' Ben Tov said, 'but I can guarantee nothing.'

'You will understand that any false move on our part, any . . . accident, will undermine our posture on the Paris outrage. The French would like nothing better than to put us in the wrong.'

'The thought had occurred to me.'

'Good. I beg you to be careful.'

'I have an exceptionally difficult task,' Ben Tov said,

making no effort to keep irritation out of his voice. 'I am doing my best. No one is forbidden to do better if they can.'

'Quite, quite, my dear Shayeh. Nothing is being imputed and no one presumes to do better. We have every confidence in your department. But please understand, I see the minister, the PM even, and they ask questions and I have to reply, and so I need to be briefed, and if you do not brief me our entire service looks as if it does not know what it ought to know. That is my problem.'

'And mine,' Ben Tov said mercilessly, 'is that I have precious men in the field who can easily be betrayed as a result of a loose word by a minister to his wife or his mistress, and thence to who knows what little friend, and so on. Our opponents are constantly delivered to us as a result of just such chains of information and I believe in learning from the other side. So I repeat: my man is still in danger and I am taking appropriate steps which, please God, will not cause political trouble.'

As Ben Tov got up to leave, the Memuneh thought yet again how he might move him into a less sensitive area where he would irritate less and give rise to fewer situations where deniability was called for.

Back in his own office, Ben Tov asked his secretary to get him lemon tea, but without saying please, nor, subsequently, thank you. Russian-style, he took a lump of sugar in his mouth, and as the tea cooled, he sucked it through the sugar, sweetening it unevenly. When his secretary asked on the intercom if she could bring in some mail, he barked at her and she shrugged and put the mail back on the corner of her desk. She knew this mood: the old man was wrestling with his better feelings. He had an unpleasant decision to make and he wasn't going to let anyone else have a tolerable day while he was making it. On this occasion, however, she was wrong. Ben Tov's decision had been made, clearly and irrevocably, the previous night. Now he was suffering a moral hangover and, like all hangovers, it would pass.

He picked up the phone and dialled a number.

'Give me Walters.'

'Hold, please.'

A moment later the American was put through.

60

'Well?' Ben Tov barked the word into the mouthpiece.

'Shayeh, you don't waste words, eh?'

'I don't. Have you thought about what I asked?'

'We have.'

'We?'

'I have talked to a good friend in the other place. It has to be done through him.'

'And?'

'And I guess we can manage something for you. I have some sort of game plan.'

'We had better meet. Can you be at the usual place in a half-hour?'

'See you there.'

When he arrived in the Sherman Garden, Walters was already there, taking a close and affectionate look at the Arp. He was shaking his head. 'Such a command of spatial relationships,' he said by way of opening. 'Such a dominance over his material. Masterly!'

'If you say so. After all, it was a gift to the city and who am I to complain about a gift in these difficult times?'

They strolled to their usual bench and sat down.

'I would very much like to broaden and deepen your artistic responses,' Walters said. 'I reckon the sum total of modern art is passing you by and you are the loser.'

'I can put up with it. Let us talk about reality.'

'Yes, well, I have been thinking about your little problem and, as I said, talking to this friend in Tripoli. A wise fellow, very experienced in selling dummies to the other side. What he says is that you can't actually *sell* a dummy to a really smart operator. You can only sell him a clue – and the more obscure the better – and allow him to buy your dummy of his own free will. There's nothing on earth that your really clever opponent clings to more tenaciously, my friend in Tripoli says, than a brilliant bit of deductive reasoning that you've helped him ever so gently to achieve. But of course, it has to be his own and not yours. If you gauge his intelligence with accuracy – since you'd be defeating your aim if you gave him a problem he couldn't crack – then nothing is likely to deflect him from holding a view he came by with such difficulty and brilliance. Then, of course, you have

61

him. So reasons my friend. He is expert in applying modern marketing theory to our trade.'

Ben Tov grunted and there was silence for a moment. 'There is nothing in all that,' he said, 'that one could disagree with or that I haven't known for fifteen years. The question is, *what* is to be our clue and *how* are you people to convey it?'

'The one is a function of the other. A good clue improbably conveyed will nullify itself. Similarly, vice versa.'

'You should save these theoretical concepts for the training manual you will certainly write together with your friend the marketing manager when they retire you,' Ben Tov said. 'Let us be practical. Start by telling me something about your channels to the other side.'

'I am not authorized to tell you, my old buddy, but I will now do so.' Walters pushed his pebble glasses back on his nose and peered round as if the breach of regulations he was about to commit required a measure of extra caution. 'We have a leak in the traffic section of our embassy in Tripoli. We have known about it for some months, and during that time it has provided us with a very beautiful opportunity to double-talk the other side. It is an opportunity our Tripoli people have seized and used well. Do you know, stuff we have pushed through that modest leak in the system has turned up in Teheran, Damascus, Paris of all places and – once only so far – in Moscow. So that it is clear to us that the Libyans are highly sensitive to anything which reaches them along that route.'

'Very useful. And why did I not know?'

'I had no clearance to tell you.'

'But you still have no clearance.'

'Ah, but Langley has decided to plug the leak. It is reckoned by my masters that if we let it run any longer the opposition will conclude that such sloppy security cannot be accidental. And in any case, you have no idea how inconvenient it can be to have someone else's asset sitting in your traffic department taking a long, hard look at most of what you transmit.'

'I can imagine it very well.'

They sat in silence for a moment, both of them peering

about them, though it was Ben Tov and not Walters who was taking a real interest in the few midday strollers in the gardens. He made a mental note to change their meeting place for the future. He didn't like the sculpture and he reckoned they'd met in the same place too often anyway.

'My friend in Tripoli,' Walters was saying, 'has offered us the use – possibly the very last use – of our leak. Wrap it up, he has said to me, and we'll merchandise it to our customer. We'll maybe package it, tie a bow on or something. That is how he put it?'

'An unusual man.'

'Yes, rather unusual. But sound. So let me have this message of yours.'

Ben Tov had already taken a small notebook out of his pocket and was scribbling in it with a ballpoint. He looked at what he had written, shook his head, crossed it out and wrote again. Then he changed a word, then another, shook his head again and stabbed the pen violently at the end of the sentence, which he rewrote carefully. A pause, and then something resembling a wintry smile appeared briefly over his mouth. Walters said nothing, shoved his insecure spectacles higher up his nose, fidgeted on the hard bench. Ben Tov was rewriting the message carefully, translating it from the Hebrew into English. He tore the sheet from the notebook, handed it to his companion, and replaced the notebook and pen in his pocket.

'There,' he said, 'send that. I am crediting all concerned on the other side with an alertness and intelligence which were the roles reversed, they would not find on my side of the fence. Also, tell your friend the marketing genius not to interfere with it.'

Walters peered at the slip of paper:

To A106 Langley: Urgent and most secret.

Inquiry from friends here regarding Frenchman Tavernet repeat Tavernet, activity unknown but believed to have Libyan contacts. Have we anything on file? Any known visit to Libya? If so, who contacted? Friends request you do not repeat not contact French colleagues in this inquiry. Please notify me securely soonest. Walters.

'I can't comment,' Walters said. 'I daresay you know what you are doing.'

'I do. But I shall need a good deal of luck if the message is to reach the person it is aimed at. If it does, I have nothing to worry about. Being no fool, he should make precisely the deduction that I want him to.'

They got up from their bench and strolled through the garden. 'Oh, and thanks,' Ben Tov said as they parted at Rabbi Akiva Street.

'One of these days,' Walters said, 'you must tell me more.'

Chapter 8

On the day following the handing over of the weapons, Rasmia and Essat did not leave the hotel. This was in line with the ruling in Chatila that once weapons had been handed out, no one associated with an action should leave their base until the action itself was due. And so they spent the morning, each in their own room, Essat leafing listlessly through a couple of magazines, Rasmia reading a paperback edition of a French novel, aiming to improve her French as the professor had enjoined her to do some time before. At lunchtime Essat knocked on her wall and called out, 'Let's eat.' They met on the landing and went down together to the ill-lit bar and ate sandwiches of unsalted bread and smoked ham, accompanied by acrid, steaming black coffee. Afterwards, as they made their way through the lobby, they passed a young man trying to book into the hotel without luggage, searching through his pockets for money to make the advance payment that the signora had demanded. He spoke to her in halting Italian thickly accented with Arabic gutturals. As Rasmia and Essat climbed the stairs to their rooms, the signora slapped a room key on to the counter with evident distaste and the young man picked it up and followed them up the stairs to the third floor, letting himself into a room almost opposite Essat's. As he did so, he called over, 'Where's the bog in this dump?'

'End of the corridor. Can't you smell it?'

The young man laughed. 'Do they have a bathroom?'

'It's down there too.'

Rasmia stood at the door of her room while the two men talked, waiting for Essat to finish and close his door.

'You here for long?' the young man asked.

'A day or two. We're on our way to Florence.'

'I'm from Tunis. Hope to move in with a pal tomorrow or the day after.'

Essat grunted, entered his room and closed the door. A moment later he heard Rasmia's door close behind her. Then he threw himself on his bed and hoped he might doze for a while. He reckoned he must eventually have dozed because he did not hear the young man's door open, nor the creaking board outside his own room, nor any sound the paper may have made as it was pushed beneath his door. But as he turned on the bed he saw the paper, retrieved it and read it:

You are to carry out your mission exactly. Action is being taken to safeguard you and intended victims. You can safely return to Damascus. Good luck.

He took a gas lighter from his pocket and burned the paper on the marble top of the bedside table. Then he carefully collected the charred fragments and put them under the stained and threadbare carpet which covered part of the floor. He did not allow his mind to dwell on the paradox: how could both he and the El Al crew be safeguarded? Did not survival of the one imply irrevocably the death of the other? He thought so, but did not care to contemplate by what moral sleight of hand Jerusalem had reconciled the two incompatibles. He stretched out once more on the bed and once more tried to sleep.

At 17.00 hours on the following afternoon he phoned the airport. El Al from Tel Aviv had landed five minutes late. Together with Rasmia he set out for the Piazza della Republica, stopped at a bar on the way for an espresso, and arrived on the piazza just before 18.00 hours. They took up a position on a bench on the western side so that they had a clear view of the traffic coming up the Via Terme and circling the piazza before entering the Via Nazionale. Essat carried a copy of *La Stampa*. For a while they sat side by side, two young people aimless in the city. They had hardly spoken to each other all that day and the day before, as if they were strangers with nothing in common. The traffic thundered and hooted its way past them in an unending stream, punctuated briefly by the action of the traffic lights.

'It should be any time from a quarter past onwards,' he said.

'Yes. I can see one of our boys over at the entrance to the Via Nazionale. He's looking this way to pick up your signal.'

'How far down is the Hotel Commendatore?'

'One block, maybe fifty metres or so.'

She was nervy and answered him sharply, as if she would prefer not to talk. But he felt the need to talk to someone, even to this cold, self-contained creature, who seemed not in the least disturbed by their mission.

'Our boys will have problems getting away in this traffic.'

'I assume they have it worked out. My guess is they'll keep the grenades to use if they're needed during the getaway.'

They sat in silence for a while, both looking at the oncoming traffic in the Via Terme to their left. The man at the entrance to the Via Nazionale on the far side of the piazza was leaning against a lamp post, a newspaper held idly in front of him. His eyes did not leave the two on their bench across the way.

'What time do you make it?' Rasmia's question betrayed tension.

'It's twelve minutes past. With the flight five minutes late and this crazy traffic we aren't likely to see them this side of their usual 18.30 or so.'

But at twenty-seven minutes past a short break in the traffic coming up towards them along the Via Terme revealed the front of a white minibus.

'There it is!'

They both rose from their bench and Essat was rolling his copy of *La Stampa* as the vehicle approached them. They could see clearly now that it was a Mercedes and that there were seven or eight people in it. It was possible to see that most of the occupants were women.

As the minibus drew almost level with them and started to make its way round the piazza, the watcher on the far side saw Essat's hand go up, holding the newspaper. He

67

turned towards the Via Nazionale and raised his own newspaper in turn.

Two automatic hand guns were carried on the El Al minibus – one by the driver, the other in a shoulder holster worn by the security guard who travelled aboard the airliner and always accompanied the crew to and from their hotels. The guard on the El Al Tel Aviv-Rome flight was a stocky youth of twenty named Avram who had developed a passion for one of the stewardesses – an almond-eyed beauty with tight auburn curls, a sensuous mouth and perfect legs. Her name was Rachel, she came from Baltimore and had been in Israel and with the airline for a year. Her indifference to Avram was total, since she fancied herself deeply in love with a purser she had met on the New York run. Her close friend Ruthie was flying with her on the Rome route and now sat next to her in the front of the bus as it crossed the space in front of the railway station and nosed its way through the heavy rush-hour traffic into the Via Terme. The driver, who had been stationed in Rome for six months and had hated every minute of it, was muttering ancient curses in Hebrew as he competed with the mannerless and dangerous drivers surrounding him. The security man Avram sat in the single seat next to the driver, his jacket undone, his big farm boy's hands hanging loosely in his lap. There were four men and five girls in his care and he liked the feeling. In a minute he would ask Rachel again to have dinner with him, expecting an excuse but hoping somehow that she'd say yes – a hope he had regularly entertained ever since she had agreed to join him for a drink during a stopover in Jo'burg. Nothing had happened between them, no sign of special warmth or interest on her part, but his imagination had fed on it ever since.

'It's pasta and bed for me,' Rachel was saying to her friend Ruthie as the minibus swung from the Via Terme into the roundabout of the Piazza della Republica. Through the window she caught sight of a handsome curly-headed young man holding a rolled newspaper above his head. Idly, she wondered what he was doing. He had a good-looking girl with him. Then the bus was past them and heading for the Via Nazionale.

'Ari asked me to see a movie with him tonight. I told him yes,' Ruthie said.

Ari was steward in first class, studied agronomy in his spare moments and dreamed of getting out of the Boeings and on to a kibbutz somewhere in the Negev. He sat now in the rear of the bus, scanning the cinema ads in an evening paper.

'Here we are then, *chaverim*,' the driver chanted as he brought the minibus in to the kerb. 'All alight here and have a pleasant stay.' As he spoke, Avram pulled back the sliding door. Immediately a youth who had been standing on the kerb with a long parcel wrapped in paper under his arm leapt into the bus, the Kalashnikov blazing, the paper blown away. At the same time another youth with a similar parcel ripped the paper from his gun, raised it shoulder-high and sprayed bullets through the side windows of the vehicle.

It was all over in seconds. Neither Avram nor the driver had the slightest chance of using their weapons. The first volley from the youth inside the bus killed them both outright. Bullets ripped into the bodies of Rachel and her friend Ruthie. Amid the screams the two youths were shouting unintelligibly in Arabic. Then they fled.

A hotel porter who tried to run after them was blocked by another young man, and an elderly man who did the same found himself in collision with a dark girl in slacks and a black leather jacket. The two youths disappeared up a side street as the first passer-by dared to look inside the bus at the carnage wrought by the automatics.

As the minibus had disappeared behind the tall building at the corner of the piazza and the Via Nazionale, Essat and Rasmia started to walk slowly down the Via Terme towards the railway station. They had gone a few paces when the familiar chatter of the Kalashnikovs reached them distantly above the roar of the traffic. They walked on without quickening their pace. Essat felt his stomach churn and realized that tears were welling in his eyes. It required a supreme effort of will to maintain the casual pace, to say nothing lest his voice should betray his emotion, not to break into a run, cry out, ram his fist into the beautiful, impassive face of this

69

dehumanized, ice-cold girl. As they walked on he risked a glance in her direction and was astonished to see a single tear shake itself from her eyelash on to the collar of her jacket.

Chapter 9

'This afternoon,' Alfred Baum said to his secretary, a Mademoiselle Pineau, 'you will not return from lunch. You will go to a shop of your choice and you will buy yourself a nice handbag.'

'Whatever for?' Mlle Pineau was a birdlike creature of uncertain age who pecked at her words in a rather disconcerting fashion. Like a bird, she was also fierce in defence of her territory on the fourth floor of the DST headquarters in the Rue des Saussaies. For her, the territory comprised, as the estate agents have it, her grim little office and Baum's scarcely more cheerful room, with all living things residing therein. And since the only living being other than herself was Alfred Baum, he had become the reluctant object of her excessive loyalty and the pretext for her pecking and swooping at others in the building. She had been with Baum for fourteen years and nothing by now was likely to change in this uneasy arrangement, much like a marriage which had become an irksome but unbreakable habit. Madame Baum viewed the whole thing with secret amusement and lent herself to two annual ceremonies. The first was the invitation to lunch at the Baum apartment in Versailles on New Year's day. Mlle Pineau, who had no living relatives, could never decide whether she was the object of the Baums' pity or of some genuine but ill-focused friendship. The annual invitation plunged her into doubt but she always turned up, bearing a modest but carefully chosen gift of wine.

The other ceremony related to her birthday. On this occasion Baum would press an envelope into her hand and

71

give her the afternoon off. In the envelope was a decent sum of money with which to buy herself what the Baums had ordained. It never occurred to Mlle Pineau to buy anything but what had been suggested and it never occurred to the Baums to ask her what she might prefer to have. The arrangement suited everyone.

But now Mlle Pineau wanted to know whatever for.

'For your birthday, of course. And may I, on behalf of my wife and myself, congratulate you most warmly.'

'But it isn't my birthday.' Mademoiselle Pineau sounded offended.

'I am well aware of that, my dear Mademoiselle Pineau. 'Your birthday is on Friday of the week after next.'

'That is correct. So why am I to go shopping this afternoon?'

'This year, I choose to regard your birthday as taking place tomorrow, and so you must buy your present today. You will forgive my presumption in intervening in such a personal matter.'

He took the traditional envelope from his pocket and pressed it into her hand. 'With the respect and affection of Madame Baum and myself.'

Mademoiselle Pineau was accustomed enough to certain eccentricities of her boss – his inordinate love of cats, though only the long-haired varieties. His tendency to wander off, up the Rue des Saussaies, on unpredictable absences which would last anything from fifteen minutes to a couple of hours. Her upbringing prevented her from concluding, as the younger inspectors had long ago concluded, that he had a *petite amie* tucked away somewhere up towards the Boulevard Malesherbes. But only fifteen minutes, including travelling time? The more worldly of his colleagues thought it unlikely. Once he had been seen sitting morosely and alone inside a bistro, a coffee before him. An unsuccessful assignation? Or a contact with an informant? No one knew. Mademoiselle Pineau was also tolerant of his other famous idiosyncracy, much advertised by the staff in Archives: his fondness for poring and muttering over obscure dossiers, often relating to cases long since wound up – as if he preferred that kind of literature to any other. Was he adding a new eccentricity to the list: the shifting of her birthday? If so, she was not going to have it. Deputy director of the DST he might be, but God he was not.

She placed the offending envelope on his desk. 'God has decreed that I should be born on the twentieth. With respect, Monsieur Baum, you cannot undo what the Almighty in his infinite wisdom decided to do.'

'True. But there are reasons of state.'

'What possible interest can the state have in the birthday of Berthe Pineau?'

'You'd be surprised.'

'I would indeed.'

'I am afraid I must order you, dear lady, to buy your birthday present today. I will not insist on your shifting your birthday, but as far as I am concerned, it is tomorrow, and if any of your colleagues comment on the matter you must say that I dated it thus, and if that was wrong, then confirmation is provided once again of the popular view that I am fast losing my senses. Is that clear?'

His eyes were twinkling beneath their bushy brows but the message was both firm and clear enough. Mademoiselle Pineau picked up the envelope. 'Please thank Madame Baum for me. I will send her a little note. And thank you very much. I will see what they have at the Galeries Lafayette.'

As she disappeared into her own room Baum allowed himself a broad smile, locked some loose papers in a drawer and pulled his bulk out of his chair and made for the stairs and the canteen two floors up. At the lift a few moments later he met Mademoiselle Pineau, dressed for the street.

'By the way, I should not in the least mind if you were to mention in the building that I have made this stupid and unforgivable mistake in the matter of your birthday. But I would be grateful if you would make it clear that you never disabused me on the subject. You happened to be able to use this afternoon on other matters, and so you let the old fool persist in his error.'

Mademoiselle Pineau nodded briefly as the lift arrived. 'If you say so.'

'I do, I do,' as the lift bore her down towards her afternoon among the handbags.

Later, Baum called the typing pool on the intercom.

'Madame Ballard, good afternoon. Baum here. I do not have Mademoiselle Pineau this afternoon, I have given her some time off on personal business, and now I find I have a couple of urgent memos to dictate. Can you let me have someone?'

'Most certainly.'

'Good. You'll send a girl up right away?'

'Of course.'

'Thank you.' A brief pause. 'By the way, who will it be?'

'Jacqueline is free.'

'Some of it is sensitive. Also, it's a foreign matter – tricky place names and so on. I found that girl Françoise very good. Is she free?'

'She has a long report from the inspectorate. It won't be finished till four.'

'I think I'll wait for her. Oh, and by the way, don't say I asked for her instead of Jacqueline. You know – I hate to foment jealousies and all that.'

'Very well.'

Madame Ballard also thought that Baum's little quirks were beginning to interfere with his work.

Shortly after four the girl called Françoise was seated, pencil and notebook poised, at the corner of his desk.

He smiled encouragingly at her. 'Shall we begin? I have this memo to the minister's office, with a copy to the director. Subject: training programme for the Senegalese security agency. Please leave a wide margin.'

He dictated rapidly from notes which lay before him. When the memo was finished he gave her another on a joint surveillance between the DST and the Police Judiciaire. As she got up to go, he started rummaging among the papers on his desk.

'Do you think you'd have time to type this short note for me?' He passed her a sheet of paper bearing two paragraphs of handwriting. 'It's to be added to a dossier in Archives and I'd like it done right away. Mademoiselle Pineau's notebook is already full up with other stuff.'

The girl took the paper and glanced at it. The heading

read: *Chatila Group – Communication from CIA, Baghdad.*
It bore a date and a file reference number.

'I'll be able to do all this before I leave at six,' she said.
She was a bright, decisive kind of girl, rather better looking
and better groomed than most of the grey ladies in the pool.
She had been seconded to the DST from the Ministry of the
Interior next door four months earlier.

Baum bestowed his most avuncular smile on her. 'Thank
you, Françoise, but don't stay late on my account.'

AIDE MEMOIRE
Ref: CH/881/27387/AB
6/87

Chatila Group – Communication from CIA, Baghdad

Hanson reports contact with agent 'Wasfi' in Damascus
within past 24 hours. 'Wasfi' believes suspicions of Professor
Hanif have been successfully centred on the man Essat
Osman, thus relieving dangerous pressures on 'Wasfi'.
Baghdad states that 'Wasfi' is shortly to travel to France.
Questioned on the purpose of the visit, 'Wasfi' was evasive,
claimed he did not know. When question of payment was
raised there was the usual trouble over his excessive financial
demands. The matter was not resolved and we still do not
know purpose of the visit. Baghdad believes 'Wasfi' may
become more communicative after further negotiation.

Source: CIA Baghdad (Agent Hanson)

Origin: Agent 'Wasfi', Damascus

Quality of Information: High, based on past experience.
Incomplete. To be pursued with Baghdad, but seek confirmation from Jerusalem.

A. Baum

Françoise typed the memo and the two longer documents,
making the required number of copies plus, in each case, one
flimsy which she slipped into her handbag and thence, later
on in the toilet, behind the waistband of her skirt where
the paper made a troublesome rustling sound. She returned
Baum's documents to him shortly before six and was thanked
and treated to another of his benevolent smiles. She trooped
out of the building with the men and women who were lucky

75

enough to finish on time, called goodbye to a couple of other typists from the pool and made her way westwards along the Faubourg St Honoré. At the corner of the Rue du Colisée, she used the telephone in a bar and was observed to do so by a young man in jeans and bomber jacket who had been sauntering up the faubourg behind her. Then she went on and took the Metro at St Philippe du Roule. The young man sought a telephone in turn.

'She phoned. Now she's taken the Metro as usual.'

'Did she see you?'

'No, chief.'

'Absolutely sure?'

'I swear it.'

'Good,' Baum said. 'You'll go to the place I said. I'll send Catherine to join you. It will look better. Hang around there until she turns up and makes contact. Eat what you like; I'll sign the chit. You can call me at home during the evening.'

'Yes, chief. Does that include the wine?'

'Yes, but don't take advantage.'

'Thanks, chief.'

The young man walked briskly down side streets to the Champs Elysées, crossed the road and walked down towards the Rond-Point. He turned into a large plastic-and-neon 'Self', lined up for a beer and found himself a table near the door. After a while Catherine joined him, a frizzy-haired girl with spectacles and too much eyeshadow, but jolly and sharp and good company for a surveillance job. It was close to seven. They lined up and pushed their trays past the display of food and drink, returned laden to their table and set to eating supper on the DST.

'How do we know she'll come here?' Catherine asked.

'It's where she always meets this guy.'

'Someone follow her here?'

'Not at all. When she comes here she takes pretty good care she's not being tailed. Anyway, the old man wouldn't risk it. We did it with a bug or tap or something. Want some of these onions?'

The girl shook her head. 'How, a tap?'

'Tapped her phone,' her companion said. 'That way we

usually know when she's got a date with this fellow. But she never gives the name of the place. Too careful.'

'For Christ's sake,' the girl said. 'Stop showing how much you know and tell me how we found out it's here and not somewhere else.'

'Postal service, wasn't it?' the young man said, enjoying himself.

The girl shrugged.

'Intercepted a letter. From him to her, that is. Couple of months ago, saying to meet here. And since then, it's always here: "Let's meet at the same place." Simple. Stands to reason.'

'Lousy tradecraft.'

The young man nodded. His mouth was full. Then he tapped her on the knee beneath the table. Françoise had come into the restaurant and was queuing at the food counter. They watched her fill her tray, pay for the meal and head for an empty table. Shortly afterwards, a middle-aged man in a gabardine trench-coat joined her from a table at the far end of the restaurant.

'Contact made,' the young man said to Catherine. 'You can see them better than I can. Tell me if she hands anything over.'

The other two were deep in conversation. After a moment, the girl took an envelope from her bag and slid it across the table. The man took it and put it in his breast pocket. The thing was done naturally and their conversation continued.

'It's all the old man needs to know,' the young man told Catherine. 'We're free to knock off when we've finished eating. Fancy a film, like?'

Catherine shook her head. 'My boyfriend said he'd wait for me till nine. Isn't he the lucky one – it's only eight fifteen. I'm off.'

'I'll phone the chief,' the young man said. They left the restaurant without being seen by the other couple, still talking quietly together.

'I must go out to phone, I'm afraid,' Baum said to his wife. He had just had the young man's call and had remembered to congratulate him on a job neatly done and ask if he'd enjoyed the wine.

Madame Baum looked up from her knitting and nodded. 'Don't be too long. Another couple of rows and I'll want to measure this across your shoulders.'

'It's splendid,' Baum said. He tipped one cat off his lap, stepped carefully over another and made his way out to the hall. 'Green,' he muttered as he went. 'I really don't know about green.'

In an access of extreme caution he walked past the bistro where he usually made his more private calls and headed into the centre of Versailles. He chose a café he used seldom and made for the phone booth.

He dialled a number and waited through the clicks and echoes of the international network. Then the ringing tone, ending within a couple of seconds as the instrument was lifted.

'Yes.'

'Paris friend here.'

'Shalom.'

'I think everything is all right,' Baum said. 'Certainly our little message has been passed on. Now we can only hope it reaches the right desk.'

'Good. I have taken steps to leak something else,' Ben Tov said. 'It will reach our target from a totally different direction. It will be' — he searched for the word in French — 'corroborative.'

'Directly?'

'Indirectly.'

His conversation concluded, Baum paid for his call and made his way back to the apartment to be measured for his green pullover.

Chapter 10

The telex message from the American Walters in Jerusalem to his friend in Tripoli had been received and decoded in the American embassy in the small hours by a US Marine named Folsom. On duty alone in the embassy's top-security room, he had had all the time he needed to take a copy and secrete it with a number of other items in his boot. When he was relieved at seven, he passed the log book and messages received during the night to the man coming on duty, signed himself out and went home to sleep.

Later that day he made his way on foot to the old city, through the maze of narrow alleys and up to the castle overlooking the harbour. As he went he took his usual precautions. He was pretty sure his rear was clean, though twice lately he had had his doubts. It had shaken but not deterred him, since he was a man acting under constraint. Those handling him had made the situation perfectly clear: he would work for them or they would send the evidence to the embassy. In his own mind he was a victim, wronged, almost blameless. How could he have known that the whole thing was a trap, that the girl was under age and her 'brother' was a professional recruiter for Colonel Jalaf's Intelligence Bureau? If he hadn't panicked he'd have been able to talk his way out with his commanding officer and they'd have spirited him away quietly to an assignment elsewhere. He was good at his job, he had his stripes, and the Marines found it harder to come by new brain than new brawn. But he had panicked, and had signed their bit of paper. Since then, for over a year, he had been passing them stuff. He did not, in his mind, face the fact that he was passing far more than he needed in order to keep them quiet, because that also meant facing the fact that he appreciated the cash. Jalaf was smart. The piece of paper ensured co-operation; the generous cash element would, in most cases, ensure enthusiasm. Men like Folsom reasoned on the sheep-and-goat principle. After all, if one was to be hanged . . .

He reached the entrance to the castle and paid for a ticket into the museum. Once inside, he headed for the archaeology section and entered the Roman gallery. Halfway down was a pediment taken from the arch of Marcus Aurelius. It was poorly preserved, its surface pitted and scarred. It had been placed inconspicuously against a wall, as if the museum was not too proud of it, and there was a narrow space behind it. Folsom took from his pocket the envelope containing the copies of the night's messages and slipped it between the ancient stone and the wall. Then he sauntered back through the galleries and out into the brilliant afternoon sunshine. Glancing down to the busy harbour below, he turned on his heel and made his way back to the modern city.

The Marine Folsom being the finest asset Libyan intelligence had had in years, the leader himself took a direct interest in the product from that source. Colonel Jalaf was the leader's cousin, thus ensuring on the basis of family loyalty that Gadafi would actually receive the material, together with relevant and reasonably honest interpretations and assessments from the Intelligence Committee. In regard to the Jerusalem message, however, no sensible assessment appeared to be possible since Jalaf's department had no idea what significance it might have. A careful inquiry at Foreign Affairs produced the nervous advice that this was one for the leader himself. And so it proved.

Gadafi studied the brief text for an inordinately long time. Then he looked up at Jalaf, standing before him. Then he rose from his chair, seized a heavy volume from his desk and hurled it across the room.

'These Palestinian dogs!' he yelled at the terrified Jalaf. 'These dangerous idiots! Scum, all of them! May their mothers curse them!'

Jalaf did not dare to say a word until the familiar paroxysm had died down. Gadafi continued to rage for what seemed to the colonel an agonizingly long while. Then he stopped as abruptly as he had started. 'I give the most confidential information to a man I trust like my own brother, and evidently he has blabbed about it and it comes back to me now through a foreign intelligence service. God alone knows through what imperialist drains and cesspools it has travelled to reach us here. And why, why? Because the dog is a Palestinian, that's why! Understand, Jalaf, Palestinians can do only one thing: they can talk! Nothing else!'

He was working himself up again and Jalaf would have edged closer to the door if he had dared. But he had learned that the safest thing during Gadafi's rages was immobility and silence. He preserved both.

'I suppose I must warn the fool,' Gadafi was shouting. 'He deserves nothing of the kind. He deserves the whip, the knout. And he's the best of them. No wonder they've been nearly forty years in the camps. It's all the dogs deserve.'

He sat down and read the offending text again. 'This cannot be a coincidence.' He spoke to himself, ignoring Jalaf. 'I do not believe in coincidences. I have had no occasion to talk about this Frenchman to anyone except Professor Hanif – to no one.'

Gadafi threw the paper across the desk and Jalaf moved forward to retrieve it. 'You know how to contact Hanif in Damascus?'

'Yes.'

'Contact him securely. I repeat, securely. Give him the contents of that telex. Tell him someone in his outfit has been talking and needs to have his tongue cut out. Tell him I do not suggest that person is himself, but he'd best look at his associates.'

Colonel Jalaf saluted his cousin and withdrew.

The decisive conversation with Gadafi which gave rise to the events here described and to the leader's present anger had taken place a few days before. Hanif had come off the morning plane from Damascus, immaculate in off-white silk suit, button-down white silk shirt, sober tie – a successful,

81

conservative figure. He had been met by a young officer and ushered into a black Mercedes flying the national flag. The car drew away from the airport and out into the traffic, the young officer beside the driver, the professor in the rear seat.

'Welcome to our country,' the young officer had said nervously, turning in his seat. 'The leader instructs me to present his best wishes. He will receive you at the command headquarters without delay.'

His passenger nodded but said nothing.

'I have orders,' the officer said, reaching over and drawing the window curtains. 'It is more secure.'

He was uncomfortable: this personage was remarkably unresponsive. He had been instructed to honour him, but how did you honour a man like this who had not uttered a word? He relapsed into silence and nothing was said on the twenty-five-kilometre drive into Tripoli.

The bedouin tent had been set up on a small lawn surrounded by hedges in the midst of the stark modern buildings of the Libyan Army Command Headquarters. Sand had been sprinkled on the ground. A brazier set between the two tent poles left a pall of thin, acrid smoke within the tent which caught at the throat. There were half a dozen low chairs for visitors, and tables on which books and magazines were scattered in disarray, there for use rather than show. On one of the tent poles hung a gleaming Kalashnikov and a riding whip. Gadafi sat in an armchair facing his visitor. He wore a colonel's undress uniform without decorations, the collar unbuttoned. He was smoking an American cigarette in a short amber holder. There was a slim gold chain round his left wrist.

'*Salaam alaykum.*'

'*Wa alaykum as-salaam.*'

'My dear professor, I am happy to see you again. You and your friends are our brothers. What is ours is also yours. You are welcome here in Libya. I am listening.'

A small cup of sugary *gahwah* had been put before the visitor, with a box of cigarettes and a lighter. He paid no attention to them. When he spoke his voice was low, the Levantine Arabic carefully articulated, the tone unemotional.

82

'It is confidential,' he said.

'Very well.'

'He should leave.' The visitor nodded his head in the direction of an aide-de-camp who stood motionless in the far corner of the tent. Gadafi gave a brief order and the man withdrew.

'A trusted man,' he said.

'I have such trusted men, but I do not trust them. Like that we are not betrayed and we survive to continue the struggle.'

'That is an unusual attitude among you Palestinians.'

'I know. It is why my Chatila group has successes. The PLO factions are riddled with Zionist spies. We are not.'

'So tell me what you want.'

'We have assessed once again the situation of the Zionist presence and the various forces opposing them. We conclude that the PLO in its politicized form is a spent force. It can talk but it cannot fight. The same is true, of course, of the Egyptians. We expect nothing from them, nor from Hussein in Jordan. A midget whose liver is yellow. An agent of imperialism with American spies in his cabinet. We therefore turn once again to you.'

'Do you need guns?'

'No.'

'More money?'

'Not money.'

'Men?'

Hanif threw up his chin in a sign of dismissive impatience.

'What then?'

Hanif removed a gold pen from his pocket and twirled it slowly between thumb and forefinger as he spoke. He had fine hands, the nails carefully manicured.

'There have been rumours,' he said, 'that the work at Tukrah has been crowned with success. That is what I want to talk about.'

'What do you call success?'

'A weapon would be success.'

'It would.' Gadafi stubbed his cigarette out carefully and lay the holder on the table before him. 'What makes you think we have made a weapon?'

'Rumours cross the desert. Like camel trains, only faster.' The pen described an arc, catching the light from the overhead lamp. 'They reach us in Damascus. They also reach us indirectly, across the Atlantic. We have a man in Washington. His sources are excellent. He tells us there is a CIA appreciation paper which states that Libya is now believed to have weapon capability.'

Gadafi smiled briefly. 'In Washington, you know, they write too many of these papers. What they do not know they invent. I believe they are paid by results – so much per secret.'

'Nevertheless, we hear these rumours in Damascus and we reason in the following way. The Zionist presence cannot be ended by conventional military means; the day for that is long past. I am not a man to harbour illusions. It cannot be ended by political means; say Zionist and you say American. One cannot shift the Americans. Therefore – and this is how we reason – only ultimate measures can succeed. These would be measures which sovereign states will not undertake but which an organization like ours has the human resources and the will to carry through. Above all the will.'

'There is nothing wrong with your reasoning, professor. Nothing at all, when viewed in the perspective of history. But I must tell you there are problems.'

'What are these problems?' The visitor's voice had a curious quality in it, as if the Kalashnikov on the tent pole were his and not the Libyan leader's.

'They are two in number,' Gadafi said. 'The first is that with every respect to the CIA our weapon is not yet ready. My technical people tell me six months but I have learned not to put my faith in technicians. The second, which is more serious, is that Zionist missiles with atomic warheads can reach us here in Tripoli within minutes. Conventional bombers can be here in an hour or so. And the Americans would look the other way, as they did when the Zionists destroyed the Iraqi installations in 1981. I cannot take that kind of risk.'

The visitor tapped impatiently with the gold pen on the edge of the table. 'I must tell you we have a sure way of delivering such a bomb into the heart of Jerusalem. It might not even be necessary to detonate it, since no government could afford to let that happen in their capital.'

'The Zionists, on the other hand, have a reputation for always detonating their bombs. You must not forget that I am a military man. I was trained to assess risk.'

'We have this unique delivery opportunity. It will not recur.'

'You are a professor of archaeology, and so you reason in historical terms – in very long stretches of time. You are too steeped in history, my friend, whereas I am steeped in the day-to-day struggle. We both know that Jerusalem has changed hands six, seven times in the past three thousand years and Allah will yet bring it back into the hands of those to whom it belongs. Unfortunately, I have to think in months and maybe decades – no more. By all means do what you can do in Jerusalem. For that you have my blessing and may Allah go with you. But I cannot allow you to expose my country to a reprisal which would destroy us. A revival of our people a century from now does not interest me.'

The visitor was silent for a moment, his face expressionless, his fingers toying with the pen. From nearby the muezzin called the faithful to prayer.

'You wish to pray?'

'Allah will forgive me.' Gadafi allowed himself a brief smile. 'Let us continue. He may also forgive you.'

'I am a believer but not devout.'

'It is usually the faith which motivates men like you.'

'You spoke of a sense of history. That is what motivates me. I look around and see eight hundred million Moslems and very few Zionists. What – maybe twelve million in the entire world? I look back in history and see two thousand years and more of strife for my people. I look at Jerusalem and what do I see there? A city which suffered under the Babylonians, the Assyrians, the Romans, the Persians, the Turks and the Crusaders. And through it all my people survived and clung to the city as they still do. I am not impressed by a Zionist occupation: I have studied too many others. They do not last.'

'This opportunity you speak of. How secure is it?'

'Very secure. I am the only one to know of it.'

'You and whoever it is that you have inside the city.'

'You spoke of faith. There is nothing like faith to sustain a man's silence. The man in the city lives only for his God. I will vouch for him because he is a fanatic.'

'I would like to help you,' Gadafi said. 'Your project is not without appeal. I will give you a name. The man is a good friend of our cause. Perhaps also a little fanatical. He may be able to do something for you. You must describe our little talk here and say I will confirm any inquiry.' He wrote carefully on a pad, tore the sheet off and handed it across the table. His visitor took it and put it in an inside pocket of his jacket without glancing at it.

'The man is a Frenchman. He can be found through a Major Savary of Service 6 of the DGSE. You may talk freely to him. He is an unusual man.'

'You trust him?'

'He has a long record of working for us. He has set up a useful shipping route.'

'Please explain.'

'He can get goods safely out of France to destinations which interest us. If you meet him and he trusts you he will tell you what he can do.'

'What motivates this man?'

Gadafi smiled. 'Money. That, and latterly the fact that having worked with us, he knows he cannot stop . . .'

'May Allah go with you.' It was all Hanif said as he rose to go. He still did not smile. It was as if nothing whatever had been transacted between them.

'Tell me,' Gadafi said as he got to his feet, 'how will you persuade the Zionists that you have an atomic device in place, that it works and that you are prepared to detonate it? After all, it is not one task but three.'

'I have plans which will be effective. I take it you would not wish me to explain them.'

'I would not.'

The Libyan leader clapped his hands and the aide reappeared. He saluted Gadafi's brief order and ushered the guest out into the sunlight.

Chapter 11

The atmosphere in the Israeli embassy in the Rue Rabelais was not good. An angry despondency had settled on the place following the disaster a week earlier. The fury directed at the French was unabated. But a sense of guilt lay below the surface of the anger: the ambassador believed his staff had not faced up to the Ministry of Foreign Affairs in the matter of the armoured car, while his associates took the view that if the ambassador spent less time trying to win friends in fashionable circles and more time on basic questions, and particularly on impressing himself on the Middle Eastern desk at the Quai d'Orsay, things might have turned out differently. To these feelings of guilt, unease and bitterness was added a sense of futility, since the embassy could do nothing more than convey to the French what Jerusalem was saying. Beyond civilizing the language and cautiously briefing their friends in the media, the embassy staff were helpless. And their attack of nerves, ill-articulated and inadequately focused, was leading them to take amiss almost anything that Jerusalem instructed them to do.

This being the case, when the decrypt of Ben Tov's message lay before the Mossad resident, it was perhaps not surprising that that gentleman viewed it with a jaundiced eye. In the first place it was festooned with prohibitions. For his eyes only. Not to be discussed at any, repeat any, level at the embassy. Reply, which was to be of the utmost urgency, not to be routed via Foreign Affairs, but to go direct to Ben Tov and to no one else. No record to be kept. And the last word on the message was PRIORITY.

There was no mention of background, purpose or any further intention. It appeared to have nothing to do with the only thing which was exercising their minds at the time – the assassinations on the autoroute. Ben Tov had not considered that this aspect of the matter was any of their damn business. He further considered that even Shimon, who was as good a resident as he had anywhere, might not resist the temptation to say to his colleagues: 'Don't worry, the old man is on to something . . . can't tell you what . . . a bit odd, but at least we've something to do.' Ben Tov wanted none of that kind of talk.

So that what Shimon did was to curse quietly to himself, re-read the message three times, reach for the intercom to summon his assistant but withdraw his hand before it had touched the instrument, and then decide that if it was that secret he'd have to look after the thing himself.

Having consulted the telephone directory and a street plan, he locked the door of his office and spent fifteen minutes immobile behind his desk and deep in thought. Then he unlocked the door, told his secretary that he would not be back, descended to the ground floor and let himself out into the street. He was careful not to take the first cruising taxi but picked one up round the next corner. On his way to the Bourse he checked regularly through the rear window: no one was following. At the Bourse he paid off the taxi and made his way down the Rue Feydeau. The fascia at No. 14 proclaimed: Ets. Dejazet. Coffres-forts. The showroom at street level was bleak. Through the rather dusty windows safes of various sizes could be seen, with further and larger safes illustrated on posters hanging on the walls. There was a counter with a man in a grey overall behind it. There was also an austere lady at a desk.

Shimon opened the door and advanced hesitantly towards the counter. The hesitation was feigned: he was not a man easily inhibited.

'Monsieur?'

Shimon shrugged and smiled in what he hoped was an expressive display of confusion.

'Does anyone here speak Hebrew?' He said this in Hebrew. The man behind the counter shrugged in turn.

'*Ivrit . . . Hébreu.*' Shimon tapped his own chest. '*Moi Yisroel.*'

The man turned to the lady at the desk. 'Doesn't seem to speak French.'

The lady shrugged and folded her hands on the top of her typewriter. If this was nothing else it was a break in the monotony.

'*Personne parle Hébreu?*' Shimon made it sound as if that exhausted his vocabulary.

The man scratched his head. 'What do you think?' he asked the lady at the desk. 'Do we have anyone upstairs?'

'Madame Altman is Jewish. Maybe she does. Why not try?'

'Good idea,' the man said. He turned to Shimon. 'Wait.' Shimon smiled and nodded.

The lady was on the phone. Words were exchanged. Then she shrugged again and hung up.

'Not a word,' she said to the man.

There was an awkward silence. Heads were shaken and hands extended in gestures of helplessness and regret. Amid this, Shimon retreated to the street. Through the dusty window he could see the man saying something to the lady and the lady laughing. If they had lost a sale they didn't seem bothered.

It was close to five thirty. Shimon crossed to a café a few doors down and managed to find himself a table in the window from which he could see the door of the Ets. Dejazet. He ordered a beer and waited for some movement across the way.

At six the man at the counter emerged minus his overall and made off towards the Bourse. Shimon slapped money on to the marble table top and moved out into the street. His only worry was that the lady at the typewriter might see him lurking there and draw unworthy conclusions. But she passed on the far pavement, her mind elsewhere.

Staff were coming out of the door in little groups. Shimon was watching for someone looking reasonably like a Madame Altman. He pictured in his mind a Jewish lady of uncertain but mature age, drab like the establishment she worked for, hard-faced perhaps, since she had not volun-

89

teered to come down and help with the Hebrew (possibly an unjust thought), and cetainly harassed since at Dejazet they worked them until six and to judge from the appearance of the emerging staff, rewarded them inadequately for their labours.

He was startled when a figure answering pretty faithfully to his mental description emerged and fell in with the crush of commuters making for the Bourse. This, he decided, was his Madame Altman.

The putative Madame Altman was indeed of mature age; Shimon reckoned sixty-plus, possibly retained by the frugal owners of the firm because viewed purely as an overhead she was a lesser evil than someone younger and more eager to be adequately paid. She was shabby in a plain brown dress and her hair fell in wisps on to the sides of her face. The face itself was pinched, timid, Shimon thought. She carried a plastic shopping bag.

Following her was no problem. She made her way to the Metro at the Bourse, changed on to the St Ouen line at the Gare St Lazare and left the train at La Fourche. Up in the street Shimon had to hang back and pretend an interest in various shop windows as she visited a grocer and bought vegetables off a stall. Then she crossed the Avenue de Clichy and made her way to the Rue Lemercier. He considered waylaying her but thought better of it. She turned into No. 37, a nondescript apartment block. He stood about for five minutes before presenting himself to the concierge.

'Altman? Staircase in the courtyard, third floor left.' The concierge slammed her glass door. Beyond, a child was wailing without commitment as if its heart was not in it.

Shimon made his way across the courtyard and mounted the uneven wooden stairs to the third. He pressed the bell by the side of the door on the left. Indeterminate cooking smells hung in the air with a hint of inadequate drains. Soon there were footsteps and the door was opened on a chain, revealing in the few inches of space the face of an old man. Shimon had an impression of mistrustful eyes and little more.

'Yes?'

'Shalom. I am from the Israeli embassy. I would like to speak to Madame Altman.'

90

'We have no dealings with any embassies. What is it about?'

'Are you Monsieur Altman?'

'I am.'

Shimon took a visiting card from his pocket and passed it through the crack in the door. There was a pause as the card was brought close to the face to be inspected.

'What do you want?'

'Could I come in for a moment? What I have to say to your wife is important.'

At that moment a woman's voice could be heard from somewhere in the apartment.

'What is it, Jacques?'

'A man wants to talk to you. He says he's from the Israeli embassy.'

'Well, let him in.'

The door closed and Shimon heard the sound of the chain being freed. Then it reopened.

'Come in.'

Madame Altman was standing next to her husband. Both looked scared. Shimon was aware of the musty odour of unaired rooms, cooking oil and human incontinence. Monsieur Altman was much older than his wife. He wore a frayed dressing gown and slippers. Beneath the dressing gown the neckband of a collarless shirt could be seen. What hair he had was unbrushed. Only the eyes, suspicious and calculating, seemed truly alive.

Madame Altman had opened the door of the sitting room and led the way in.

'Please sit down.'

Shimon sat on a hard chair and the Altmans ranged themselves before him on a sofa. The old man was muttering. His hands moved constantly, plucking at the edge of his dressing gown.

'I am an attaché at the Israeli embassy,' Shimon repeated. 'We have a problem and believe you could help us with it, madame.'

'I? Surely not.'

'You work for the safe manufacturers Dejazet?'

'Yes.'

91

'Then you can certainly help.'

'How do we know you are from the embassy?' The old man's voice was squeezed out of him past obscure bronchial impediments.

'You have my card, and you can check on me if you wish by phoning the embassy.'

'Jacques, let the gentleman talk,' Madame Altman said.

Shimon had rehearsed in his mind what he would say, but instinct told him now that he had best bring the old man into the scenario.

'Monsieur Altman, you are possibly not in the best of health. I must apologize for intruding.'

'My health has not been good for over forty years now. I am seventy-nine years of age, monsieur. I am a survivor of Buchenwald.'

'Jacques, the gentleman doesn't want to hear old tales.'

'He's from the embassy, he said. So why shouldn't he want to hear? Have you no interest in talking to a survivor of Drancy and Buchenwald?'

'On the contrary, I am deeply interested.'

'My health you asked about.' He was wheezing, perhaps as a demonstration of what genuinely ailed him. 'My lungs – almost finished. Also, my nerves are bad.'

'He hasn't been able to work since he returned. His nerves; he can't stand any kind of strain, any anxiety, you understand.'

'I understand.' Shimon turned to the old man. 'Those were terrible days. My mother's family ... from Rumania, you know, all gone.'

'Do you want me to tell you what it was like there, in the camp?'

The eyes were glistening, eager. Eternally hungry for an audience, Shimon thought. Reliving it; unable to move beyond the monstrous event. He turned to the wife. 'Could we perhaps talk alone?' He realized he was addressing her as if the husband were not there.

'No, no. My husband must know what you have to say, otherwise he will be worried, upset.' She turned to the old man. 'Please, Jacques, let the gentleman speak. He hasn't come to hear about us.'

The hands plucked at the dressing gown. The eyes were fixed on Shimon's face.

Now the rehearsed story, so much closer to the truth than Shimon, in inventing it, could have realized.

'At the embassy we are doing what we can to bring to justice the terrorists who killed our people last week on the autoroute.'

'Terrible, terrible,' Madame Altman rocked her head from side to side.

'It is very important for us to be able to examine the contents of a safe used by those believed to be responsible. We have established that the safe was supplied by Dejazet.' He took a sheet of paper from his pocket, handed it to her. 'The details of the safe.'

Madame Altman looked at the paper and handed it back. 'A model we stopped making ten years ago.'

'Was it exported?'

'I believe so. To many countries.'

'Could one check the destination of a particular safe from the registration number?'

'Of course. We keep very careful records. We are a businesslike firm.'

'And what if the present owner of the safe lost the key and needed a new one?'

'He would have to provide Dejazet via the people he bought it from with proof of ownership and we would supply a new key.'

'What constitutes proof of ownership?'

'The registration document, accompanied by a letter witnessed by the civil authority.'

'And what if such a procedure could not be followed?'

'Then we would naturally not provide a key. We aren't fools. Many people try to obtain keys by fraud.'

'Of course.'

He paused. The eyes were still watching him. The crucial part lay ahead. He cursed himself for not having approached her before she had reached home. He hadn't reckoned with the old man. What if he broke off now, waylaid her in the morning on her way to work? He decided that what he had to say would probably feed the old man's obsession with the

93

wrongs against him in the past and what Shimon judged to be a consuming desire for justice, revenge.

'Madame, we have access to the safe in question but we have no key. We need to obtain a duplicate key from your office.'

'But it is impossible, monsieur, without the documents.'

'Is there no way, madame, that someone in possession of the serial number could have the key cut in your workshops?'

'I can see no way.'

'What if someone inside the firm who believed as we do that these killers must be brought to justice — what if such a person was willing to help, despite the absence of documents?' He paused for as long as he dared. The old man was watching, still silent. 'What if you, madame, were willing to help in this important task?'

'*No!*' The old man was trembling and there was spittle on his parched lips and down the front of the dressing gown. 'She will not do it. You have no right to come here, involving us in these schemes. We are quiet people. We keep out of trouble. Have I not had enough trouble in my life? The camp — I will tell you about the camp, monsieur.' His whole body was trembling now. His wife had placed an arm round his shoulders and was trying to calm him.

'You see what you have done, monsieur? It is clear that I cannot help you.' And to her husband: 'Please be quiet, Jacques. I am not going to do anything for this man.'

'Do you think we can risk her losing her job?' He was shouting now, struggling to free himself from his wife's restraining arm. 'We have no money, monsieur. I cannot work. I was a skilled man, a tailor, but since then I cannot work. We depend on my wife's income, you understand. We are poor people. Leave us alone.'

'You had best go,' Madame Altman said. 'Forgive us. It is not always possible to be helpful.'

'I understand.' Shimon rose from his chair. 'I will see myself out. Thank you for listening to me.' Then he left the apartment and walked slowly down the stairs, cursing himself for a fool.

Next morning he phoned her at her office.

'Forgive me, madame, I owe you an apology. I would like to make it in person.'

'It is unnecessary.'

'Please meet me for lunch. Even if you cannot do what I asked yesterday evening, I think you could help simply by answering a few more questions.'

There was a silence. He could hear typewriters in the background. 'Very well. I do not wish to be unhelpful.'

'I am grateful. Do you know the Brasserie de la Banque in the Rue Réaumur?'

'Yes.'

'I will be there at one.'

'Very well.'

Later, when she approached his table she was wearing the same brown dress with a grey cardigan. He rose to greet her and she smiled at him. The smile revealed that she had been a beautiful girl long ago.

When the food was before them, he forced himself to return to his topic.

'I am very sorry to have upset your husband. I had no idea – I thought he might welcome an action which could be seen as a defence of our people . . . to ensure there are no more Buchenwalds, you understand.'

'He is afraid I would lose my job. It would be very hard for us.'

They ate in silence for a while.

'You are not a religious person?'

She shook her head. 'Neither of us. Before . . . before the camp, I understand my husband had been religious. Orthodox, in fact. But when I met him and we married – that would be in 1946 – I remember he said to me many times, "I have proof that God does not exist. At Buchenwald I saw the proof." We are not religious.'

'In recent years there have been many attacks against Jews, and not only Israeli officials. Many have been in Paris.'

'I know.'

'Does this not concern you?'

'What can ordinary people do?'

'Sometimes ordinary people can do something truly useful. I believe you can, madame.'

There was a long pause before she said, 'In what way could I help?'

'First of all, please tell me exactly what routine is followed when your office receives a request for a new key.'

'We check the papers and if the request is judged genuine by our office manager, the release of a key blank is authorized. That is the first security check. The workshop cannot create new keys without blanks. They are held in a locked cupboard in the sales department.'

'And then?'

'The blank will go down to the workshop on the ground floor behind the showroom. With it will be a chit giving the serial number of the safe. The workshop manager will check that number in his records and that will tell him the configuration of the cut key. Then he puts the job out to one of the workmen and the key is cut. It goes back to the sales department and the transaction is recorded before the key goes out to the customer.'

'And where do you work?'

'I am a clerk in sales.'

Shimon allowed time to elapse before he put the next question.

'If you agreed to help us, would you be able to obtain a key?'

More time. Then: 'It would be dangerous for me.'

'But possible?'

'Possible, yes.'

He felt that he was drawing her by gentle, tentative steps towards him.

'What would it involve?'

'I would have to obtain a blank and send it downstairs with the serial number. That would be on the chit, which I would have to take from a drawer in our office. Then, when the key came back, it would have to be intercepted before it reached the manager. It would probably mean finding an excuse for collecting it downstairs. Perhaps urgency – something like that.'

'When does your office manager take his summer holiday?'

'He is away now.'

'Does that make it easier or harder?'

96

A silence. 'Easier, I suppose. His deputy is not all that conscientious.'

'And if you were willing to help, how long would all this take?'

'We give a good service. Often customers need a key over-night. It can be done during the course of one day.'

'Madame Altman, I believe you are going to help me.'

Again, a long pause. She had finished her food and she sought refuge from what he was asking in an elaborate search through her handbag for a handkerchief.

'And what would the Israeli embassy do for me if I lost my job?'

'We look after our friends.'

'That is not really an answer.'

'I need authorization, but you can take my word that we would not abandon you.'

'You see, my husband . . .' Her voice trailed off. Shimon nodded but said nothing. Instinct told him that a decision held by a fragile thread.

Suddenly she said: 'I will try.'

He reached across the table and took her hand. 'Bless you, madame.'

They had arranged to meet the next evening just after six in a bistro a few minutes' walk from the Dejazet office. Again she was dressed in her brown dress and grey cardigan. She carried a plastic bag.

She refused Shimon's offer of a drink.

'I have done it, but do not ask me again for such a service – ever.'

'I promise. It must have been a great strain.'

'I am exhausted with worry. There was a very difficult moment. I will not bother you with the details.'

She took an envelope from her handbag and handed it to him. Inside he could feel the outline of a long, slender key.

'The safe was sold through our Middle East agent who worked at that time from Beirut. The records give the owner's address as Damascus.'

'Thank you. Israel is deeply indebted to you, madame.'

'One has to help. Even a woman like me can be called

upon to help, I suppose. I would not have felt right if . . .'
She did not finish the sentence.

'You have my card. If there is any trouble, please call me.'

She smiled at him and again he saw the beautiful girl who had married the young survivor from the camps who had never been able to rejoin the mainstream of life.

As they left the bistro and she turned to bid him farewell, he leaned forward, kissed her gently on the cheek, and slipped an envelope into her hand.

'That may help a little.'

Chapter 12

In France the army is not the career of choice of the ambitious, the confidently able and the well-born. Rather, it is the refuge mainly of the petty bourgeois and the mediocre. An army career carries little prestige, meagre financial rewards and scant opportunities, save in time of war, for adventure and heroics. The younger, often duller, sons of provincial shopkeepers or of run-down rural gentry become career officers in the French army. The system has produced over the years significant and often dangerous outbreaks of political and social beastliness by the military.

General Boulanger in the 1870s attempted a coup and failed incompetently. The Dreyfus case exhibited the army at its most rancorous, socially envious and reactionary. In the thirties the colonels and generals had close connections with the upstart fascist movements, the Cagoule and the Croix de Feu. It was the army which tried to kill de Gaulle for disentangling France from her hopeless colonial pretensions in North Africa. And in war after war – 1870, 1914, 1939 – the French officer corps displayed its inability to accept the present in preference to the past. It was a French military court that condemned de Gaulle to death *in absentia* in 1940 and the timorous and mediocre Marshal Pétain who led France into collaboration with Hitler.

Through this cadre of officers and petty officers the regular intakes of conscripts pass like doses of salts through a living organism. The analogy is distasteful but not unapt. And it is from this organism that the staff of the DGSE – France's main intelligence service – is largely drawn.

The DGSE, which grew out of the turmoil of the Liberation and the subsequent social and political upheavals of the fifties and sixties, is perhaps the oddest nest of spies and covert operators in the world. Its leadership is heavily tainted with the political ambitions and social obscurantism of the army officer class. And as one sinks down the levels of the DGSE hierarchy one encounters a degree of ethnic variety and even of foreign involvement unknown in any comparable service. In the rank and file of hitmen, mercenaries, petty informers and 'ultimate' interrogators are to be found North Africans and Senegalese, Germans and Italians dredged from the ranks of the Foreign Legion, white trash from the former colonies, and of course Corsicans from the Paris *milieu*.

All this, oddly enough, is relevant. Without it, Major Claude Etienne Savary of Department 6 of the DGSE cannot be understood.

Savary's father had been a career officer in a famous cavalry regiment. The cavalry charge, in his view, was a paradigm of the military virtues – courage, discipline, *élan*. He had not taken kindly to the replacement of the horse by the Hotchkiss and Renault tank and like his fellow officers had regarded Colonel de Gaulle's theories of tank warfare as so much upstart rubbish. When de Gaulle was promoted general he and his friends had snorted in the mess. When, too late, the upstart was made under-secretary for war the elder Savary's regiment was being smashed to pieces by Von Kleist's panzers east of Paris. With de Gaulle in England setting up the Free French, the elder Savary had agreed with his fellow officers that the man was a traitor. Then, with the Germans occupying two thirds of France, he had been summarily retired. In his native town of Douai he found employment as manager of a home for delinquent boys. His predecessor's name had been Levinson and this name had earned the family a place on a list prepared by the local police at the request of the Gestapo. Nothing more was heard of them. The older Savary, a decent and patriotic man, had deplored the fate of the Levinsons, the grasping violence of the German occupation, the deep disgrace of France. All this he attributed to the venality of politicians and communist efforts to demoralize French society. In his mind it had no connection with the tactics of tank warfare or the competence of the general staff. He did his best to instil in his only son, Claude, a view of his unhappy country's plight which coincided with his own. In this he achieved a substantial measure of success.

Young Claude Savary was on military service at the time in the fifties when France was in some political and social turmoil: it frightened right-thinking citizens to see so many inhabitants of unknown industrial suburbs chanting slogans in the very centre of Paris as if they meant every word. The Communist Party could call half a million people on to the streets of Paris. The colonies were stirring uneasily. Governments were once again falling like skittles. But now de Gaulle, the upstart and traitor of 1940, was seen by the Savarys and their kindred spirits as France's only hope of national self-respect and stability. Claude Savary elected to stay on in the army, passed through St Cyr with modest distinction and was posted to the intelligence branch as a second lieutenant. 'Sound' was the epithet to be found on his passing-out assessment.

First Djibouti, then Saigon, and then Oran as the Maghreb erupted in furious national fervour and the bombs started to explode in the towns and cities of the North African littoral. It was in Oran that Savary had crossed the thin line from intelligence to interrogation and from interrogation to the routine extraction of information and confessions by the use of torture.

As a captain in military intelligence at the Lyautey barracks in Oran, Savary earned himself a reputation for extreme diligence in the hunting down and bringing to punishment of the young men and women who had taken to the bomb and the hand gun where politics had failed them. Whereas the administering of repeated electric shocks to the more sensitive parts of the body was the method favoured in virtually all the French interrogation centres at the time, Savary was an exponent of the *baignoire*, made notorious during the Occupation by Klaus Barbie and other Gestapo torturers. To be taken repeatedly to the verge of death by drowning in a session lasting for several hours was, generally, sufficient to break all resistance and to produce, when

101

combined with savage beatings, any kind of confession from any kind of suspect, including those picked up by mistake by a thoroughly frightened police force motivated by the sight of nasty nationalist excesses against the French population. The promise, carefully and sympathetically made by Savary, of a daily repetition of the macabre sessions in the blood-spattered bathroom, indefinitely into the future, would usually break even the strongest spirit. One route of escape from the prospect of unending agony was to drown deliberately. It was often tried, but the torturers had become expert at foiling such moves. Another was to attempt suicide back in the cells by other means. It was difficult. Best and worst of all, was to talk – give names, any names, confess – sign anything . . . There was after all a limit. Even amid the religious and national fervours of the North African liberation movement there had to be a limit.

De Gaulle had left politics in disgust and returned later with a promise to maintain the French presence in North Africa. But though de Gaulle looked like a general he thought like a politician. He proceeded to pull France from the brink of colonial disaster by granting the North Africans an independence that they were in process of winning for themselves. For Savary and his friends this was the Judas touch – betrayal at the moment of victory. The victory of the *baignoire*, the generator and the *nerf de boeuf*, the knout.

Savary joined the OAS, the conspiracy of army men against the regime. Friends mentioned his name in Paris. A sound man. In the intelligence community, after the flight from North Africa, he won his extra pip, attended a few secret OAS meetings, had dealings with those who believed political assassination, even of the Old Man himself, was now the way forward. But things settled down. From being the enemy, de Gaulle became the main bulwark against the students of 1968, the anarchists of the Left Bank, the communists from the suburbs.

Yet another shift in allegiance followed. The patriots of the right, men with nostalgia for an imaginary past, looked upon the post-colonial alignment in the world and hated what they saw. Perhaps, in his excessive way, Hitler had

102

been right about the Jews. Consider Israel, aggressive and intransigent. Consider the Rothschilds, back in their banks.

The DGSE became one of the forces in the complex process which shifted France from her pro-Israeli stance during the seventies. If the new-found affection for the Arab cause was, for Savary, a personal contradiction, so be it. If a pro-Arab policy coincided with Soviet policy in the area . . . but, ah! Was it not astute to woo the Moslem world away from the Soviets? Savary espoused the new cause with the ruthless singleness of purpose with which he had previously hunted Moslems in Oran.

A contradiction? A lack of principle? Or that useful concept, *raison d'état*?

All this is necessary in order to understand in some measure the Savarys and Tavernets and the role they were prepared to play in the story of Chatila and its ambitions. It will also explain the care with which Section 6 had placed its agents within the DST to keep an eye on the Wavres and Baums and other friends of the Jews. Savary had met Saad Hayek in a bistro not far from the DGSE headquarters in the Boulevard Mortier. He had listened to him, asked a couple of questions, told him he would see him again that evening. Back in his office he had checked with Tripoli and made a local call. Later the two men were together again.

'So your boss wants to meet Tavernet?'

'Yes.'

'Why?'

'I don't know.'

'Come on now, aren't you a close associate of his?'

'I still don't know. We don't talk more than we have to.'

'I have spoken with Tavernet. He says yes.'

'I must meet him first.'

'Why?'

'They are my orders. I am to fix things up direct.'

'Wait.'

Savary went to the public telephone and was back a few moments later.

'Here. Tomorrow morning at eleven. He's short, about your age, a bit bald; wears strong glasses, smokes a pipe, and he'll carry a copy of *Le Figaro*. He'll say the major sent him.'

Next morning the meeting of Saad Hayek and Tavernet took place as promised and arrangements were made. When the men parted Saad Hayek returned to his room in the Place Genty and transmitted to Damascus. The operator in the Syrian capital had instructions for him: stay in Paris and raise us daily at midday.

As for the extra carbon of Baum's aide memoire, this had reached Savary via the typist Françoise and her contact later the same day. He wasted no time. His channel of communication with Professor Hanif was via the DGSE resident in Damascus, who was instructed to pass on the contents of the note person to person. This he did. 'Any reply?' the Frenchman had asked. 'Say I will still keep the appointment in Paris,' Hanif replied. The Frenchman had gone away.

'I have had reports which point to Saad,' the professor said to Rasmia.

'What about Essat?'

'My reports point the other way. Also, you tell me that Essat carried out his duties in Rome in a proper fashion.'

'I doubt if that is any kind of proof. It looked as if they failed to contact him.'

'Of course it is not proof. It is simply an indication which is to be borne in mind. I have to consider it in connection with the reports which point to Saad.'

'What are they?'

'I will tell you,' the professor said. 'On certain matters I believe the instinct of a woman is worth consideration. You will give me your opinion.'

He told her of Alfred Baum's memo, dictated to the girl Françoise who was working for the DGSE. There was a long silence while Rasmia sat motionless.

'Is it not just a shade too neat?' she asked finally.

'I admit it is convincing to the point of being dubious – a meeting of opposites, as it were.'

'Could not someone be playing a double game?'

'I am told that is not a possibility, but who knows?'

104

'Then perhaps our friends are being fed information. Is it not what we might do in the circumstances?'

'Of course, and I have considered that. But here again I am told it was chance alone which brought us this information. I know all about chance which turns out to be nothing of the kind, but I have no way of checking further.'

Rasmia tossed her head impatiently. 'I think I do not like it, really. Too – too fortuitous, tidy. I do not know how to express my thought.'

'Very well. Now consider the second element in this story, and please bear in mind that the very fact that we are looking at two elements where only one might be expected must in itself be regarded if you will as yet a third element. Hence, we have three matters to consider.'

He told her of the message from Gadafi via Syrian Intelligence. 'I find this altogether more interesting,' he said. 'Gadafi and Jalaf are not fools. Their source is described to me as first rate. Now, what is the CIA doing suddenly asking questions about the Frenchman Tavernet?'

'Has Essat heard his name?'

'No, he was with you when I briefed Saad.'

'I have to say,' Rasmia said slowly, 'that this information from Tripoli is more convincing, but it would have been more convincing still if it had not reached you within hours of the Paris information coming in. The coincidence is disturbing. I think your so-called third element must weaken the value of both stories. I believe they call it overkill.'

'And if there were no evidence of any kind against either Saad or Essat but we still had to choose, which would it be?'

Rasmia paused again. 'You have no right to ask me such a question.'

'I have every right. We are not playing at cops and robbers, you and I. Do you think there aren't many decisions to take which are just as difficult as that one? I demand an answer.'

'And I will not give it. You cannot drag me into the liquidation of a comrade who may be perfectly innocent just because his personality inspires less confidence than someone else's. Women's intuition has nothing to do with such amateur guesswork.'

'And yet,' the professor said, 'I have to take such a

decision, and you have done what you can to undermine my confidence in the facts I have at my disposal.'

'You should not have asked me.'

There was a silence.

'If we are to deal with Saad it must be done right away, there in Paris, before he has the opportunity of doing us any more harm. But if I give the boys orders to deal with him there will be small hope of getting a confession to settle the matter once and for all.'

'Can't they interrogate him?'

'It would be better done here.'

'You must decide.'

'I will do so. Also, I must be in Paris myself next week. Saad set up a meeting for me with this man Tavernet.'

'A trap?'

'Perhaps a trap, and I naturally do not plan to meet the man precisely as arranged. But I think that can be managed.'

'So?'

'In my life I have found that cancers are best cut out clean, with a stroke of the knife. With cancer one should never wait. So the doctors tell us.'

'Will you confront Saad in Paris?'

'I will see none of our people in Paris. What we are doing now is to be kept strictly apart from our operations in Europe. Only you and I are involved in it.'

'Essat?'

'Not Essat. He will stay here while we are in Paris and he will not have access to the house.'

A world away, on the following day, which chanced to be a Sunday of brilliant sunshine in Versailles, the Cat Club was holding its annual show. Here Alfred Baum, a member of the committee, past president, a winner of trophies and a thoughtful judge of a cat, was busy with his duties as judge in the long-haired class. In the congenial company of the ladies of the fancy (there were few male members of the Versailles Cat Club) he was able to be himself – twinkling, but with a touch of that sardonic style native to all good Frenchmen, quietly knowledgeable, a portly figure in a creased suit of uncertain beige, pushing into the mid-fifties.

Madame Baum, whose interest in cats did not extend beyond the affectionate, was at home with friends. Days like this were necessary, Baum believed, to his peace of mind, his sanity. 'The relationship between cat and man is a moral benchmark against which we may judge the quality of relationships between people. Mutual trust, within reason and with appropriate precautions taken; a sensible degree of affection; mutual dependence, whereby the cat trades its comfort and sustenance against the companionship and aesthetic pleasure it can give; finally, a quality of peace and quiet in which neither side strives for advantage. This is what exists between man and cat and should serve as a model for all our relationships.'

He would treat his wife to homilies of this type and she never knew how seriously to take him.

'You should have been a philosopher, Alfred. Or a vet.'

'I would have liked to study philosophy, but as you know, my father made me waste two years training for the priesthood. I suppose you could say that neither theology nor philosophy is entirely excluded from my work.'

Now he was passing down the line, judging the entrants proudly displayed by their owners – nearly all ladies of a certain age and all concealing a burning desire for victory behind a studied politeness to the other members of the fancy.

Baum was examining a Lilac-Point Birman.

'I am impressed by this animal,' he told its owner. There was a silence as he held up the head, checking the slope of the forehead, the fullness of the chin. 'A nice expressive face and well-set ears. Good eye colour.' Baum was talking to himself, making an occasional note on his pad, ignoring the cat's anxious owner. 'Good proportion between body and tail.' He examined the paws. 'Almost clear pink. Very good.' He turned to the cat's owner.

'I congratulate you, madame. His fur colour is possibly the best I have seen in the breed – no shading at all and the gloves are pure white. Also the eyes – almost a violet, very fine.'

He stepped back, cocked his head, taking visible pleasure in the animal.

Out of the corner of his eye he caught sight of the small, round figure of his wife. She was signalling to him, holding her hand to her ear, miming a telephone conversation.

'Excuse me, madame, a message for me.'

He smiled apologetically at the owner of the cat and crossed to his wife.

'Alfred, I'm sorry, it was Allembeau. He says you are to call your friend. I came as fast as I could. He said it was urgent.'

Madame Baum was fanning herself with the programme of the show which someone had thrust into her hand at the entrance to the hall. She had hurried and the day was hot.

'Thank you, my dear, I shall deal with it. But Madame Jacob will be upset if I interrupt my appraisal. A very fine animal, actually.'

He returned to the cat, made his notes, explained to his fellow judge that he must telephone, and made his way to the bistro opposite the hall.

Ben Tov was impatient. No shalom. 'There are developments. Please note. Hanif is in Paris. With him is the woman Rasmia Burnawi. Do you need descriptions?'

'We have dossiers on both, with descriptions.'

'Hanif is without a beard. The girl's hair is long.'

'Right.'

'We do not know what names they are using. Also, they are unlikely to stay together. My information is that they will not use a safe house; they will be in hotels.'

'So how can I find them, since I cannot use our police?'

'I have my own worries.'

There was a pause. Baum wished he could get back to the cat. It had a good chance of the Prix d'Honneur. He knew his day was ruined. He sighed into the mouthpiece and the sigh could be heard in Abarbanel Street.

'I know,' Ben Tov said, unbending a little, 'it's how I feel. Did I interrupt anything?'

'I was assessing a rather fine Lilac-Point Birman.'

'A what?'

'Never mind. Tell me, what nationality passports do they use?'

'Never Syrian. Usually Iraqi or Turkish. Lebanese or Egyptian are possible. If I were Hanif I'd have the girl on a passport of different nationality to mine.'

'Would they come in on the same flight?'

'Our man says he heard her refer to "our flight". It's possible.'

'Where from?'

'I have no idea – anywhere they could get a connection with Damascus but certainly not direct.'

'And would the girl stay round the corner or well away?'

'As close as possible but almost certainly not in the same hotel. So I believe.'

'Hanif's dossier speaks to me of a man more likely to put up at the George V than a fleapit.'

'You are right.'

'Very well. We will do what we can. Do you reckon the pressure is off your man?'

'For the moment, yes.'

They bade each other goodbye. Alfred Baum returned to the hall, made his apologies to his friends, recommended the Birman for first in its class, and after returning home to change, make a call to the duty officer at the Rue des Saussaies, and shrug helplessly to his wife, caught a train for Paris, jostling with the city folk on their way home from a day trailing past the splendours of Louis XIV's preposterous palace.

Chapter 13

The French Police de l'Air, part of the frontier force, have their headquarters in a severe block tucked into a corner of Charles de Gaulle airport. Here the DST had friends. It was one of these friends that Baum called on the radio in the car sent by the office to meet him at the Gare Montparnasse. He disliked using the DST's radio network, which shared a wavelength with the police. He therefore confined himself to announcing that he was on his way to the airport. It was a stroke of luck that the man he could safely talk to was on Sunday shift.

The DST car threaded its way north from Montparnasse, across the river and through the sparse Sunday-evening traffic on the boulevards, out of the city and on to the autoroute du Nord. It passed the spot where the boys had fired their Rexims. The masonry where the road passed under the Rue du Landy was chipped and scored. There were no other signs of what had happened. Baum was thinking, his eyes closed. Normally he chatted to his drivers. 'We should know what they are saying in the car pool. It's the nearest we get to real people in this damn trade.' It was one of the things he enjoined upon his senior inspectors. 'If you are leading an army, even a platoon, you should listen from time to time to make sure they are still following you.' And again, 'When you start listening to yourself instead of other people you are on the way to early retirement and a rocking chair somewhere on the Marne.'

But now he was listening to himself and not his driver. By a process of internal questions and answers he was feeling his way to solutions, picking up and discarding tactics. He had come, tentatively, to one or two conclusions by the time the car drew up at the headquarters. With him, conclusions consisted largely of a series of questions to be answered. And the questions were usually contained each one within its predecessor like a nest of Russian dolls.

'Thank you. Please wait for me.' They were the only words he had spoken to the driver, a DST veteran who was used to his ways and would have driven him to the gates of hell and waited for him there if asked to do so.

Baum found his contact in an office on the first floor. He explained what he wanted and the man reached for a world flight directory.

'Can we assume the point of origin was Damascus?'

'Yes.'

'And that they reached Paris with only one interchange?'

'It's probable. Let's see where we get on that assumption.'

The policeman consulted the directory. Between them they built up a list of probable cities where Hanif and the girl could catch connecting flights to Paris. There were nine of them. The policeman called traffic control at the airport. There had been twenty-two incoming flights from the nine on the previous day.

'Do they have EEC passports?'

'No – let's say Iraqi, Turkish or Lebanese. We may have to extend the list later.'

'They will have filled in immigration cards. Also, their arrival will have been added to their computer file. Let's see.'

He turned to a VDU on a table next to his desk and punched keys.

'If you had the names it would be simple. As it is, we have to go hunting. May take a while.' He lit a cigarette and offered the pack to Baum. 'Sure it can't wait?'

Baum shook his head. 'Would I come on a beautiful Sunday evening if it could wait?'

'You'll know that the immigration cards are distributed daily to the police in the areas the travellers have indicated as their destination. It's Paris, I gather.'

Baum nodded.

'You'd probably get quicker results at the Préfecture.'

111

Baum shook his head. 'You know we have paranoia at the Rue des Saussaies. The police are to be kept out of it.'

'Well, I can call up the data by flight. Shall we link up the printer?'

'I can never get used to those damned screens. We have them all over our office and no one over the age of twenty-five knows what to make of them.'

The policeman busied himself and print-outs started to spew from the printer.

'I'll use your phone.'

Baum set in motion the procedures whereby DST staff could be torn from their loved ones at a moment's notice and brought grumbling to the office. He reckoned he needed half a dozen people capable of staying awake on black coffee, probably well into the small hours. All from his private list of staff he considered reliable.

'This is how we will proceed,' Baum was saying. 'Our tools are these – ' he tapped the neat pile of computer print-outs lying before him on his desk, ' – and your telephones.' He was addressing the four men and two women crowded into his office. They did not look pleased. Three of them had been called out for one thing or another on the past four Sundays. The embassy of the People's Republic of Rumania was under close and continuous surveillance on a hunch of Georges Wavre that something was about to break – a contact to be made, a Rumanian diplomat to be foot-faulted, a defection . . . ? There were rumours in the department but no hard information from on high.

'Come now, *mes enfants*.' Baum tried a smile. A girl named Josianne smiled back and tapped her ballpoint on her teeth. It was the only response he got. 'We are seeking persons connected with the autoroute du Nord murders. A nasty affair. We will all feel proud to have played our part in clearing it up. Above all, in preventing a repetition.'

He explained what he wanted and presented the variables: twenty-two flights; a man and a woman on the same flight; probably Iraqui, Turkish or Lebanese passports; probably a different-nationality passport for each of them; immigration data indicating hotels in Paris.

112

'You will each take four print-outs, and using the variables I have given you, plus the native intelligence without which I would have called not you but six of your colleagues . . .' Josianne smiled again ' . . . you will come back to me here with marks against those names on the print-outs that you consider interesting, and you will give me your reasons for so thinking. We will then take things from there.' He paused, looked amiably round the room. The atmosphere had thawed a little. An *affaire*, almost any *affaire*, had about it some of the excitement of the chase.

'Any questions?'

A burly inspector who had missed the last course of a splendid family dinner raised a finger.

'Would this pair be so bloody stupid as to put their true destination on their cards?'

'Why not, if they felt sure of their cover?' someone said. 'If there were trouble later they might have a problem explaining their cards away.'

'We will assume the stated destinations are the true ones. If we draw blanks we shall have to make the other assumption. Always eliminate the easier options before you go looking for difficulties,' Baum said.

'What happens when we've built a suspect list?'

'We all get to work on the telephones.'

'What do we know about their ages?' It was Josianne.

'A very good point. Archives tell us the man is believed to be forty-five and the girl is in her early twenties. Dates of birth on their passports, and therefore on their cards and finally on the print-outs, will be close enough to be credible. Let us say forty to forty-eight or so for the man, twenty up towards thirty for the girl. A very good point.' Josianne was a promising girl.

'No more questions?'

There were none.

'Right, *mes enfants*, to work. No doubt one of the ladies will organize coffee. I leave you with a tip. Look first on the lists for the girl. Fewer women in their twenties travel than men in their forties. So, the girl first, then check for a man with the appropriate characteristics. Method, always method.'

After they had left him Baum sat for a long while immobile. Coffee in a white enamel mug was brought and he found it an effort to smile and say thank you. He was sipping the steaming, blackish liquid when an idea came to him. 'I talk to them about method,' he said to himself. 'They should be talking about method to *me*.'

He found a number in a notebook, dialled and spoke.

'I'm sorry to call you so late Aziz, but I need you urgently. Yes, at the office. Yes, for the rest of the night. Fine, thanks.'

As he replaced the receiver in its cradle he reflected that he had plugged a potentially troublesome gap.

Method, indeed!

It was not to prove a successful night. By one a.m. they had checked through the print-outs and had identified six girls travelling on the same flights as six men, all of about the right ages and all coming from relevant destinations. Of the twelve, only nine had given their intended addresses as hotels, and of these only six had turned up at the hotels indicated on their immigration cards. By six a.m. small surveillance teams had been set up at all six hotels and men had started making inquiries at the three remaining private addresses.

When Aziz turned up, looking happy at the thought of being wanted, Baum said: 'My dear fellow, how good of you to come out at such short notice.'

'Monsier Baum, I count myself your friend. What can I do?'

'We are looking for a man and a girl from Damascus.' He gave Aziz a description. 'It struck me that they may have checked in at one of the rooming houses favoured by your co-religionists. I think it unlikely, but I can't leave that particular avenue unexplored. Can you make inquiries?'

'Of course.'

'Without raising any kind of suspicion whatever?'

'I can do what I did for you in the Tunisian business last year.'

'That was very well done.'

'Thank you.'

'How long, do you think?'

114

'There are maybe ten, twelve likely places full of illegals and therefore discreet. It would take me a day.'

'Use taxis and charge them.'

'Thank you. I will do my best.'

And Aziz, a small sallow creature in disreputable clothes, had smiled broadly and departed.

Neither Aziz nor Baum's team came up with anything remotely promising. None of the girls acted in a manner that the DST men could describe as suspicious. One proved to be a whore who must have gone home to see her family and was now back on the beat in the Faubourg St Martin. Only one of the others bore the slightest resemblance to the personal description in Rasmia's file. Similarly, all the men save one were quite unlike Professor Hanif's description, and the one who might conceivably have passed for him turned out to be the head waiter of a commercial hotel on the Left Bank.

None of Aziz's informants in the Arab underworld of Paris had anything useful to say.

'It was worth trying,' Baum said gloomily to Allembeau later. 'You should always try, and just occasionally you get lucky.'

'How did they slip past you?'

'They may have separated when they changed planes. It would be a pretty obvious thing to do. Added to which, they probably played it doubly safe by putting false destination addresses on their immigration cards. But as I say, it was worth trying.'

He turned with a sigh to a pile of papers on his desk. The top sheet was a typed note from his secretary:

Please sign the diplomatic list. The quai d'Orsay have rung twice.

M. Pineau

Foreign Affairs would send a weekly list of diplomatic accreditations to the DST, who would signal receipt by signing and returning a covering note. The signature of the deputy director was mandatory. Normally, Alfred Baum took a deep – some said an obsessive – interest in these lists of Vassilis, Borises, Dwights and Achmeds, often calling for files, seeking concordances, disparities, coincidences –

115

anything that would turn a name into a person and a person, conceivably, into a subject of interest to the DST.

'The Archives — always the Archives,' he would tell the recruits. 'Without them you are mere policemen without uniforms. With them, you are effective defenders of the state.' These wise saws of Baum's were meant to jolt the minds of the young men as they chewed the ends of their ballpoints and tried to look more intelligent than they were.

He rang for Mlle Pineau.

'I am very sorry,' he said, 'I have been too busy. It will not happen again.'

He signed the form, handed it to her, and glanced down the list of names, each identified by country and function. The Rumanians had paused for breath. He noted that a Bulgarian had been sent by Sofia and accepted by Paris to replace a first secretary who had been drunk and disorderly at the Ritz once too often. There was one Russian name:

Igor Vassilievich Belaiev: USSR. Temporary accreditation as second secretary, commercial affairs. Arrived 15 June.

'I would swear,' Baum said to Mlle Pineau, 'that Mr Belaiev is KGB.' He pointed a stubby finger at the name on the list. 'Please ask Archives to send me the I.V. Belaiev file.'

'And if there isn't one?'

'There is one. My memory has not retired before I have.'

There was indeed a file for one I. V. Belaiev, who had spent a short six months at the Paris embassy four years earlier, when he had been identified as KGB by a defector from a Soviet trade mission, some at least of whose revelations had stood the test of time. The file itself contained little of interest on what, if anything, I. V. Belaiev had achieved for his masters, but Archives had kept themselves abreast of his travels. Since his last stay in Paris he had been in Moscow and Teheran. For the last two years he had been in Damascus.

Baum wondered idly why a middle-ranking KGB man (he deduced the rank from age and experience) should be assigned temporarily from Damascus to Paris. The geography was odd. The Russians were not masters of logistics, but even the KGB did not move their men around like pawns in a crazy game of chess.

'See that comrade Belaiev's dossier is brought up to date,'

116

he told Mlle Pineau. Then he looked up at Allembeau, still sitting stolidly on the far side of the desk.

'I have one of my hunches.'

Allembeau suppressed an urge to smile. Instead, he composed his face into what he hoped was an expression of polite interest.

'A Russki – KGB – is transferred from Damascus on temporary accreditation. As far as we know, he is not an expert on anything legitimate in the commercial field. Nor is there anything happening between France and Syria which could interest the Soviets. *Ergo*, the KGB has developed some Damascus-Paris interest of its own. That is my hunch. I want this Igor Vassilievich Belaiev put under close surveillance. And while we're about it, let's see if we can get a few nice pictures. The mug shot we have from his passport is very poor. I'd like a better view of his ears. Also, I suspect from the eyes that he normally wears glasses. Let's get him with his glasses on, right?'

'Day and night?'

'Day and night.'

'I haven't the men.'

'Then give the Rumanians a little breathing space. They must be heartily sick of us.'

'The boss won't like it.'

'You can leave that to me.'

It was in the small hours of that night that four young men drove up to the tenement in the Place Genty to carry out their orders. The time was soon after 01.00 hours and the young men made no attempt to keep their presence quiet. Three of them clattered up the stairs to the room occupied by Saad Hayek. They stayed for close to an hour, while the fourth man stood watch at the street door. Despite the extreme brutality of their treatment, Saad Hayek did not talk, since he had nothing to say.

Chapter 14

It was after nine the following morning when the local police appeared at the tenement. The place was almost deserted, the illegals having no stomach for an inspection of their papers and even less for any kind of role in a murder inquiry. But the police inspector in charge of the investigation eventually found his way to an apartment with signs of life. An old man shuffled reluctantly to the door as the policeman beat a fist on it, then retreated to a room almost devoid of furniture, where a seemingly even older woman sat motionless on a kitchen chair.

Had he heard anything during the night?

He shrugged, implying that perhaps he had.

All right then, what sort of noise? The inspector had assumed the hectoring tone he reserved for people of this type.

The old man said it was the most terrible scream he had ever heard. It ended in sobs, he said. A sort of choking, then sobs. Then there was what sounded like someone pleading. That was when he knew it was a man, for the scream, which had woken him, was high-pitched and it might have been a woman. But it was a man pleading.

'In Arabic?'

Yes, in Arabic. Then another scream, the same as the first one. There were many screams, he thought.

'What about other voices?'

'I heard no voices.'

'Not even one?'

'I heard no voices.'

'What did you see?'

'I was in my room. How could I see anything?'

He shuffled from foot to foot – irritable or frightened, perhaps both.

'We were afraid to look,' his wife said. 'Round here, you keep to yourself.'

'Shut up,' the old man said. 'Was anyone talking to you?'

'It was the voice of agony,' she said, ignoring him. 'I know what agony sounds like. Wasn't I in Constantine in sixty-one? I tell you it was the voice of great suffering.' She rocked her head from side to side.

'What do you know of this man who calls himself Abu Afa?'

'Nothing,' the old man said.

'Was it his real name?'

'How should I know?'

'How long had he lived in the building?'

'They come and go. How can one know? We keep to ourselves. These days there's no one fit to talk to. Scum. Illegals, all of them.'

'Ever talk to him?'

'No.'

'How long had he been here?'

'I don't know – a few days, a week or so, maybe less.'

'Did he have visitors?'

'I never saw any.'

'A woman, perhaps? Surely he had a woman, a man like that, on his own.'

The old man shrugged and wiped a drip off the tip of his nose with the back of his hand. 'Scum,' he repeated. 'A fat slug.' He belched loudly.

'And that night, you saw no one come or leave?'

'I told you, we were in our room. Asleep.'

'Yet you heard a man pleading in Arabic.'

'It was loud. The words were not clear but it was Arabic.'

'What words?'

'Maybe he called on Allah. Maybe he cried "no" many times – *laa* . . . *laa* . . . *laa* – like that. I don't know for sure. There was the wall between us, wasn't there?'

'And you?' to the woman.

119

'She heard nothing. She covered her head when the screaming started. Anyway, she's half deaf. Pay no attention to her.' He swore at her in Arabic.

The woman sniffed. 'Such agony was beyond belief,' she said, shaking her head. 'I heard *wa-hyaatak . . . wa-hyaatak* – please . . . please.'

The inspector from the Brigade Criminel sighed and turned to his sergeant. 'We're wasting government time. Is there anyone else?'

'The others won't even admit to the screams. They're all deaf for the duration.'

'As usual,' sighed the inspector, who had not wanted to join the brigade, having a strong antipathy towards all things North African, Middle Eastern, Corsican – indeed anything south of Marseilles. He was a conscientious-enough policeman but he was inclined to favour a quieter kind of life and lacked his sergeant's earnest approach to the job. He attributed all crime in Paris to Mediterranean influences.

'Looks to me like another of their routine little differences of opinion.'

He looked with distaste at the old man and his wife, fidgeting before him.

'But think what they did to him,' the sergeant said.

'Expect they got a bit irritable. Lost patience. Maybe he forgot to offer them a coffee.'

The inspector waved the old people away. 'Animals, the lot of them. The things they do to each other.'

'Our papers are in order,' the old man said. 'We live here legally. Twenty-two years we've been here. Never had any trouble with the law.'

'Yes, yes.'

'We won't be in trouble, then?'

'That's all right, grandad.'

'Come,' the old man said to his wife, 'you heard what the gentleman said – get moving and show them out.'

'We think,' the commander of the Brigade Criminel said carefully, 'that this is certainly a case for the DST. The victim had an Iraqi passport issued in Baghdad. His immigration card gave a false address.'

He sat across the desk from Alfred Baum, the dossier, such as it was, on the desk between them. There was precious little to be learned from the three sheets of paper and the half-dozen photographs which lay between the buff covers, and rather than hand it over right away he wanted to talk this one down. So he did not push the folder across the metal desk top towards Baum. Instead, he pulled a pack of Gauloises *maïs* from his pocket and teased out a cigarette without offering the pack. He was not a man to bother over-much with small politenesses, even when he wanted something.

The commander lit his cigarette and, dragon-like, blew a great cloud of smoke through his nostrils.

'Not a nice story,' he said. 'Not at all a nice story. An Arab, or similar, thirty-six according to his passport, which could be telling the truth on that score if on no other. Apparently, he had a room in one of those tenements they've started to pull down in the Place Genty to make way for the new Gare de Lyon. They're full of North Africans, Iraqis, Palestinians, you name it. Mostly illegals, so no one will talk, of course. In any case, most of those at No. 18, where he was killed, have moved out in the past week or two. It wasn't much of a dump in the first place. My men traced one old couple and that's about it.'

'Useful?'

The commander shook his head. 'My inspector got nothing out of them and wrote it up at length. It's in there.' He nodded towards the folder.

'What's so special about the case?'

'What's special is the pathologist's findings from forensic. Terrible. Absolutely terrible.'

The commander had not seen the corpse but his men who had done so had returned ashen-faced and one of them had vomited in the car taking him back to headquarters.

'You'd better tell me.'

'He'd been emasculated.'

'Not uncommon, I'm afraid, in those circles.'

'They left the knife. A bread knife with a serrated blade. Not sharp.'

'I've heard of that before.'

121

'No prints.'

'Of course not.'

'They had his eyes out too.'

Alfred Baum shook his head sadly as if to say he already knew there was no limit to human wickedness and he himself was now on the far side of astonishment. He shifted uncomfortably in his chair, hoping the commander did not intend to dwell on the details. But the commander seemed to think the details had significance. Or perhaps this was his way of cleansing himself spiritually after contact with such enormities.

'The man's testicles had been thrust into his eye sockets and they'd somehow jammed his passport of all things halfway down his gullet. A curious thing, that. Then they'd trussed him up and left him to die. No one heard him after that and no one dared go into the room. These illegals without papers are mostly terrorized by the bully-boys of this or that faction. After all, they hadn't even bothered with a gag. They let him scream.'

'To encourage the others, no doubt.'

'No doubt. Also, they did certain other things to him. It's all there. They have strong stomachs in forensic.' He shoved the buff folder across the desk and pulled on his cigarette. 'Odd, though, about the passport.'

Alfred Baum opened the folder, holding a corner delicately between thumb and forefinger as if it could contaminate him in some fearful manner. His brows knitted together, he appeared to be reading. In fact, he was giving himself time to think. 'The thing smells of West Beirut, the Beka'a valley, the lunacy of Teheran. Interesting to us, perhaps, but then a vast number of things are interesting to us.'

He looked up quizzically from under his brows, covering the obscenities of the pathologist's dead prose with the flap of the folder. Then he smiled.

'My dear fellow, this is surely one for you and not for me.'

'An Iraqi illegal? With a Walther PK and plenty of ammunition. What was he doing here?'

'Not visiting the Louvre I grant you. But why bring all this to me when you could go to that admirable chap Dupace,

122

whose job it is to ferret out foreigners with guns?' He tapped the folder with a plump forefinger.

The commander felt the time had come to play his ace. 'Also a transmitter, code equipment, a one-time pad. Your kind of stuff.'

Baum hunched his shoulders and his head seemed to sink into them as if he were about to hibernate as a way of avoiding what had been put before him.

'But I am not equipped here to solve murders, you know.'

'We'll lend you someone. Speak to Dalmette.'

Baum appeared no longer to be listening. Pursuing his own line of thought, he suddenly said: 'I presume there was something ritualistic about the passport in the mouth. You think it was meant to have special significance?'

'Probably.'

'And the other thing with the eye sockets?'

The commander nodded.

'Where is the passport?'

'With the corpse at the police mortuary on the 12th *arrondissement*. It wasn't in a fit state to go into the dossier. Dalmette has the other stuff.'

Baum let his gaze wander round the grey walls of his office as if solutions to the problems of the day were to be found there, pasted up. The President of the Republic stared back at him from his cheap oak frame, infinitely contemptuous and powerful, still demanding action. Baum averted his gaze, brought it down to the commander sitting hopefully before him, a far less daunting figure. The commander was puffing smoke out of his nose and mouth as if there were a damp fire somewhere inside him.

'Obviously,' Baum said, 'the passport had deep significance for his torturers. Punitive killings in the Middle East often include stuffing the genitals into the victim's mouth. It is some ultimate kind of insult which escapes the Western mind. But here they clearly thought an honoured custom normally considered *de rigueur* had to make way for a more specific statement.' He paused, tapped two fingers on the metal desk. 'What were they saying? "*This* is what we think of your passport, for we know you are not the person your passport says you are." Which is more, my dear commander, than you or I know.'

'It looks that way.'

The commander was hoping that Baum was reasoning himself into accepting the dossier, but it could equally well be going the other way. No excessive enthusiasm must therefore be shown until one knew where all this was leading.

'If we are right in making such an assumption, what are we left with? A man who has betrayed, or is believed to have betrayed, his comrades? Possibly. And who are these comrades of his? A very confident bunch of cowboys. Mere criminals? I think not, since criminals don't feel strongly enough to go to such lengths.'

The commander felt the argument was beginning to go his way after all, and nodded encouragingly.

'But whose handwriting can one detect in this *grand guignol* of the eyes and the testicles and the passport? I fancy we need advice from someone who is more familiar than we are with these abstruse tribal rites.'

He paused and looked at the commander, who thought he could detect a touch of humour in the pensive brown eyes.

'I will interest myself in the matter, though I am bound to add that you scarcely deserve it, my dear fellow.'

The commander was lighting a second *maïs* from the butt of the first and chose to ignore the jibe.

'Excellent. Fellow by the name of Masset at the mortuary has the corpse, and as I say, Dalmette will help.'

He got up to go, extended a hand. 'We'll send the transmitter and the other stuff over later today.' They shook hands and as the door closed behind him Baum was already reading the dossier carefully. As he read he extended a hand to the internal phone and looked up briefly to dial a number.

'Archives?'

'Yes, *patron.*'

'Get the Saad Hayek dossier while I hold. In the Palestinian section.'

He was still reading when the voice came back over the line. 'I have it here.'

124

'Look at the personal description. What does he weigh and how tall is he?'

'It says approximately ninety-eight kilos and one metre sixty.'

'Identifying marks? Anything about a wart?'

'It says here, "wart or similar on left cheek".'

'Thanks.' Baum replaced the receiver and made two small marks in the margin of the sheet he was reading. He read to the end, glanced with distaste at the police photographer's half-plates and got to his feet. He locked the dossier into a drawer in his desk and made his way to the lift and out into the Rue des Saussaies. A few minutes later he was installed in an airless phone booth in the basement of a café in the Rue d'Astorg, where he was known as the uncommunicative regular for very early *casse-croutes* and a number of long-distance phone calls.

He dialled ten digits. When he heard the ringing tone he closed the door of the booth carefully. The receiver was lifted at the other end.

'Yes.'

'Paris friend here.'

'Shalom. Can you talk?'

'I can. They appear to have done the job. Very messily, I'm afraid, but done.'

'You're sure it was him?'

'Sure.'

'Good.'

'Poor devil.'

'We're all poor devils.' Shayeh Ben Tov grunted. 'And the professor?'

'No luck, I'm afraid. We haven't traced him or the girl. Without using the police it was difficult.'

There was a silence. Ben Tov's disapproval was conveyed in some mysterious way through the international telecommunication system.

'I see.'

'I'm sorry. We are still working on it but I have small hopes.'

'But the other thing – that has not been bungled.' There was emphasis on the 'that'.

125

Baum allowed a smile to crease the corners of his mouth. 'I understand how you feel, my friend, but let not you and I make a diplomatic incident out of it. That sort of thing is best left to our governments.'

Another silence. Then: 'You are right. I am too outspoken. Thank you for what you have done. And please call me if your men find something after all.'

Chapter 15

'Yusef is here,' the old man said.

They were at the far end of the Ommayad mosque and there was a conveniently busy crowd around them. Essat stood against a wall, a book open in his hand. He did not look up.

'Where is he?'

'By the next column to your right. He wears Western clothes. Also glasses. He is shorter than you.'

Essat glanced up, saw the young man. He could have been a worshipper or a visitor from some neighbouring country, probably both. He appeared to be absorbed in an examination of the brilliantly coloured wall tiles, but for a moment he looked towards the others and their eyes met.

'Okay. Any message?'

'There is an instruction. No risks to be taken. None at all. Those are the words: "No risks — none at all." '

There was a pause.

'I can look after myself,' Essat said, 'but I am worried about the risks you take. Running a transmitter for so many months is risky. They can be getting a fix on you.'

'I transmit only briefly, and we always vary the times.'

'They aren't fools. If they catch you it will be terrible for you.'

The old man shuffled his feet and shrugged impatiently. Then he gestured angrily at a group of babbling children.

'My heart is weak. The doctor says a strain will finish it off. If I am caught, the sight of the branding irons and all

127

that stuff will kill me before they can make me talk. They don't give you a medical before they start lashing you.'

He shuffled off, muttering to himself, and Essat walked slowly towards the young man in the Western suit.

'Shalom.'

'Shalom.'

'I shall be in the Garden Café in Independence Square at midday. Come to my table, greet me openly as if you hadn't expected to find me. I'll invite you to join me and you will do so.'

The young man nodded briefly and Essat walked away.

Later, in the Garden Café, Essat asked: 'How did you enter the country?'

'Algerian papers. I am not allowed to tell you more.'

'How is the boss?'

'Difficult, as usual. He sends his greetings.'

Their table was well back, both of them facing the door.

There was a large crowd in the place, polyglot and noisy. Essat lit a cigarette and offered one. The young man calling himself Yusef refused.

'What's the job?' Yusef asked.

'We will enter a house. There will probably be a number of locks – the back door, then a couple of rooms inside. Also the safe.'

'Alarms?'

'I can deal with them.'

'And when do we do it?'

'Tonight.' Essat was watching a man alone at a table by the door who had a newspaper spread out before him. From time to time the man's eyes would scan the crowded room like radar. Essat thought he had detected a flicker of interest in the expressionless eyes as they focused on the two of them before moving on. He wasn't sure.

'Also, we may have to neutralize the opposition. Do you have a gun?' Essat asked.

'No.'

'I will bring one for you. You can shoot?'

The young man nodded.

'You have what you need – keys, tools, you know?'

'Not everything. The boss said I might not be able to buy

128

my way through customs. We'll manage. I have the key to the safe.'

'The camera?'

A nod. 'A Minox with flash.'

'And the drug?'

'I have a bottle of aspirin tablets. Among them are ten slightly smaller. They are the ones. They can be crushed and dissolved. They act in about forty minutes, depending on the size of the person. Ten will kill. Two will give about six hours unconscious.'

'Pass them to me under the table.'

The man by the door was reading his newspaper. If he was Security there'd be another like him somewhere nearby. They worked always in pairs since an operative alone could not be trusted. Essat pretended to look round for a waiter. There was another man alone at a table to their right. This one had his profession stamped all over him. There was no way of knowing who it was that the two of them were interested in. It wasn't unusual for Security to be watching someone or other in such a place.

'What's your cover story?' Essat asked.

'I'm a freelance journalist from Algiers, interested in doing a series on the Arab capitals faced with Zionist aggression, starting here in Damascus.'

'We'll leave together,' Essat said. 'There are two men from Security here. In case of trouble you're an old acquaintance, met me in here by chance, hadn't seen me since seventy-nine, when I was in Algiers and a mutual friend introduced us because you were writing about the liberation struggle.'

'Where did my piece appear?'

'It didn't. Find a reason.'

'Right.'

They got up and walked slowly, one behind the other, to the door. The man with the newspaper looked up briefly as they passed him. His eyes were expressionless. They couldn't see his colleague on the far side of the room. Then they were outside, shaking hands and protesting mutual affection a shade more loudly than necessary.

But neither man from Security had followed them out.

'It looks all right but watch your tail,' Essat said. 'I'll meet

129

you at eleven thirty tonight across the road from here. It's always a crowded spot. If you see anything you don't like try for a rendezvous a half hour later at the northern side of the mosque. So long.'

He walked away, recovered his moped and drove off carefully towards the Chaghou Jouwany quarter. At the approach to the Madhat Pasha soukh he turned down a narrow lane and into a labyrinth of streets behind, threading his way among old men with carts, youths on bicycles and housewives on their way to and from the local market. He stopped at a modest house, its windows grimed with dust, the door open to a dank passage. A brass plaque, mildewed and almost illegible, announced: Aleppo Export-Import. Y. Khalil. A small child sat half in the doorway, a line of mucous running from its nose down to its mouth, flies unhindered on its face. The child was playing listlessly with a stick, banging it on the doorstep to no apparent purpose.

Essat stepped past the child, giving it a gentle shove to one side and meeting no response. At the end of the corridor he mounted a flight of stairs to the first floor. A radio was coughing out a news bulletin at full volume from a room at the rear of the building. Essat opened the door and went in.

The room contained a desk and a filing cabinet. A row of hard-backed chairs stood against a wall. A slim youth in army fatigues was sitting on one of them, the radio next to him. Beyond it lay a knapsack. An automatic leaned against the wall by the youth's elbow. He was grooming his nails with a splinter of wood, looked up when Essat entered the room, and turned the radio off.

Essat sat at the desk, noticed the knapsack.

'You taking food to the guards?'

The youth nodded. He had the delicate features and fine skin of the desert Arabs. His smile revealed pale, even teeth.

'Let's see what you've got in there.'

'No need to see. Just the usual – bread, sausage, things like that. What they asked for.'

'And drink?'

The youth fidgeted and giggled. 'I know the rules: no alcohol. There's a couple of bottles of lemonade.'

'Let's see.'

'You don't need to see. It's lemonade.'

Essat got up, went over to the knapsack and opened it. In the bottom, as he knew, would be two bottles of beer. He pulled them out.

'What are these?'

The youth giggled again. 'You know, the boys like a drink. A beer doesn't hurt anyone. They said they'd smash me up if I didn't bring it.'

Essat took a step forward and brought his open hand down hard on to the youth's face. The blow jerked his head back. A whimper escaped him. He said nothing.

'You know the professor's rules?'

'Yes.'

'You know what he does with those who disobey him?'

'Will you report me?'

'Of course I'll report you when he gets back.'

'But they'll throw me out.'

'They'll give you a hiding first.'

'Please. I'll do anything. I don't mind a hiding, but I want to stay in the group. I've given good service. I'll do anything.'

'Go out and get two bottles of lemonade. I'll think about it.'

The youth leapt out of his chair, made for the door and was gone. Essat closed and locked the door behind him. He took the bottles of beer to the desk, took an opener from a drawer and very carefully prised open the bottle caps. Then he emptied the contents of the aspirin bottle on to a sheet of paper, selected four of the smaller tablets and put two into each of the bottles. He used pliers to fasten the caps back on to the bottles. The task was completed as the youth's footsteps echoed up from the stairs. Essat unlocked the door and was sitting at the desk, the bottles of beer before him, when the youth entered, carrying two bottles of lemonade.

'I got them.'

'Come here.'

The youth approached the desk, uncertain whether to draw up a chair. He stood awkwardly, grinning, a bottle in each hand.

'How old are you?'

'Sixteen.'

'You're a good-looking fellow. Made any girls happy yet?'
The giggle again. A shrug. 'Sure.'
'I don't believe you.'
'I have. Ask my brother. He knows.'
'Like it?'
'Of course.'
'I think you prefer cock.'
'I don't.'
'What if I say you do?'
'Then I suppose I do.'
A silence, with the youth shifting from foot to foot, uncertain what to do with the bottles.
'You're a good-looking lad. I propose to find out. What do you say to that?'
'Then can I stay?'
'Yes, if I find you're to my taste.' A pause, with the youth smiling in what he imagined to be an encouraging fashion. He could see his salvation ahead and the route didn't worry him overmuch.
'Shall I put these in the bag?' holding up the lemonade bottles.
'They can have their beer,' Essat said. He handed over the bottles. 'If you brought lemonade they'd know something had happened, wouldn't they?'
'I suppose so.'
'Which means you always take them beer?'
The youth shrugged.
'The idiots throw the empty bottles over the wall. There's a pile of them on the open land next door. They must think I'm blind.'
'Oh.'
'If you say a word of all this to anyone it will get back to the professor. He has his private informers in the group and no one knows who they are.'
'I swear I won't say a word.'
'And you'll meet me here at ten tonight and we'll see if you prefer cock. It's what you're going to get from now on. Now take the food and get out.'
The youth collected the bottles of beer and put them in the knapsack, which he slung over his shoulder. Then he

grabbed the gun and at the door turned to give Essat what he imagined was a signal of sexual complicity.

The youth was waiting in the narrow street when Essat drove up in a Japanese pickup truck. He nodded as he came to a stop and the youth climbed aboard. He drove off and nothing was said until the houses had fallen away and they were in open country with the dim outline of cypress groves on either side of the road.

'Everything all right at the villa?'

'Yes.'

'Did you talk?'

'No, I swear I didn't talk.'

The pickup turned off the main road along a track which led up an incline through a grove of walnut trees. A half-mile along, Essat brought it to a halt. Here there were disused quarry workings on their left and open scrubland to the right. The lights of the city threw up a pink glow on the horizon.

'We'll get in the back,' Essat said.

The youth opened the door of the cab and jumped down, leaving his automatic inside. As Essat climbed down on the far side he handled the gun in the pocket of his jacket. It had a silencer fixed to its snout. As he walked to the rear of the pickup he eased the safety catch. He was trembling because he had no feelings of anger or hostility against this youth, no desire to kill, no stomach for the task at hand. 'It's them or us,' he repeated to himself for the tenth time since he had formulated the plan that afternoon. The pretty El Al girls raked with bullets in the Mercedes in Rome, and now this innocent teenager who wanted to serve his people, only to be snuffed out on a dusty track outside Damascus because he'd be the only witness.

When Essat reached the back of the pickup the youth was standing awkwardly, not knowing if he was expected to climb aboard.

'What do you want me to do?'

The question was not answered. The gun came up slowly and deliberately and from a few inches away Essat shot him between the eyes. It was too dark to see his expression, too dark, please God, for the boy to have seen the gun at all.

He fell without a sound. Essat bent over the body, slumped awkwardly in the dust, and fired again into the head. Then he dragged the dead youth to the edge of the quarry. The body scarcely made a sound as it rolled down the steep incline of rock. He returned to the pickup, took the youth's automatic from the cab and flung it down towards the body. Then he climbed into the cab, turned in a clearing and drove back to the city.

At the appointed time he was in Independence Square among the evening crowds. He saw Yusef, idly pretending to examine a board bearing international exchange rates in the window of a bank. What interested him more was a man devoting equal attention to the contents of a shop window a few yards away. It was only when the man had finished his inspection and moved on, to be lost in the crowd, that Essat approached Yusef.

'Follow me round the next corner. I'll wait for you there.'

When Yusef had joined him, he said: 'We do the job an hour or so from now but we'd best wait up near the house.'

They climbed on the moped and made their way westward out of the city centre. Soon the neon and wailing music lay behind them and they were travelling along tree-lined residential streets with little traffic. They came to a vacant plot where a house had once stood, to be replaced by a wooden shack, now abandoned in its turn. Essat wheeled the moped off the road and out of sight behind the shack. Then he beckoned to Yusef and pushed open the door. The hinges screamed at him. With the door shut behind them he took a torch from his pocket.

'Sit on that box. I'll sit here. We can't risk a light. We've got time to kill so I might as well describe the house. There's a security fence linked to an alarm but I've got the right gear to get through it. Where I'll need you is for the back door of the house and any doors we find locked inside. Also, there are a couple of guards – youngsters – who sleep in the front hall. They should be drugged, but we have to be careful in case something went wrong in that department. If necessary they're to be shot. But the game plan is to get in and out

134

without leaving any sign that the place has been entered at all. If we achieve that the whole operation doubles in value.'

'Where's the safe?'

'In a first-floor office.'

They sat in silence until Essat said, 'All right, let's go.' Then they emerged into the moonless night, wheeled out the moped and covered the remaining distance to the villa in a few minutes. The moped was concealed on the open ground next to the villa. Essat detached a saddle bag.

'Follow me. I know every inch of the place. I'll tell you of any obstacles.' They advanced slowly towards the low wall, topped by a fence, surrounding the professor's property. The fence was crowned with barbed wire at a height of six feet or so.

'There's an electric circuit running round at two levels in the fence. I'll make a loop and we'll be able to cut our way through.'

He took wire cutters and lengths of electric flex from the saddle bag. They were at a spot at the rear of the villa which was out of sight of the road. He handed a torch to Yusef. The beam was dim but enough to work by. He fixed a length of flex to a wire running just above the base of the fence and the second flex to a similar wire three feet higher. Then the ends of the pieces of flex, which were six feet long, were attached to the wires, creating by-passes at both levels. With the wire cutters he then cut a gap in the wire netting. They both climbed through.

'We can mend it on the way out. It'll be years before anyone sees the netting has been cut.'

At the back door to the house Yusef got to work. It took him some ten minutes to deal with the two locks on the door. It swung back noiselessly. And now they were inside the house with the door closed gently behind them. Essat led, using the torch. When they reached the hall the heavy breathing of the guards could be heard.

'Sounds all right. Let's have a look.'

On a low table stood the two beer bottles, empty, with the remains of a meal.

'If your stuff actually works we should have no trouble

from these two. Let's go. I'm interested in two rooms and I don't know what I'm looking for until I find it.'

'Aren't there any servants in this place?'

'They come in at six. No one sleeps in.'

The lock of the professor's study on the ground floor did not yield easily. Yusef worked in silence, cursing from time to time under his breath. 'If I'd been able to bring all my gear, we'd be inside in three seconds. There's nothing tricky about the lock.' He worked on, interrupted by the metallic sounds coming from the lock mechanism as his keys probed within. At last they were rewarded with a decisive click, the handle turned and the door yielded.

'While I'm in here,' Essat said, 'try your luck on the first door on the right on the first floor. It should be much the same. Can you work without the torch?'

'Yes.'

In the study Essat concentrated on the desk. None of the drawers was locked, but he found nothing of interest, save that in a bottom drawer the professor had stored two books on the Neturei Karta and Satmarer movements. Essat wondered why he should be interested in Orthodox Jewish extremists. Perhaps it fed his dislike of the Jews. With the books was a street plan of Jerusalem and a map of Israel. There was nothing else in the study he did not know of already.

He made his way up to the first floor by the light of the torch. Yusef had opened the door of the office where Rasmia worked. Together they crossed to the safe, squatting against a wall in the far corner of the room.

'You have the key?'

'The Old Man gave it to me just before I left. How the hell he got hold of it I've no idea.'

The key slid comfortably into the lock and activated the tumblers smoothly. The door of the safe opened without a sound.

'We'll take the stuff out item by item to make sure everything goes back in its place. They mustn't know we've been nosing inside.'

Essat removed a buff envelope. Inside was a sheaf of decoding sheets covered in groups of five digits.

'I want pictures of those.'

Yusef laid them out on the desk and busied himself with the camera.

'Pull the curtains and keep the number of flashes to a minimum,' Essat said.

While the photography was being done he was searching carefully in the safe. There were bundles of banknotes in several currencies and a large envelope full of passports and passport photographs. At the back of the safe were two hand automatics and a container of pills. Essat knew they would be there: cyanide for use *in extremis*. Beneath the envelope with the passports was a sheet of paper, folded into four. Essat opened it out. On it, a plan of several streets had been drawn. At the top were the words, hastily scrawled, 'Third from left'. Street names had not been written in. There was a crude sketch of a building topped by a dome.

'Take a picture of this. I'll make a note of it myself.'

The paper was transferred to the desk and soon the flash and click of the camera mechanism coincided.

There was nothing else in the safe save a bunch of keys.

'That's it. We'll put the stuff back and lock up again.'

They relocked the safe and left the office, locking the door behind them. Downstairs they locked the study door. The heavy, regular breathing of the guards could still be heard as they let themselves out of the house, securing the back door behind them.

The black of the night was turning to an iridescent mauve on the eastern horizon as Essat finished working on the perimeter fence, wiring the gap they had cut and detaching the electrical by-pass.

'Neat job,' he said as they made their way across the waste ground to retrieve the moped. 'Give me the keys. I'll get rid of them. You don't want to risk anything on the way out.'

Yusef handed over the bunch of keys.

'What about the camera?'

'My instructions are to ditch it. I've good concealment for the film in my bag.'

Yusef removed the film and the minature camera was pushed into a hole hacked in the rough ground.

'What are your plans?'

'I've got a booking for tomorrow morning.'

They rode back into a quiet part of the city and said goodbye on a street corner near Yusef's hotel.

At ten the following morning Yusef got out of a taxi at Damascus airport and made for the check-in desk. He held a ticket on Alitalia's 11 a.m. flight to Rome. The girl at check-in had a short list of names in front of her, out of sight of the travellers. The name on the ticket presented by Yusef appeared on this list. Before processing him on to the flight she pressed a button beneath the edge of her desk.

'Gate 4,' she said brightly. 'Boarding at 10.45. Have a good flight.'

Yusef did not see the two men follow him to passport control. One moved ahead of him into the short line waiting to have their passports processed; the other moved in behind him. As he reached the desk and held his passport out to the officer, the man behind him thrust forward. He was hustled between the two men, his arms were gripped and pulled behind him and he was dragged, struggling and quite help-less, into an office a few yards away on the air side of the barrier.

He heard the click of the handcuffs behind him as he felt the steel on his wrists. Then they emptied his pockets and shoved him backwards into a chair. There was a fat, exhaus-ted-looking policeman in a soiled uniform seated behind a desk on the far side of the room. He now looked up as if he had only just noticed the disturbance.

'Who are you?'

'My name is Shahid Osman. I am an Algerian. You'll find it in my passport.'

One of the men who had jumped him passed the passport over to the fat policeman, who glanced at it without interest.

'We think you are not.'

'I am, and I demand to be freed and allowed to board my plane.'

'You will not be boarding your plane. You will be telling us now who you are, or we will take steps so that you will be telling us shortly.'

'I demand to know why I have been arrested.'

'I am not authorized to tell you. I am merely authorized to hand you over to our security people for interrogation.'

The policeman nodded to the two heavies. Yusef was yanked to his feet and dragged to a further door, leading back to the concourse.

Out on the roadway a car was waiting. He was bundled into the back and the two men got in on either side of him. He noticed that his holdall had been thrown in next to the driver.

The car pulled out and headed back to the city.

'If it were up to me,' the man on Yusef's left said to his companion, 'I'd kill all the fucking Zionists. Kill the women but cut the balls off the men first.'

'Good idea,' the other man said.

The first man turned to Yusef, thrusting a heavy, unshaven face at him. 'What do you think, friend Osman from Algeria?'

'A tall order, that.' Yusef tried to sound as if he'd be in favour of the thing if it could be done.

'Hear that? Our Algerian friend says it's a tall order. Eh, Osman?'

A painful thrust in the side from the man's fist. 'But you'd do it if you could, eh Osman?'

'No doubt, no doubt.'

'He favours emasculating the Jews,' the other man said. 'You're a witness. He said "no doubt".'

A stab in the ribs from the other side.

'Soon,' the first man said, 'there'll be a chance to see whether you tell lies about these things or the truth, eh?'

The car was speeding along the highway back into Damascus. Yusef did not think he would be able to withstand what awaited him at interrogation.

'So you are Shahid Osman?'

'Yes.'

'From Algiers?'

'Yes.'

'Journalist?'

'Yes.'

'But you are unknown at the Ministry of Information in Algiers.'

A shrug.

'Answer me, Shahid. Those who do not answer are treated very badly. What happened to you this afternoon will seem like paradise.'

'I am a journalist come to write about life in Syria and other countries.' The words came out stubbornly, without conviction now.

His mind was numb, not functioning properly. There seemed to be a sheet of glass between the interrogator and himself — the questions coming through indistinct, remote, almost irrelevant. And the slightest movement in the chair was agony as the fabric of his shirt pulled at the wounds in his back to which the garment had adhered, embedded in his blood. The beating had lasted as long as consciousness remained. Twice they had brought him back with injections and continued until he had sunk into oblivion again. There was hardly an inch of skin left intact between his neck and buttocks.

'I would like some water. My mouth is too dry to speak.'

'Water comes later. I repeat: They do not know you in Algiers. We contacted them while you were having your little treatment this afternoon.'

'I am from Algiers.'

The interrogator rose from his chair, came round the desk and kicked at the chair on which Yusef was sitting. The young man screamed as he fell to the ground, unable to save himself with his manacled hands, falling on the side of his head, his back in agony again.

Almost gently, the interrogator lifted him back on to the chair.

'I am losing patience. If you do not talk sense to me now you will be handed back to the men you met this afternoon. It is now six and your treatment will last through the night. We will burn you, my friend, and we will cut you in terrible places. After it you will no longer be a man. You will no longer have your health, and certainly not your beauty. Why be so foolish?'

Yusef knew now that he was not of the élite who with-

140

stood such things. How, then, to minimize the damage from what he would tell them? He had followed instructions, had held on to his cover story as long as strength remained in him, could scarcely recall now what the next stage of cover was supposed to be. Through the pain and terror he tried to remember, unaware that the interrogator knew more of these matters than he did; knew that when the first cover story has been broken, brutal speed would almost certainly drive a way through the next protective layer.

'What do you want to know?'

'You already know that. First, your name.'

'My name is Yusef Livneh.'

'Where are you from?'

'Tel Aviv.'

'Who do you work for?'

He remembered; never tell them you work for the Mossad. Say the Ministry of Foreign Trade, industrial spying. But he knew they would not believe it. He couldn't face unnecessary suffering any more. He would tell what lies he could, but not transparent nonsense like this.

'I work for the Mossad.'

'What was this mission?'

'I had a message for a man here. It was coded. I don't know what it was about.'

'I am about to ask you how you contacted this man, but I want you to think carefully before you reply. What you tell me is to lead to an arrest. If it does not, you will go back to treatment, as I described. I am not interested in the standard evasions – rendezvous in this or that spot, arranged in advance, no arrangements for meeting again, no names, nothing, nothing, nothing . . .' The interrogator had come round the desk again, was standing over Yusef, bending so that his face was a few inches from the face of his victim. 'Here we come to the heart of the matter. This decides your fate, my friend. I am interested in a name and I am interested in a further arrest. Only so will I know whether you are being honest with us at last. Isn't that so?'

Yusef nodded.

'I am inclined,' the interrogator said, 'to return you to my colleagues for an hour or so, just to make that point abundantly clear to you. Or are you ready now to tell me things which will lead to an arrest?'

Yusef nodded.

'Very well, we shall see. Describe to me your arrangements for making contact. And remember, if we find subsequently that this first version was inaccurate, untrue, a lie, we will smash you to a pulp even when we have the truth out of you. We will do that simply as a remonstrance – a way of showing our displeasure at being taken lightly by Zionist scum.'

'I will tell the truth.'

The interrogator returned to his desk and sat. 'I am listening.'

It was the point at which Yusef abandoned the struggle; the point at which the interrogator always calculated that he would win or lose, though with this young man he had never doubted that he would win.

'We met in the Ommayad mosque.'

'How did you recognize each other?'

'There was an old man – I think he kept order there. He sent my contact to me.'

'Describe your contact.'

There was a glimmer of hope in Yusef's mind that here at least he could fool them.

'A dark man with straight hair. Maybe thirty-five. In Arab dress.'

'His name.'

'I swear I never knew his name.'

'What happened?'

'I handed him the message. He took it and went. That is all.'

'I assume you could identify the old man and this other contact?'

Yusef nodded.

There was a pause while the interrogator looked at him pensively, deciding perhaps for or against monstrous agony. Then he seemed to make up his mind.

'You will be taken away and perhaps you will get a little water and some attention to your back. You will sign a confession which I will draw up. You will co-operate with

142

us further in ways that will be explained to you. But I repeat: if we make no arrest your situation will deteriorate sharply. You will beg us to give you a beating instead.'

Later, in his cell, he was presented with a statement drawn up in Hebrew. The facts were as he had described them. The conclusion was a promise to co-operate and a renunciation of the Mossad and what it stood for. It had already been signed by his interrogator, and he now signed it himself. Then they brought him a tin mug of water, followed by a man in immaculate white shirt and fawn trousers who said he was a doctor. Tending the wounds on his back was almost as painful as the beating and he fainted twice before the doctor had finished with him. He then lay on his belly, his face resting on the foul surface of the stone floor, sobbing and unable to sleep.

Later that day they found the undeveloped film concealed in the handle of his holdall. The interrogator, who lacked experience, allowed genuine anger to take hold of him. He had told the colonel in charge of the case that he had broken his man and was getting the truth. It now appeared that what he was getting was lies. He joined the two specialists responsible for the 'treatment' and in their collective fury they killed Yusef before he had a chance to tell them of Essat, the break-in and the safe. Cause of death: cardiac seizure aggravated by suffocation on a gag, though it could equally well have been severe trauma to the brain resulting from heavy blows to the head (in the absence of an autopsy the death certificate stated laconically 'heart failure').

Their luck was no better with the old man, whose prediction that his heart would not stand up to harsh treatment proved accurate. He, too, was mercifully dead before he could talk. When, later, they found the radio and code books in his room, the discovery was concealed from the colonel in charge for fear of greater official anger.

'Must have been a false trail after all,' the interrogator said. 'There was nothing at the old fellow's lodgings.'

The experts could make nothing of the prints they had blown up from the roll of developed film.

143

Chapter 16

Major Savary had taken his precautions. One of his men from the DGSE was in the bistro near the Odéon, leaning on the bar over a pastis. He was dressed as a building worker, even to the cement dust on his dungarees and in his hair. He was a man who believed in dressing for the job, taking the thing seriously. He had been there for twenty minutes when Tavernet came in, chose a table opposite the bar and ordered a beer. He took a pipe from his pocket, put it in his mouth but did not light it. Rasmia had been told about the pipe and had been given a description: a short, bald man with steel-rimmed glasses – strong lenses – wearing a dark suit. She walked straight to his table and sat down facing him. She nodded briefly, looked round the almost deserted bistro.

'Will you drink something?'

'Thank you, no.'

'It would look better.'

'A coffee. Black.'

The DGSE man at the bar dropped his cigarettes and managed to get a look at the girl as he picked them up. It was only in profile.

The waiter retreated after serving the coffee. Rasmia did not touch it.

'Is it secure here?'

'Yes.'

'You know who sent me?'

'I was told. What do you want?'

'I am only here to arrange a secure meeting for the man

who sent me. He would like to see you without fail later today.'

'What does he want to talk about?'

'I do not know.'

'I do not like these arrangements. Two meetings where one would presumably do. Mystery about the subject matter. If anyone but Major Savary had arranged all this I would have refused.'

'I am sorry. We have learned caution.'

Tavernet put his pipe back in his pocket and drank some of his beer. His movements were slow, even ponderous. He had a habit of looking over the top of his spectacles, and this gave him the air of an unsuccessful schoolmaster – unsuccessful because there was no distinction about him. It was a manner not so much furtive as tentative, self-deprecating. Also cautious.

There was a silence as Tavernet drank again. 'Does your friend know the Rond Point des Champs Elysées?' he asked.

'Of course.'

'On one corner is the Drugstore. Just beyond it, horse-drawn cabs are parked. They take tourists for rides round the gardens, down towards the Place de la Concorde. At seven this evening I will stand on the pavement where the cabbies wait. When I see your friend I will climb into a carriage and he will join me. Describe him, please.'

Rasmia gave a description of Hanif. 'It does not sound secure,' she said.

'You will permit me to know better.'

'But a horse cab in the centre of Paris . . .'

'My dear mademoiselle, what is significant about a horse-drawn carriage?'

'I don't know. Its speed, I suppose.'

'Precisely. How do you tail such a vehicle, which is far too slow to be followed by a car and slightly too fast to be tailed on foot without the hurrying person drawing a good deal of attention to himself? An ideal conveyance for our purpose.'

'But it is very visible.'

'Not at all. Serious people do not look inside cabs. In any

case, your friend can wear a panama hat — something like that.'

The man at the bar could hear nothing of the conversation. When the girl showed signs of getting up to leave he followed his orders and left ahead of her. He waited in the doorway of a nearby shop and followed her when she came out of the bistro. But the girl obviously knew about tails. She lost him within ten minutes.

'You should never have accepted such a ridiculous arrangement for a meeting,' Professor Hanif told her later. She said nothing. 'You had better cover for me. What time is it for?'

'Seven this evening.'

'You will be at the Rond Point at six thirty. Conceal yourself and make sure this man Tavernet hasn't been followed. And be sure no one is there ahead of him. If you have any doubts at all we will abort the whole thing. You simply come up to me when I arrive and we go off together. Is that clear?'

She nodded.

Later that afternoon Tavernet called Savary and told him of the meeting with the girl and the arrangements for that evening. 'Get one of your men to keep an eye on things.'

'I have been doing that.'

'I imagined so.'

When Rasmia arrived at the Rond Point at half past six there was the usual summer swarm of tourists, augmented by the rush-hour crowds making for the Metro and the buses. There was no way of knowing whether the café tables bunched on the broad pavement contained nothing but innocent drinkers. She did not see the man Savary had sent to keep an eye on the proceedings, and when Professor Hanif appeared promptly at seven she was able to nod to him from the position she had taken up on a bench beneath the plane trees. She had seen Tavernet arrive a few minutes earlier, exchange a few words with the cabby who headed the short row of cabs, and look carefully around him. He was wearing a felt hat with the brim low over his eyes.

Then contact was made and Rasmia watched Hanif climb into the cab after Tavernet. The cabby flicked his whip,

146

clucked at his horse, and manoeuvred the cab out into the traffic.

As it made its sedate way down the Avenue Gabriel Hanif explained what he wanted.

'I understand that you have access to weapons.'

'What manner of weapons?'

'Shall we say ultimate weapons?'

'Please proceed.'

'I am thinking of weapons of low yield because the size has to be the minimum possible. Maybe something like the warheads used in a mobile missile system.'

'But atomic?'

'Atomic.'

'What is your purpose?'

'I am not prepared to discuss that at this stage. First, I need to know whether we have anything to discuss at all.'

There was a pause, punctuated by the reassuring clip-clop of the ancient horse's hooves on the tarmac. The cabby flicked his whip and the nag tried to show a pathetic burst of speed as they turned into the Avenue de Marigny, heading for the Champs Elysées.

'We have something to discuss,' Tavernet said. 'Under certain conditions.'

'I have resources.'

'It is a very risky business. There are heavy expenses. Others have to be looked after.'

'I know it is risky and I expected it to be expensive. As for the others, that worries me. I do not believe people can be trusted.'

'They can, if they do not know what they are doing. In such a case only I would know.'

'So how expensive?'

The other did not reply. Instead, he sat in silence for a moment, apparently contemplating the trees along their route. Then: 'Have you considered another option?'

'What do you mean?'

'If you had contacts in a friendly country with facilities – say Pakistan, maybe Libya – you might find it easier to acquire the raw materials and let your friends make up the weapon. The problem today is uranium enrichment, not the

147

manufacture of the bomb. That can be done by almost anyone since the technology became known.'

'I prefer to acquire a weapon.'

Tavernet ignored the remark. 'You see, there is a curious dilemma here. Buying enriched uranium is difficult but, relatively speaking, the likeliest route. Consider how much has been spirited away despite the rule books. A hundred kilos of the stuff went missing from a Pennsylvania plant in 1966 and another eleven kilos from the Apollo plant in the same area in 1977. A few plutonium bars disappeared from Dounreay in Britain in September 1973. And I can give you an even more interesting figure: back in 1982 it was officially reckoned that eight hundred kilos of enriched uranium were unaccounted for at Oak Ridge alone in the thirty-seven years since the plant was built.'

He paused again to let his remarks take their effect. 'Those eight hundred kilos would make you eighty-five bombs, my friend, and you only need one.'

'Two.'

'Very well, two. But my point is that there is a market – admittedly a difficult market – in enriched uranium, plutonium. Very, very expensive, but possible. And not all that risky when you consider what we are dealing with. Whereas acquiring two complete weapons . . . Risky; highly risky. Therefore costly.'

'My need for secrecy precludes your alternative route.'

There was another pause. Traffic surged past the cab as it advanced slowly down the Champs Elysées towards the Place de la Concorde.

'I must know more about your purpose,' Tavernet said.

'I am engaged in anti-Zionist activities.'

'Where?'

'In a number of places. But we are talking about Israel itself.'

'I see.' Another silence. 'And what assurance can I obtain that you are what you say you are and that your present purpose has to do with Israel and not some crazy scheme to take hostages here in Paris?'

'Via Savary you can get all the assurances you could need from Gadafi.'

They rode in silence while Tavernet took out his pipe and with slow and deliberate movements procured a pouch from another pocket, carefully filled the pipe and tamped the tobacco down. Then he used a lighter to light it. They were approaching the Concorde.

'You'll turn back at the Concorde,' Tavernet shouted to the driver. The man nodded and flicked his whip at the horse as if passing on the message.

Tavernet turned slightly towards Hanif. 'Subject to what the Libyan has to say and after the careful consideration that I will necessarily give to your project, I can tell you now that I would need five million dollars US, half to be deposited in a Swiss account on concluding the deal, half to follow on delivery.'

'I am told you can deliver outside France.'

'Under certain circumstances.'

'Israel?'

'To Israel I deliver subject to discharging the merchandise, which is to be handled by the purchaser.'

'And what flag?'

'French. The Israelis accept their imports from France in French or Israeli vessels only.'

Hanif raised his eyebrows. 'A French vessel and you claim it is secure?'

'The owner is my man.'

'And the crew?'

'There is no problem with the crew. We have been running difficult cargoes for some time. We know what we are doing.'

Tavernet had identified a Marseilles shipping company with six of its eight vessels laid up and with promissory notes in the hands of one Emilio Lavazzi, a baron of the Marseilles *milieu*. The company was unable to honour the notes on due date. A proposal was made: the company would sell the *Croix Valmer*, a 4,000–ton general-cargo vessel, to the Société SARAP with a registered address at the office of a lawyer in the Boulevard National and no visible activity in shipping or anything else. The *Croix Valmer* would be chartered back to its original owners, complete with crew. Further, SARAP would put business in the company's way and the *Croix Valmer* would carry the cargoes involved. The arrangement had run for two years.

There was a silence. Then, without turning his head, Hanif said, 'The price is absurd.'

'Nevertheless, it is the price.'

'One million in advance and one million on delivery.'

Tavernet shook his head. 'We are wasting each other's valuable time. Go elsewhere.'

The firm tone belied the man's flaccid persona.

'Whatever the ultimate price, the advance element is far too large. How do I know you won't simply pocket the money and disappear?'

'You don't know. I advise you to ask Savary how likely that would be. Then you must make up your own mind.'

'Whatever the figure we finally agree,' Hanif said, 'it is not reasonable to expect me to trust you to the tune of one half of that sum. I do not impute dishonesty. There can be a failure of nerve, a disaster which aborts the project. What then?'

'Firstly, I honour my commitments. I repeat, ask Savary. Secondly, there will be no failure of nerve. On that point, too, Savary will have an opinion. As to disaster, if that landed me in trouble I would regard the money received as small compensation. That is why there has to be half in advance.'

'It is scarcely reasonable.'

'It is not negotiable. The risks I run in such a situation are greater than those run by you.'

'One million, and two later.'

'You will forgive me,' Tavernet said evenly, 'I am a Frenchman; you are from the Mediterranean. We do business differently. You bargain whilst I do not. You have my price. If it interests you we can talk. If not, not. We will have had a pleasant ride together and you have my word that I will immediately forget everything that has been said.'

'If we reach agreement, at what point am I to make the first payment?'

'It is a preliminary payment and preliminary is a word with a clear meaning. We will shake hands on the deal and I will then give you details of the bank and account number.

You will then go away to make the transfer. When the bank notifies me that the funds have been received I will proceed. It should take me up to a month, perhaps a little more, maybe even a shade less. It will depend partly on the acquisition of the weapons, partly on the availability of transport.'

'I will need a detailed specification for the weapons – exact dimensions, yield, triggering mechanism and so on.'

'I can supply the atomic warhead of our Pluton suface-to-surface missile. It will carry a plutonium fission charge of fifteen megaton capacity. In case you do not know, that is about fifty per cent higher than the rating of the Hiroshima bomb.'

'And the dimensions?'

'About forty-five centimetres diameter and one metre sixty-five long. The exact dimensions are mentioned in the technical specification. The weight of a Pluton warhead is about fifty kilogrammes. Will you need timers for delayed arming and detonating?'

'Yes.'

'I will supply them.'

'If you will be loading in Marseilles we must suppose there is a risk that the authorities will search the dock area with detectors which pick up the radiation.'

'That point has obviously been considered. These are plutonium bombs. The main emission, I understand, is that of alpha particles. The bombs will be coated by us in rubber latex, which is painted on. This is an effective barrier against these particles. In any case, the emissions are not powerful and it is not easy to detect them against normal background radiation.'

Professor Hanif pondered the reply.

'And how will I know that what you deliver is the genuine article?'

'Your own expert can examine the merchandise before the second half of the payment is released. You will be required to place it in escrow at a bank of your choice at the same time as you pay over the first sum. It will be released to me on receipt of both your authorization and mine.' There was a thin smile. 'Trust is essential in business, but a bank holding

151

money in escrow is a great help in the process of creating trust.'

The cab was approaching the Rond Point once more.

'I will think about it,' Hanif said. 'How can I contact you around midday tomorrow?'

'At twelve thirty I can be in the Restaurant de l'Etoile in the Rue Balzac, just off the Champs Elysées. I will be downstairs, at the back. It is a convenient place with two exits.'

'Very well. Please tell the driver to stop here.'

Tavernet issued an order, the cab stopped and Hanif got out. Nothing more had been said. Then the cab drove on, to deposit Tavernet back at the Rond Point. As he alighted and paid the fare there was no expression on his face and he did not respond to the cabby's 'goodnight'. After spending a moment looking carefully about him, he joined the crowd moving slowly up the Champs Elysées and presently descended the steps into the Metro.

Chapter 17

Shortly after the Libyan hit squads started operating on a regular basis in Paris in 1981, a third-floor apartment at No. 16 Rue Lamoureux had changed hands. It had come on to the market on the death of its occupant, a reclusive lady of advanced years, and had been snapped up at the asking price by a lawyer by the name of Benoit. M. Benoit was someone who did favours of this kind from time to time for the DST. On this occasion he was also successful in buying the apartment's contents, thus avoiding the undesirable spectacle of removal vans and the transporting of furniture in the street below. The staff of the Libyan embassy across the street was thus unaware of the change of ownership and were further misled by Alfred Baum's decision not to relinquish the room manned by the DST's watchers at No. 24, thirty yards further up the street.

'They know about No. 24,' he said to the head of the detail which tried to keep an eye on the Libyans. 'They are perfectly happy trying to mask their entrance from our cameras, so why disappoint them? Let them concentrate on No. 24. It can do no harm.'

Thus, cameras, directional mikes and other electronic listening equipment were taken into the new apartment quietly over the course of several nights, and the new surveillance post was manned intermittently, whenever Baum thought it was worth deploying some of his men.

Just before nine on the morning after the conversation in the horse-drawn cab, the man who had come on duty a couple of hours earlier at No. 16 was jolted from a reverie

153

about the fishing of trout by the arrival of a taxi at the embassy door across the way. The occupant must have prepared his money and handed it to the driver as they drew up, for he alighted immediately, crossed the pavement with his head bowed and after pressing the electric door release was out of sight again in a second or two. The DST man cursed the fact that he had not got a shot of the visitor, but he had seen him clearly enough in profile; a tall, slim figure in well-cut clothes, maybe forty-five or so, black hair, swarthy complexion. He looked very much like the one who'd been described to him a couple of days earlier. He picked up the phone and dialled the office.

Shortly after his arrival had been notified to the DST in this manner, Professor Hanif was installed at the telex keyboard on the top floor of the embassy. The Libyan diplomatic network is equipped with a telex system incorporating encoding and decoding devices. An operator had linked him to Gadafi's headquarters. There was an exchange of messages.

'I have been offered what I need by the man you recommended. I have no way of knowing if he can and will deliver. What is your opinion?'

'The man is politically well motivated and has always been found reliable. He has co-operated effectively with our commandos in France. If he fails he will know that we are in a position to expose him or to take measures against him.'

'I am required to hand over two and a half million dollars in advance and the same again on delivery. What is your opinion of this?'

'I am aware that this individual is hungry for money.'

'I have tried to get the sum reduced. I have made no progress.'

'You will not make progress. He is a hard man in this as in the matters which he will be required to do for you. My opinion therefore is that the deal is reasonable.'

'I do not have such a sum at my disposal.'

'It will be transferred from certain funds we have. Please give details.'

'The payment is to be made in Switzerland. I will have details later today.'

'It will be done.'

Hanif tore the uncoded print-out from the telex machine and handed it to the operator. 'Burn this, please.'

The man took the roll of paper to the marble fireplace, set fire to it with a lighter and watched it burn in the grate.

'My presence here is not to be subject for gossip,' Hanif said.

'Very good.'

'Tell Rabah I am ready to leave.'

When Rabah, the head of security, appeared, Hanif said: 'I would prefer to get out of the building unobserved. What can you do?'

'It is not difficult. We have an embassy car in the inner courtyard. You can lie down at the back and you will be driven out.'

The DST man had been instructed to make damn sure his camera was ready when the visitor came out, but all he was able to get was a meaningless shot of a black Fiat and a note of the car's number, which was already well known.

The DST car which had been sent racing through the streets of Paris from the Rue des Saussaies had been reduced to a crawl in the morning rush-hour traffic. It arrived in the Rue Lamoureux several minutes after Hanif had been driven away.

The man at No. 16 ignored his instructions and instead of reporting back direct to Alfred Baum, got the switchboard to put him through to Allembeau in the belief that he would thus be subjected to less disapproval. Allembeau listened in silence, called the man an idiot and rang off. Then he made his way to Baum's office.

'A balls-up,' he said, and told the story.

Baum sighed as if he were past caring. 'What other good news do you have for me, my friend?'

'Nothing good, but you may be interested to hear how we are getting on with that Russki from Damascus, comrade Belaiev.'

'Tell me. It will take my mind off more troublesome matters.'

'I'd guess he's someone's handler,' Allembeau said. 'My men say he wandered straight off to the Bois de Boulogne.

Went again the following day, that was yesterday. Pissing with rain, wasn't it? So it can't have been for the exercise, but he never made contact.'

'Where did he go?'

'Same area each time, around the western end of the big lake. We've staked it out today to save following him there each time.'

'Good. Switch your teams around so they don't get bored, lose interest and miss the big moment.'

'It's what I'm doing.'

'How many men?'

'Two men and two girls on foot, plus a couple of cars.'

'When contact is made, try to get a picture or two. He may lead us to someone we'd like to meet.'

Allembeau wondered idly why the Russians had gone to the trouble of bringing in KGB from Syria when they already had plenty of KGB in Paris.

When Hanif arrived at the restaurant Tavernet was already installed at a table in a far corner downstairs, the remains of a drink before him. During most of the meal they said very little. Over the cheese Hanif felt it appropriate to come back to the bargaining.

'It will be very difficult for me to raise so much money. I could reach one and a half million – no more.'

'Then I fear we have nothing more to say to each other.'

'Would you consider a final payment some months after delivery?'

Tavernet was inspecting the piece of Camembert on his plate. He shook his head. 'I am afraid my position is not negotiable. For enriched uranium you would pay – what – ten million a kilo. It is about the going rate. And it would be easier. So you see, five million for two weapons is cheap, even absurd.'

'So why are weapons cheaper than uranium if uranium is easier to come by?'

Tavernet was eating his cheese, biting into it from the end of his fork.

'Simple. To obtain the weapons and transport them I have to make some payments, but they are manageable. To obtain uranium I have to buy, and there is always a chain of sellers, each of whom is running grave risks and requires to be rewarded accordingly. Also, there is a market, since others also buy. Therefore, there is a market price. So you see – no contradiction.'

'How would I know that you had delivered weapons in working order?'

'You will appoint your own expert and I will provide specifications for him to examine. This can be done at the dockside. If, at the end of the inspection, your man pronounces himself satisfied, the sum which you will already have placed in escrow at the bank will be released to me by means of our joint telexes.'

The coffee had arrived. The restaurant had filled up while they were eating and Tavernet, his back to the wall, glanced regularly around him.

'I consider myself well informed on the arms dealing community,' Hanif said. 'I have never heard of you.'

'I am not an arms dealer.'

'What can you tell me about yourself?'

'There is only one significant fact about myself: I am the brother of a well-placed man. That is all.'

'And your political views?'

'I have no political views. I am a businessman.'

'And does this brother of yours have a view, say, on the Middle Eastern question?'

'He does. That is why he is willing to undertake this scheme. His position could be said to parallel that of Savary. Also, he will naturally share the financial reward. After all, the greatest risk of all is taken by him.'

'You have driven a hard bargain,' Hanif said.

'No one is obliged to do business with me. Maybe elsewhere you could find it cheaper.'

'It is a deal.'

Tavernet took a slip of paper from his pocket and pushed it across the table. 'That is the bank account into which the transfer is to be made. I start work when I receive the bank's notification.'

'And what about further contact?'

'There is a phone number written there. It is mine. If you

157

call and ask for a meeting I will know it is here. You just give the time.'

'Very good.'

'We will leave separately, please.' Tavernet rose, brushed the crumbs off the front of his shirt, extended his hand. Hanif shook it, surprised at the limp and passive handshake.

He left the restaurant a few minutes after Tavernet and made for the lower end of the Champs Elysées.

Chapter 18

'You know,' Baum said, 'that I consider you without equal when it comes to a *pied de porc*, accompanied by a salad of broad beans. Absolutely without equal.'

'If that is so, why are you toying with it as if it turned your stomach?'

'That's the whole point.' He put his knife and fork on his plate, lifted his wine glass, thought better of it and replaced it on the table. 'My stomach is in fact turned, not by your dish, which I acknowledge to be delicious, but by something mysterious. I don't know what it is.'

'Your old trouble?' Concern had crept into Madame Baum's voice.

'I fear so.'

'You are worrying again, Alfred.'

'It is not uncommon.'

'Your pills?'

'My pills.' He got up heavily from the table, rummaged in a drawer of the great oak sideboard, found a box of pills and returned to the table.

'But should you take them with wine?'

'If I had to take both pills and water I would end it all. Simply not worth the discomfort.' He extracted two small white pills from the box and swallowed them, taking more wine than the exercise called for. 'These pills are useless.'

'They soothe you.'

She removed his plate, with most of the pig's trotter still intact. 'Maybe it will keep in the fridge until you feel yourself again.'

159

'Maybe. But the way things are it can be a long time.'

'A bad day?' she asked as the fridge door closed.

'Naturally. I was at the Elysée with Georges. They are not attractive people there.'

It was true. That afternoon Baum and Wavre had been summoned to the president's office to report progress. There had been no progress. The icy Vallat, stand-in for the president, was displeased on his master's behalf.

'The president had expressly ordered speed in this matter.'

He said this as if the timetable were fully under the control of the DST.

'We are not dispatching trains,' Wavre said, exhaling a great cloud of tobacco smoke as if he were. 'Our opponents unfortunately show no interest in helping us. Nor do they appear to be helping Duparc here.'

The head of the president's anti-terrorist unit looked at his knees and seemed to find little comfort there.

'Can we have a report, please?' Vallat looked balefully at Wavre, Baum and Duparc in turn. 'I do not mind who produces it provided I have something to tell the president . . .' he paused a moment, a master of offensive timing ' . . . who is angry and shows signs of becoming angrier.'

Wavre and Baum having prepared a scenario for this moment in the proceedings, the former turned to the latter and said, 'Alfred.'

Baum shifted uncomfortably in his chair, cleared his throat and turned his amiable gaze on the gaunt and charmless figure of Vallat.

'I think you might tell the president that our sources indicate that the Chatila group has no present plans for further terrorist action on French soil. My foreign source takes that view and I concur.'

Vallat turned to Duparc, who was now looking a shade more cheerful.

'We know nothing to the contrary,' Duparc said.

'Information has reached me,' Vallat said, 'that leading personalities from this group are believed to be presently in France.'

160

Baum managed with difficulty to keep his half-smile in position on the lower part of his face.

'What is your source?' The tone did not gell with the smile.

'The police.'

'Is that a reliable source,' Baum asked mildly, 'given their performance so far in this affair?'

'I did not say it was reliable. I merely answered your question. I now ask you whether I am to discount that information and tell the president that the DST denies its authenticity.'

'As far as we know, it is not true. We all know that our country leaks like a sieve in both directions. We further know that we can get no co-operation from the police in tracing incoming travellers in this instance. Nevertheless, and despite these shortcomings which lie outside the province of my service, we have no evidence that the Chatila leaders are presently in France.'

On their way back to the Rue des Saussaies after more fruitless exchanges, Wavre asked: 'True or false, what you said in there?'

'I don't want to embarrass you.'

'For once I can stand it.'

'In that case, false.'

'Completely false?'

'Perhaps not completely. You will have noticed that I said we had no evidence. But what is evidence?'

Wavre did not choose to answer the question.

'We get a message from Israeli intelligence,' Baum said. 'Then a dark man visits the Libyan embassy. The first could be a mistake, the second could be Gadafi's cousin. Scarcely evidence. So maybe what I said was only a shade false.'

'Philosophically interesting but operationally dubious.'

Baum sighed. 'I fear so.'

They walked on – two portly men at odds with the hot summer day.

'You didn't follow our brief, Alfred. I never agreed to telling lies, or even half-lies to the President of the Republic.'

Baum looked quizzically at Wavre from under his brows. 'I felt in the circumstances that the president was in need of a greater measure of reassurance than we are in a position

161

to grant him. I therefore . . . extended the brief, though not by a great deal. And I do not believe that either Duparc's men or anyone else is likely to find the man Hanif before I do.'

'I hope so, Alfred,' Georges Wavre said as they reached the unimpressive portals of the DST offices. 'My presence associated me and therefore the department with your little untruth. You realize that?'

'I do. Perhaps it was unwise to invite me along.'

'Perhaps it was.'

'If it is any consolation to you in these difficult days,' Baum said as they waited for the lift, 'I do not expect to find the man Hanif and his companion myself.'

'How can that be a consolation?'

'If I find them it will be living proof that either I lied or I, and through me our department, was ill-informed.'

Wavre grunted.

'Despite which,' Baum concluded cheerfully as he alighted at the fourth floor, 'I am sparing no effort to locate these wretched people.'

The iron lift gates clanged shut on the unhappy figure of Wavre as the antiquated mechanism lurched into life and bore him up to the fifth.

Seated in his own office, his tie loosened and a handkerchief mopping his brow, Baum asked Mlle Pineau to find Commander Allembeau for him. He needed someone to talk to.

'How are the Germans?' he asked when Allembeau was installed on the far side of his desk.

'You handed me a dog there, Alfred.'

'Absolutely.'

'There's a little progress. Do you want to hear?'

'No. Any kind of progress on any *affaire* currently makes me jealous. No, I want you to listen to me, and I assure you that I'd talk to you from a couch if I thought that would make me feel better.'

'I am no psychiatrist.'

'A pity. My self-diagnosis is anxiety neurosis with a touch of paranoia. Nevertheless, please listen.'

162

He brought Allembeau up to date on Chatila, told him of Ben Tov's fears of a nuclear conspiracy.

'Every security man in the world is paranoid about nuclear weapons,' Allembeau said. 'You mustn't allow the Israelis to drag you into that overheated madhouse of theirs.'

'I take it seriously. Please bear with me while I tell you what I propose to do. But first a question. Could our men mount an effective surveillance on Savary at the DGSE? I have an opinion but I would like to hear yours.'

'I think not.'

'Why?'

'For a start, that damned complex in the Boulevard Mortier is impossible to keep under observation. In the boulevard itself the Mortier barracks lie opposite and there's no vantage point from which one can keep the DGSE gates under observation. Then, in the Avenue Gambetta they've taken over the buildings opposite their back entrance and their cars are always parked here and there along their frontage. As for the Rue Fargeau on the third side of the triangle – hopeless. We tried back in eighty-three. Made fools of ourselves.'

'I thought maybe we'd learned from that foolishness.'

Allembeau shook his head. 'All I learned was that we shouldn't try it again.'

'Maybe from Savary's home?'

'Maybe, but useless. What's the point of tailing him from his home if we can't tail him if he chooses to slip out of his office to meet someone?'

'We could try, of course,' Baum said with no conviction in his voice.

'It would take a dozen men and several cars to make any sense at all. A waste.'

'As you say, a waste.'

Baum tried again.

'A tap on his phone?'

'I can't believe a man like that would allow himself the luxury of incriminating phone conversations.'

'Nor can I.'

'And his mail is bound to be innocuous.'

'Bound to be.'

163

They sat and stared at each other for a while, as they often did when a case was deadlocked, a foreign foe too agile, a rival department too troublesome.

'I have one last idea,' Baum said.

Allembeau waited for more but knew better than to ask what the idea might be.

'A contact of mine,' Baum said. 'A little private arrangement I have found useful once or twice.' He looked up suddenly and treated Allembeau to a broad smile. 'This confounded wretch Savary, what are his – er – tastes, his vices? To what is he susceptible, eh? The dossier only gives us a few bare bones.'

He reached into a drawer of his desk, pulled out a familiar grey folder. Turning the few sheets that it contained, he stopped and read out: 'Married 1964 to Louise Allard. No offspring. Occasionally seen alone or with unidentified female companions at high-class restaurants (beyond his means) and on one occasion at the Club Bleu, Montparnasse. General impression from fragmentary information is that subject has sources of income beyond his salary. In Tunisia he had reputation of high-living womanizer. Was involved in scandal surrounding death of young woman in Tunis nightclub under mysterious circumstances. Woman had suffered multiple rape and torture. Case led to arrest of several members of armed forces who were subsequently released without charges when police closed investigation. Dossier on case not available.'

Baum looked at Allembeau.

'Vulnerable, I would say.'

Allembeau nodded.

Baum replaced the file in the drawer.

'I think I must speak to Jaloux about all this. I didn't want to bring any of our other people in, but if someone has the crazy idea of stealing bombs, atomic material, I don't know, then it's his department.'

Inspector Jaloux, head of department 7D, was in charge of the DST unit responsible for the security of atomic installations in France in co-operation with the security directorate of the Atomic Energy Commission.

'What do you say?'

'If you don't involve Jaloux and something bloody awful happens they will make an auto-da-fé out of you.'

'I had thought of that. Perhaps I'll send for him.'

But he hadn't sent for Inspector Jaloux. 'I must be true to my paranoia about security – or rather to Ben Tov's paranoia. Who am I, after all, to sneer at the neurosis of my distinguished Israeli colleague?' He had reasoned thus to himself as he made his way back to Versailles that evening, and now all this had caught him in the liver. At any rate, true Frenchman that he was, he held the traditional Gallic view that the liver was where God punished you for excess. He had read many expert articles to the contrary by a new and manifestly unreliable breed of doctor. 'If they knew *my* liver they'd take a different view,' he told his wife when she had suggested dyspepsia, that being her own favourite ailment.

He spent the rest of the evening in his easy chair, the cats stretched elegantly at his feet, listening in a distracted fashion to the clicking of Madame Baum's knitting needles. Having finished his green pullover and stored it away against the coming winter, she was now producing socks for the indigent charges of the Sisters of Mercy. From time to time Baum reached for a pad on the nearby table and jotted down a few words. A little later he would reach again and cross them out. Soon he turned on the television news, but at the sight of the forceful figure of the President of the Republic greeting a Central African potentate and telling him that what France truly wanted was yet closer ties with his ramshackle country, Baum muttered impatiently and obliterated the president and his apprehensive guest from the screen.

Later, just before falling asleep he made a mental note to the effect that his stomach seemed a shade better (possibly a new-found efficacy on the part of the pills) and, further, that he knew what he must do on arrival at the office next morning. He must, after all, speak to Jaloux.

'A bad liver and an auto-da-fé – too much,' he murmured into the pillow.

But before speaking to Jaloux next morning he undertook

the ritual which would lead to a phone conversation with Ben Tov in Jerusalem.

'I am sorry to have to tell you that we have had a setback.'

'I am the expert on setbacks. I have more than anyone else.'

Ben Tov was being magnanimous and it did not promise well.

'The setback relates, unfortunately, to the man who interests you. Not only have we failed to locate him and his companion, but we believe he visited the embassy that you would expect. Regrettably, when he left my men were unable to keep him under observation.'

There was a long silence, which Baum took to be the time necessary for Ben Tov to get his feelings under control.

'I am no longer the leading expert. I bow to your superior expertise.'

This time the silence was Baum's.

'We are still trying,' he said at last. 'I have some of my best men on the job.'

'God forbid it should be otherwise.'

'Be reasonable. You know the difficulties. From the point of view of my own department the setback is equally disappointing.'

'That I appreciate. But whereas here we face a possible disaster of truly historic proportions, there in Paris you face merely trouble with your superiors. I have that kind of trouble every week of my life. You must allow me my strong emotions.'

'Of course.'

'Furthermore I have great anxiety for my man on the other side. I sent to him another man who has not returned. I fear the worst. If I am a little sharp with you, you must forgive me. My capacity to absorb thoroughly bad news is not unlimited.'

And the conversation had tailed off. Baum paid the phone bill at the bistro and returned, dejected, to the office, where he sent for Inspector Jaloux of department 7D.

The apt word for Inspector René Jaloux was perhaps nondescript. He had come into the DST from the Ministry of National Defence across the river some ten years earlier and had the reputation among his colleagues of being steady, colourless and well fitted to a job which offered no excitement of any kind whatever. He would disappear regularly on his rounds of inspection at atomic installations and would draft, on his return, reports in which tedium struggled fitfully with nitpicking for ascendancy. A man admirably suited, Baum reflected to Wavre, to a job in which nothing ever happened.

'And what if, one day, it did?' Wavre had asked in his usual pessimistic fashion.

'He would write an irreproachable report,' Baum had replied.

Jaloux sat across the desk from Baum, a notebook poised on his knee, a ballpoint in his hand. A grey figure, Baum reflected. What sort of life did he have, if any, outside the office? Did he ever smile? Or say anything that was not tedious? Did he ever make love to anyone?

'What I have to tell you,' Baum said, 'is to be regarded as top secret and must not be discussed with any other member of the department.'

Jaloux nodded.

'Put that away, please.' Baum indicated the notebook and pen. 'There is nothing to write. The facts are simple.'

He spent ten minutes explaining that whereas there was a solid case for placing all atomic installations on yellow alert, in fact this could not be done. Nevertheless, certain precautions must be taken. There were grounds for believing that an attempt would be made by persons unknown to obtain either plutonium or even a warhead – he did not know which. Nor did he know when or where such an attempt might be made. In fact, he knew nothing at all save that such an attempt was on the cards, and if that was an inadequate brief he was sorry but it would have to do. Were there any questions?

Jaloux said he thought there were indeed some questions, which he proceeded to ask. To none of them was Baum prepared to formulate a reply, save to one: What must he, René Jaloux, do about it?

'First, I want you to provide me with a list of the establishments from which an opponent of hostile intent might steal either a bomb or the fissionable material with which to construct one.'

'Very well.' Jaloux was clearly finding it difficult to resist the urge to write these matters down for the record.

'Second, you are to communicate at once with the heads of security of these establishments and instruct them to check over their arrangements because we have reason to believe that something may be tried by an Italian terrorist group. You can say we have had a tip-off, and although we do not rate the information highly, we think precautions are called for.'

Did that include units holding military stockpiles?

It did.

And what about the Atomic Energy Commission?

'They are not to be alerted. They leak to the press.'

'Very well. You will have the list this afternoon.'

'Thank you. Please make it as soon as possible.'

And Jaloux had disappeared from the room almost as if he had never been there.

Then Baum called a friend who worked in the anonymous building in the Rue Beaujon which housed the central police computer.

'Jacques, this is Alfred, I hate to bother you.'

'A pleasure.'

'You remember you checked the name Tavernet for me the other day?'

'Yes, and found nothing.'

'It just occurred to me, maybe the computer carries the name with a slight variation – you know, keyed in as Tabernet or something close by a tired girl on a Friday afternoon. Worth checking?'

'Afraid not, Alfred. When we call up a name the programme gives us all near spellings. It's much like the reservation programmes the airlines use. If Dupont goes in as Dumont, it will come up on the display.'

'The wonders of science,' Baum said, 'have knocked all the excitement out of life. There was a time when one of my little brainwaves could actually serve some purpose. But no longer. Thanks anyway.'

'Not at all. Any time.'

When Mlle Pineau brought in a cup of black coffee, Baum had his head in his hands and there were two small white pills lying on the blotter in front of him.

'Is there anything I can do?' Mlle Pineau asked solicitously.

'No thank you. It is very kind. Just bring me a small glass of water.'

The time was later that day.

'Please understand,' Baum said, 'I am not asking you to allow matters to reach the point where you get hurt. Absolutely not.'

The woman sitting opposite him in the drab café in the Rue du Temple nodded but said nothing.

'But we have reason to believe from his record that this man has a certain sadistic element in his personality. His deeds in Tunisia show as much. Such a man probably has few if any outlets for tendencies of that kind here in Paris, and in his present job he must avoid any kind of scandal. Nevertheless, I believe he can be tempted by a companion who can hold out, however distantly, the prospect of a little S/M . . .'

He allowed his voice to trail off into silence, unhappy with what he was having to say and the way in which he had expressed it.

'I see,' the woman said. 'I'm afraid S/M is not my turn-on.'

'I would never suggest it,' Baum said, flustered. He looked into his half-finished glass of beer, trying to break out of the distasteful impasse in the conversation. 'It is a question of, er, holding out . . . expectations. Nothing more.'

'You must know, Monsieur Baum,' the woman said, 'that certain men grab at expectations of that kind and feel free to behave like savages. At that point it is useless, indeed laughable, for a woman to protest. The man regards it as a very stimulating part of the game.'

Baum looked unhappy. 'How can I deny it? Nevertheless, I put it to you: We will take all possible precautions; you will be in constant touch with one of my men, and indeed with me; and I believe from what I know of you that you will be able to manage the situation. After all, you recall the Codreanu case. That you managed brilliantly.'

The woman's metal-blue eyes were fixed on Baum's paternal features. 'Monsieur Baum, for such a charming man you are very ruthless. I need to know two things. What will this mission of yours bring me in the way of a reward? And what if I refuse to have anything to do with it?'

'We will pay you ten thousand francs for a successful outcome.'

'And if there is no success despite the best that I can do?'

'I think we can find something for you. Perhaps five thousand. I will have to trust you with such an arrangement.'

'You have not said what will happen if I refuse.'

'My dear Nadia,' Baum said, 'I am an official of the state. I do what is needed on behalf of our country. I do not do what I, personally, might wish. All this is distasteful to me – extremely distasteful. But I have to tell you that if you refuse my department will have no choice but to allow the police to proceed with your case. At the very least you would be deported.'

'And is this how I am to live the rest of my life?'

'It will be the last case,' Baum said.

'Why should I believe you?'

'When I say that, I speak as myself, not as an official of a government department. You have my personal word for it, my dear Nadia, and bringing all this to an end will take a great load off my conscience.'

'I daresay it will,' the woman said.

She was strikingly beautiful, with blue-black hair pulled back and gathered at the nape of her neck. The high cheek-bones and aquiline nose, the fine eyes set far apart and the high forehead gave her an air of extreme distinction: a woman of spirit who knew men and would be expensive.

'Very well,' she said suddenly, 'since I have no option. Now will you please tell me what I need to know.'

'The whole matter is extremely urgent,' Baum said, and proceeded to tell her what it was that she would have to do.

Later, in the office, Allembeau appeared.

170

'Have you a minute to hear about Belaiev and look at some interesting pictures down in photographic?'

They went down to the lab where the DST photographers worked. There was new electronic equipment standing against a wall – a unit housing a long rotating cylinder and control panel and a large visual display unit with its own controls standing nearby. Both were linked to a computer. A group of lab technicians were gathered round the VDU. Displayed on the screen was a colour shot of a man walking among trees, a girl by his side. There were cars on a road in the background. The shot had been taken from a distance with a telephoto lens and there had been camera shake.

'Not too good,' Baum said.

'We can enhance the detail,' a technician said. He pressed buttons on the control panel. The colour contrasts on the image changed as the digital scanner responded. Detail emerged from the areas in shadow. There was now a clearer view of the man's profile.

'Belaiev?'

Allembeau nodded.

'The ears at last,' Baum murmured.

'That's about the best we can do with that one,' the technician said. 'Any more detail in the dark areas and we'll lose the highlights. We can try another.'

The image was wiped from the screen. Another built up, line by line. Gradually, the shadows were clarified, detail emerging on the faces of the girl and the man.

'Not enough for a positive identification,' Baum said, 'but it's a good general impression. Can we have prints for the file?'

'No problem.'

The girl, who was taller than Belaiev, was facing the camera but her large sunglasses made it impossible at the distance to see what her face was like. She wore a skirt and blouse and carried a bag. The picture was clear enough to show that the bag was in a shade of brown or cream with a broad diagonal stripe across it.

'Get someone to fetch the print of the girl Burnawi.'

When it arrived, Baum studied it, looked up at the

171

enhanced picture on the screen and down again at the poorly focused shot snatched by the Israelis in an Athens street.

'High forehead, straight nose, rather long neck – what do you think?'

'Not impossible,' Allembeau said.

'I want the profile shot as well. The ears.'

'Pardon?'

'I said the ears. We should have more pictures of ears on our files. They can't wear sunglasses over their ears. It helps.'

Back in the office he said to Allembeau: 'The most we can assert with any confidence is that it *could* be her. Circumstantial evidence, not positive identification. Assuming we've identified her correctly, we have a very simple situation: a KGB asset within an Arab terrorist organization. Banal, boring even. Chatila is a client of the Syrians and the Syrians are clients of the Soviets. There is nothing improbable in the Soviets keeping an eye on these Syrian-backed outfits, just as they keep an eye on the Syrians themselves. Further, our records tell us she is an Armenian. You may ask why she isn't shooting diplomats on behalf of the Armenians instead of the Palestinians. Answer: because she does what she's told.' He paused, eyebrows raised, querying. 'Shoot that down.'

'The Soviets aren't crazy enough to sponsor a group which tries to use nuclear devices.'

'Who spoke of sponsorship? I thought I said they'd be keeping an eye on these people.'

'On the other hand,' Allembeau said, 'the Russians and Czechs are arming the Syrians and the Palestinians. They can't deny that they support what Chatila is fighting for.'

'Support for a certain end does not necessarily imply support for any and every means to that end.' Baum paused, shook his head. 'That is too facile. Who am I to decide what the KGB will and will not do?' He paused again. 'If this whole business is not a piece of psychopathic terrorism after all, but some move in big-power chess – something large and diabolical – then I fear we are in very deep trouble indeed.' He sighed and rose heavily from his chair. ' I shall be out for maybe half an hour. I have some phoning to do.'

He spent a long time in the airless phone both at the

café nearby, testing his theory on Ben Tov. Later, when the enhanced prints came up from the lab, he sent a set round to the Israeli embassy as requested.

The mechanics of the transaction between Tavernet and Professor Hanif took several days to complete and are of small interest in themselves. An instruction by an innocuous trading company with its offices in the Sharia Magarief in Tripoli to the National Commercial Bank of Libya was translated, by telex, into a further instruction to the Union de Banque Suisse in Geneva. This in turn led to the transfer of two and a half million dollars US from a numbered account at that bank to an equally anonymous account at an equally solid bank in Zurich. As these processes got under way, Hanif had a further meeting with Tavernet at the restaurant in the Rue Balzac. At this meeting they arranged techniques for future contact.

'I leave Paris tomorrow,' Hanif told Tavernet. 'I will return as needed.'

This was not true, since he and Rasmia had arranged separate flights out of Charles de Gaulle that afternoon.

'Since our last meeting I have made some preliminary inquiries,' Tavernet said. 'If we are successful at the first opportunity, the weapons can be acquired as I indicated to you, within a month. If this proves too risky, then we must await a further opportunity. That should occur about one month later. We are governed by certain movements which take place on a fairly regular basis.'

'And how long after that can I expect delivery?'

'It depends if the vessel has sufficient cargo. At present she is at sea and I expect her to dock in Marseilles within ten days. She will be turned round quickly since some cargo to Haifa has already been booked.'

'Tell me about this vessel.'

'The *Croix Valmer*. Registered in Marseilles. Some four thousand tons. Takes containers as well as mixed cargo. You do not need to know the name of the owners nor who she is chartered to.'

The two men left the restaurant separately, and that afternoon Hanif and Rasmia left the country unhindered. This was on the day following Alfred Baum's conversation with Inspector René Jaloux. Also on that day Tavernet had two further meetings. One with Major Savary. The other was with his brother.

'Do you think these people intend to use the weapons?' Savary asked.

'I cannot tell. It seems possible. At all events, they will threaten to use them. Otherwise they will have wasted five million dollars.'

They were walking in the Bois de Boulogne, near the Château de Madrid. Savary had picked up a taxi in the Boulevard Mortier outside the main gates of the DGSE complex. He had paid off the taxi at a point half a kilometre from their rendezvous and had been cautious.

'And you can deliver?'

'There is a good chance. I always reckoned the day would come when I'd have an opportunity of this kind. My brother and I have often discussed it. This is what they call the historic opportunity. I have no intention of letting it slip.'

'You will ship the weapons out of Marseilles?'

Tavernet nodded.

'Your crew is secure?'

'It is unchanged, therefore secure.'

'I will want two of my own men signed on.'

'No problem.'

They had walked on for a while and before parting had discussed money, reached an arrangement and shaken hands on it.

While Savary was crossing Paris again from west to east to return to his office, Tavernet, whose real name was Alexandre Jaloux, regained his apartment in the Rue Spontini and waited there for his brother.

There are four depots through which warheads are routed to the units of the three French fighting services holding atomic weapons in their arsenals. At regular intervals – on average once a month – convoys travel from these depots to the twenty-odd units in question. On their outward journeys they carry newly-assembled or re-armed atomic warheads.

On their return they carry weapons whose warheads contain decayed fuel which needs replacing. The convoys, which travel by night, include escorts provided by a specially trained infantry battalion of the French army. Their journeys are meticulously logged and regularly reported to the Atomic Energy Commission and department 7D of the DST.

'I got your call,' Alexandre said to his brother. 'I assume it was important, otherwise you wouldn't risk coming here.'

'Very important. I saw the deputy director. They've got wind of this thing. I'm to alert the depots.'

'What do they know?'

'I don't think they know much. I'm to tell the security people there's a vague rumour of an Italian terrorist interest in getting hold of a weapon. They're to tighten things up but there's no yellow alert. I had to supply a list of the installations involved.'

'Did you do it?'

'Yes, yesterday afternoon. But I took a precaution. I left Meyrargues off the list.'

'Good.'

They were drinking beer in the drawing room of the Rue Spontini apartment. The furniture was expensive and vulgar. A glass-fronted cabinet contained shooting trophies and mementoes of rifle clubs. There were no pictures on the walls, but a calendar over a desk carried the portrait of an eager terrier, head cocked. Alexandre Jaloux was a bachelor.

'How do you assess our chances now?' he asked.

'I see no reason not to proceed.'

'Risky for you.'

'It always was. In any case, if things get too hot I shall disappear. One can do nicely for the rest of one's life with a million or so in the bank and a beach house somewhere.'

'If one doesn't gamble the lot away,' Alexandre said drily.

'I'm finished with all that.'

'It's what you said when the syndicate got nasty and I hauled you out of trouble.'

'This time it's a new life. With decent money I don't need to gamble to pay the bills.'

'The bills you were paying were gambling debts.'

'I'm not here to be lectured.'

175

'Forget it. What are your plans?'

'I set out for the south tomorrow: Narbonne, Marignane, Aubagne, Toulon and Meyrargues. I will make the necessary arrangements.'

'When will I know dates and what we need in the way of back-up?'

'As soon as I get back next week.'

'What will things cost down there?'

'Maybe three hundred thousand francs, maybe up to half a million.'

'You're sure Meyrargues is the best place?'

'Positive. For once, you'll have to have confidence.'

'I've no choice.'

René Jaloux finished his beer, wiped his lips carefully on his handkerchief, and hiding his distaste for his brother, forced a wan smile on to his face as he said goodbye. Then he left the apartment, closing the front door carefully behind him. Down in the street he looked equally carefully in each direction before making his way towards the Metro in the Avenue Victor Hugo. He always felt shaken up inside when he had been with his brother. He could never reconcile himself to the fact that another human being – even if it was his own brother – should know anything about him. Anything at all.

Chapter 19

In the Libyan embassy on Adnan al Malky Avenue in Damascus Hanif was once more in telex communication with Gadafi. He asked for the services of an expert capable of verifying a nuclear device. The man would be needed in France at a date to be specified. Details were discussed and further communication arranged. Hanif left the building and drove back to the villa, having decided on his next moves.

'The French business is going forward,' he told Rasmia. 'I shall want Essat to go to France, probably in three or four weeks.'

'To Paris?'

'Not to Paris. Probably to a rendezvous in the south.'

'You are bringing him into this project which is supposed to be so secret?'

'I am.' Rasmia said nothing. 'You are doubtful?'

'You yourself had grave doubts about him. Then you came to the conclusion that Saad Hayek was a spy. Perhaps he was, though we still do not know for certain. But does that prove beyond a doubt that Essat is not?'

'No. But one cannot get proof of such a negative proposition. Prove to me that you are not an agent also.'

'I cannot. But then, I have not been under such strongly founded suspicion.'

'You are hostile to him, and your hostility is based on some subjective feminine principle that I do not appreciate. I am satisfied that I can now work with him.'

Rasmia shrugged. 'Please yourself. I will carry out my orders as usual.'

'The time has come,' Hanif said, 'for me to take you more fully into my confidence in this matter.'

'I do not want to hear anything I do not need to know. Unlike the others, I have no curiosity.'

'That is well. But now you must listen.'

When he had finished talking Rasmia shrugged again. 'I will do whatever is needed,' she said.

'You understand the risks?'

'Of course.'

'You are not frightened?'

'Is that a question you would put to one of your men?'

'Please stop sparring with me. There is serious work to do and you and I must work together. My instructions to you are that you will co-operate fully with Essat within the limits that I shall set from time to time.'

'Very well,' Rasmia said. 'I have expressed my reservations and I will not return to the subject.'

'There are broken fences between us,' Essat said. 'We must try to mend them.'

He was in Rasmia's office, kicking idly at the base of a packing case, wondering how he could change the relationship between them. Rasmia was at her desk and did not look up at him.

'I am not aware of fences, broken or unbroken.'

'That's what I mean. We are comrades in arms, are we not? And yet everything I say is analysed and demolished, just as if we were on opposite sides.'

She looked up. 'I have nothing against you, any more than I have feelings against the youngsters on the gate. It is just that I am busy. I have no time for what they call personal relationships.'

She said it, he thought, with little enough conviction. He smiled at her. 'Couldn't we perhaps be a shade more friendly? If not friendly, then at least relaxed?'

'I feel I am relaxed.'

'If you are, I'm not.'

'I'm sorry.'

There was a silence and he noticed that she did nothing to drive him out of the room.

178

'Have dinner with me this evening and we'll see if we can't demonstrate that I am human and quite a nice fellow really.'

He thought it might earn him a smile. Instead, she looked down to her papers again. 'Very well. I shall be in town and can meet you at the house there at eight.' It was said as if the thing were a business appointment, dismissively.

Essat found himself in the Chaghour Jouwany quarter by seven with time to kill before meeting her. He wandered in the Madhat Pasha soukh, going northwards beyond the lane which led to the house. He allowed himself to be inveigled into a shop by a trader. He was offered coffee and shown rugs. He pretended an interest: the coffee was good and the man entertaining. A pleasant half-hour was passed in mock-angry bargaining for a rug worth a quarter of what the trader sought for it. Essat got away from the shop with difficulty. As he emerged into the soukh and started to push his way back through the crowds, he thought he saw Rasmia ahead of him, walking in the same direction. He was about to overtake her when he noticed that she appeared to be walking alongside a short, thickest man, a European, he imagined. And then, without any farewell sign from either of them, the man turned off to the left and Rasmia continued until she reached the lane leading to the house. Perhaps they had not been together after all.

She had turned the corner by the time Essat reached it. A few minutes later they were together in the first-floor room. He said nothing about having seen her. For some reason it excited him.

'Let us eat at the Greek place near the citadel,' he said.

He noticed that she had put on a dress which revealed the outline of her body. Her fine eyes were enhanced with eyeshadow. She wore no lipstick. There was something about her of the woman who is not indifferent to the effect she has on her companion.

At the restaurant Essat was surprised at the ease with which their conversation flowed. Although they had spent many hours, days together before, they had never talked to each other beyond the communication of essential, practical information. Even on missions together there had always been restraint, a clear distance between them. But now she

179

smiled, and several times he made her laugh. She told him something of her childhood and her student days, though she had nothing to say about her relationship with Hanif. When she asked him about himself he had the impression that there was genuine interest behind the inquiry.

'The professor will be talking to you about a trip to France,' she said.

'With you?' She shook her head. 'A pity.' She looked at him solemnly and then she smiled.

'Perhaps I was not supposed to tell you that.'

'I won't reveal that I know.'

He asked her the purpose of the trip but she said she didn't know. Was it connected with her own mission to Paris with the professor?

'I have no idea. You must ask him.'

They drank ouzo and talked for the first time of trivialities like any young couple engaged in discovering each other.

They parted outside the restaurant.

'That was very much overdue,' he said.

She smiled. 'I suppose it was.'

'You see now that I am not such a terrible fellow.'

'I never thought you were.'

'Thank you for coming this evening.'

'I liked it,' she said, and reaching up she lightly touched his cheek and kissed him below the point where her fingers rested on his face. Then she turned quickly on her heel and made off before he had a chance to say anything more.

The old man was not there at the usual time in the morning. Essat wandered cautiously among the crowd at the mosque, wary of asking the old man's whereabouts from the youth who appeared to have taken his place and was trying to keep order. Perhaps he was ill. The thought was no comfort because Essat had no faith in it.

Early in the afternoon he returned to the mosque, deciding that he must get news of the old man. The youth was still there.

'I haven't seen you before.'

'I usually work in the office,' the youth said.

'Where's the old boy then?'

The youth put on what he imagined to be a conspiratorial expression. Then, in a stage whisper: 'They came for him here yesterday.'

'Who is they?'

'Security.'

'Why would they be interested in an old boy like that?'

'No one knows. Anyway, they took him away and that's all we know. We sent someone down to the police to find out, but they wouldn't say anything.' The youth shook his head. 'Maybe he was a spy.'

Essat walked towards the far end of the mosque, trying to maintain the general demeanour of a worshipper lingering in the holy place after saying his prayers. On the far side of the mihrab he turned to look back. A man was talking to the youth. Essat could see his face in profile; it looked vaguely familiar. He eased back, keeping among the crowd, to get a better view. When he was some ten yards away the man turned in his direction. The face was certainly familiar, but Essat couldn't place it. There was nothing noteworthy about the features, save their familiarity. Long, sharp nose, clipped moustache above a thin mouth, black hair brushed back. The suit was nondescript. The whole spelt Security. And then he remembered: the man with the newspaper at the Garden Café where he'd met Yusef. The eyes scanning the crowded café, flickering as they rested for a second on Essat's table.

The youth was talking to the security man. No doubt Essat had been seen questioning him, and no doubt it was Essat that they were after. And that must mean the security man had colleagues with him, dispersed among the crowd in the mosque, maybe stationed at the exits.

Essat was within a few feet of the great door leading out towards the soukh al Hamidieh. He could see no obvious security types between himself and the doorway. If he broke and ran, they'd see the commotion and be after him. But if he moved slowly and was already under observation they'd have a better chance of catching up with him.

He decided to back his own superior speed. He slipped as smoothly as he could between the worshippers coming towards him through the doorway, pushing ahead of those heading for the outside courtyard. Out of the corner of his

181

eye he noticed a sharp movement in the crowd to his left. That would be another member of the team. They often worked in threes when there was an arrest to be made, leaving a space in the car for their victim once he was caught.

Now Essat had reached the courtyard, bathed in blinding sunlight. Quickly, he bent to pick up the desert boots he had discarded as he entered the mosque. The security men were also without shoes in the holy place. They would have placed them in the most accessible spot in the lobby. Essat made for the rows of footwear nearest the doorway, kicking the shoes and slippers at random across the floor.

There was a thirty-yard sprint ahead of him before he could reach the soukh with its winding alleys spreading out like tentacles from the main thoroughfare. He decided to cover the distance without putting on his boots. As he dashed ahead there was a shout close behind him. One of the security men had reached the door. There was no time to glance back, but Essat reckoned all three of them were likely to be close to the door, reaching the courtyard by the time he had come to the far side and was plunging into the crowded soukh. He had no idea where he would make for. There was no room in his mind for anything but the idea of escape. And now, with the shouts redoubling behind him, he was among the crowds at last and pushing and charging his way down the main thoroughfare, looking for a likely turning and fearing he would choose a blind alley in his haste. Then he crouched in a doorway and pulled his boots on, tying the laces as fast as he could. As he finished the shouts of the security men were close at hand.

The spectacle of a young man pursued by police types was common enough in the soukh. It excited neither great interest nor any desire to help the forces of the law. Thus, the crowd closed behind Essat as he ran and jostled his way forward, presenting an unyielding obstacle to the pursuers. Essat devoted ten minutes to dodging down alleyways before flinging himself, exhausted, into a doorway to rest and ponder his next move. They had lost him. The danger now was that they'd call up police manpower and block the exits from the network of alleyways leading out of the soukh. There was no time to rest or to think. The soukh itself abutted at its far end on the broad As Sawrah Avenue. There would certainly be police waiting there. On its right it ran along the edge of the mound topped by the Citadel. Essat was in the network of alleys to the left. Beyond them lay the Madhat Pasha soukh and farther to the south the crowded Chaghour Jouwany quarter where he would be safe for a while, provided they hadn't yet established who he was. But what if they had? What if Yusef had panicked, forgotten his cover story, talked? In that case they'd be lying in wait for him at Aleppo Export-Import. So had he not best try to move northwards and away from the Chatila hideout? But what about the truck? He needed to be mobile; his moped was back at the mosque, beyond his reach now. Perhaps he could make a careful approach to the hideout. It was a ridiculous risk to take, but the minutely planned escape arrangements for just such a crisis as this had one weakness: he needed the truck. The keys of the truck would be in the office on the first floor, the truck itself parked on a piece of waste ground behind the old house. Essat knew the territory. It was worth a try.

He moved out of the doorway and followed a deserted lane southwards. It led him to the Mou' Awiyah, a thoroughfare running parallel with the soukhs. As he crossed it he caught sight of two policemen fifty yards away and walking towards him. They must have seen him, for one of them shouted something and both broke into a run. Now he too was running, this time down a narrow alleyway between dilapidated warehouses. Before the police reached the head of the alleyway he must get out of sight; it might lead them to believe he had darted down the next one. But the buildings had no open doorways.

One of the policemen reached the entrance to the alleyway just as he got to the far end and turned the corner. There was a shout: he must have been seen. A policeman in uniform and town boots was unlikely to be faster on his feet; Essat was in fine shape, wore desert boots, had a life to save. He could outrun his pursuer, but where was the policeman's companion? Essat reckoned he'd stopped to radio the sighting and seal off the southern exits of the Chaghour

Jouwany. If so, hiding out was no longer an option. His mind, now, was racing.

Assumption: They didn't know his identity. From which it would be safe to assume they didn't know where he was heading.

Assumption: Only one man was on his tail.

Given the assumptions, the conclusion was clear.

He was racing down another deserted lane, the local people presumably asleep while the sun was still high in the sky. The policeman was proving to be faster on his feet than Essat had reckoned for; the gap between them remained stubbornly at fifty yards. From time to time there was a shout from the policeman. Venturing a glance over his shoulder, Essat saw that the man had lost his cap and had drawn his revolver. He had a fleeting impression of a macho moustache and a head of thick black hair. Looking forward again he saw a turning a few yards ahead and decided this was where his plan would have to take shape. Racing round the corner into a somewhat wider street he saw at once that he was in luck. A few yards ahead was a cart piled high with bales of old rags and waste paper. There was no animal between the shafts and no one in charge of it. He clambered on to the low tailboard and from there to the top of the stinking pile. He managed to sink down out of sight between the bales as the policeman appeared at the corner, and neither seeing his quarry nor hearing the thudding of his footsteps, stopped, gasping for breath, guessing that the quarry had gone to ground.

The man advanced cautiously along the middle of the road, the revolver held before him. Essat had a narrow field of vision diagonally across to the house opposite and dared not widen it by pulling a bale aside. Suddenly, the policeman came within sight. He had a walkie-talkie in his left hand and was bringing it up to his mouth.

Essat grabbed the penknife from his pocket and lifting his arm above the bales, threw it against a window of the house across the way.

A metallic sound echoed out into the silent street. The policeman stopped, dropped his walkie-talkie, crouched in the way he'd been taught, and brought his handgun up, his left hand clasped at his right wrist. But whereas they had taught him that in street battles you sought cover first and then identified your target and having found it, you took careful aim and fired, he had crouched in mid-street and now let off three rounds in the hope that his quarry might be somewhere in the line of fire.

The single shot from Essat's gun struck him in the back of the skull as his third shot was fired, sent him lunging on to his face on the cobblestones. He was already dead as his body finally came to rest and his gun clattered against a wall and lay still. The bullet had lodged in the brain, taking bone splinters in with it.

Essat leapt from the cart. The shooting had brought the neighbourhood to life and shutters were flung back, heads appearing at windows. A dog nearby started to howl, and a ragged child, not knowing yet that there could be death on a city street, poked its head out from a doorway and took a step out into the sunlight.

No one else had the courage yet to come out on to the street, but the urchin advanced towards the policeman's corpse and stared down at it as if it were the kind of thing he had seen many times before and therefore of only limited interest.

Essat raced down the street and away from the area from which he knew the dead man's companion would be coming. As he went he heard a police whistle and, soon, the pounding of boots on the cobbles. For five minutes he ran, always southwards, dodging at one point past market stalls and the few people who had braved the heat of the middle day. Fugitives were not uncommon in the streets of Damascus: no one tried to hinder his progress.

All appeared to be quiet as he crossed the Madhat Pasha soukh, reducing his pace to a fast walk, but there was some kind of commotion at the northern end beyond the Al Khazna fountain. As he turned southwards into the lanes leading to the house, he told himself the commotion must be a police patrol, advancing down the soukh. If so, there would probably be another patrol moving in from the far end.

When he reached the house the narrow lane was deserted.

185

The ragged child who usually mounted a kind of guard at the door was nowhere to be seen and the dogs were staying out of the blistering heat. Essat's shirt and jeans were soaked in sweat, clinging to his body, and the sweat was streaming down from his forehead and into his eyes. He had tucked the gun away. They had not connected him yet with Aleppo Export-Import. He stood for a moment outside the door, checking both ends of the lane and the windows and doorways opposite. Then he pushed the door open and went up to the room on the first floor.

Two youths were seated against the wall. One was cleaning an automatic while the other took swigs from a can of Coke. If they were surprised at Essat's dishevelled appearance, neither showed it.

'Hi.'

'Hi. I've come for the pickup. Is it here?'

Both youths nodded and one of them got up, went to the desk and took the keys from a drawer.

'Thanks.' Essat caught them as the youth flipped them across the desk to him. 'I'm going up to the villa.'

'Is the boss in?'

'None of your business, is it?'

The youth grinned. 'Sorry.'

Then he was down the stairs, taking care not to hurry. The lane was still quiet. He turned left and left again, coming to the open space behind the house. The truck was there. He found his hand was trembling when he inserted the key in the ignition. The petrol gauge showed a full tank and he knew there were a couple of cans, kept full, in the back. All he needed now was a little luck. And since they were not looking for the driver of a pickup truck and probably had only an approximate description of him, luck might not be too hard to come by.

He took a careful route round the west side of the city, watching for police patrols along Shoukry Al-Qouwatly Avenue, where the traffic was heavy now as the population returned to work in the cooling end of the afternoon. At the roundabout at the end of the avenue there was a squad car with two uniformed men sitting inside. It was facing down

186

the avenue, watching the traffic as it slowed down at the approach to the roundabout. Essat made no effort to speed past. As he drew level, the driver said something to his companion, and as the truck moved slowly past, Essat saw the mike come up in the man's hand. The squad car's engine must have been running; as Essat slipped into the roundabout he saw in his wing mirror that the police car had pulled out across the traffic stream and was now moving into the line of traffic behind him. The cars were solid at the approach to the roundabout and the police car was caught in the jam. As its siren started to wail, Essat pushed the truck through the mass of moving cars and trucks slowly rotating around the central reservation. Spotting an opening, he jammed down on the accelerator and took the exit into Adnan al Malky Avenue at sixty. Along the straight and almost deserted road he pushed the truck up to seventy-five. The siren, now, was wailing in the distance. The police might not have chosen the right exit from the roundabout.

A few minutes later he was in Ach-Cherkassyeh, with its rows of cypress and poplars, the villas and foreign embassies standing in their gardens of scented flowers and shrubbery. The Dutch embassy stood in a quiet street north of the Tora river. He left the truck at the end of the street and walked the fifty yards to the embassy. There was no policeman on duty outside; the Dutch were not considered politically glamorous enough for the Ministry of the Interior to want to log their comings and goings.

Essat asked the pretty girl behind a counter in the lobby for Mijnheer van der Beck.

'You have an appointment?'

'No. Please tell him it is Jonathan.'

She used the phone.

'You may go up. You will be met on the first floor.'

On the first-floor landing a pale man with glasses was standing. Without speaking he extended a hand to be shaken and beckoned Essat through a door which stood open. On the far side of the door was a sparsely furnished office. Eastern music wailed and sighed from a cheap radio. Essat was waved courteously into a chair.

'Mr van der Beck?'

'At your service.'

'I bear greetings from your friend Shayeh C5.'

'A very good man.'

As he said this, the Dutchman leaned over to the radio and, formalities satisfactorily completed, turned the volume up.

'I take it you know what message to send?'

'I do. When do you want to rendezvous?'

'Tomorrow night.'

'They know where?'

Essat nodded.

'Do you need anything?' The question was asked as if to say the questioner hoped not.

'I am short of money.'

'I am afraid I am not authorized to advance money; only to pass on a message in an emergency.'

'You should not have asked, then, if I needed anything.' Essat, the Sabra, the cactus, was not inclined to ask twice.

'Very well. The message will be on telex immediately after you leave. The Hague will be asked to re-transmit at once.'

Essat got to his feet.

'Thank you.'

Outside, the street was still deserted. He regained the truck, turned and headed north out of the city, snow-capped Mount Hermon just visible far over on his left, orchards and market gardens on either hand. There were secondary roads that he knew well in this area – roads he had reconnoitred months before in readiness for this day. They led him northwards, on to the road which ran along the foothills of the Anti-Lebanon range. The time was close to seven in the evening, the light had turned to a pale gold and would soon show tinges of purple. Soon he would cross the motorway linking the city with Homs and Aleppo to the north. Travelling eastwards across the Jebel Haymoor, he would reach the desert as the desiccating heat of the day gave way to the cooler night. The distance he had to cover was something over 200 kilometres.

Chapter 20

The duty officer at the Ministry of Foreign Affairs in Jerusalem was handed the telex from The Hague at 20.00 hours, checked the appropriate list to see where he might find Shayeh C5, saw that it was at the Ministry of Defence and got busy on the phone. To his surprise, the switchboard at Defence put him through at once to an extension occupied by an irascible voice.

'What is it?'

'Foreign Affairs here. Duty officer speaking.'

'Yes?'

'We have a short telex from The Hague addressed to Shayeh C5. Is it for you?'

'Read it.'

'It reads, "Exit plan tomorrow Tuesday 21.00 hours onwards." No signature. I hope it makes sense to you.'

'It does. Now destroy it.'

'Don't you want confirmation?'

'I said destroy it.'

'Very well.'

Ben Tov rang off without saying 'thank you'. The duty officer shrugged, glanced again at the telex and put it in the bag destined for the shredder.

Ben Tov, working late despite his wife's dinner arrangements, dialled a number and was drumming on the desk with his fingers as it rang.

'Lev?'

'Who is this?'

'Ben Tov here. Shalom.'

'Shalom.'

'Do I interrupt your dinner?'

'You do.'

'Never mind. Worse things will happen. I need to speak. May I come round?'

'We have company. Can it wait?'

'It cannot wait. Give me two minutes in a side room. Your wife will look after the company.'

'Very well, come now.'

'Thanks.'

Later, he sat in General Lev Shapiro's study. He refused a brandy, lit a cigarette despite his pledges, leaned forward, his elbows on his knees, his strangely angry eyes fixed on the other man.

'My man needs to get out of Syria.'

'How soon?'

'Tomorrow night, as soon after 21.00 hours as your plane can make it.'

'A tall order at short notice. I don't know what we have available.'

'That is why I came this evening, to give you all the time in the world to fix things.'

'This you call all the time?'

'Also, I have to play it safe. We need the diversion.'

'But that's a matter for cabinet. Not even the air staff – '

'Look, my dear Lev, I have no time. More than my man's life hangs on this – far more. The cabinet would think for six days and then say no because of the peace process. They don't want the Syrians hopping mad and the American senate passing resolutions.'

'Can't we dispense with this damn diversion of yours?'

'You yourself said it was too risky. If the plane stays under the radar screen there are observers on the ground, especially along the Jordan-Syrian border.'

General Shapiro got to his feet and started pacing back and forth among the chairs.

'But how can I fly a sortie over hostile territory without any kind of political sanction? You know the Syrians – they'll claim we bombed hospitals.'

190

The two men were silent. Ben Tov fished in his pocket for cigarettes.

'The minister?'

'It isn't Sharon nowadays. Forget it.'

'How long will your people need to set up the diversion?'

'We can do it in three hours if we're pushed.'

'Would you be willing to order it, subject to ministerial approval? You can abort at the last minute if I fail to get the OK for you?'

There was a pause. The eyes were still angry, still peering intently at the general, who sighed and moved to the telephone, dialled a number.

'General Shapiro here. Pass me the base commander's office.' Then, after a pause: 'Where is Kahan? Who am I? I am General Shapiro. How do you know? A good question. You don't know, but Kahan can call me at home to get confirmation later. All right? Good. I am glad to find our air bases are security conscious. Now, you will find Kahan immediately and tell him I want operation C5 for tomorrow night. Yes, you heard correctly, C5. Tell him there can be no ifs and buts, and if he hasn't got an aircraft he is to find one. Where? I don't care where he finds it. Also, remind him that this thing calls for superlative flying skill, so he should allocate a good man – his best man. Also, the diversion. Tell him it's on, according to plan. He is to contact me in the morning.'

The general replaced the receiver. 'Is that good enough for you?'

'I hope so. I'll call you in the morning at nine to see what has been arranged. Now may I use your phone?'

He crossed to the instrument, looked up a number in a pocketbook, stood grim-faced while the number rang.

'I want the minister, please. Tell him it's Ben Tov of the Mossad. Tell him I disturb him because I have no choice.' Then, a few moments later: 'Minister, it is good of you to come to the phone. This relates to the matter which the committee discussed recently, when I attended. Yes. Why not the Memuneh? He is at home, having dinner no doubt. Unorthodox? Yes, sir, but these are unorthodox times. I would like to come over to see you for ten minutes. Yes,

191

now. Thank you, minister. I will be with you in fifteen minutes.'

'Such determination?' General Shapiro said.

'My dear Lev, I will not have that young man tortured to death; that is one point. I will not pretend this is not a life and death matter for the country; that is another point. And I will not be tied down in red tape and protocol. There will be no protocol at Armageddon; that is my final point. Good night and God bless you.'

In the promised fifteen minutes he was at the defence minister's villa in Givat Hananya. The minister was a former army general who had come up through the Herut party, having learned all the politics he needed along the way. He sat now on the verandah, drinks before him, staring impassively at Ben Tov.

'Isn't this irregular?'

'Yes, minister.'

'The Memuneh must be informed in the morning.'

'Of course.'

'So tell me what brings you to disturb my evening in this way.'

Ben Tov sipped from his glass of soda water, leaned forward in the wicker chair, and for ten minutes told the minister things he did not want to hear. Then he sat back and waited as if ministerial approval could now only be a formality.

'Impossible,' the minister said. 'Absolutely impossible.'

'With respect, absolutely essential. My man has information that we have to have.'

'You will have to get him out as best you can without this ridiculous diversion.'

'It reduces his chances, say by fifty per cent. It is unacceptable.'

'And a bombing sortie over Lebanese and Syrian territory – is that not unacceptable, with talks due to resume in Washington next week?'

'You refer to talks, minister. I refer to survival. We speak different languages.'

'We do, Ben Tov, we do.' The minister's tone had hard-

192

ened, and as it did so, Ben Tov decided that he would get no further.

'Have I your permission to speak to the prime minister's office?'

'Permission refused.'

'Can you not reconsider that, minister?'

The minister got to his feet. 'I repeat, permission refused. You could not have expected any other answer.'

Ben Tov rose from his chair. 'Curiously enough sir, I did.'

'You are placing yourself in jeopardy.'

'It is a matter of indifference to me. The political process will smell like a bad joke if these people are not stopped. Good day, minister, and thank you for your time.'

Ben Tov walked slowly down to his car, got in and headed for home, devising what he would say about the fact that he was late, had not called to tell his wife, and would arrive smelling of tobacco. Also, he had no idea what he would do next.

By seven thirty Essat had crossed the motorway at a straggling village called Qutayfe. Villagers stood idly in the dust, watching the sparse traffic along the motorway. Occasionally a child would throw a handful of sand at a passing vehicle in a gesture of futile defiance. Leaning against the wall of a house built of breeze blocks and left unfinished, a young man watched as the pickup turned eastwards off the motorway. Then he disappeared into the dim interior of the house and picked up a walkie-talkie from a table.

A half-hour later Essat decided that in the failing light he could no longer keep moving. He put the truck into four-wheel drive and took it carefully off the road and along the bed of a wadi until the road was out of sight. There he stopped, hoping he could snatch some sleep.

Chapter 21

The Memuneh next morning was at his worst. As Ben Tov sat facing him he fussed with the items on his desk as he fussed with his words. The minister of defence had called him late the previous evening, demanding to know why he couldn't control his own people. This had reached the Memuneh where it hurt most – in that area where his perception of himself and his ability to command were uncertain. And now Ben Tov was sitting there, mutinous, self-assured and seemingly unrepentant.

'You place me in an impossible position,' the Memuneh said.

'I am sorry, but it can happen in the work we do.'

'Why did you not call me first?'

'To be frank, because you would have refused permission. In your position I would have preferred not to know.'

'It is highly irregular and the minister is angry, very angry.'

'All this is of no interest to me. I cannot understand how it can interest you unless you take the view that the threat from Chatila is of no significance.'

'I do not take that view.'

'Then how can you let the tantrums of a politician stand in the way of what has to be done?'

'These are not tantrums. Disciplines have to be maintained in government. The minister is right.'

The Memuneh was aware that once again Ben Tov had captured the high ground of the argument. The questions were flowing in the wrong direction.

'In any event, I am now giving you an instruction at the

194

minister's insistence. For political reasons the diversion can not take place. You are not to approach the prime minister's office, since you will only get the same response there and it will be inconvenient for the minister, just as what you have already done is inconvenient for me.'

'How can the word "inconvenient" be used at all in a context such as this?' Ben Tov's voice was quiet but he was clearly having difficulty with his own feelings.

'That was an order. I am not prepared to discuss it further.'

'Very well.'

'What will you do?'

'I will arrange the rescue of my man. You are not suggesting we should leave him to have his eyes put out? They scoop the eyeball out with a teaspoon, then they tug on it until the optic nerve snaps.' He looked steadily at the Memuneh. 'You would not want that.'

'Arrange the rescue, but put an end to this nonsense about a diversionary action.'

As Ben Tov marched out of the room the Memuneh sighed and decided yet again that something must be done about this rogue elephant in the department.

Back in his own room, Ben Tov dialled the cabinet office and asked for Mordechai Poran.

'Mordechai, Ben Tov here. How are you since last Thursday?'

'Not well. It takes more than a week to recover from such a hiding.'

'So I play better poker. Reconcile yourself.'

'What can I do for you?'

'I am coming round right away. Please be there.'

'Where else?'

Later, in Poran's office, Ben Tov said: 'Listen, Mordechai, I need your help as I have never needed help before.'

'What are friends for?'

Poran, a small dapper man, former schoolfellow of Ben Tov and now head of the prime minister's staff, smiled encouragingly. An old affection between them had survived regular Thursday-night poker sessions in which the silent games were punctuated with fierce polemics.

Ben Tov took Poran as far into the story as he had to and

no further. What he left unsaid he covered with the formula: 'This you must take on trust, on what you know of me for thirty years.' When he had finished there was a long silence.

'The prime minister,' Poran said, 'has a short fuse.'

'I know.'

'An equally short attention span.'

Ben Tov nodded.

'Also, he doesn't enjoy inner-cabinet trouble. Combative he may be, but he doesn't go looking for it.'

'That I also know.'

'And you want him to override Defence?'

'I do.'

Poran scratched his head and rocked it gently from side to side.

'You don't know what you are asking.'

'I know perfectly well, my dear Mordechai. I am relying on my belief that beneath the prime minister's terrible personality there is a patriotic man lurking – a *concerned* man who cares more for the harsh realities than the niceties of protocol.'

'And the peace process?'

'I rely on his not giving a highly dubious process precedence over a simple matter of survival like these other idiots I have to deal with.'

'You ask a lot.'

Ben Tov shrugged, said nothing.

'You want to see him yourself?'

'It's the only way.'

'Wait.'

Poran rose from his chair and left the room. During the time he was away Ben Tov rehearsed in his mind what he might say to the prime minister, how he might cope with the interruptions, the disconcerting way in which one was peered at, thrown off the point by mannerisms designed for that purpose. Then Poran returned.

'You are lucky. He remembers you from the Security Committee. It looks as if you made the right impression. He will see you right away. You have ten minutes, no more.'

'This is highly irregular,' Ben Tov said with a grin.

'If the boss decides you're crazy it will do me no good,' Poran said.

'If you lose your job I'll still be your friend.'

They walked the few steps to the prime minister's office across the corridor.

'He wants me to stay,' Poran said as the red light over the door changed to green and they entered the presence. 'My advice is keep it short and do not fudge anything. Appearances to the contrary, he cannot shoot you.'

The prime minister sat in his shirtsleeves, his desk clear save for a pile of red folders. As they approached across the room he was changing his spectacles, waving them both to chairs at the same time. Then he peered intently at Ben Tov through the glasses he had just put on.

'So you break all the rules, eh? Is that a way to run a department?'

'Necessity, prime minister,' Ben Tov said. He found his voice was steady, his nerves well under control. Somehow, he liked this irritable little man who seemed to terrify his colleagues.

'I am listening.'

Ben Tov started to go over what had been revealed in the Security Committee, but halfway through he sensed impatience. 'You will recall what was said, of course,' he concluded.

The prime minister nodded.

Ben Tov filled out the rest of the story. 'Everything we have been able to learn so far points to a nuclear conspiracy. I cannot be sure, but what is more important, I cannot guarantee the contrary to you. I must therefore proceed on the assumption that my role is to defeat this conspiracy, and if that is so, my duty is also to test my plan up to the highest level – in this room. At lower levels I have been denied the resources I need, presumably on the grounds that you would object.'

'Why should I object?'

'I am told that a military diversion would upset the peace process, particularly since you are to be in Washington next week.'

'It will.'

197

'I have to say to you, prime minister, that I cannot guarantee the security of the state against Chatila if my agent is to be lifted out tonight without benefit of a diversion. The military appraisal is that the chance of success would be reduced by fifty per cent. General Shapiro will confirm.'

The prime minister was being surprisingly calm. The ten minutes was up and ignored.

'You may be right about the peace process, but that is a matter for me and Foreign Affairs.' He took his spectacles off, tapped with them on the leather top of the desk, put them back on his nose. Then he peered long and hard at Ben Tov, saying nothing. The stare was returned. This man, Ben Tov decided, was in the job because he was probably the best of a bright bunch, all with jumbo-sized personalities. Did these people never show human characteristics – indecision, puzzlement, fear, even?

'I will not call the minister of defence while you are with me,' the prime minister was saying. 'It would not be seemly, perhaps, for you to overhear such a conversation. Poran here will let you have a decision within the hour.'

'Thank you, prime minister,' Ben Tov said, as if the decision were bound to go in his favour.

'I am extremely displeased, my friend, at the way you have manipulated the system in order to reach me. Poran here had no right to take up my time in this way. As for you, it is a case of gross insubordination, is it not?'

'Yes, prime minister.'

'Let it not happen again, eh?'

'Certainly not, sir.'

'Now go and rescue this man of yours, and may it all have been worth while. I repeat, Poran will tell you within the hour.'

The game, Ben Tov decided, was won.

What he did not know – indeed, what the minister of defence did not know either – was that the prime minister had his own fish to fry, and here, doubtless as a result of divine intervention, had come a man with a proposition which would raise the temperature nicely in the frying pan. Put bluntly, the prime minister had been seeking, so far without success, an abortifacient for the peace dialogue in

198

Washington. The meeting had been fixed with the US president some time before but the timing had become inconvenient, dangerous even. The Jordanians were about to make concessions which would be embarrassing in their amiability. In the deadly game at which the prime minister was so adept, ideas had been floated publicly in the belief that Jordan would say no and the Americans would perforce line up with the Israeli position. But obscure pro-Israeli sources in Amman now knew otherwise. What the prime minister did not want was yet another round of talks in Washington in which growing anti-Israeli sentiment in congress would be fuelled by his intransigence in the face of sweet reason from the Arab side. The prime minister was, when it came to the problem of the West Bank, defending the indefensible and most of the world knew it perfectly well. This kind of confrontation in Washington he could do without. For reasons such as these, a sortie over Syria and the Lebanon was something he could contemplate with equanimity. Arab tempers would flare, the Jordanians would have to look to their rear, and amiability would be off the menu. But it was also something he could not debate in these terms in cabinet, where the hawks were forever attacking the doves and the doves were fluttering their wings and issuing angry statements to the media. By temperament, the prime minister was not a committee man and only just a democrat.

Also, he had no time at all for enthusiasts, to whose number this fellow from the Mossad appeared to belong. If things had been different in Washington, he would have had no compunction whatever about saying no, on the ground that this was yet another example of the foolhardiness and improvidence of the Arab Affairs section. But now it suited him to say yes, which he said forcefully to his minister of defence, through whose mind the idea of resignation blew briefly like an icy wind and almost immediately dissipated itself.

'We will get a lousy press,' he ventured.

'You are right.'

'It will be yet another strain on the goodwill of our friends.'

'Again, you are right.'

'I have to tell you that there are urgently needed spares for our Phantoms which the Americans could embargo.'

'So we will wait.'

'But, prime minister – '

'Listen, Eli. You have misconceptions on the question of time. The world pays attention to our excesses and those of our opponents for how long? Maybe three months. Six at most. It depends on the enormity of the event. Sure, Chatila and Sabra dragged on because we ourselves went ferreting and getting into all sorts of judicial nonsense. But the killings at Rome and Vienna? Three months? All right, maybe four. Then they forgot. I tell you, the world has supped full of horrors, as the saying is, and its digestion has learned to cope with the diet.'

The prime minister was not above taking a literary allusion and embroidering it to suit his purpose. He liked to do the same with the bible when he could devise something apposite.

The defence minister made no reply. He was busy promising himself that the man Ben Tov would, in due course, have to be brought to account.

By five the eastern horizon turned from black to a shimmering purple and then to vivid orange as the rim of the sun appeared above the dunes. By the first light Essat busied himself wiping a handkerchief over the glass and metal surfaces of the truck, soaking up the condensation and squeezing the water into his mouth, trying to ignore its stale, metallic taste. He had no food.

Then he deflated the tyres for desert use until they showed bulges at their base and made a rough check on the dashboard compass against the sun's position: the compass had been corrected to account for the truck's own magnetism, and now he threw out anything he could find that was metal and could spoil a compass reading.

Carefully, he turned the truck in the narrow wadi and drove it back on to the track, heading east.

The going on the track was fair. Much of it had been compacted by vehicles, and where the surface ahead softened and was treacherous Essat could detect the typical blurring of the sand tracks and slow to a cautious crawl. An hour later and forty kilometres on, he reached Sab a Biyar. The village sat astride a more substantial road running due east and west. Essat followed it for two kilometres, watching on his left for a track running to the north. The layout of the terrain was clearly imprinted on his mind.

It was as he was approaching the track that he heard above his own engine the deeper growl of a low-flying aircraft. It was coming up from behind, following the road. There was thin scrub and occasional clumps of trees along the roadside but nothing which could give him cover. The plane must be doing well over a hundred; there was no point in accelerating and putting his front suspension at risk among the potholes and stray boulders on the road's surface.

The plane overtook him, banked steeply and returned on a course parallel to the road so that the pilot could get a better look. He did this twice, the second time as Essat reached the track to the left. The plane must be a spotter. If they were looking for him, it would radio back the presence of a truck heading east and no doubt, if they thought the truck worth investigating, someone would be sent out by road. Essat drove past the turn-off and kept moving until the plane disappeared over the horizon behind him. Then he turned, dashed for the track and turned off on to it, keeping his speed as high as he dared along the crumbling surface, slipping repeatedly into deep-worn tracks from other vehicles, skirting boulders and dropping speed, perforce, where the hard-edged tyre tracks blurred as they traversed soft sand. There were no more roads to be crossed. He might feel naked and exposed, now that he was deep into the desert, but he knew that finding him again would be a daunting task unless they had more luck than they deserved; and God, surely, was not that hostile to his chosen people. It was a thought which, on past evidence, offered little comfort. There was more comfort in the thought that they'd be looking for him further along the road he had just left.

Sixty kilometres on, the track petered out at what had once been a watering hole at the end of a dried-out wadi. This part of the desert consisted of dunes of fine sand which shifted with the wind. Driving was a lottery. What looked like firm sand would turn out to be soft, offering no purchase for the wheels, which would spin wildly. Essat would then reverse the truck and attack the dune ahead once again. The sun, rising higher in the cloudless sky, was becoming intolerable, heating the truck itself so that touching any metal parts became impossible. And in the fierce, almost blinding glare from the sun as it climbed overhead, Essat found that all shadows, and hence all detail, disappeared from the landscape. With it, his ability to judge distance had gone, and twice he ran the truck into steep sand slopes, believing he was still on level ground.

He had been travelling due north, knowing he had to cover another sixty kilometres before heading exactly north-west. Watching the odometer for the sixty-kilometre reading, he stopped at the edge of a plain which stretched endlessly ahead of him with the dunes at his rear. His throat was parched, his eyes smarting and the skin of his face sore. He knew the danger of heat stroke and dehydration. He decided to rest for a couple of hours to wait for the return of the crucial shadows. And maybe he could lose some body heat if he did not advance into the hot desert air for a while. But as he brought the truck to a halt, he realized something else: the air was not still. A wind had sprung up from the south, and the southern horizon had disappeared. The *hamsin* was bringing a sandstorm with it.

He turned the car so that its rear faced the oncoming wall of sand: they had taught him that a car facing a sandstorm head-on would have its windscreen and headlamps sand-blasted and made totally opaque. Then he crouched down on the floor, fitting himself with difficulty in the space between seats and dashboard. With his handkerchief tied over his mouth and nose, he waited.

The sand arrived two minutes later, starting an incessant roar of sound as the rising wind flung the millions of particles against the vehicle. The whole truck vibrated. The sand filled his ears, clung to his eyelids, got into his nostrils. And despite the protection afforded by his position on the floor, the sand bit into his skin until he felt he must scream. People died in sandstorms, choking to death, their lungs full of sand. Many became delirious with loss of body fluids, unable to lose heat. Essat wondered how long he would last.

Several times he looked up: he could see the blue sky above him, but visibility in every other direction was nil – a dirty, grey wall offering nothing on which the eyes could focus.

He had remembered to put his watch in his pocket for fear the glass would be rendered opaque. He dared not take it out to look at it. How long had the storm been raging? An hour, two hours, three? He sought consolation in the thought that if they were looking for him after the sighting on the road, they'd never find him now. But what if the sand had drifted and the truck was half buried? And the engine would be choked with sand.

He realized suddenly that the racket had lessened and there was now little vibration. The storm was passing on. He stole a glance at his watch: it was just under three hours since the storm had blown up. A half-hour later it had passed. He rose painfully from the floor of the cab, coughing, his throat raw, his exposed face and forearms a vivid red and agonizing.

The paint on the rear end of the truck had been blasted down to the bare metal. The truck itself had been shifted by the wind through ninety degrees. It was full of sand.

Essat raised the bonnet. Sand covered every surface and crevice inside, as if there had been no protection at all. He removed the distributor head and cleaned the sand out, cleared the plugs and cleared as much sand off the engine as he could. Then he went back to the cab, switched on the ignition, and knowing no appropriate prayer, muttered the blessing of the wine as recited on the sabbath eve. The familiar words seemed a comfort.

The engine coughed twice as the starter turned it. The battery was OK. He tried again. At the third attempt it came to life, uncertainly at first, and then, as Essat coaxed it with the accelerator, roaring into life at last. Sand had piled up behind the rear wheels, partly burying them, but the drive on the four wheels pulled the truck clear. Essat steered it carefully around until it was heading north-west. The time was 5.15 and he had another sixty kilometres to cover before the sudden desert sunset.

The going now was easier. The soft, shifting sand had given way to a gritty, compacted surface on which the truck's tyres could maintain a grip. The landscape was featureless, inhospitable, terrifying.

Once, on the far horizon to the east, he saw a bedouin camel train – twenty or so of the animals advancing nose to tail like solemn black insects. Perhaps they were returning from the coast, loaded with salt. Essat dared not abandon his compass route to seek water from the bedouin. After five minutes they were lost to sight.

Close to sundown the odometer reading told him he had covered the sixty kilometres. He should be forty kilometres south of Palmyra. And now he sought level ground free of boulders and depressions. A few minutes driving due west brought him to ground he judged flat enough. He stopped the truck and flicked the headlight switch. No response. Frantically, he tried again, then again. The electrics had packed up. No doubt the sandstorm had broken a connection somewhere.

In the failing light he searched for the fault, checked fuses, tormented himself as he rummaged through his indistinct memories of how to deal with an electrical breakdown.

A half-hour later, with the light almost gone, he gave up in despair. The time was 21.15. Searching through his pockets he failed to find a lighter. He would have to fall back on a trick they had taught him at the Mossad training school at Tulkarm – *if* he could remember it, if he could manage it in the dark, and if it worked.

It was a case for another prayer.

Chapter 22

At midday Poran called to say that the prime minister had agreed to the diversion, having checked with General Shapiro as to its precise nature. Hearing that the bombs were all to be dropped in the Beka'a valley though the planes would violate Syrian airspace in both directions, he expressed to Shapiro the thought that if a stray bomb were to drop not on Lebanese territory but on the Syrian side of the border, he would not subsequently raise any objections. 'But don't hit houses,' he had added. 'Just the symbolic thing with an explosion, maybe two, in the Syrian desert. Something to annoy.' General Shapiro, scarcely believing his ears and fearing a later charge that he'd done the thing unauthorized, had asked for confirmation. He was even more astonished to get it an hour later, copy to the minister.

'You see,' Poran said to Ben Tov, 'the ways of politics are mysterious. Who would have thought . . . ?'

'*I* thought,' Ben Tov said. Then he called Shapiro, discussed details, and shortly after three set off for the air base at Ramat David, 130 kilometres to the north.

The base lies off the Haifa-Nazareth road, on flat land which, further northwards, merges gradually into the Galilean hills. To the south lies the Jezreel valley. The base itself is much like every other air base, characterless, ringed by electrified fences and barbed wire, with sentries on the gates. Ben Tov's pass took him through to the car park and thence to the office of Colonel Kahan, base commander.

'The rescue plane will leave from here,' Kahan told him.

'A little later, 134 squadron will scramble a flight of F.16s from Mahanayim, up by Lake Kinneret.'

'I know. What plane are you using?'

'A little Swiss job we received last year, a Pilatus Porter. It takes off and lands on a handkerchief, will dawdle at a hundred feet or less, and has the latest Decca navigator. We use it for rescue jobs, spotting, stuff like that.'

'This has to be done after dark, and your pilot has to find my man in the desert.'

'No problem. But did you have to fix a rendezvous so far north with all the desert to choose from?'

'We assumed that if this happened they'd be after him. So where would they be most vigilant? South of Damascus, reckoning he'd make for the frontier. Once we decided he'd move north-west I had to get him beyond the dunes to flat ground where your plane can land. I took advice. So you have to head for the plain south of Palmyra.'

'No problem, I just wondered.'

'I take it the pilot can do the whole thing in the dark?'

'The plane's Decca equipment gives us automatic chain selection. The Decca is programmed before take-off and it gives the pilot all the information he needs, taking account of wind drift. Incidentally, the *hamsin* is blowing in off the desert. You can feel it here.'

'Will that raise sand?'

'Unusual at this time of year, but it might. But our flight will be at one hundred feet which keeps us below the radar screen. You probably know that sandstorms are only fifteen to twenty feet deep.'

'All right for the plane; not so good for my man.'

Kahan nodded.

'And what happens to the landing if a storm is still blowing tonight?'

'We can't land. The plane will return.'

'The plan says try again next night.'

'So we'll try again.'

'By the way,' Ben Tov said, 'your plane should carry first-aid supplies, water, food – you know. My man will have been in the desert for twenty-four hours or more. He may not have had time to lay in supplies.'

206

'I'll see the medic.'

'Don't forget heat stroke, severe dehydration, things like that.'

'We know the desert,' Kahan said.

There was a pause. 'If he's dead,' Ben Tov said, his voice chill, 'your pilot is either to bring him back, or if there's a reason why that can't be done, he will strip the corpse and bring back the clothing. All of it, including the boots.' He was silent for a moment. 'We have a drill for these things.'

Kahan nodded. 'The operation from Mahanayim,' he said, 'looks to me like a bit of overkill. I'd have thought we could do it with a lot less fuss.'

'I gather Defence welcomes the opportunity to go after a target in the Beka'a.'

'At night? Much simpler by day.'

Ben Tov shrugged. 'Who knows what motivates these crazy fellows on the air staff?'

The little Swiss plane looked like a starling among falcons as it stood alongside the Phantoms on the apron. The pilot, a youthful, gangling creature who said his name was Shmuel, grinned bashfully when Ben Tov told him this was the most important mission he was ever likely to fly.

Ben Tov turned to Kahan. 'And this is your best pilot?'

'My best pilot.'

Shmuel shrugged and waved his hand dismissively. The nature of the mission had somehow dissolved military protocol among them. It was an adventure, perhaps an Entebbe in miniature.

'Take-off is at 20.00 hours,' Kahan said. 'It will give time for darkness as he crosses into Jordan to follow the Jordan-Syrian frontier, flying east to longitude 38.20, then north across the frontier into Syria. He should rendezvous in just under three hours. Wind's a good deal stronger now – something like thirty knots, coming at us from the desert to the east. It doesn't help.'

'Sand?'

'None that the met people know of, but we don't get good met intelligence from Syria. We've been trying to pick up their radio traffic, looking for a mention of the weather. Nothing so far.'

Shmuel uncoiled himself and got to his feet. His heels clicked and he saluted. 'Reporting for duty, sir,' suddenly remembering the ritual.

Kahan and Ben Tov rose and the three walked out to the plane.

'Good luck,' Ben Tov said. Then he turned on his heel and walked wearily back to the building. He stood there, watching as the ground engineers concluded their ministrations. Then the howl of the compressors winding up reached him, followed by the throb of the propeller. Shmuel, waving through the cabin window, taxied her out on to the runway. A few minutes later she was airborne and banking to turn eastwards for the Jordan valley and the frontier.

Inside, Colonel Kahan's phone rang. He picked it up, listened, grunted several times and rang off.

'The flight from Mahanayim will take off in thirty-five minutes for the Beka'a, flying an eccentric route. They'll cross the Syrian frontier at thirty-five thousand feet and Syrian radar will have no trouble at all in tracking them.'

'Will the other side send up interceptors?'

'Usually, they don't. But sometimes a few go up and go through the motions. Their night-fighting capacity is damn nearly nil. The ground-to-air stuff is what we have to watch for.'

'I must get back to Jerusalem,' Ben Tov said. 'Thank you for your help and please call me at any time tonight when you have some news.'

'I will.'

'And may it be good news.'

'God willing,' Kahan said.

Essat rummaged behind the dashboard, found a length of wiring and tugged it away from its clips. Then he cut off a metre length, stripped away the insulation and drew out a single strand of wire. There was a pencil in the dashboard stowage. He wound the fine wire round the pencil, creating a coil, and then slipped the pencil out. He twisted one end of the coiled wire round the positive pole of the car's battery.

Then, gingerly, he touched the other end to the negative pole. The wire glowed. The trick worked and he would be able to use it later in the dark.

By last light he saw that it was close to 21.30 hours. There would probably be a couple of hours to wait, maybe more. He got on with the preparations.

Fumbling awkwardly in the dark, he stripped the truck of everything that might conceivably be inflammable. There were bits of paper, a couple of road maps, a tarpaulin, the seat upholstery and a bit of carpet that someone had installed in a half-hearted attempt to make the place comfortable. All this Essat piled up a short distance away. Then he placed a can of petrol nearby in readiness to be poured over the bonfire. He had no idea how long he could keep such a bonfire alive.

He had retained the best of the paper. This he screwed into a number of tapers and stuffed them into a pocket. Everything depended now on the speed at which he could ignite the paper, convey the flame to the bonfire without extinguishing it in his haste, and get the rubbish burning.

He sat on the ground, leaning against the truck's front wheel, and waited. A thin slip of paper, secreted in his boot, carried his notes: all he could remember of the contents of the safe. He felt very ill.

The *hamsin* had blown itself out and the desert was absolutely silent. Nothing moved. The silence, normally oppressive, became a positive hostile presence as he strained his ears for any break in the wall of non-sound. A thin, pale moon had made an appearance; it gave enough light to reveal bulk – the outline of the truck. It yielded no detail, no sense of perspective, and offered no comfort. Essat's skin was raw, his throat and mouth dry, his thirst was a torment. He was aware that he no longer had control over his thought processes, for what came into his mind was unbidden and refused to be driven out. Yet with part of his mind he managed to know at every instance that he must listen, listen, listen . . .

Waves of nausea rose from his stomach. He retched repeatedly. He could not stop the trembling of his limbs.

He had been hearing the murmur of the plane for some

time before he realized that it was what he had been waiting for. Then he struggled to his feet, turned to the open bonnet of the car and reached for the coil. His hands were shaking, his knees weak. It struck him that even if he got a taper alight he would probably extinguish it as he stumbled towards the bonfire. A sense of failure, of approaching disaster, seized hold of his mind: what he was doing with his hands was dictated by earlier mental processes, not by decisions he was taking now.

Still trembling violently, obsessed now by the thought that the plane would miss him, he touched the wire to the pole of the battery, holding the end of a taper to the point at which it glowed whitest. The taper was too tightly twisted and would not ignite. He loosened it, tried again. This time a flame flickered at the end of the taper and gradually took hold. Shielding it with his hand he made for the bonfire. Almost there, the flame guttered and went out. Back at the car he tried again, this time holding the two remaining tapers together, trying to ignite one from the other. The sound of the plane was louder. It seemed that it would not fly overhead but would pass by his position maybe a mile or two to the east. The pilot must be looking out for a signal, which they would have told him was to be a vehicle's headlights.

The two tapers alight, Essat moved as fast as he dared back to the bonfire. Applying the tapers carefully, he managed to get a piece of rubbish burning dully. Then he turned to the can of petrol, opened it, stood back and flung some petrol at the fire. With a roar a sheet of flame sprang from the bonfire and ran back along the line of petrol which had spilled back to where he stood. A wall of heat advanced towards him, plunging his face and forearms into agony. He stepped further back. The bonfire was well alight now, with points of flame shooting up into the blackness above. Over the crackle of the fire the sound of the plane's engine was getting fainter, now lying well to the north-east.

Was the pilot able to see anything back behind him? If not, would he turn back after a while to follow a search grid? Essat poured more petrol on the flames, worried now that the material would burn up before the plane returned.

Silence in the sky. The crackling of the fire was deafening

210

in the surrounding silence of the desert. Essat stood watching the beacon, trying to shield the raw skin of his face from the heat, coming to terms with the fact that the plane had missed him, would return to base and report mission failure, would be sent again tomorrow night, when there would be no signal of any kind.

He had already decided that he could not risk losing consciousness and being found by the Syrians. They would revive him and he had no illusions as to what they would do to him. He had his revolver: he would use it as soon as he had decided that the rescue tonight had failed.

He thought at one moment that a light had appeared on the horizon, but even as he stared at it, it disappeared. Then he heard what he took to be a bird chorus. As he listened more intently, it ceased. At moments he diagnosed his condition as heat stroke; at others a kind of euphoria seized him in which current reality ceased to matter and he saw himself aboard an aircraft heading for home. He wept but there were no tears. Several times he shouted, as if the pilot must hear him, but only a strangled scream came from his throat. Automatically and at appropriate intervals he doused the now waning fire with petrol, as if this were the only rational act of which he was any longer capable.

He did not become aware of the sound of the returning aircraft's engine until it was drumming loudly in his ears. For a moment he was confused, unable to associate what he heard with what he had hoped for. Then, the realization rushed at him and he flung the rest of the petrol on the guttering fire, waving frantically as if the pilot must see a gesture so passionately performed.

It was when he saw Shmuel's navigation lights winking, red, green, white, that he grasped that he had been found and would be saved.

The plane circled, losing height. The engine noise seemed deafening now, as if the plane would crash into the fire itself. Shmuel had banked gently and brought the plane to within thirty feet of the ground, watching the readings on his altimeter. As he closed the throttle, Essat below was aware of the change in the engine noise. Shmuel put his undercarriage down and extended the flaps. The pitch of the engine was deeper and the glow from the exhaust was clearly visible below. Then the Pilatus's wheels felt the rough ground, the tyres took a grip, accepted the weight of the plane, and the landing had been achieved. Shmuel turned her and taxied back towards the fire, came to a stop and opened the door. In the plane's lights he saw a staggering figure, gesticulating and trying to reach him. The figure collapsed and did not move. Shmuel ran to the spot, lifted Essat in his arms, carried him back to the plane and managed to heave him into the cabin. He spent ten minutes applying to the unconscious Essat what meagre first-aid knowledge he had.

He kept the run for take-off as short as he dared, leaving the ground at 100 metres. He was airborne at 50 knots. He headed the plane due south and left the rest to the Decca. Essat, behind him, was slumped in the passenger seat and appeared to be sleeping.

Associated Press, Beirut, 15 July
ISRAELI PLANES RAID BEKA'A. LEBANESE & SYRIAN PROTESTS
Bombs were dropped last night by Israeli fighter-bombers in the Beka'a valley. According to Israeli sources, terrorist bases were hit and all the aircraft returned safely. The targets were found in the area of Zahle and Marj'ayoun. Lebanese government sources report at least eight civilians killed and over 200 wounded. These sources claim that no military targets were hit. It is understood that bombs were also dropped on the Syrian side of the frontier, near the village of Kanaker. A communiqué from Damascus protests strongly against what is described an 'an act of war, in which habitations were destroyed and many civilians killed'. There is no confirmation of the damage done. It is understood that the Syrian government will be protesting to the US government and will raise the matter at the United Nations in New York at the earliest opportunity.

Associated Press, Washington, 15 July
MID-EAST PEACE PROCESS SAID TO BE HALTED BY ISRAELI RAID

212

White House sources confirmed this evening that yesterday's raid by Israeli planes on targets in the Lebanon, and the presumably accidental bombing of a village in Syria, will have put back the president's efforts at promoting an Israeli-Jordan accord. Talks were due to resume here next week but it now seems likely that they will be postponed. Congressional sources have expressed dismay at what is felt to be an ill-considered and hostile act by Israel at a time when signs were forthcoming that King Hussein of Jordan had adopted new positions on the problem of the West Bank.

Asked whether the projected talks would proceed, a White House spokesman declared: 'With Arab opinion inflamed by the bombing the president may decide to ask both parties to postpone the resumption of the talks to a later date. You can't talk peace when bombs are dropping.'

There was no comment from the Israeli or Jordanian embassies here.

Chapter 23

The post-war history of the extreme right in France is confused and complex, since it has the chameleon ability to change its forms, aims, allies and enemies to suit the day. It is made up of many groups, tendencies and political parties. It has always been able to call on an extensive sub-culture of gangsters, bent policemen, ex-legionnaires and paratroopers without a vocation, students from the faculties of law and medicine who are mesmerized by the philosophical writings of Pareto, Sorel and Spengler, and politicians of dubious repute.*

It was in this underworld of disaffection, adventurism and twisted ideology that Tavernet had his contacts. Now he knew where to turn, who to see, how much to pay.

Having heard by telex from the Swiss bank that the first half of the money had been received, he took a taxi to the

---

*For instance, the Service d'Action Civique (SAC) was formed in 1958 to defend 'Gaullism'. From 1961 to 1967 it battled against the OAS, which had set out to keep Algeria in French hands and, ultimately, to assassinate General de Gaulle. In 1968 the SAC and its offshoots were unavowed police auxiliaries, beating up left-wing students on the streets of Paris. They had a fleet of their own official-looking ambulances in which they carried casualties away from the scenes of clashes, took the wounded students to their own cellars in the Rue Solferino and beat them up, extracted information and threw them back on to the streets. Later, the SAC degenerated further into blackmail, kidnapping and fraud. Further to the right, fascist, royalist, anti-semitic and terrorist groupings remain active to the present day.

Rue de la Forge, near the Arc de Triomphe, and walked the short distance to an unremarkable building set among the apartments and modest shops which lined the street. Unremarkable, save for the fact that instead of the usual wooden doors leading to the courtyard, No. 87 had steel gates. The ground-floor and first-floor windows had grilles. A plaque listed the occupants:

Club Nationaliste.
Jeunesses de la Patrie.
'Europe-Victoire'.
Imprimerie Nouvelle.

Inside there were young men in black leather jackets stamping about the courtyard in their parachutists' boots. From the building at the back came the metallic throb of printing machinery. There were cars and vans drawn up in the yard: the rear windows of the vans were covered in wire mesh. Tavernet made his way up the bare staircase to the first floor where a pale girl in a smock sat at a desk, guarding a telephone switchboard. He asked for José Caracci.

The girl nodded towards a row of chairs and reached for the phone.

'Your name?'

'Say it's Alexandre.'

'He says his name's Alexandre,' she announced into the phone, as if she did not believe it. Then she nodded towards a door to her left.

Tavernet spent a half hour with Caracci, at the end of which the two men shook hands on the agreement which had been reached. Then Tavernet descended the stairs and was let out through the gates by one of the men in black. The place smelt like a barracks and Tavernet allowed himself a slight shiver of disgust as he emerged into the street and made his way up the Avenue de la Grande Armée in search of a taxi.

Nadia had managed the accident with skill. She had picked out Major Savary's grey Peugeot in her wing mirror as it travelled south down the Avenue Gambetta, and pulled out, giving no signals, as he came abreast of her car. Neither her beauty nor her evident distress did anything to abate Savary's fury, which only dissipated when a policeman pushed his way through the crowd of onlookers. Nadia, in tears which were in part genuine, exchanged insurance details with Savary. The policeman decided it was not a police matter, having no stomach for filing a lengthy report. The damage to both cars would mean a tidy insurance claim.

'I am dreadfully sorry, monsieur,' Nadia kept saying. 'It is my fault.'

'And you'll pay for it,' Savary shouted.

'Yes, monsieur, I'm sure my insurance company will take on your repairs as well.'

They managed to drive away.

Next day she phoned him.

'Forgive me. I found your name in the phone book. I would prefer to pay for the damage to your car direct. I would have trouble with my insurers.'

'You are insured, I take it.'

'I am.' She managed to make it sound as if she were not. 'Will you send me the repair bill?'

'How do I know you'll pay it?'

There was a silence. Then: 'Do you want me to pay you something in advance?' She had introduced panic into her voice.

'It would be appropriate.'

'How much?'

'Say four thousand.'

He heard her gasp, as he was meant to. 'Surely it's not going to cost that much.'

'It surely is.'

Another silence. Then, in a small voice: 'Perhaps we could discuss it. Four thousand would be difficult.'

And they had arranged to meet.

Nadia sensed that the note of anguish in her voice had intrigued him. She sustained it when they met at a café in the Avenue Gambetta near the spot where the accident had happened.

'What were you doing there?' he had asked suddenly.

She had not been ready for the question, but luckily remembered that there was a florist a few steps from where she had parked.

'I had some flowers sent to a relative in hospital. He's in a very bad way. I was thinking about him and that was why I wasn't paying attention to the traffic.'

'Which hospital?'

'St Louis,' she said at random.

She looked at him with her splendid blue eyes, dropping them as he returned her gaze.

'Perhaps we can come to some arrangement over this thing,' he said.

'What arrangement?'

'Why not dine with me tomorrow and we'll talk some more.'

As they parted she had suddenly looked up and given him a radiant smile which said: Maybe I am available. Maybe there is quite a lot I would do to save four thousand francs.

This was a proposition which had become clearer over dinner at Fouquet's the following night.

'I could overlook the repair bill,' Savary said. 'I would not wish to cause distress to such a very beautiful woman.'

She smiled and said nothing.

'We could perhaps get to know each other better. Then it would be inappropriate for money to change hands between good friends.'

'Perhaps,' she said, and later took him back to her apartment and there found him to be an aggressive and self-absorbed lover.

'I have known worse,' she reported to Baum next day on the phone. 'A very boring person.'

'I am sorry, Nadia.'

'Please don't keep apologizing, Monsieur Baum. Didn't you say you are only doing your duty?'

'That is so.'

'I didn't see your men.'

'From today you can have them whenever he visits you. Just call and tell my secretary you have an appointment that evening. Today we will install the listening devices, say at five?'

'Fine.'

'My men will be in a car below, picking up the signals from your apartment.'

The third time they met Savary told her that his wife was away visiting her mother in Douai and he planned to spend the night with her. At two in the morning she had slipped out of bed, taken his pocketbook from his jacket and spent ten minutes in the bathroom copying out initials and telephone numbers. There were strings of numerals in the book, but she had no time to copy them, fearing that he would wake up. She replaced the pocketbook and returned to bed without disturbing him.

'Very useful,' Baum said later, 'but I am interested in the other numbers as well. Can you manage it again?'

'I will try.'

Later that day Savary called her. 'My wife isn't back yet. I will come round again this evening.'

When she phoned the DST, Baum's secretary was not at her desk and Nadia left the message at the switchboard. The operator failed to deliver it.

On the same day Savary had had occasion to consult his notebook and was surprised to find that it was not lying in his pocket with the spine to the left, which was the way that he always placed it. He concluded at once that Nadia was not all she seemed. He left his office during the afternoon, walked down the Avenue Gambetta and paid a visit to the florist. He gave the owner a date and time. A search through the order book showed no dispatch of flowers to the hôpital St Louis.

That evening in her apartment he suddenly looked at her and smiled.

'And your relative who is ill, how is he?'

For a moment her mind was a blank. Then she recovered herself. 'He's better, thank you.'

'Did he get the flowers?'

'Oh, yes.'

'So you've seen him since?'

'Yes.'

He rose from his chair, crossed the short distance to where she was sitting. He had a brandy and soda in his hand. He took her chin between thumb and forefinger, forcing her head upwards. Then he flung the remains of his drink in her face. As she gasped for breath he released her chin and swung

218

his left hand, knuckle foremost, hard against her cheek. Calmly, he returned to his chair.

'Now you will tell me.'

'I – I don't understand. How dare you hit me! What have I done?'

'Don't waste my time. I have long experiences in making people talk. Especially women. I advise you to tell me voluntarily what I can make you tell with great pain.'

A patch of purple was already spreading on her cheek. She sat, terrified, trying to recall what Baum had said: 'If you find yourself in trouble, do not mention the DST. You are an agent.' And he had given her a cover story.

Now she prayed for his men to arrive. They would have heard the exchange, picked up by the bug in the room. They had instructions to intervene if she were in trouble. They would be on their way up, surely, and she must play for time.

'But I have nothing to tell,' she said.

'Why did you lie about the florist?'

'I – I don't know. Often I say the first thing that comes into my head.'

'So what is the second thing that comes into that head of yours? What were you doing in the Avenue Gambetta?'

There was a silence. Then, 'I was seeing a man. It didn't seem suitable to tell you. I thought there could be something nice between us.'

He laughed briefly. 'Good, but not good enough. Try again. The time for voluntary talk is running out.'

'But it's true. I swear it's true.'

Where were Baum's men? Surely they should be at the door by now.

'Tell me about this man of yours. What's his name?'

'Jacques,' at random.

'His surname.'

'I don't know. I'd only just met him.'

'So you go whoring?'

'No. It was just someone I met. I fancied him, that's all. Just as I suppose I fancied you.'

'His address.'

Where were the DST men? What would she do if they didn't turn up?

'It was the apartment house close to where I was parked. He took me there. I never noticed the number.'

He smiled again. 'All this is fantasy, isn't it?'

'It isn't fantasy. I swear it isn't.'

Slowly he withdrew the notebook from his jacket.

'Seen this before?'

'Your notebook? No.'

The men. Where were the men?

He got to his feet again and took the few steps towards her.

'No, no, don't hit me. Please don't hit my face again.'

'If we don't make progress you will be begging me to hit your face instead of what I shall be doing. How will you get by in life without your beauty, eh?'

He grabbed at her hair and hit her with his knuckle on the other side of her face, jolting her head back. His signet ring cut through the flesh of her cheek and she started to scream as he brought his hand up and clapped it over her mouth.

'If you make a noise I shall use this on you before anyone can get here.' He picked up the brandy glass, struck it against the edge of the coffee table and held it up for her to see the jagged edges.

He went back to his seat. 'Tell me,' he said.

Nadia was sobbing hysterically, unable to catch her breath. She tried to talk but the words would not come. She dabbed with her fingers at the blood which was oozing slowly from the wound in her cheek.

'Take your time,' Savary said. 'But not too much time, eh? Meanwhile let me say that anything you tell me that sounds improbable will be tested. Painfully. So you can save yourself much agony by telling me the truth now and not later.'

Baum's men weren't coming after all. Suddenly, she hadn't the nerve to use the cover story: an agent working for Todorov at the Soviet embassy. She knew this man could not be fooled. And hadn't the DST let her down? The men hadn't come and her life was in danger.

'I was forced,' she said. 'The DST have a hold over me

220

because I am not a citizen and there is something I did — something troublesome in my past.'

'Who gives you your instructions?'

She was still sobbing, gasping for breath.

'I said, who gives you your instructions? *Answer me!*'

He picked up the brandy glass, the jagged edges glinting in the light. He was smiling.

'I get my orders from Monsieur Baum.'

'How is the girl?' Allembeau asked.

'I got her the best care I could. We've put her in the safe house out at Marly. She'll be all right.' Baum shook his head.

'Did he do much damage?'

'She'll have a scar on her face, I'm afraid, and when he started punching her he broke a couple of ribs. I suppose he controlled himself just in time. He was probably afraid he might kill her and have a scandal on his hands.'

'Did she talk?'

'Didn't have the nerve to stick to her cover story. He knows she worked for me, but she says she told him all I got was a list of his appointments. Even saying that took some courage.' Baum reached in a drawer for his box of pills, shook two out and swallowed them with some water. His stomach was troubling him. 'Poor creature,' he said. 'I feel bad about the whole thing. I've sacked Frachot downstairs for not passing on her message.'

'Do you believe she didn't tell him she'd given you phone numbers?'

'I don't know. Maybe. In any case, they aren't genuine numbers as they stand. They've gone down to Danoux for cryptanalysis.'

'I don't imagine that Savary will make any kind of complaint,' Allembeau said.

'I don't imagine so. He wouldn't look all that good.'

Later, Danoux returned the list of numbers, suitably analysed. 'Not all that difficult,' he told Baum. 'A common device was used. The last digit of each number was increased by a sum which varied with the order in which it was inscribed on the page. Then the number was reversed. Thus the genuine number 816 4542 has had 2 added to the last

221

digit since it appears second on the page. This made it 816 4544. Then it was reversed, giving us 445 4618. Not difficult.'

'How do you know what we have now is right?'

'I checked at random with the telephone company. Take 816 4542, which became 445 4618; it had the initials R.A. against it. The telephone people tell me the subscriber is one Robert Amieux, whoever that might be.'

'Thanks,' Baum said. 'Great work.'

'I prefer something which stretches the mind,' Danoux said.

There were fourteen phone numbers in all. Baum told an inspector to get the subscribers' names from the telephone company's security people. When he had the list he searched first for a Claude Hébert. It was duly listed.

'Our little Françoise from the typing pool,' he murmured. 'Françoise Hébert, who lives with her parents. Father's name: Claude Hébert. Very good.' None of the other names meant anything at all.

He sent the list down to Archives, calling for whatever dossiers there were. Five came back and Baum settled down to read.

'See that no one disturbs me,' he told Mlle Pineau. 'And please phone my wife to say I will be late this evening, exact time unknown. Offer my apologies.'

There was nothing he liked better than a session with the archives, not knowing what he sought, but his senses alert to anything that stirred a memory, seemed in any way out of place, out of character, or merely interesting in its own right. It was recognized by all ranks at the DST that no one could distil information – relevant information – from a dossier like the Old Man. 'Almost everything you will ever need to know,' he would tell new entrants at the DST school, 'is to be found down on the first floor, in Archives. If we are interested in someone it is because they have done something against the security of the country. And if they have done that, the chances of their already having done something worthy of our attention will be high and will have led to the creation of a dossier. I have proved it many times.'

Now he set out to prove it once more.

222

By the time he had to leave the office to catch the last train to Versailles, Baum knew that this time he would prove nothing of the kind. Not that the five dossiers were without interest. But there was another precept that he would offer to the students and which he firmly believed: if you are after a man because you think he has stolen the plans of the latest submarine, do not be diverted from your objective when you discover that he is a rapist, has strangled his mistress and is deep into financial fraud. All this will have its relevance, but you are not there to do the job of the police. That can follow later. Keep submarines and nothing but submarines in your heart and mind.

For this reason, he kept his interest in the dossiers well in hand. It was interesting, for instance, to find that Major Savary of the DGSE had the phone number (in code) of a socialist deputy who had earned himself a dossier in Archives as a result of associating too closely with the Algerian liberation movement long before it had become fashionable to do so. Did this mean that the man was, after all, some kind of DGSE provocateur? And why would Savary have the number of a second secretary in the consular department of the US embassy when it was no part of his responsibilities to maintain liaison with the CIA, of which the consular official was a known member? Also, what about an inspector Emile Narjac of the Brigade Criminel? And a counsellor at the Syrian embassy who also figured in the pocketbook? And there was the phone number of Europe Victoire, bearing the initials J.C, which Baum recognized from close familiarity as those of José Caracci.

All this was interesting enough and much of it warranted brief addenda to the dossiers in question. But none of it was, as far as he could see, of much use in the present case.

Wearily, he told himself that they'd have to work their way laboriously through the remaining nine names – those which did not crop up in the Archives despite Baum's well-known thesis. Even there he'd probably draw nine blanks. But he couldn't assume anything of the kind. Tomorrow he'd have to put a couple of bright lads on to the thing to ferret their way through it like any pair of police detectives. And unless they got lucky and hit pay dirt at once, that would take time. The more so since he had no clear idea of what he was looking for, nor whether he would recognize it if and when it turned up.

When he got home his wife was asleep. He helped himself to a cold beer and managed to get to bed without waking her.

Chapter 24

'You are looking,' Baum said, 'for anything odd, anything that is not what you would have expected. You will ask yourselves why a high officer in our intelligence services should have a relationship with the person or organization in question. You will not presume to offer an answer to such a question. You will refer your suspicions to me and I alone will be the arbiter. Nor must you hesitate: the worst that will happen to you if you come forward with something that turns out to be stupid is that I shall say so. No one died from being called a fool, though quite a few have as a result of being afraid to be thought one.'

The two young men smiled. It was the Old Man's home-spun philosophy again. They would not have been surprised to learn that philosophy was what he would dearly have liked to study in his youth.

'You will take half of these names each. You will find out what these people are, what they do, their vital statistics, and any apparent reason for their being in touch with the DGSE. Also, you will not speak to any of your colleagues about the assignment and you will not leave your notes on your desks. Any sensitive phoning should be done away from the office. Any questions?'

There were none.

'Right, off with you. I shall want verbal reports each morning at nine.'

It was the day after his fruitless search through the dossiers. He was not happy. He felt that somewhere he had probably made a mistake, may have missed something that was staring at him from the grey files. Also, he had small faith in the search he had now set in train. But if the search were not done he would torment himself even more with the conviction that if only they'd looked hard enough . . .

His stomach was still far from settled. Though he had no faith in the white pills, he shook two more from the box and asked Mlle Pineau for water.

'You really should see the doctor, Monsieur Baum.'

'Indeed, I should.'

'It is not enough to say you should and then do nothing about it. You have been doing that for at least a dozen years.'

'It's my liver. There's nothing for the doctor to discover. And there is no known cure for liver trouble.'

He took the pills and tried to compose himself for other tasks. Then a thought came to him and he picked up the phone and dialled Allembeau's office.

'Baum here. A thought occurs to me.' Allembeau said nothing. 'I see that our friend Savary carried the phone number of one Mustapha Khelou around with him. The man's a counsellor with the Syrians. My thought is this: the Syrians are beginning to figure large in this *affaire* of mine. I think I owe it to myself to pay some attention to Mustapha, at any rate for a few days. Please put a couple of good men – maybe Léon and a mate of his – to keep an eye on the fellow.'

'Very well.'

'They can report in writing to me daily. I want to know who he meets and where.'

On the same day, Savary met Tavernet once more at the Château de Madrid.

'We must change the place,' he said. 'We have been here too often.'

'Do you have any reason to be worried?' Tavernet asked.

'Some reason. The DST put a spy on to me. It was a close thing.'

'Did they get anything?'

'I'm not sure. Probably not. But the elaborate operation they mounted shows that they have their suspicions.'

'What exactly did they get hold of?'

'Going into details will serve no useful purpose.'

'Then how am I to judge the degree of danger?'

'I am the one who judges, and I am telling you that the only risk, and it's a faint one, is that they may get hold of your office phone number. You'd better warn your staff.'

'Are you saying I should keep away from there?'

'For the time being, yes. Above all, no one from the DST must hear the name Jaloux. It will take Baum straight back to your brother.'

'Obviously. I will do whatever is necessary.'

'I will try to find out what they know. I have a source. If your brother is in danger I will let you know.'

There was a pause; Savary looked hard at the other man. 'Well?'

'What do you mean?' Tavernet asked.

'You are now active in this matter, are you not?'

'I am.'

'And so is your brother?'

'Yes.'

'But you would not be active unless you had received the first payment.'

'Of course not.'

'So you will have brought the first tranche of my commission with you.'

Savary was smiling. The other man did not find the smile pleasant.

'I am waiting for a bank transfer.'

'I find your approach unacceptable. I want the money by the morning.'

'I doubt that the transfer will be through by then.'

'In which case you will advance the sum from your resources here and recoup it when your leisurely banking procedures have been concluded.'

'It is not customary in a deal of this kind.'

'I don't give a shit what is customary. Use your Jewboy tactics with other people. With me you pay up – sharp!'

Tavernet shrugged. 'If you insist on being difficult . . .'

'I do.'

They parted, walking in opposite directions to find taxis.

Tavernet met his brother later in a café near the Pantheon. He repeated what Savary had told him.

'We now live dangerously,' he said. 'There is no way of knowing whether Savary is fooling himself or even deliberately fooling me about what the DST may or may not have gathered. He was edgy when I asked for information.'

'If the DST find their way back to you,' his brother said, 'I am finished. At the first sign of trouble, I get out. Have you made the bank transfer in Geneva for me?'

'I have. And that was another thing. Savary was aggressive about his commission, as if he felt he was in some danger from now on. It confirms my view that he's worried about what the DST already knows.'

There was a silence as René Jaloux looked round the deserted café, as if they were already after him.

'So what progress have you made?' his brother asked.

'I got back from my tour to the south last night. I made contact with my man at the Meyrargues depot. No problem there. And I have the transport schedules for the next couple of weeks, which means that I have a date for you: the night of 22 July. Have you lined your men up?'

'No problem. I saw Caracci. I can have whatever I need.'

'I think it can be done with six men of the right type. They'll need automatic weapons. Tear-gas grenades would be useful.'

'They'll have them.'

'And the vehicles?'

'Also fixed.'

'In the next day or two I'll have the exact spot and a detailed game plan.'

'And the merchandise?'

'Two fifteen-kiloton Pluton nuclear warheads.'

They parted, arranging to meet again, and Tavernet conveyed what his brother had told him to Hanif in Damascus, using the Libyan diplomatic facility.

'The time has come,' Hanif said, 'for you to take a fuller part in this venture. Doubly so, since you were right about the traitor Essat.'

228

Rasmia said nothing. She was surprised that she felt no satisfaction in being right.

'And by extension, about Saad Hayek also.'

Rasmia still said nothing.

'Why are you silent?'

'We killed a good man. There is nothing to say.'

'You must not dwell on such matters. I have told you in the past,' he said, 'that these commando operations of ours in Rome and Paris are purely marginal. They can have no ultimate influence on the frontiers in the Middle East; they cannot eliminate the Zionists; and they certainly cannot influence world opinion in our favour. Obviously, they do the opposite. No, the ultimate question of power can only be resolved by means of superior power. And that cannot be achieved by frontier raids, or even by local wars with conventional weapons. It has been tried repeatedly and it has failed. And if the Zionists had been on the point of losing any of those wars – the Seven Days, the Yom Kippur – they would have used their atomic weapons to settle the matter. In the event, they did not need to. We all know about the US airlifts which saved them. So, in view of these facts, only a *fait accompli* can achieve a decisive result. And what is a *fait accompli*? A situation in which Israel would be effectively destroyed if the Zionists refuse our demands. And that requires the deployment of our own atomic weapons. That is what we will acquire in France.'

'Will you need to detonate such a weapon?'

'I do not know. If necessary, yes. We will do whatever is needed once the Zionists confront the alternatives we will face them with. But meanwhile, there is work to be done. I shall leave tomorrow for Tripoli and France. Very soon I shall want you to be in Israel itself.'

He gave her his instructions. She asked very few questions, knowing that he would offer few answers.

'Tell me,' she said, 'do you think the traitor Essat got wind of this plan of yours?'

'It has never been mentioned in front of him.'

'Is anything written anywhere?'

'There are notes on certain aspects in the safe. They are coded.'

'He could not have had access to the safe?'

'Impossible.'

She said nothing.

'Does the idea of going to Israel frighten you?'

'It would be foolish to pretend there was no fear in me. The point is that I can master it.'

Chapter 25

Ben Tov had gone home at midnight. His wife was in bed and asleep. He sat in the living room, papers spread on the table before him, and tried to work. He could not concentrate. He picked up a book on military history and settled in an armchair. A half-hour later he snapped it shut, went to the telephone and called Ramat David.

Was there any news? No, no news and none expected until three or later. He returned to his book, helped himself to yogurt from the fridge, ate an apple. The thought that this was the best he could do in the way of self-control made him ashamed of himself. He thought of waking his wife; he needed someone to talk to. He decided against it and tried once more to attend to his papers.

When the phone rang at 3.45 he sent his chair flying as he dashed to answer it.

'Your man is safe.' It was an officer from the Ramat David base.

'What condition is he in? Can I talk to him?'

'His condition is poor. Our doctor has looked at him and says he'll be all right, but he wants him taken to a good hospital right away.'

'Take him by ambulance to the Hadassah, I will call them to make arrangements. Do I need to describe his condition?'

There were sounds of a consultation, then: 'Second-degree burns to parts of the body. Heat stroke. That seems about it, as far as we can tell right now. He'll be aboard an ambulance within fifteen minutes.'

'Is he conscious?'

'Delirious. He will be sedated. The doctor is dealing with it.'

Ben Tov rang off, called casualty at the Hadassah and pulled his rank. 'The Ministry of Defence requires a private room for this man. He should reach you within the next hour or two.' He described Essat's condition. 'You will notify the administrator right away.'

'It won't be necessary, we'll take care of the patient.'

'I repeat: you will notify the administrator.'

There was considerable menace in this voice from the ministry. 'Very well,' the duty doctor said, 'right away.'

Ben Tov, a broad grin on his face, put out the lights and went up to the bedroom. He shook his wife into semi-wakefulness.

'We saved him,' he declared. 'He's OK. We saved him.'

Next morning he called at the Hadassah. Essat, still heavily sedated, was dozing fitfully and managed a wan smile. Feeling awkward and out of place in the immaculate side ward, Ben Tov allowed himself to be shooed aside by a tiny nurse who busied herself at the bedside, demanding that Essat drink more. 'Your kidneys demand it,' she said. 'Let us have no more nonsense. Now, drink.'

Essat managed to swallow more water as Ben Tov looked on, much like a father at the bedside of a sick offspring.

'Where are his clothes?' he asked the nurse. 'I ordered that they should not be removed from the room.'

'In the wardrobe,' she said, without looking round.

Ben Tov took possession of them. Essat raised a hand and Ben Tov approached the bed.

'Boot,' Essat said. Then he closed his eyes again.

'I will come back later,' Ben Tov said. 'Get well.'

'He is to sleep,' the nurse said. 'You may return between six and seven this evening.'

Ben Tov found himself unable to argue with her.

Later, in his office, he found the slip of paper beneath the inner sole of one of the boots. What was written on it meant nothing to him. He locked the paper in a drawer of his desk. Then he went to the Memuneh's office and made his report.

'What do we know?' the Memuneh asked.

232

'I cannot say until my man recovers sufficiently to talk to me. That will be tomorrow.'

'You will keep me informed.'

'Naturally.'

'You realize that if the information is of little value, there will be great difficulties with the minister. I have already had strong representations.'

'My main objective was to save this young man from being tortured to death in a cellar in Damascus. That has been achieved. There can therefore be no basis for complaint.'

'The minister naturally expects information which can avert this threat from Chatila.'

'The minister, also both of us, and the prime minister – we all expect, hope for, pray for such information. If we get it, fine. If we do not, we will seek it elsewhere. I gave no guarantees.'

The Memuneh was about to reply and thought better of it. As the door closed he hit on an effective rejoinder, but it was too late.

Instead of going to his office, Ben Tov made his way out of the building and along the hot streets to the house in Abarbanel Street. There he performed the ritual which led, fifteen minutes later, to a conversation with Baum in Paris.

'I have to tell you that we have lifted our man out of Damascus. We had to: another agent of mine was caught and must have talked under torture. My man got away by the skin of his teeth.'

'Did he bring information out?'

'Some. It has not been assessed. I do not know its significance.'

'You will tell me what I need to know?'

'When I know it myself.'

'So you have no one inside now?'

'No one. I am more than ever dependent on you.'

'We are working on a lead. It is not all that promising.'

'Do your best.'

They said shalom to each other and Baum sighed heavily as he replaced the receiver. He walked slowly back to the Rue des Saussaies, head bowed, thinking about the dossiers in Archives and their refusal to yield up the secrets which he felt entitled to know. Once again he had the feeling that he had gone wrong somewhere. Reports had started to come in from his two young men and none of them so far seemed to have any significance. What was the way forward? Indeed, was there a way forward at all? One thing was clear: he would not after all get to the meeting of the federation of cat clubs at Chartres this weekend. He had been invited to give a paper on the Maine Coon and to do a little judging. He was looking forward to it. But he would not be able to justify his absence. A double shame, for the people in Chartres always laid on an admirable lunch.

He sighed again, and reaching his office, asked Allembeau to join him for a chat.

'Germany?' Allembeau asked as he sat down.

'Not Germany. Please spare me the Germans of all people until I am feeling better.'

'I'm sorry.'

'I wish to leak something to this swine Savary. Tell me how I do it.'

'Our little Françoise downstairs?'

Baum shook his head. 'I spoke just now to Ben Tov. Their man in Damascus has had to get out. It means that Savary will know that what I fed to him via Françoise about a spy in Chatila was fraudulent. He won't swallow anything coming from that source.'

Allembeau scratched his head. 'Difficult.'

'Why else would I take you away from your love affair with the Germans?'

They looked at each other. Neither had anything useful to say. At last Allembeau felt the need to break the silence.

'I don't suppose you could do something via Jo at the Brigade Criminel?'

'No . . . Yes! Why not, my dear fellow? Why ever not?'

'I don't see how.'

'But I do. Your idea is brilliant.'

'Such brilliance comes easily, since I only said it for the sake of saying something.'

Baum was already dialling a number. 'Thank you, my dear fellow. Now back you go to the Germans.'

When he had a connection he asked for Jo Leduc.

234

'Jo? Alfred here. Can you meet me in half an hour? At the usual place? Splendid.'

If only, he mused to himself, we were able to devote to the enemy the time we are forced to devote to the unsatisfactory people on our own side . . . what might we not achieve!

He met the man called Jo Leduc a half-hour later in a bistro in the Rue de Berri. He bought two beers and they sat at a back table. He wasted no time in small talk.

'You know an inspector in the Brigade called Narjac – Emile Narjac?'

'Of course. A nasty bit of work. Bent, and everyone knows it.'

'My problem is this. This bent copper Narjac's name has turned up in the address book of an equally nasty bit of work over at the DGSE. I know nothing of the relationship, but whatever it is, I need to use it to get some information to the man at the DGSE.'

'How the hell am I to do that for you?'

'Can you find a pretext to go drinking with this fellow?'

'I can but I won't enjoy it.'

'Your enjoyment will come from helping me to crack a particularly hard nut.'

'All right, tell me more.'

'You will get drunk together. Only he will be drunk and you will merely appear to be drunk. Possible?'

'I suppose so.'

'In your inebriate state you will let fall certain remarks that I will now reveal to you, together with a plausible reason for being in possession of such information. It is tricky and must be done with care. Further, the man must not be so drunk that he promptly forgets what he has heard. Which means that you must appear more drunk than he is. Possible?'

'I don't see why not.'

'The DGSE man is a Major Claude Savary. What you have to convey is that we are in possession of details of his forthcoming appointments and for some reason we're investigating a couple of the people he is due to see. Only you don't know which ones.'

Baum then told Jo Leduc precisely how the thing was to be done.

'Care is required,' he said finally. 'Care and speed. It is very important to us and very urgent.'

'Okay, Alfred,' Jo said. 'And I expect you to do something equally tricky for us at the Criminel when the need arises.'

'It will be my particular pleasure.'

On his way back to the Rue des Saussaies Baum had the impression that he was feeling slightly better in himself. But it was still a pity about Chartres.

By the following day he had reports on all nine subscribers on Savary's list of phone numbers. Some, on the face of things, were interesting; some, at first sight, offered nothing. Thus, it was useful to know that Savary had the home numbers of employees at the Libyan, Moroccan and Senegalese embassies, none of whom had dossiers at the DST, but all of whom were now to have their own grey folders in Archives. A further three numbers belonged to right-wing politicians who also now qualified for dossiers. One number belonged to a private company called Inter-State Consultants, one to a known dealer in sado-masochistic pornography, and one to a lady who figured in the appropriate police files as a prostitute. 'Rather surprisingly downmarket for such a man,' Baum observed of the lady in question.

'What can interest us in all this?' he asked himself as he re-read the notes prepared by his young men. 'The lady? I am doubtful. The porno dealer? About the same probability as the lady and for the same reasons. The man at the Libyan embassy could bear closer examination. The deputies? A low probability, I would have thought. They are unlikely to be people for whom Savary would arrange a clandestine appointment with Chatila. With the PLO, maybe, but hardly with a maniac who wants to blow the Middle East to bits.'

He had told one of his young men to find out what he could about the ownership of Inter-State and to take a discreet look at its offices. The information in the Register of Companies told him that the sole proprietor and shareholder was a Dominique Soult and that the company carried on business as commercial and industrial consultants. Inquiries in the building where it occupied a modest suite of offices further revealed that the staff consisted of two ladies and that a gentleman often came to the office. Name unknown by the elderly North African who cleaned the building and tended the boiler. Or so he claimed.

A telephone call was answered by a lady whose only response to inquiries as to the name of the director was: 'Please write in, stating your business, and it will be dealt with.'

With modest expectations, Baum decided to mount a daytime watch on the building. There was nothing in Archives on Dominique Soult. He decided against a full-frontal assault with interrogation of the two employees. He still hoped to get what he wanted without alerting Savary. Later, he willingly recognized that this was the cardinal mistake of the entire enterprise. The watch was to yield nothing beyond the shopping habits of the two ladies, and a half-hearted attempt by Baum's young men to scrape acquaintance with the least plain of them foundered on her icy indifference. Attempts to trace Dominique Soult failed when it was found that that mysterious person had long since left her registered address.

'The very blandness of all this is what must interest one,' Baum said. 'We will examine this Inter-State in greater depth. Unfortunately, it will take time. I am giving it three days. By then, I want this Soult person identified, the nature of their business clearly explained to me, and the identity established of the man who is said to visit the office. Why can no one get closer to one of the ladies – buy her a beer, take her to the pictures, kiss her, I don't know . . .'

'I have tried,' the young man said.

'At your age, I would have succeeded,' Baum told him.

'But *patron*, you haven't seen her.'

'And the other one?'

'She looks like an aunt of mine,' the young man said. 'I couldn't.'

'You have three days,' Baum said. 'And if you want to be well thought of around here, you'll give me my answers in two.'

Afterwards he said to Allembeau: 'It is difficult for them. They aren't policemen and they haven't police resources. It is always like this when we are forced to do pettifogging police work. It makes everything twice as slow.'

It was not a good day, but he felt it was partly redeemed the following morning when Jo Leduc called him.

'You remember that assignment you gave me?'

'Of course.'

'Well, I carried it out last night.'

'What impression do you have?'

'It could be OK. I distinctly saw the little bastard's eyes light up, drunk as he was. Actually, I think he was playing tight, just as I was, though I've no idea what he expected to get out of it. Anyway, I did the necessary.'

'Thanks.'

'Remember what I said: one day you can do something for the Criminel.'

'Of course.'

To Baum it felt like an unexplained move in a game of chess played against an invisible opponent on a board which kept shifting around.

Unhappily, he devoted some time to his papers, among them two days' reports from Léon. The Syrian counsellor, Mustapha Khelou, had done nothing, seen anyone or gone anywhere of interest. Baum thought of dropping the exercise entirely. Then he thought better of it despite the manpower crisis in the department.

In his office in Jerusalem that morning Ben Tov took the sheet of paper from the drawer in his desk, placed it carefully in an envelope and slipped the envelope into his breast pocket. Then he went down to his car and drove himself to the Hadassah. The two days since his flight from Syria had seen a marked improvement in Essat's condition. Ben Tov had resisted the temptation to ignore medical instructions, which had been clear: This man is to be left to rest and regain some strength for forty-eight hours. The forty-eight hours now being up, the debriefing could take place.

Essat was sitting up in bed, smiling carefully, the creasing of his face causing pain to the burns on his cheeks and

238

forehead. The skin was still raw in these areas and on his forearms and the backs of his hands.

'So now we can work,' Ben Tov said.

Essat nodded.

Ben Tov took the paper from its envelope and placed it in front of Essat on the sheet.

'Tell me.'

'Those are passport numbers from unused passports. There were more, but most are there. The letter I indicates Iraqi and E Egyptian.'

'Useful.'

'The other numbers are copied from a sheet of paper in the safe. I have no idea what it all means – just numbers. There were no other marks on the paper.'

'A code of some sort. We'll have to see what the boys make of it.'

Essat turned the paper over, revealing a rough sketch.

'We took a picture of this one, so I only did a very rough version as a precaution. It looks to me like a section of a street plan. As you'll see, there are no street names or anything else to identify the spot, save for single letters here and there, maybe indicating street names. I've no idea if we can make anything of it.'

'What is this in the middle?'

'It looks like a rough sketch of a building with a dome. I think I copied that pretty well as it was in the original.'

'A mosque?'

'Presumably. Most domes are on mosques.'

'So maybe this is a plan of a few streets in an Arab quarter?'

Essat nodded.

'And these words – "Third on left"?'

'They were written on the sketch.'

'Tell me what else there was.'

Essat described what he could remember of the contents of the safe.

'Do you think,' Ben Tov asked, 'they can possibly find out that you have been at the safe?'

'I don't think they can.'

'Now tell me everything you know of the man Hanif. Start

239

wherever you like and keep talking. I want to *feel* these people – the way they talk and think and act, what motivates them, what are their strengths and weaknesses, everything. Here, take a drink.'

He passed a glass of water to Essat, who drank briefly. Then he took a notebook from his pocket and made occasional notes in it as Essat talked.

'And what about the girl Rasmia?'

'What shall I tell you?'

'Everything – anything that comes to mind.'

After Essat had been talking for five minutes, Ben Tov interrupted impatiently. 'Does she possess a handbag – one of those large soft ones with a strap, in some light colour, with a darker diagonal stripe?'

Essat looked startled. 'As a matter of fact, she does. It's yellow and a sort of brown.'

Ben Tov took a photograph from his pocket and handed it to Essat without a word. It showed Rasmia and Belaiev. Essat studied it, looked up, nodded.

'It's her.'

'The man,' Ben Tov said, 'is KGB. Now in the light of that information talk to me some more about the girl.'

There was a silence as Essat searched his memory, wondering why he was not surprised at the news. What could he recall about her that was odd, significant?

'In Rome,' he said, 'there was this man on the bed on the first floor of the hotel.' He told Ben Tov of Rasmia's expedition during the night, which he'd thought was connected with her suspicions of him.

'What else?'

'In Damascus, in the south, just before I had to get out.' He told of seeing her with a European, then walking away without a farewell gesture.

'The man in the picture is from Damascus. Could it have been him?'

Essat examined the picture again. 'I never saw his face.'

'And the build?'

'The build is right.'

The debriefing continued for a further two hours on the following morning. Meanwhile, the fragment of street

240

layout, if that it was, had gone to the cartographers at the Ministry of the Interior with a request that it be matched against the street plans of the Arab quarters of Jerusalem and all other towns with an Arab population. The list of numbers from the safe had gone to the decrypt section of Mossad, and the passport numbers had been distributed to the frontier police and, in an exercise supervised by Ben Tov personally, to Alfred Baum at the DST.

But at Interior an unauthorized step was taken. Following standard practice, and despite Ben Tov's covering note 'for our own use exclusively', a go-go young official passed the list of passport numbers on to Interpol in Paris.

Interpol, following established procedure in turn, circulated the numbers to the anti-terrorist organizations of its member countries. This included the Italian Ministry of the Interior, where a clerk took a private note of the numbers and passed them on to the two anti-Israeli groupings from whom he received modest retaining fees. The Rome representative of one of these groups — he did not know its name — was a studious-looking youth with glasses who answered to the name of Khaled. He took delivery of the list of passport numbers, for which he paid cash, and transmitted the information to Damascus the same evening.

The Mossad analysts got nowhere with the numbers from the safe which Essat had listed. Not knowing what they were looking for, and confronted with inadequate data, they were unable to offer solutions of any kind or to deal with the withering scorn which emanated like a black cloud from Ben Tov's office.

From the cartographers there was nothing but silence, save for a comment from the head of the section: 'The request is crazy and anyway my staff have better things to do.' Nevertheless, staff was put to work after the minister's private office had intervened.

Chapter 26

The French army's Pluton mobile ground-to-ground rocket system is deployed mainly along her eastern frontiers. The missiles with their nuclear warheads are launched from super-heavy eight-axle trucks. However, one unit of the tactical nuclear force is deployed in the south – at Aubagne to the east of Marseilles. Aubagne is a major military centre, containing among others the headquarters of the Foreign Legion. A few kilometres to the south lies the Compiagne firing range. To the west is the air base at Marignane and to the south the naval bases at La Seyne and Toulon. The thinking behind the deployment of Pluton within this southern military complex is not altogether clear. The use of such a resource against Spain is clearly improbable. It must be supposed that the French high command has, among its atomic scenarios, one which would be played out on location in North Africa.

The Pluton warheads stored underground at the Bourgace military base on the southern outskirts of Aubagne are rotated regularly: they are taken fifty kilometres north by road to the depot near Meyrargues, where the decaying nuclear fuel is replaced, after which they return to Aubagne. Once a month a twenty-ton container lorry makes the night journey, accompanied by a military truck with a detail of six men of the 124th infantry regiment stationed at Bourgace. The journey, part of which is along winding mountain roads, takes a little over two hours. The villagers who live along the route have long since become accustomed to the heavy rumble of the lorry and its escort and no environmentalists have poked their noses in and raised the issue of safety.

The depot at Meyrargues is under the joint control of the army and the Atomic Energy Commission. It lies some four kilometres to the west of the ancient town with its eighteenth-century castle standing high above a heavily wooded gorge. The depot consists of galleries driven deep into the mountainside, with service roads extending from the two gallery entrances to the N556 which runs due south across the Durance river and down towards Aix. Security at the depot is tight.

Before going off duty at 18.00 hours, the day shift had loaded twenty re-armed Pluton warheads on the container lorry, together with a supply of detonators and ancillary equipment which had been requisitioned by Bourgace. The driver and his mate drove up from Meyrargues in a 2 CV, arriving shortly after 20.00 hours. Within fifteen minutes the sound of a military truck could be heard, labouring up the N556 and turning off on to the service road. It came to a halt at the entrance to the main gallery. On board were six men in battledress. They were carrying sidearms. They were joking in desultory fashion as they leaned over the sides of the truck, shouting mild obscenities to the men on guard duty. The detail had come up from Bourgace that evening. They would not be in bed much before one or maybe two a.m. Guard duty, even, was preferable.

The container lorry's load was signed out by an officer. The driver and his mate climbed into the cab. The driver, a short, wiry man in his forties with something of the weasel about him, seemed impatient to get going, and started cursing when the military truck failed to move off on time.

'Take it easy,' his mate said. 'What's the bleeding hurry?'

'No hurry,' the driver said. 'They fuck about. Get on your nerves.'

The officer signalled, the lorry's diesel started up and the big vehicle turned slowly and nosed down the service road. The military truck fell in behind. The headlights of the two vehicles stabbed into the darkness, picking out the giant oaks which lined the road. The driver had lit a cigarette and let it hang loose from his lower lip.

'About two hours, eh?' His mate was inclined to chat about nothing.

The driver nodded, not bothering to comment.

'Your bird expecting you?'

The driver had a wife in Meyrargues and a side interest in a block of flats in the centre of Aubagne – the wife of a sergeant in the Legion who was more often in Africa than at home.

He shrugged. It was no one's business whether he'd see her tonight or not. In fact, she was expecting him but he knew that on this occasion at least he would be standing her up. More than that, he had plans, far-reaching plans which involved the lady in question and were equally no one's business but his. Perhaps that accounted for his impatience, perhaps not. Whatever the reason, his mate reckoned he was edgy this evening and decided to leave him alone. He noticed that their speed was inclined to exceed the regulation forty.

In the military truck, advancing seventy-five metres behind the lorry, the men had taken up their positions, facing to either side and back towards the empty road behind them. Their weapons were slung across their chests, safety catches on. No one was particularly alert: the thing was routine, boring, probably not necessary. There was sleep, drink, women, gambling to think about. Intermittently, as the road ran straight for a short stretch, the lorry ahead was flooded in yellow light from the truck's beams. Then it would disappear round a bend and be lost to view. The night was oppressively hot. The roar of the two engines drowned the familiar night sounds.

There is a steep incline coupled with a series of sharp turns on the N556 two kilometres before it drops down to join the more important N96. It was here, as the lorry disappeared round a bend ahead, that the army driver suddenly felt the wheel wrench in his hand. He stepped on his brake as the truck slewed over to the left. There was a chorus of curses and laughter from behind the cab. The driver sounded his horn to alert the lorry ahead. There was no response.

'You can laugh,' the driver said, 'but you're the ones who'll

244

have to change the wheel.' He had climbed down from the cab and a moment later let out a yell of pain. He had stepped on a metal star with fiercely sharpened points. It was one of hundreds strewn across the road. One of them had punctured a tyre and two others were embedded in another tyre.

'Call the lorry on the radio,' he shouted to the corporal who was in charge of the soldiers. The corporal activated his transceiver, which crackled at him and gave no joy.

'Christ, talk about interference.'

He failed to raise the lorry. Cursing, he ordered his men out on to the roadside.

As they jumped down on to the roadway two tear-gas grenades, lobbed out of the undergrowth by the roadside, landed among them. The men, cursing and retching, staggered away from the vehicle. Some of them let fly with their automatics until the corporal in charge managed through his coughing to yell at them to stop for fear of shooting each other. Among the trees two men slipped quietly away with their electronic jamming gadgetry, their mission accomplished. It was twenty minutes before the soldiers had recovered sufficiently to clear the road of stars, change the wheel and set off.

It was a kilometre further down the N556 that the headlights of the container lorry picked out a number of logs lying across the narrow road. The driver brought the vehicle to a standstill. The fag was still hanging, smouldering, from his lip. He did not seem startled.

'What the bloody hell?' his mate asked. 'And where's the escort?'

'Fallen behind.' The driver leaned out of the cab, trying to see into the woods on either side. 'Looks like some kind of ambush.'

'Call them up on your radio,' his mate said.

The radio produced garbage and nothing else.

In the lorry's beams two figures appeared. They were in khaki battledress. Their faces were hidden behind balaclavas. They carried automatics, which they were pointing at the cab.

'Get down on to the road with your hands up. Come on – move!'

245

'Better do it,' the driver said. 'The bastards will shoot us.'

The two men got down, one on either side. Two other figures appeared from among the trees. The driver and his mate were prodded with the guns. Then they had their hands tied behind their backs with rope.

'Who has the keys?'

'They're carried by the escort.'

A fist was smashed hard into the face of the driver's mate.

'Now who has the keys, or do you want a bullet in your skull?'

The man was grunting with pain. 'I tell you the military carry the keys.'

They turned to the driver.

'D'you want the same treatment?'

'He's right. We're not trusted with the keys. Stands to reason, with that stuff aboard.'

They were hustled to the side of the road, flung to the ground, and their legs were tied. Masking tape was plastered across their mouths and they were dragged a few metres into the woods, out of sight of the road. Meanwhile, the logs were being pulled off the road and they heard the engine start up. Beyond it they could hear a car engine come to life. Then the sound of the vehicles receded.

The lorry was driven three kilometres down the N96 and on to a side road leading eastwards into the Bois de Ligoures. A kilometre into the dense forest it halted at a clearing. A team got to work on the bolted and padlocked rear doors. They yielded after five minutes. Inside, like sinister giant-sized metal cigars, the Plutons lay strapped into wooden racks. Alongside were wooden crates containing their detonators. The Plutons shone dully in the yellow light of the men's torches.

The men selected what they had been instructed to take. The transfer into a van which had stood concealed under the trees took moments. Then the van was driven back on to the N96, heading southwards, back towards Aubagne. But soon it forked right on to the motorway and covered the twenty kilometres into Marseilles in a little over seven minutes. Racing through the eastern industrial suburbs of

246

the city on the urban motorway, it headed for the docks. Soon it was nosing its way through the maze of deserted streets behind the warehouses. The driver paid no heed to the one-way system and crossed intersections at speed. Emerging from the back streets, the van gathered further speed along the Chemin du Littoral, the walls of the docks on its left with, behind them, the towering silhouettes of the dockside cranes. The driver braked sharply as he approached Dock Gate 4.

'Can this thing go off?' his companion asked.

'Christ knows. For all I know it could be timed. The sooner we offload the better.'

At the gate, the driver sounded three short blasts on his horn. The nightwatchman opened the door of his cabin and stepped out into the road.

'From Jo-jo,' the driver said, handing over an envelope.

The watchman nodded, returned to his cabin, emerged with heavy keys on a ring. It took him half a minute to unlock the heavy metal gates and heave one of them back. The van was driven through and the gate was eased back into position.

'Which warehouse?'

'Opposite the eastern quay: 47D.'

The water slapped against the quayside to their right as they drove carefully past the cranes and the rows of containers waiting at the dockside to be loaded. The hulls of the cargo vessels loomed above them with here and there a light throwing long shadows across a deck. Warehouse 47D was a long, grey building fronted by corrugated doors. The van stopped. A man came out of the shadows to the left.

'Max?'

'You got it first time.'

'Wait, we'll open the door.'

There was a sound of casters on metal rails as one of the doors was trundled back. The driver and his mate had climbed down from the cab and had the back of the van open. It took a few minutes to transfer the load from the van to the interior of the warehouse. Then the van was driven back to the dock gates and out on to the road, soon

247

to lose itself in the labyrinth of narrow streets around the Vieux Port.

Inside the warehouse one of the men opened a case of instruments and got to work on a technical inspection. After thirty minutes he announced himself satisfied, shook hands with the other two and was let out on to the quayside. He walked to Gate 4 and was let out by the watchman. The two men then got to work with welding equipment, files, rubber solution and black paint. It was soon after 3 a.m. when one of the men straightened up and wiped the sweat off his face with his sleeve.

'That's about it. Give old Ali whatsisname the signal.'

The other man moved out of the warehouse on to the quay. He could make out the bulk of a vessel moored level with the building. He picked up a bolt from the ground and tossed it up. It fell, clanging, on to the fo'c's'le. He took a torch from his pocket and directed a narrow beam at the poop. Soon there was a shout. He returned to the warehouse and together with his mate manhandled the Plutons out to the side of the vessel. The gangway which had been winched up, was let down, the ropes and blocks creaking in the almost silent night. The cargo was taken aboard and the gangway was hoisted back into position. The two men walked to Gate 4 and were let out.

It was 6.30 on the following morning before the news of the events on the Meyrargues road had percolated up to the military command in Aubagne. By 7.30 the news had reached the Ministry of the Army in Paris, where a colonel attached to the minister's private office, summoned by the duty officer, recognized the event for what it was: a political and public-relations disaster of impressive potential. It was close to 9.00 a.m. before a meeting could be assembled in the minister's room. Meanwhile, the colonel, who was very bright and suitably political, had been issuing orders. He had been careful to do nothing overt himself, since he could not imagine any outcome to the crisis which did not include a commission of inquiry and a pack of journalists in search of a scandal. He therefore instructed an adjutant to call Aubagne.

'Tell them to do nothing until they receive our orders,' he

said. 'Meanwhile they will confine to barracks all personnel who were involved.'

'Shall I telex?'

'No. Use the phone. And tell Aubagne the military police may examine the site but are not to involve the civil authorities in any way. Is that clear?'

'Yes, sir.'

'If the DST make inquiries they are to contact us.'

'Very good, sir.'

'I repeat, use the phone.'

The minister, who had been given the bare bones of the story before setting out from home, was every bit as shrewd and twice as cautious as the colonel. He used the half-hour during which he was being driven through the Paris traffic to think out a course of action which, should it succeed, would meet what he deemed to be the needs of public policy, and should it fail, meet the equally insistent need for personal survival in the political arena. As the official car swung into the courtyard of the ministry, he came to the conclusion that he knew what had to be done.

The meeting at 9.00 a.m. was carefully restricted to the colonel, the minister himself, and the member of the general staff responsible for all units with a nuclear capability. The latter was a two-star general famous for the doctrinaire fashion in which he interpreted the army's disciplinary code and its famous sense of military honour.

'We want no one else poking their snouts into this calamity until we have things under control,' the minister said. 'It will have to go to the presidency later this morning. It had better go in a suitable condition.' The others nodded. 'We want no loose ends. Understood?'

It was understood.

'Your report, Alain.'

The colonel gave his report, including details of what precisely had been stolen and what orders he had given.

'Who else knows about this thing?'

The colonel explained how careful he had been in the matter of transmitting orders to Aubagne. The minster, who knew his man, did not need to wink.

'I will give the news direct to my colleague at the Ministry of Defence, whose task it will be to inform the president's office. Meanwhile, I would be glad if you, general, would take charge personally down at Aubagne. Our task is, of course, to recover what has been stolen, but above all to prevent any leak of information. To this end the military personnel involved will continue to be confined to barracks until further notice.'

'Certainly, minister.'

'I suppose,' the colonel said, 'it would be too risky if we simply suppressed the entire episode. After all, if there is an explosion the evidence disappears, and if there is not, the evidence remains hidden.'

'Too risky, Alain. But in the public interest we have perhaps to minimize the significance of what has occurred.'

'Two Pluton weapons complete with detonators,' the general offered. 'It will not be easy to minimize.'

'What if we chose for security reasons to say one weapon with no detonator, general? No doubt under the *Secret Défense* regulations you could guarantee me silence down at Aubagne?'

'I can. In the army orders are obeyed.'

'Very good. That is all, gentlemen, thank you.'

When they had left, the minister called his colleague and superior, the minister of defence, and told him of the Pluton missile, minus its detonator, which had been stolen that night on the Meyrargues road.

'I suppose we will have to call in the DST?'

'Certainly.'

'The police?'

'It will amount to calling in the press.'

'Best leave it to the president to decide.'

'You realize this is political dynamite for the coalition?'

'You don't mean anything as obsolete as dynamite, my dear fellow.'

The minister of defence tried a polite laugh at his colleague's weak jest.

'The president will not be pleased.'

'That will be the one fixed point in this sorry tale.'

Chapter 27

Later that morning the President of the Republic chaired the meeting at the Elysée himself. At his right sat the imperturable Vallat, chef de cabinet. At his left the minister of the interior slumped, defensive and truculent by turns, with Wavre and Baum beyond him. Next to Vallat was the unfortunate Duparc, head of the president's very own anti-terrorist squad. He was staring fixedly at some invisible point on the table before him. Beyond him, a bald three-star general from the Ministry of Defence was gloomily running over some notes on a sheaf of papers which he clutched in his left hand as if someone would seize them if given the chance. The minister himself had been excused on the grounds of a pressing official engagement elsewhere.

The atmosphere in the president's office was alarming.

'What you are telling me,' the president was saying, as if talking to these people at all was costing him an effort, 'is that it is altogether possible for a group of unknown persons to seize from our arsenals a nuclear weapon, and then to vanish – *pouf!*' He made a gesture designed to convey disappearance.

He turned to the bald general. 'Do I understand you correctly, *mon général?*'

The general shifted uncomfortably in his chair and managed to keep all expression off his face. 'It has certainly happened, Mr President. And now we have to recover the device. Elements from the army's security branch are working on the case. It can only be a matter of time.'

'That does not follow,' the president said darkly.

'I will be taking all necessary steps,' Duparc said.

The president ignored him.

'Tell me, general, can these people get hold of a suitable detonator?'

'The detonators are custom-made for the Plutons. They would have to steal one. As it stands, the weapon is unusable.'

'It is difficult to believe,' Vallat said in his doom-laden voice, 'that a group smart enough to pull off a coup of this magnitude would overlook the crucial question of the detonator.'

'Were there any detonators in this shipment?' the president asked.

'I think not.' The general appeared uncertain. 'At all events, I am informed by the army that no detonators are missing.'

'But we may now expect an attempt somewhere or other to steal one?'

'We will take – '

'Yes, yes, all necessary steps. I hear a lot about such steps. I cannot pretend I am impressed.' The president turned to the minister of the interior. 'We must keep this out of the papers, Gaston.'

'I will do my best.'

'Regrettable as the theft of one of our nuclear devices undoubtedly is, it would be even more regrettable if the fact were to be discovered by the media and therefore the world at large. The political consequences of such a leakage would far outweigh the event itself in the damage it must cause.'

There was a silence. Baum could be seen, though not by his president, to be smiling quietly to himself, as if the political process were offering once again a supremely ironic and fascinating entertainment.

The bald general, who had never attended a presidential meeting before and therefore lacked all caution, plunged on, oblivious to the political semaphore which was signalling around the table.

'It seems to us essential to get this device back with the minimum of delay. Otherwise, we might be accused of being dilatory.' He paused, foolishly, for effect. 'The army,' he pronounced proudly, 'is not dilatory.'

'Only incapable of looking after its own weapons.'

'Security during transport,' the general ventured, 'is ultimately the responsibility of my friend Wavre here and the Atomic Energy Commission.'

'So the army washes its hands of the whole matter, is that it?'

'No, no, Mr President. Absolutely not at all. It was merely – '

The president's hand came down on the table with surprising resonance. 'Can no one understand what the true nature of this disaster is? You talk about getting the thing back when what you should be telling me is how to keep the media out of it. Do you realize what trouble the government will have in the Assembly? Do you have any conception of what the Americans will make of it? And the Russians? What do you think the Russians will say?'

There was silence, since no one knew what the Russians would say.

'They will say,' the president announced, 'that it was not a theft at all, but a manoeuvre by us to get such a weapon into the hands of whatever state it suits the Soviets to pick out of the hat. That, my friends, is what the Russians will trumpet around the world.' He sighed. 'It is something we can do without. That, and the inevitable hysteria from Jerusalem.'

Silence again.

'I will deal with the media,' the minister repeated.

'You had certainly better, and right away.'

'May I suggest, Mr President,' Georges Wavre said, 'that the inquiry be left to the DST. We do not leak.'

'Those involved can be told that the weapon has been recovered,' the minister suggested. No one chose to pursue the idea.

The president sighed. 'The DST is responsible. Duparc here will give whatever help is required. The army will stay out of it, general, and so will the police, except insofar as Wavre here decides to call upon them.' He looked hard at Wavre and Baum, the two plump DST men into whose lap the mess had been tipped. 'Who, in your opinion, is responsible for the theft, gentlemen?'

Wavre and Baum shook their heads in unison. 'I do not know, Mr President,' Wavre said quietly. 'Baum and I no doubt have our ideas, but without evidence I would not wish to mislead you with speculation.'

'Arabs? Italians? Lunatic Germans?'

'I cannot speculate.'

'You will report daily,' the president said, removing his glasses from his nose. It was a sign that the meeting was over.

'Any ideas, Alfred?' Wavre and Baum were walking back along the Faubourg St Honoré towards the DST building.

'Oh, yes, I have ideas. But I, in turn, would not wish to mislead you. Or to speculate.'

'Your man Jaloux will no doubt be on the carpet.'

'He was, this morning.'

'And?'

'He seems to think because procedures were followed, signatures duly appended to documents and the regulation guard was present, that nothing really went wrong. I pointed out that all that was splendid, but what about the little matter of the hijack? He said it was regrettable and had no idea how it could have happened.'

'Do we have many like that?'

'A few, a few. I am dealing with all this myself, of course.'

'Leads?'

'Well, it has to be an inside job. Apparently this gang knew when the stuff was being moved and by what route. We shall take a close look at all those involved.'

'The Chatila people, do you think?'

They crossed the Place Beauvau in silence as the minister's car swept through the great gates of the Ministry of the Interior, the sentries saluting sharply.

'Chatila or not,' Baum said, 'I think our friend Vallat made an interesting point back there.'

'About the detonator?'

'About the detonator. I fancy there will be no theft of detonators in the period ahead.'

'Because they already have one?'

'It would be altogether like the army to lie about it. After all, what have they ever defended successfully but the honour of the army? In a mess like this, it must have been the only thought that occurred to them.'

'You will follow up this idea of yours?'

'Difficult as that will undoubtedly be, I shall.'

Back at the Rue des Saussaies each went unhappily to his office and Baum set in motion the machinery required to give effect to the president's decision. In a painful telephone conversation with Jerusalem he informed Ben Tov of what had happened, though he said nothing about detonators. Then he called the military in Aubagne and announced his imminent arrival together with two of his inspectors.

There were papers on his desk. He glanced through them. Near the bottom of the pile he came across Léon's report for the previous day on the surveillance of one Mustapha Khelou, counsellor at the Syrian embassy:

' . . . subject was followed to No. 14 Rue Lamartine and took the lift to the second floor. Subsequent investigation indicated that one of the two apartments on that floor is occupied by a Claude Savary, the other being unoccupied. Subject remained for approximately forty minutes and was observed to leave. A short distance from the Rue Lamartine the trail was lost under difficult traffic conditions.'

Baum took the sheet and locked it in a drawer of his desk. Then he sat, immobile, staring at the grey wall of his room, thinking, trying to get a mental grip on the mess of random facts the *affaire* was constantly throwing up. He was jolted from this reverie by the phone.

'Yes?'

'Monsieur Baum, here is Kovacs.' The voice carried traces of a mid-European accent; it was low, measured, with an odd mixture of deference and self-assurance.

'What can I do for you, Kovacs?'

'Let us meet, Monsieur Baum. It would be a pleasure to have a chat about mutual friends, old times . . .' The ingratiating voice trailed off.

'Would you call it a pressing meeting?'

'I think so, yes.'

'I can be at the Rotonde at seven.'

255

'Excellent. I hope you will do me the honour of being my guest for dinner.'

'That is most kind.'

'My pleasure.'

That evening, at a table at the back of the crowded restaurant Kovacs allowed the meal to go by without further reference to either mutual friends or old times. Instead, he had an endless fund of opinions, anecdotes and homilies, which he offered freely until brandies had been placed before them. Then he leaned forward and tapped Baum gently on the back of the hand, his expression suddenly serious and his voice businesslike.

'I have information for you.'

'On what topic?'

'Are you at all interested at the moment in tactical nuclear devices – missing from your arsenal at Aubagne?'

'I know nothing of such matters.'

'Quite. You cannot be expected to share sensitive information with me. Nevertheless, may I proceed?'

'Please do. I am always willing to listen.'

'My understanding, Monsieur Baum, is that what is missing from Aubagne will be shipped out of Marseilles.'

'When will this be?'

'I do not know. We do not have that much detail. But I imagine it is imminent. Indeed, it may already have happened.'

'And you got this . . . ?'

'From our friends.'

'You were specifically asked to . . . ?'

Kovacs raised a finely manicured hand. 'Please, let us not get into specifics. When I talk to you I do so because it is felt in another place that it would be mutually helpful. No one, my dear Monsieur Baum, has an interest in an atomic catastrophe. No one but madmen. And so I repeat: a ship from Marseilles – ultimate destination Israel. That is all I am authorized to say. That, and the absolute necessity of not revealing your source of this information.'

'Would you mind if I leave you immediately?' Baum asked. 'I have many things to do.'

'I imagine so.'

'Thank you for a very pleasant meal.'

'The pleasure was mine.'

Baum drank the remains of his brandy at a gulp and almost ran through the crowded restaurant and out to hail a taxi.

Back at the office he got busy on the telephone to Marseilles. Later, he called Ben Tov at home.

'My news is not good.'

'Nevertheless, tell me.'

'We believe the weapon will be shipped out of Marseilles. All our efforts – '

'Yes, yes. And what do you know about the vessel? What flag?'

'We know nothing at present, but I am personally in charge of the case and I will do everything I can.'

'I am sure.'

'At least you can now concentrate your own efforts on every ship arriving in Israel from Marseilles.'

'They can trans-ship elsewhere, so that the damn thing arrives on a vessel with a totally different port of origin. They can get it off the vessel in our waters and row it ashore in a dinghy. They can call at Larnaca or somewhere else and get it on to a plane. How do I know what they will do?'

'Nevertheless, I am sure you will investigate all ships reaching your ports.'

'Obviously,'

'There is one more thing,' Baum said. 'I got this information from a tip-off.'

'A leak in their organization?'

'I have a source which feeds me from time to time with what a certain other power wants me to know. It came from that source and it means that these other people are closer to this thing than we are. It is surprising.'

Ben Tov took a long time replying. 'I am grateful to you for telling me something as sensitive as that. I will respect your confidence.'

'Thank you.'

'You do not suspect a provocation?'

'I do not.'

'Or American guesswork?'

'It is absolutely not the Americans.'

'I see.' He was about to ask a further question, thought better of it.

'Shalom.'

'Shalom.'

The meeting of the defence committee in Jerusalem on the same day had proved to be no more urbane or amiable than the proceedings at the Elysée. The Memuneh had thought long and hard about whether he should share with the committee what Ben Tov had told him about the theft. On the one hand, there would be trouble, anger, fury even, which might ultimately prove to have been pointless, since no one knew for sure that the weapon had been stolen by Chatila, nor whether it might not be recovered by the French. There was thus a case, and a seductive one, for saying nothing until more was known. But on the other hand, what if it had indeed been stolen by Chatila, was not recovered by the French and subsequently turned up somewhere in Israel? In that event no one would be seduced by the argument that it had been premature, unnecessarily alarming, not truly useful to notify the committee. And the Memuneh could name several politicians who would assert against all the evidence that if they had been told in time, this or that measure could have been taken and all would have been well. So that, all things considered, it was perhaps best to bite on this particular bullet now and suffer the resultant toothache. He had spent an unhappy morning considering all this and cursing an unkind fate which had fixed a committee meeting for that very day. The only mitigating step that he could think of was to tell Ben Tov to attend the meeting. Let the anger be diffused a little.

And anger there was, offered initially by the minister of defence who had an axe to grind and had decided to grind it in committee.

'Is this not an intolerable failure of the Mossad?' he asked.

'The theft took place on French soil, minister. I do not see how we could have prevented it.' The Memuneh hoped his voice demonstrated confidence, but it emerged as self-righteous.

'Since when,' the prime minister asked, 'have we considered that the defence of Israel takes place only on Israeli soil?'

'We do not get co-operation from the French. The committee will be aware of French policy.'

'Curiously enough, French policy is something with which I am tolerably well acquainted.'

'It has made working with the French security people very difficult.'

'And yet,' the minister of defence said, getting comfortably into his stride, 'the government grants facilities to the Mossad far in excess of what can reasonably be expected, including extensive air support, even to the point of interfering with the peace process.'

Developing his thesis, he failed to notice the expression on the prime minister's face. 'It would appear that the Mossad's elaborate measures to maintain surveillance on this Chatila group have proved to be a waste of time, resources and political capital.' He looked round the table. 'It is not at all satisfactory.'

'I would remind you, Eli,' the prime minister said, 'that I personally authorized the intervention of our air forces in the rescue of the Mossad's man. As I told you at the time, it seemed to me to be the right thing to do. Any criticisms on that score should therefore be addressed to me. I am listening.'

'Perhaps,' the secretary to the committee ventured, 'we should concentrate on what can be done next.'

'May we have your appreciation?' The prime minister had turned to the Memuneh, whose hopes had risen in proportion as the politicians' squabble took on pace and spirit. This, he felt, was a suitable moment at which to make use of Ben Tov's presence.

'My colleague Ben Tov will report,' he said.

'Sometimes,' the prime minister said unkindly, 'one could be forgiven for thinking that Ben Tov is running the department. But no matter.'

'We have information from my man,' Ben Tov said, 'and I would like to thank the prime minister for enabling us to save him and thus to gain possession of this information. As

259

to its value, it is too early for me to say whether it will prove to be decisive. But the fact of the matter is that what my man brought out is the only thing we have. I repeat: the only thing. Our only other asset is the co-operation we are getting from our friends in the French service. That is genuine but seemingly of limited value.'

'Is it your view,' the prime minister asked, 'that the French nuclear device was stolen by Chatila?'

Ben Tov looked round the table. The silence was tangible. The Memuneh, not one to appreciate drama, fidgeted with his papers. The prime minister's head was thrust forward. He was staring at Ben Tov.

'It is my view,' Ben Tov said, 'that Chatila is now in possession of an atomic warhead, that there is a better than even chance that the French will not find it, and that we should therefore reckon with the possibility of it being transferred successfully on to our soil. Please bear in mind that Pluton warheads are not large and could be smuggled ashore here without insuperable difficulty. That being so, I submit that the danger to the state is immediate and exceedingly grave.'

The Memuneh had stopped fidgeting. The prime minister had not shifted his gaze from Ben Tov.

'What do you need from us?'

'At the moment, nothing,' Ben Tov said, well aware that he should be deferring to the Memuneh. 'But I would like to feel free to ask at any time for whatever support may be needed.'

'Any questions?' the prime minister asked.

There were no questions.

Chapter 28

At the Bourgace barracks south of Aubagne the instructions from the ministry in Paris had been received and understood. Within three hours they had been acted upon. The stores unit was relieved of its duties and shifted to similar work at the Compiagne firing range a few kilometres to the south. Between their departure and the arrival of the replacement unit, the records of weapon movements had been modified, the sheet showing sixteen Plutons booked in on the previous day being removed to be replaced by a new delivery sheet showing seventeen. The record of detonators was adjusted accordingly. The young captain who had been put in charge of the operation reported his mission accomplished and his superior officer spoke to him sharply about *Secret Défense* and the solidarity of the army in the face of external interference. To this was added the news that Paris would be sending men from the DST to look into something which – and here his superior slapped him on the back in a flattering way – something which those of us who had chosen an army career knew was no one's business but ours.

'Yes, sir,' the young captain said. He was impressed – flattered to be brought into this conspiracy to defend the integrity of the service.

In Marseilles, the harbourmaster received instructions from the ministry: no ships to leave without the approval of a DST officer who was installed in the port authority offices and whose word would be law.

The search of the docks and the shipping tied up there began. Teams of customs officials, port police and DST men moved methodically along the wharves and jetties, opening up the warehouses, searching containers on the quayside and going aboard the vessels tied up alongside. Amid a good deal of cursing from the shipping interests in the port area they insisted on opening up the reefer containers, endangering the contents as the temperatures were allowed to drop. Anything destined for the Middle East was poked, opened, taken apart. Bales were prodded. Crates were prised open. Geiger-Müller counters, clicking intermittently as they picked up background radiation, were run over every surface.

When they came to warehouse 47D the DST man in charge of the team indicated the containers he wanted opened. Several hours were spent amid engineering parts, bags of chemicals, knocked-down Hotchkiss guns and foodstuffs. The same performance was repeated with containers awaiting the gantry cranes on the quayside. Then the DST man expressed himself satisfied.

'We're coming aboard,' he signalled the master of the *Croix Valmer*.

The crew members were hanging over the rail, watching the game. The DST man and half a dozen others climbed aboard.

'Make yourselves at home,' the master said. 'There's nothing suspect aboard this ship.'

They started in the bows, looking everywhere, opening everything. Men climbed into the lifeboats, inspected the winch housings, ordered the deck cargo opened up. One of them clumped about among the pipes and air shafts inside the funnel while others worked their way through the holds. A stock of hashish was found in the bosun's stores but no one bothered. The lamp room, crew quarters and bridge were visited. In the engine room the customs men poked about behind the diesel, in the shaft tunnel and in the bilges. On the fo'c's'le gas bottles and coils of rope were shifted about. Nothing was found and nothing significant was registered on the Geiger-Müllers.

'You're clean,' the DST man said at last. 'We'll be leaving one of our men to check that nothing goes aboard that we haven't already taken a look at. When do you sail?'

'Now that I can finish loading I should be ready by

tomorrow morning. You've made me twenty-four hours late as it is and I'll be in trouble with the owners.'

'What's your destination?'

'Haifa.'

'You can make up the lost time at sea.'

'With this old tub?'

They shook hands and the inspection unit moved on to the next vessel. The master stood at the rail watching them go. 'No problem,' he said to the first mate, standing next to him.

'I admire your nerve.'

'No point in getting upset when you're dealing with ass-holes like that.'

Alfred Baum and his two inspectors, installed in offices at the barracks, spent the whole of the following day interviewing everyone connected with the events on the Meyrargues-Aubagne road. They spent hours with the soldiers who had been in the truck, interviewed the commanding officer of the depot at Meyrargues and the personnel in transport at Bourgace. Baum himself spent most of his time with the driver of the container lorry and his mate.

'What about your driver?' he asked the mate. 'Everything normal there?'

'What do you mean?'

The driver's mate was a young man in his twenties, swarthy and compact in the manner of the local people, not talkative.

'You two have worked together for over a year, right?'

'Right.'

'So you must know each other pretty well.'

'He doesn't let on much.'

'Still, you know the usual things. He's married?'

'Why don't you ask him?'

'I have, but I like to choose the questions, so I am asking you too. What about his girlfriend?'

'He told you that too, did he?'

'Maybe.'

'She's some bird he has here in Aubagne. I never met her. He seems stuck on her, far as I can tell. I know he spends.'

263

'How do you know?'

'Showed me stuff he bought for her, didn't he.'

'Expensive stuff?'

'I'll say. Daft, spending like that on a tart like her. Half the garrison have had their leg over. So I heard.'

'Cast your mind back a bit. The other night, would you say your mate was his normal self? Please think before you answer.'

The man seemingly didn't need time to think. 'No. He was jumpy as hell.'

'Before the attack?'

'Yes.'

'Please explain.'

'Usually he's a lazy sod. This time he was impatient to get off, cursing because there was a hold-up. Then on the road he kept going over the limit. I said something but he told me to fuck off.'

'And when you were attacked?'

'Well, all I know is the bastards hit me and didn't hit him.'

'Anything else?'

The man shrugged and said nothing.

'Tell me,' Baum said, 'do you think there was a tip-off?'

'Stands to reason.'

'Why?'

'Well we set out at a different time each journey. How could they mount an operation like that unless they had the time and the route, let alone the date?'

'Anything else?'

'Like I say, we were doing over the limit. Must be a reason.'

'Maybe your driver was in a hurry to see this woman.'

'Maybe.'

'Did you hear the truck's horn when it had to stop?'

'I did.'

'What happened?'

'I said, "Sounds like their horn." He said, "You're imagining things." Then he revved up the engine and turned the cab radio on, as if he didn't want to hear.'

'Why didn't you insist?'

'I'm not in charge, am I? If I fall out with him my job could be on the line. He's only got to put in a lousy report.'

'All right,' Baum said. 'Stay around. I may want to talk to you again.'

He called in one of his inspectors as the man left.

'Did you check on the driver with the Meyrargues police?'

'He's got form. Must have been a bit of a tearaway in his youth – three convictions for taking vehicles, one for causing an affray. Then there was a breaking and entering charge, but they couldn't make that stick. The record ends about eight years back, when he moved to Marseilles. He only came back to Meyrargues eighteen months ago.'

'What do the Marseilles police say?'

'I haven't been on to them.'

'Any special reason?'

'No, *patron*,' the inspector said lamely.

'This is not the best work, is it?'

'I suppose not.'

'You had better give me the answers from Marseilles within the next half-hour.'

The answers were interesting. The driver's name was linked with the Lavazzis, who headed one of the three Mafia families in the city. They controlled the classic mix of criminal activities and legitimate businesses. The driver had kept out of jail but he'd been up for questioning twice. 'A bad lot,' the Marseilles policeman said.

When Baum had the driver slouched defiantly in a chair before him he adjusted his style to suit the opinion he now held of this man.

'Your behaviour on the night of the hijack was highly suspicious.'

The driver said nothing.

'Why did you ignore the sound of the truck's horn?'

'I never heard it.'

'Your mate said he drew your attention to it.'

'He can say what he bleeding likes.'

'You still claim you didn't know the truck had stopped?'

'You heard me.'

'You're lying.'

The man said nothing.

265

'This woman you have in Aubagne, they tell me you spend a lot of money on her.'

'Maybe.'

'Where do you get the money?'

'I earn it, like you.'

'Do you know the Lavazzis?'

'Never heard of them.'

'Why were you in such a hurry the other night?'

'I wasn't.'

'Others say you were.'

'Fuck 'em.'

Baum sighed. 'You are obviously not aware that you are making things pretty bad for yourself. Here you are, a man with a lot of form, well known to the police, involved now in a very serious situation indeed – the only person of your type so involved. Naturally, my suspicions fall fair and square on you, and I have to tell you now that you will be detained here and questioned for as long as it takes to get at the truth, and the truth will either land you in jail on a most serious charge or, of course, it will clear you. Personally,' Baum said, as if it were a mere afterthought, 'I do not believe for one moment that the truth will clear you. On the contrary.'

'What charge?'

'It depends. But whoever gave the gang the tip-off – and for all I know that person may be far more than a mere informer in this little business – that person is going to spend a long, long time in a cell somewhere. Meanwhile, you will be detained here until I have established the facts.'

'How long will that be?'

'It depends on you, just as the ultimate punishment depends on you. Co-operate, and I will do all in my power to minimize things. And my power in that respect is considerable.'

'I don't believe any of this crap.'

'Your mistake,' Baum said, 'is that you think you are dealing with just another branch of the police. In fact, you are dealing with the DST. It is a very different matter, my friend. No influence can be exerted, not even by the Lavazzis.

And we will hold you for as long as we choose. I now intend to have you taken to the guardhouse and locked up.'

'I want my rights,' the driver said. 'I want to see a lawyer.'

'You have no rights and you will see no lawyers. You are in deep trouble, and I trust a night or two in the lock-up will bring the fact home to you. When it does, we will talk again.'

The driver's woman friend contradicted the picture of her that Baum had built up in his mind. She was not blonde, she was not smeared in heavy make-up and she was neither defiant nor sulky.

'My husband will kill me.'

She kept repeating the litany. It was clear that she had been crying. It was difficult to see what the driver, let alone the garrison, had seen in her.

I never seem to understand these things, Baum said to himself. To the lady he said: 'Please compose yourself, madame. There is no reason why your husband should be involved in this business.'

'But I don't even know what it's all about. They came to fetch me but they wouldn't tell me anything.'

'It is merely that your boyfriend is in a good deal of trouble and I need to ask you a few questions.'

'Marc, where is he?'

'He is with us. If you wish him at all well you would be advised to answer my questions fully and truthfully.'

'I have nothing to hide, monsieur.'

'Good.' He offered her a cigarette, which she refused. 'Tell me, madame, how long have you known this man Marc?'

'About two years.'

'You are lovers?'

She nodded.

'Has he been a generous man?'

She nodded again.

'Did it surprise you that a driver could afford to give you nice presents and still keep a wife and family at home?'

'He earns a lot of overtime and bonuses for dangerous work.'

'Do you know what that work is?'

'No.'

267

'Now I want you to answer my next question very carefully. Do you think he had plans for the future, for both of you?'

For the first time a wan smile spread briefly over her face. 'Oh, yes, he told me that he had come into a legacy of some kind and would have some real money and we'd go away together – make a clean break.' She paused, as if the morality of the venture needed justifying. 'My husband is a brute.'

'And when would this money be available?'

'He was to meet me the other night to tell me all about it, but he never turned up. I understood the formalities were nearly completed. We were planning things for next month.'

'Did he ever mention the sum involved?'

'No. He's a secretive person and I don't ask questions.'

'Thank you, madame, that is all. You will be taken back home.'

It was shortly after she had left that one of Baum's young men came on the line from Paris.

'We got lucky, *patron*. It's a hell of a story.'

'I don't need preliminaries. Just say what you have to say.'

'We trailed one of the ladies of Inter-State Consultants after she left the office yesterday. She ended up in a bistro near the Gare de l'Est. She was joined there by a well-dressed middle-aged fellow. We thought at first it was some kind of assignation, but from what we could tell from a distance it was more like a business meeting. They were looking at documents. It struck me that maybe this was the director of Inter-State. So we decided to follow him rather than her after they parted. It was a difficult decision to make but – '

'I must teach you how to stick to essentials, my friend. I am interested in the outcome, not your thought processes.'

'Sorry, *patron*. Well, after about half an hour this man left the bistro and hailed a taxi. We got lucky, like I said. We managed to get a taxi to follow them. The driver did a beautiful job. We ended up in the Rue Spontini, in the 16th. We thought it safest not to check with the concierge, seeing that you said the other side mustn't be alerted to the investigation.'

'Very wise.'

'Today we got a list of residents from the town hall. There

are ten households at 26 Rue Spontini. Do you want me to read you the names?'

'Have you checked them in Archives?'

'Yes. There's nothing.'

'Any of the names strike you in any way?'

There was a silence at the other end.

'Well?'

'It's just that it's an odd coincidence, like.'

'What is? Come on, man, I have work to do and so have you.'

'Well, *patron*, I'm not suggesting there's anything in it, mind, but it is a bit odd. You see, one of the apartments belongs to an Alexandre Jaloux.' There was another silence. 'We just thought it a bit odd, that's all, seeing that Inspector Jaloux – '

'Jaloux is not an uncommon name,' Baum said quickly. 'You will not speculate about a colleague. Is that clear?'

'Of course, *patron*.'

'I hope you haven't been broadcasting this around the office.'

'No, *patron*.'

'Lock your list of names in a drawer. I am returning to Paris this evening. One of you will wait for me at the office.'

After ringing off, Baum sent for the driver again.

'In the last ten minutes,' Baum told him, 'I have been on the phone to Paris. Our investigations there have thrown up new facts which are very damaging for you.' He looked hard at the driver, preparing carefully for what he hoped would be the moment of truth. The man stared back at him, signalling unconcern.

'We have been talking,' Baum said carefully, 'with Inspector Jaloux.' He was watching the driver from beneath his bushy brows. There was a benevolent look on his face, as if he badly wanted his man to save himself. 'I have to tell you, my friend, that Inspector Jaloux has been talking to us about you.'

'The fucking bastard!'

'I must admit we put pressure on the inspector,' Baum said. 'Anyway, he made it clear to us that you and he had entered into a little transaction.'

The driver had relapsed into silence, only now the corner of his mouth was twitching and there was an expression in his eyes which Baum diagnosed as a mixture of anger and fear – mostly fear.

'I can offer you a deal, my friend, and I advise you to take it.'

'What deal?'

'You will tell me the truth and I will do my best for you. That is the deal.'

'And if I keep my mouth shut?'

'I will do my best to get you the heaviest sentence that the law permits. And if I judge it not to be heavy enough we'll see what we can add into the indictment to sharpen it up. I repeat, you are in the hands of the DST. It is not a soft option.'

'The bastard!'

'I understand your distress. It may be some satisfaction to you that what you have to say will undoubtedly ensure that the inspector gets his just deserts.'

It seemed to settle the issue.

'I was paid to tell them the departure time and route and to close my eyes to whatever happened.'

'Who handled the money?'

'One of Lavazzi's boys.'

Baum took a chance. 'But according to the inspector, you've done a good deal more than that for them.'

'I contacted Henri Lavazzi. It isn't against the law to talk to someone.'

'So you know where the weapon has been taken?'

'No idea. Why would they tell me a thing like that?'

It sounded like the truth.

'Who else is in this thing?'

'No one else. Just Lavazzi and his people. But the impression I had was the hijack was to be carried out by the boys from Paris.'

'With Lavazzi looking after the stuff once they'd got it.'

'I don't know.'

'All this will be written down and you will sign it,' Baum said. 'Once we have it all down on paper, and always

270

provided you don't try any tricks later, I will keep my promise. Now I will have you taken back to the guardhouse.'

Later, Baum called for the written records and asked to see the man in charge of the stores unit which received deliveries from Meyrargues.

'You booked in the delivery from Meyrargues yesterday?'

The man had his instructions. 'Yes, sir.'

'At what time precisely?'

'I understand the container lorry was located around midday.' The man consulted a sheet of paper. 'The delivery reached us at 13.05 hours.'

'You supervised the unloading?'

'Yes, sir.'

'And you filled in the delivery sheet?'

'Yes, sir.'

'Show me.'

The man handed over the sheet. He was a sergeant. Near retirement, Baum reckoned. None too bright. An old sweat who'd been pushed on to quartermaster duties where he couldn't do much harm. Most of the military affected a swagger of one type or another when confronted with those services which could not boast a uniform, stripes and pips, coloured service ribbons . . . But this man wasn't comfortable.

Baum was looking at the document. 'Your handwriting?'

There was a silence. Then, 'Yes, sir.'

Baum tore a sheet from his notebook, pushed it across the desk with his pen.

'There, sergeant, be kind enough to copy out the line relating to detonators received.'

The sergeant had had no instructions on a point such as this. He didn't see how he could refuse a request so firmly made. And for all he knew, this fat little man could be more important than he looked.

He copied out the line of figures and handed back the paper and pencil.

Baum glanced at it, looked again at the official sheet, then up at the sergeant, who was staring straight ahead of him.

'Not your writing, eh?'

'My writing, sir.'

Baum sighed. 'Very well. Now tell me, how long have you been in this job?'

'Exactly one year, sir.'

This was something on which he had been briefed.

'So you must know my inspector who visits this place regularly.'

'Yes, sir.'

'What's his name?'

Silence. Eyes front.

'Never mind, you must have forgotten. It's Bertrand, isn't it?'

'Yes, sir.' The man exuded relief.

'Thank you, sergeant. You have been most helpful.'

The sergeant saluted, turned on his heel in a style betokening thirty years of practice, and made for the door. Baum waited until he had grasped the handle, then: 'By the way, sergeant, it has just struck me that the law permits me to have you up before a civil court on a charge of obstructing the course of justice. Would you be interested at all in a confidential chat which could avoid proceedings which might have you dismissed from the army?'

The man turned.

'I have done nothing wrong.'

'Your superior officers will not stand by you, sergeant. Your pension rights will not interest them.'

The man said nothing, but the sightless military stare had gone out of his eyes.

'Tell me, when do you retire?'

'Next June, sir.'

Baum shook his head sadly. 'Not a good time to tangle with the law.'

'I am only carrying out my officer's orders.'

'I do not doubt it. But to me you must tell the truth and I will treat what you say in confidence.'

'If my officer knew, I'd be up on charges, sir.'

'Your officer will not know.' Baum paused, tried a friendly smile. 'Now tell me, when did they put you into this job?'

'Yesterday, sir.'

'Write down there the name of the man you replaced.' The man took the pen and wrote. 'Where is he now?'

272

'I was told he'd been transferred to Compiagne.'

'Thank you. You have nothing to fear.'

Baum was shaking his head sadly as the man left the room. Then he collected up his papers, called in one of the inspectors and gave him detailed instructions in respect of the man named by the sergeant. After which he bade the inspector goodnight and made his way to the commanding officer's room to thank him for courtesies extended.

He could not be expected to know that the corporal in the military police who was on duty in the guardhouse that night was accustomed to carrying messages for small rewards in cash. It was something that the driver, who had an instinct in such matters and was, after all, a southerner like the corporal, quickly established. He gave the corporal a Marseilles phone number and a simple message: 'Tell Henri that Jaloux has blabbed.'

He got the corporal to repeat it back to him to make sure he had it right. During his break for supper, the corporal wandered out to a public call box and delivered the message.

Within an hour of the corporal's call being received in Marseilles, Tavernet and Savary were together in Paris.

'My brother will have to get out tonight,' Tavernet, alias Alexandre Jaloux, said.

'They'll be watching for him at the frontiers.'

'He has a useful passport. I think he can get through.'

'Have you been in touch with him?'

'I thought it wise to see you first. I'll go to him from here, but it's tricky. They may have a watch on his place already.'

'If the message is correct and they've got him to talk, you realize . . .' Savery left the sentence unfinished.

Tavernet nodded. The two men looked at each other.

'He is, of course, your brother.'

'That cannot enter into it.'

'Who will you see?'

'Caracci.'

'Can he set it up quickly?'

Tavernet nodded.

'And what about the transaction down in Marseilles? Is that in danger?'

273

'I think not.'

It was close to 1 a.m. when two men forced the front door of Inspector René Jaloux's modest apartment in the 17th *arrondissement*. It was done with hardly any noise and Jaloux did not stir in his sleep. One of the men stayed by the front door while the other went to the second door on the right, which he had been told was the bedroom. The sleeping man did not hear his approach and had no time to feel the cold steel of the automatic's silencer on the back of his neck. The single shot, almost noiseless and professionally aimed, severed the spinal cord and killed him instantly.

On the following morning, soon after dawn, the pilot arrived at the quayside, mounted the gangway and stepped aboard the *Croix Valmer*. He was welcomed by the master. The crew were preparing to cast off. The pilot went up on the bridge and amid the customary shouts and signals the windlasses and winches turned, their machinery clanking and screeching in the silent morning air. The ropes were lifted clear of the bollards by the shorehands and slowly the *Croix Valmer* eased herself out of her berth and headed for the mouth of the harbour.

The black pilot launch came alongside in the Estaque roads and the pilot prepared to climb down the ladder.

'Goodbye.'

He shook hands with the master.

'Goodbye. Why all that fuss back there?'

The pilot shrugged, shook his head. 'May see you on the next trip.'

When the launch had pulled away the *Croix Valmer* headed out to sea, picking up speed as she went. At her customary fourteen knots she would make Haifa in something over four days. Among her crew were two men nominated by Savary. Among the gas bottles stowed in a cluster on the fo'c's'le were two slightly thicker and longer than the others, freshly painted.

Chapter 29

When Tavernet, alias Alexandre Jaloux, stepped out of the lift on the third floor of 26 Rue Spontini he was confronted by two heavy men in plain clothes. One of them offered a sight of an ID.

'We are from the DST, monsieur. You are Alexandre Jaloux?'

'I am.'

'You will kindly come with us. Our boss would like to have a little chat.'

'What is it about?'

'I understand it is to do with your brother.'

'What about my brother?'

'I have no idea, monsieur. Our instructions are to bring you back to our office.'

The DST men had a car waiting below. Twenty minutes later Alexandre Jaloux was sitting opposite Alfred Baum. He had not been allowed to call his lawyer and was protesting about it.

'All in good time, monsieur,' Baum said. 'First, a few questions.'

'I have nothing to say until I have spoken with my lawyer.'

Baum looked at him quizzically. The bushy brows knitted slightly, and though there was what might be taken as a smile around the mouth, the eyes were curiously steely.

'The charge,' he said evenly, 'will be high treason. Also a number of other counts.'

Alexandre Jaloux produced a persuasive imitation of a roar of laughter.

'Utterly preposterous! I am a respectable businessman.'

'Not according to your brother.'

'But – '

'Yes?'

'Are you saying my brother has been . . . denouncing me?'

'Yes, monsieur.' There was a silence. 'The job,' Baum said quietly, 'was botched. Your brother is seriously ill but he has talked to us.'

'I haven't the faintest idea what you are talking about. What illness?'

'As you know very well, your brother was shot last night. But the gunman's aim wasn't all that good. You and your friends should demand a refund.'

'You must be mad. I know nothing about my brother being shot. Who shot him? Where is he?'

'He is in hospital.'

'I demand to see him.'

'You are in no position to make demands.'

'There will be an almighty scandal about this.'

'I daresay there will. We have thick skins at the DST and we are used to scandals. Now, are you prepared to answer a few simple questions regarding the attack on your brother and related matters?'

'I will not answer any questions whatever on any subject. I demand to see my lawyer. In his presence I may be willing to help your inquiries so long as they do not tend to incriminate me in any way. That is all.'

'Now,' Baum said, 'let us be sensible. Your brother tells us that you and Major Savary have been selling a very dangerous weapon to foreigners and that the weapon in question was stolen from our arsenal. He has given a lot of details. You are in very deep trouble, monsieur.'

Jaloux's face betrayed no sign of dismay but Baum noticed that his knuckles were white as he gripped the arms of his chair.

'I have nothing to say.'

'I would not be surprised,' Baum added amiably, 'if we were able to add a charge of attempted murder to the rest.'

'I have nothing to say.'

'Very well. I am not prepared to waste any more time on

276

you. You will be taken downstairs and we will talk again tomorrow if I feel so inclined. Meanwhile, my people will no doubt make you tolerably comfortable.'

Later he said to Allembeau: 'I'm afraid my little trick with the dead brother hasn't worked so far. He looked astonished and possibly frightened to hear his brother was alive but it did nothing to make him more communicative.'

'How long can we hold him?'

'A few days, I imagine. We'll keep him under lengthy and very boring interrogation. Maybe we'll locate a chink in the armour, though at the moment I could not tell you where it is to be found.'

But Baum's estimate of how long Alexandre Jaloux could be held proved optimistic. The following morning, the private secretary to the minister of the interior, next door in the Place Beauvau, phoned Georges Wavre and asked him to be good enough to step over. When Wavre was in his office, the private secretary looked embarrassed.

'I am sorry to appear to intervene in DST matters,' he said, 'but the minister has had strong representations from the ministry of defence. It appears that you are holding one Alexandre Jaloux.'

'So I understand.'

'Defence tell us that this man's release has been urgently requested by the DGSE. It appears that he is involved in a mission on their behalf. You know how it is with these intelligence outfits: one cannot ask what the mission is or how important the individual may be to its outcome. At all events, the minister has promised that the man Jaloux will be released at once.'

'Very inconvenient,' Wavre said. 'He is a material witness in a most serious case in which the president of the republic is taking a personal interest. Perhaps that fact should be conveyed to the minister.'

'The minister has expressed the view that the man can always be contacted later and he has had the assurance of Defence that he is not the type of individual who would become a fugitive. The DGSE has apparently been reassuring on that point.'

'I will want a memo from the minister. I am not prepared to release Jaloux except under instructions from above.'

'I can arrange that, *monsieur le directeur*.'

'I am sorry, Alfred,' Wavre said to Baum later. 'The boss says let him go, so we must let him go.'

'As a matter of fact,' Baum said, 'I think he may be more useful to us at large than he is in here. He won't talk and I have no real confidence in my ability to get him to do so in the few days I can hold him. But I am glad you objected officially. It could come in handy later.'

'No doubt.'

'Over at the ministry did they say anything about him beyond the order to let him go?'

'No.'

'Nothing about how he is to be treated in the future?'

Wavre narrowed his eyes and looked at Baum as if to say he knew there was a dangerous ploy in the latter's mind and he, Wavre, was not going to stand for it.

'They said nothing about the future, but that does not give you a free hand, my dear fellow, and you know it.'

'I need a free hand.'

'What are you planning?'

'Consider,' Baum said. 'It is clear to us that this man is a dangerous crook. A very dangerous crook indeed. The usual wire-pulling has forced us to let him go. But is anyone seriously suggesting that we simply put him out of our minds? Do nothing? Shrug him off?'

'Come on, now, what are you getting at? I am used to your softening-up technique. It does not impress me any more.'

'I want to put tails on him. Day and night. I want to harass him until he gets nervy enough to do something stupid. Then I shall want to pull him in again, and hopefully they won't dare try the same trick twice.' He smiled disarmingly. 'That is all I want to do.'

'And will you personally go over to Defence and calm them down when the trouble starts?'

'If you wish.'

They looked at each other. Slowly, a broad grin spread across Wavre's face. Baum looked solemn. Unspoken signals

278

passed between them, based on mutual trust and some affection.

'Get out of my office,' Wavre said at last. 'Don't come in here babbling about these wild schemes of yours.'

'You don't want to know?'

'I don't want to know.'

Downstairs in his office, Baum called in Allembeau and two of his inspectors and organized a detail of eight men with transport whose task would be to make Tavernet's life thoroughly miserable.

'When he breaks, as he will,' Baum told them, 'we have to know, and know at once. Otherwise the whole effort will be wasted. He will decide to go somewhere. I do not know where, nor how he will travel. But sooner or later they always make a dash for it and that is the moment of truth. If he disappears from under your noses I shall make myself exceedingly unpleasant and I wouldn't be surprised if those responsible found themselves back on the beat somewhere in the provinces.' He looked amiably round the room. 'In uniform.'

He dismissed the inspectors and signalled Allembeau to remain.

'I propose to delay the release of our friend until after midnight tonight. Before that time I want a bug planted in his apartment. It had better be undetectable by those electronic gadgets they supply, which means putting it in the telephone. And that will suit me because it is phone conversations that interest me. Who is free?'

'Massé is the only one you can rely on to do the job properly and leave no trace.'

'Fix it for me. It will have to be done around midnight, which is a tricky time because people are coming home from their evenings on the town. Impress upon Massé how sensitive the whole thing is.'

'There will be an almighty row if it goes wrong.'

Baum bestowed a broad smile on Allembeau. 'You are most perceptive.' He allowed the smile to fade from his face. 'And so, nothing whatever must go wrong. You will tell Massé that. And fix up the listening post with your usual

279

care, only don't use men in cars parked outside Tavernet's front door. That man's not a fool.'

'One of the radio vans?'

'Possibly. But for God's sake place it round the corner or in a parallel street. You've got what — a couple of hundred metres' range?'

'That's about it.'

'Keep a personal eye on it for me, old fellow.'

As Allembeau left his office the phone rang. It was the inspector in Aubagne. He sounded excited.

'I handled it the way you said, chief, and in the end the fellow talked.'

'So?'

'Detonators are missing.'

'In the plural?'

'Yes, chief; and it's not the only thing in the plural.'

'No riddles, please.'

'Sorry, chief, but he swears two Plutons were taken, not one.'

'You believed him?'

'Yes, chief.'

'Right, come home. I will sign for the money.'

Baum rang off and made his way back to Georges Wavre's office on the floor above.

'The question,' he said, 'is do we tell them at the Elysée that two missiles with detonators have been taken, and not the army's one unusable missile?'

'And that the army is telling lies?'

'A clear inference.'

'I would welcome your opinion.'

'We don't tell.'

'What are you telling Jerusalem?'

'The truth. I have to.'

'Will they keep their mouths shut?'

'Yes. They don't need a public quarrel with us and they don't need panic at home until they are obliged to have it, as they will be.'

'If the president learns the truth,' Wavre said, 'we'll have one of his famous explosions. I have no desire to be placed

in charge of a training school for traffic policemen somewhere in Brittany.'

'Isn't it odd,' Baum said, 'how those in power contrive to
be told all these lies?' He smiled and shook his head. 'From
the point of view of my inquiries I think the lower profile
presented by a single relatively harmless Pluton would suit
me best.'

'And what about your inquiries?'

'I have close to thirty of our inspectors deployed in Marseilles and we have put a special search on all merchandise
being loaded in the port. It is, of course, a physical impossibility to open up every container or to search every cargo
hold, so we've been concentrating on ships sailing for Mediterranean ports. Even there, we have done hardly more than
an extended spot-check, but I am being as thorough as I
can.'

The DST progress report to the Elysée that day spoke
reassuringly about the Marseilles deployment. It said nothing
on the subject of detonators or a second bomb.

Baum's telephone rang as he prepared to go home to
Versailles that evening.

'Kovacs here, Monsieur Baum. I think we should meet
again, if you can spare the time.' Despite the studied politeness, Baum detected an unusual undertone of urgency in
Kovacs' voice.

'By all means. Let us make it a half-hour from now at the
bar near the Madeleine.'

'Excellent. I am much obliged to you.'

The bar in the Rue Vignon was much patronized by
middle-priced hookers exchanging anecdotes about their
tricks. Now it was empty. Kovacs did not waste time over
small politenesses.

'I am to tell you that at least one member of the group
which interests us is travelling very soon to Israel.'

'When?'

'I was not told.'

'Do you know the identity?'

'Her *nom de guerre* is Rasmia Burnawi.'

'We know the lady.'

'She will arrive at Ben Gurion airport. I do not know the name under which she will travel. And now comes the important part.' He leaned forward to add emphasis to what he had to say. 'I am to tell you most insistently that the Israeli authorities would be well advised to let her through.'

'Why?'

'All I can say is that it will greatly increase the chance of avoiding a catastrophe.'

'You cannot expect the Israelis to take such a risk on the word of a consistently hostile power.'

Kovacs sighed. 'Surely, my dear Monsieur Baum, there is someone in Jerusalem intelligent enough to understand what we are trying to do here. My friends find themselves in a difficult situation politically. That they are permitting me to give you information of this kind, however, is a measure of their concern. Is it not obvious?'

'It may be obvious to you and even to me, but I doubt if they can see it that way in Jerusalem. Surely the thing smells of double-cross?'

'What can I say?' Kovacs shrugged expressively. 'All we need is someone in Jerusalem to realize that the lady in question is – how shall I put it without betraying confidences – not all she seems? Yes, not at all what she seems can perhaps sum it up.'

'I will do my best.'

'You must, Monsieur Baum, you really must.' And Kovacs got up, extended a hand, shook Baum's heavy paw, and made an elegant exit from the seedy bar.

Later, from his usual bistro in Versailles, Baum told Ben Tov in Jerusalem what Kovacs had said.

282

Chapter 30

In line with the regulations the MV *Croix Valmer* cabled her position report to the Israeli Ministry of Transport when she had reached a point fifty miles from the coast. The report gave her name, position, course, speed and her destination, which was the port of Haifa. Soon afterwards she radioed the same information to the port operation services in Haifa and received permission to proceed. When she was still seaward of the harbour's main breakwater she slowed to take a pilot aboard, the crew busying themselves with preparations for berthing, the master filling forms to meet the port regulations. The pilot saw her safely to a cargo jetty in the main harbour. A crane was moved forward in readiness to take off her containers. On the quayside the crew looked down on the usual group of officials concerned with health, immigration, customs and commercial matters. But on this occasion there was a larger group of port security men and uniformed police.

After she had tied up, the gangway was lowered and the crew watched as the Israelis climbed aboard.

'Exceptional measures, captain,' the security officer in charge announced as he shook hands.

'What measures?'

'There's been some kind of alert here. My men will be searching the ship, including the cargo. No one goes ashore until we pronounce you clean.'

'That's very inconvenient. How long will your search be lasting?'

'No idea. Maybe until nightfall, maybe longer. If I have your co-operation things will go as fast as may be.'

'Naturally, you have my co-operation.'

'Cargo will be examined at the dockside. Containers will be lifted off and opened before being cleared for onward movement. Meanwhile, we will be looking over your ship.'

The captain shrugged. 'I hold you responsible for any damage to the vessel or its cargo.'

'I have no instructions on that point, captain. We will try not to smash things up.'

The search, which resembled the search in Marseilles though it was far more thorough, lasted throughout the day until nightfall. This time there was no question of spot-checks. Every container was opened up, the contents taken out, examined and stacked, and then returned. Bales and crates were opened and the goods inside scrutinized. Meanwhile, a team of close to twenty security men and police went through the *Croix Valmer* from bows to stern. The Geiger-Müllers were passed over everything. Nothing was found.

No identity cards were issued to the crew by the port police and the crew remained on board throughout the day and overnight. By midday the following day the search was complete.

'Okay, captain, everything is in order. Your cargo is released and you can go ahead with replacing ship's stores.'

'And my crew?'

'Port police will issue identity cards for those who want to go ashore. Thank you for your co-operation.'

They shook hands and the officer went ashore and moved on to a vessel from Livorno in the next berth.

Shortly afterwards a young man detached himself from the gang working on the cargo on the dockside, mounted the gangway and climbed up to the bridge. He spent a few minutes with the captain before returning to his work.

Later in the afternoon the gas bottles were cleared from the fo'c's'le, lowered on to the quayside and loaded aboard a lorry for transport to the company which held a contract for refilling them. The lorry was driven out of the port main gate and covered the short distance to the bottling plant in a few minutes. By the time it arrived the plant was closing down for the night. The lorry was driven into the yard.

'We'll unload in the morning,' the foreman said. 'Leave it at the back of the yard.'

The driver parked the lorry and made his way out on foot, cursing the fact that for some reason the master of the *Croix Valmer* had delayed clearing him until it was damn nearly closing time.

Shortly before 2 a.m. three men drove up to the gates of the plant and forced their way in with a crowbar. They searched through the cluster of gas bottles in the lorry, using a dim torch. Two of the bottles, slightly larger than the rest, were manhandled down and carried out to the car waiting in the roadway. They were stored in the back and covered with a blanket. The gates were closed and the car was driven away southwards along the coast road, striking inland at Hadera, just ahead of a roadblock which had been set up south of the junction.

It was that evening that Ben Tov had his big row with the Memuneh – a row that had been gestating for months.

'It serves me right,' Ben Tov said to his wife when he got home. 'It was nothing but stupid pride. Arrogance even. I didn't want to be thought to be failing.'

'So?'

'So I told that *nebbich* my plans. Just to show I had plans.'

'And?'

'And naturally, he ordered me to change them. Why? Because otherwise he had no role to play, and for him a role is always needed, to prove to himself he is the boss. No is his favourite word.'

'And is this unknown change to a plan of which I am totally ignorant so disastrous for mankind?'

'Yes.'

He pursued his meal in silence, attacking the food as if it shared the blame. His wife knew the signs, said nothing until he had finished.

'And how bad was this row you had with the Memuneh?'

'Bad. I told him the truth.'

'What truth?'

'That only his stupidity prevents him from perceiving how incompetent he is.'

'You said that?'

'And more.'

'I do not want to hear.'

Later she said, 'So you will lose your job. There are other jobs. Many of them with less anger.'

'I can't help it. I bring the anger to the job, not the other way round.'

'Meanwhile . . .'

'Meanwhile they will not move me until this case is settled one way or the other.'

'And you will defer to the Memuneh in this change of plans?'

'Of course not.'

The row had been about the Chatila case. More specifically, about Rasmia. With a momentary lack of caution Ben Tov had told the Memuneh: 'We will let her in. She will lead us to the bombs.'

'Unwise,' the Memuneh had said. 'If they are risking sending her here it is because she is needed in order to make this atomic blackmail succeed. What if you lose her?'

'What if the sky falls in? Since when can we guarantee success in such a business?'

'The risk is disproportionately high.'

'No doubt,' Ben Tov said drily, 'you are wondering what you would say to the minister in the event of failure.'

A red flush rose slowly from the Memuneh's neck, ending just beneath his eyes.

'You will withdraw that imputation.'

'I impute nothing, but I withdraw if that is your wish.'

'In any case, if we pick the girl up on entry we can make her talk. Hayesh's unit . . .'

'You do not understand the fanaticism. These are committed people. We'll have a nasty-looking corpse on our hands – that and a tape with sickening sounds on it but no information.'

'I do not agree and I order you to organize the arrest.'

Ben Tov decided that he had to take a chance with the Memuneh. 'There is more to her,' he said.

'What more?'

'I am informed that she is KGB.'

'And is that an additional reason for letting her in? You must be mad.'

'I am also informed that the Russians do not want atomic explosions in Israel.'

'You would have to prove that to me.'

'Obviously, I can't prove it, but I would have thought it was obvious. That crazy they aren't.'

'How can I be expected to sanction a plan to admit an Arab terrorist who is also KGB?'

'I admit, it would take imagination.'

'It would take criminal irresponsibility.'

And it was at that point that Ben Tov had made his remark about incompetence and the Memuneh had ordered him from the room. Back in his own office he realized the full significance of what he had done. He picked up the phone and dialled the Memuneh's number.

'I have considered what you said. I see the point. The girl will be arrested on arrival.'

Like that, they wouldn't take the thing out of his hands, give it to Section 2 and ensure they got hold of her for interrogation. Like that, he could see that his men let her through.

'I know no other way,' he muttered to himself, justifying his insubordination, his anger.

An MTB had set out from the Lebanese coastal village of Jounie soon after 23.00 hours. Its course was a shallow arc, giving it a landfall some thirty kilometres south of Haifa. It hove to some three kilometres offshore and put an inflatable dinghy over the side. Four men exchanged embraces with the man driving the MTB and climbed over the side and into the dinghy. They had paddles; the dinghy had no motor. Dipping their paddles carefully, they made for the shore, heading for a light which flashed at thirty-second intervals. Their weapons and radio equipment were in waterproof bags strapped to their bodies. A few hundred metres offshore they sank the dinghy, slipped into the water and struck out for the beach from which the signals were coming. They did not

287

expect to survive the operation and thus had no further use for the dinghy. It was 03.40 hours when they emerged from the water and joined the man who had been operating the signals.

'You were lucky,' the man said, 'there's an alert here, with extra troops along the coast and some new radar.' He spoke Arabic haltingly.

Dry clothing was distributed and the men changed hastily. The weapons and equipment were unpacked.

The man who had welcomed them said, 'Let's go. It's a hundred metres to the road. The car's waiting. Follow me.'

The El Al flight from Rome had landed on time, and as the tenders were driven up to surround the 707, the passengers hustled themselves into a dense phalanx, shuffling forward to the desks where the Israeli immigration procedures were being applied by young men with immobile faces. On either side of the barrier were more young men in uniform, each with a hand firmly gripping the butt of the automatic slung round his shoulder. All this was the visible sign of Ben Gurion airport's tight security. There were other links in the chain, but not visible, these. There were baggage handlers who looked too alert for the job. And there were civilians hanging about who appeared to be waiting for flights which never arrived, or perhaps never took off. On this occasion much of this additional activity was under the control of Ben Tov, as were certain taxis and some youths on motorbikes who idled in the mid-afternoon heat of the airport's arrival zone.

As the crowd on the air side were squeezed into two columns ahead of immigration they came within the field of view of two television cameras feeding twin screens in one of the airport security offices. Essat watched intently as, each in turn, the passengers came into view and then passed out of camera range.

Rasmia had almost passed out of the frame of the TV screen before Essat realized with a start who he had been looking at. She resembled one of the Scandinavian blondes who seemed to thrive – for a short time – in the savage heat and harsh work routines of the Negev kibbutzim. The hair of the blonde wig hung down her back. The large, fashionable sunglasses hid the upper part of her face. A Scandinavian sun freak; or maybe the dark skin denoted the north of Italy, where they also grew tall blondes nowadays. It was the bag that gave her away — the dark diagonal stripe.

The deal between the Mossad and immigration and the security police was clear: it had been supervised by the Memuneh in person. Essat would signal Rasmia's arrival to the men at passport control and she would be followed through the baggage hall and customs. If she made contact in the arrival concourse the arrest was to include whoever met her. If there was no contact they would take her on her own.

'What you will do,' Ben Tov had said, 'is this. You will watch every incoming flight until you see her. You will then signal another girl on that flight — any girl who could be said to resemble her and could conceivably be an Armenian. Try to pick one of our nice Israeli kibbutzniks who'll be able to prove easily that there's been a big mistake. Meanwhile, your Rasmia should get through quite comfortably with all the bright security lads plotting their little arrest of our decoy. As for the Rasmia girl, you'll arrange a suitable signal with our own boys. Understood?'

'Understood.'

'God forbid that we should lose her. Oh, yes, and don't forget to apologize for your mistake afterwards. Blame it on the lousy quality of the television image.'

As the double line of passengers shuffled slowly towards the immigration desks Essat kept his eyes on the screen, looking for his kibbutz Armenian. Into the frame came a young couple, the man a lanky blond, the girl dark, a floppy hat partly obscuring her face. Essat picked up the phone.

'The one in the big hat in the left-hand line. She has a dark shoulder bag. The man with her has an armful of magazines and papers. They're out of the frame now.'

'I can see them. You're sure?'

'That's her all right.'

'And the man?'

'No idea.'

Rasmia reached the desk and slid her passport towards the officer. It was Italian. He flicked it open, searching for visas and entry stamps, then back to the page bearing a photograph. He looked at it, looked up at Rasmia, then back to the picture.

'Signorina Pecelli?'

'Yes.'

'Why are you in Israel?'

'I am a tourist.'

'Where will you visit?'

'Jerusalem. Also, I hope to tour to other places.'

'Your first time in our country?'

Rasmia nodded.

'Please remove your sunglasses.'

Her hand was steady as she held the glasses away from her face for a moment. The man looked at her. Satisfied, he snapped the passport shut and handed it back.

'Enjoy your stay.' He said it mechanically as he turned to a matron who was next in line. The manual said welcome them.

Rasmia replaced her glasses, took her time retrieving the passport and dropping it into the striped bag. Then she moved on towards the baggage hall. As the carousel began to trundle its load past the waiting travellers, Essat was instructing his men and several had passed through the baggage hall to take a look at their quarry.

Meanwhile, the dark girl who had been fingered by Essat had retrieved a holdall from the carousel. Together with the young man, whom she had met during the flight, she made her way out and into the crowd waiting to greet the arriving passengers. When she fell into the arms of her fiancé – like her, a native Israeli from Haifa – the security men, pistols drawn, advanced from several directions and arrested all three of them.

Rasmia emerged from customs carrying a small bag. As she threaded her way through the waiting crowd towards the exit she looked carefully around her. Ben Tov's men were surprised at what happened next. She was approached by a youth with the deathly pale, raggedly bearded face of the seminarist. He wore a skull cap. His side curls dangled limp and greasy almost to his shoulders. They exchanged a few words, then she handed him her case and they made off together, out towards the car park and the waiting taxis. As they went, a taxi driver was talking quietly into his microphone. Then he started the cab's engine and began to roll slowly towards the car park. As he passed a young man standing idly by a motorbike he nodded, and the man got astride his machine. When Rasmia and the youth had reached a yellow Ford the taxi driver activated his mike again.

'Shmuel here. The car's a Ford Cortina. Battered. Yellow, with a lot of dust. I am trying to get the registration number but the plate's filthy. Probably intentional. I can see a seven . . . a seven two, and I think zero. You'll have to make do with that.' There was a pause. 'They're in the car . . . driving out of the car park . . .'

The radioed messages continued intermittently until the yellow Ford was out of the airport and heading towards the junction where airport traffic joined the Tel Aviv–Jerusalem highway. The taxi which had been following them carried on south towards Ramla, while the young man on the bike followed the yellow car northwards on to the Jerusalem road. Another car was parked on the hard shoulder a couple of kilometres up the road, and the girl in the driving seat was monitoring the messages. When she heard that the yellow car had left the junction and was on its way towards her she drove on to the road.

'He's doing sixty. I suggest you do fifty-five and let him overtake you. Then keep after him.'

'Understood,' she said into the mike and moved her speed up towards fifty-five. Soon she saw the yellow car in her mirror and allowed it to catch up with her gradually. The young man on the motorbike then overtook Rasmia's car and speeded northwards. When the Cortina had overtaken the girl's car she allowed it to get a few hundred metres ahead of her and then gradually increased her speed to keep it in sight.

The manoeuvre was repeated as the Cortina approached the intersection with the Ramallah road, where a van took over, and again as they passed Kiryat Ananim at the approaches to the city. As they came into the suburbs the car now on the tail of the Cortina was a scruffy Mercedes which handed over to a motorcyclist as the Cortina emerged from Weizman Boulevard and moved down the Jaffa Road towards the city centre. But it suddenly struck northwards on side streets and the motorcyclist nearly lost it at a set of traffic lights and again in the thickening traffic on Malchei Israel.

'They seem to be heading for Me'a She'arim,' he radioed.

'Hand over at Shivtei Israel.'

But the Cortina never got that far. It stopped sharply at one of the gates into the Me'a She'arim religious quarter and the young man and Rasmia got out.

'They're going into Me'a She'arim. Do I follow on foot?'

'Follow on foot. We have a couple of men in a car at the corner of Shivtei Israel. They'll join you. Do a careful job.'

'Understood.'

The Me'a She'arim quarter, outside the walls of the Old City, is inhabited exclusively by the ultra religious. It is a warren of dusty lanes, synagogues, of which there are dozens, and seminaries – *yeshivas* – where children and youths are taught the holy scriptures and prepared for a life of devotion. Among the many religious groupings in the quarter are fanatical sects which yield nothing to the Moslem fundamentalists in passion, violence and religious mania. There is no traffic in Me'a She'arim, no entertainment, only a resolute clinging to the past and a desperate, all-enfolding yearning for the coming of the Messiah.

Rasmia and her escort walked rapidly up one of the cobbled streets. There were few people about. An old man sat alone in the sun, rocking slowly to and fro, muttering. There were mangy cats, straggling vines covered in dust, walls patched, plaster crumbling, the smell of spices, and floating above it all the wailing and muttering of men and boys at their prayers.

'I am a Jew, not a Zionist' said a notice in Yiddish on the wall of a house. And across the way: 'Zionist desecration of Jewish graves'.

The men wore broad-brimmed hats, long black coats and leggings. Their side curls hung below their ears. The women wore head scarves. Their arms were covered. 'The Torah obligates to dress in a modest manner', on a poster peeling from an ancient wall. The notices and posters were in Yiddish, fulminating against the government, enjoining the inhabitants to live a pious life free from sin. Nowhere was there a word of Hebrew. A man stood, his palm outstretched. 'For the poor of the neighbourhood.' It was a statement, not a request.

The young man who had ridden the motorbike was afraid to approach too close. 'They are not, repeat not to know they are being followed,' he had been told at the briefing. 'Nor are they to be lost.' He wondered now if the two instructions were going to be compatible. The conditions in the quarter were impossible. No shops. No cover, and above all, no crowds in which to lose oneself. And where were the two others he'd been promised?

Rasmia and her companion were walking fast. They disappeared round a bend in the lane and the young man broke into a run to get them back into sight. But when he reached the corner they were nowhere to be seen. Panic seized him. He'd lost the quarry and there would be blue murder back at the unit. Ben Tov would go crazy. There were two narrow lanes leading off the cobbled thoroughfare. He tried each of them in turn. Nothing. He inspected the houses on either side. Two were seminaries, other seemed to be dwelling houses, and there was a small synagogue. Outside, a group of old men were muttering to each other, heads shaking, beards wagging in disbelief. One stood alone, thumbing through an almost derelict prayerbook.

'Have you seen a young lady and a man just go this way?'

The old man stared at him with rheumy eyes then returned to the book.

'Grandad, I asked you, a young woman and a man.'

The old man looked up again. 'Go away. I saw nothing.'

The young man returned to the cobbled lane, retraced his steps, despair in his heart. He had lost the quarry. Ben Tov would go crazy.

'At least,' Essat said, 'we know they are somewhere in Me'a She'arim. Can't we do a house-to-house?'

'We'd need a hundred men. And we're not supposed to be looking for anyone.'

'But if she's what we're told she is, surely she'll make contact?'

'Certainly, provided my friend in Paris was right, which requires his informant to have been right and also the Burnawi woman to be what they think she is, plus her being able to contact us. Which is a dubious proposition when you consider that she must now be surrounded by her colleagues in the Chatila gang.'

There was a long silence in Ben Tov's room. They looked miserably at each other. The storm about the mistaken arrest at Ben Gurion had not broken yet. There were no more incoming flights that day and Essat was back in Jerusalem. He would return early the following morning to resume his watch at the airport.

'It's a pity about the car,' Essat said. 'It might have yielded a clue.'

'It's a pity about many things, including the car, and the Arab-Israeli conflict, and Gadafi and the Syrians, and our own lunatics who like tó kill Arabs – all this is no doubt a pity.'

When Ben Tov's men had returned to examine the yellow Cortina, abandoned at the edge of Me'a She'arim, it was no longer there. Someone had planned matters with care. Ben Tov had been particularly biting about this further failure.

'I expect it can't be long now before Chatila makes its demands known, and at that point everything changes. I will devise a way of liberating you from your ridiculous vigil at Ben Gurion,' he told Essat.

Later that evening he expressed his regrets to the Memuneh over the understandable but troublesome mistake about identities at the airport.

'And you still expect this woman to arrive?'

'I know nothing to the contrary,' he told the Memuneh.

Chapter 31

At 9.05 on the following morning an envelope was delivered at the editorial office of *Le Monde* in Paris. It was addressed to the foreign editor and marked NEWS RELEASE IMMEDIATE. The foreign editor was not in his office and the envelope found its way to one of the journalists on the foreign desk. He tore it open absently, joking with the girl at the desk next to him. Then he glanced at the sheet of paper it contained, half expecting that it would end up on the spike. The message had been crudely typed on a page torn from an exercise book. The headline read: CHATILA DEMANDS ON ISRAEL. Then he read on:

This message is to be conveyed to the authorities in Jerusalem without delay. Chatila states the following:

Two atomic bombs are now securely planted on the soil of Palestine by Chatila. For the Zionists it is the moment of truth after forty years of genocide. Unless all our demands are met promptly and in full, one of these bombs will be detonated 36 hours after this ultimatum is received in Jerusalem. We assume time of receipt to be 13.00 hours today. These demands are as follows:

1: The West Bank and Gaza will be evacuated by all Jewish forces and civilians within three days. There will be no scorched-earth policy.

2: Zionist stocks of atomic weapons will be surrendered to a United Nations force and will be removed from the country under UN supervision.

3: All Arab detainees in the jails will be released at the Lebanese frontier within 24 hours.

4: The Zionists will themselves dynamite the West Wall within 24 hours so that no trace remains of this symbol of the illegal Jewish control of Jerusalem.

5: As a token of sincerity in carrying out these conditions, 50 mayors of Jewish-controlled cities will present themselves at the Syrian frontier within 24 hours to constitute themselves hostages in Syrian hands. We will then formulate our longer-term political demands which will deal with the question: What Jewish state, if any, will henceforth be permitted in part of Palestine.

These are our conditions. The authorities in Jerusalem will broadcast their response on their regular news bulletins. It should be understood that the above demands are not negotiable.

The Zionist are to understand that this, at last, is their moment of truth – the battle of the great day of God Almighty when there fell upon men a great hail out of heaven. Their history surely teaches them that this day was to come. On this day their iniquities will be punished unless they redeem themselves at the last by accepting in full our just demands, made in the name of the oppressed Palestinian people.

Chatila

The ultimatum reached Jerusalem at 12.15 hours local time. By then the morning radio and television programmes in France had been interrupted for news flashes. Within an hour the BBC in London and broadcasts throughout Europe were running the story and newspapers and television companies around the world were getting their crews on to planes for Tel Aviv.

The president of the United States had been aroused from his sleep to approve a statement in his name. It took the form of a solemn warning to any country which might harbour Chatila or act as an intermediary. Syria was told that the US would regard the accepting of Israeli hostages as complicity with Chatila. An hour later contact between the White House and the Kremlin had been established.

'The Russkis seem to want to play ball,' the president's security adviser said. 'They claim Chatila is not one of theirs.'

296

'Are the sons of bitches lying or what?' the president asked.

'I guess they're telling the truth. They sound as scared as hell about escalation in the Middle East.'

'Me too,' the president said. 'What are our options?'

He was told that their options were few and not impressive. But several units of the 6th fleet would be in Israeli waters by the following morning.

'It'll probably have to be a rescue operation of some kind,' someone said.

'Christ, we can't lift off a whole population.'

'If these lunatics explode their bomb the only useful thing will be to rush in doctors and medical supplies.'

An aide was told to get contingency plans moving and to call the International Red Cross in Geneva.

The president's mind worked in short bursts of simple, even stark, ideas, which did not always relate usefully to each other. 'Can we tell 'em we'll hit the Syrians if they explode the damn thing?'

The security adviser sighed. 'The word for that, Mr President, is escalation. The Soviets couldn't stay out. You'd be heading for a war situation.'

'But if a Syrian group threatens an atomic attack on Israel, surely we should tell the bastards we'll drop one on Damascus?'

'But would we, Mr President?'

'Why the hell not?'

'Moscow, Mr President. Moscow couldn't stand by and watch it happen. And in any event, once Israel had been nuked there'd be no point in doing anything but clear up the mess.'

'But we can't sit on our asses and do nothing.'

'Our problem is how to send a credible signal to the Syrians ahead of the event. This Chatila group is based in Damascus and no one can tell us the Syrians don't know what's going on in their own capital.'

The president's attention span had been exceeded. 'Prepare me some options and we'll talk some more over breakfast.'

The Israeli cabinet met early in the afternoon, the Memuneh and the mayor of Jerusalem in attendance. The sole topic on the agenda was the threat facing the country. The members of the cabinet had received a report from the Mossad. It said nothing of how the bombs had entered the country – since the Mossad did not know – and nothing of Rasmia.

The prime minister called on the minister of defence.

'If we assume for a moment that this report is well founded,' the minister said, 'it seems to me that we have two courses of action open to us, both of which must be pursued. The first is to redouble the efforts of the intelligence arm to locate those controlling the weapons; the second is to mount in the immediate future a total search of the country and particularly of the city, which will involve house-to-house searches everywhere and the examination of all other buildings. For this we will mobilize the army, the police and other appropriate services. Also, we need to appoint a sub-committee of the cabinet to supervise the exercise. As to the demands, they are clearly unacceptable.'

'An atomic explosion on our soil is equally unacceptable,' the prime minister said. 'We must try to negotiate.'

'You realize,' the minister of the interior said, 'that we are faced with an unimaginable panic. There is no precedent anywhere in the world for such a situation. I fear keeping order in the streets may become the first priority.'

'The search will have to go forward rapidly. When can we start?'

'We will start right away,' the mayor of Jerusalem said.

'What other proposals do I have?' The prime minister turned to the minister for foreign affairs. 'We have not heard from you, Chaim.'

'I am puzzled,' the minister said. He lifted a sheet of paper and waved it at his colleagues. 'I have a telex from our people in Paris. They say there are strong rumours in press circles that a single Pluton warhead is missing from a French arsenal – a warhead minus its detonator. Our people believe the story has been leaked deliberately by the French defence department, presumably to defuse a bigger story of some kind, or maybe to dampen a possible scandal about French security in the atomic field.'

'Are you suggesting this group got one bomb from the French and one somewhere else?'

298

'That, or the second bomb does not exist, or there are two French bombs.'

There was a silence as the assembled ministers wrestled with the complications of this theory.

'Chaim, your ingenuity is well known, but this goes too far. What would be the point?'

'I have no idea. All I know is that I do not believe a terrorist group could have the resources and skills to steal two atomic weapons from different sources. One is already a triumph.'

'We have to check out this French rumour,' the prime minister said. He turned to the Memuneh. 'Something for you, I fancy.'

The Memuneh nodded.

'What else, Chaim?'

'Are we to say anything publicly about the French origin of the bomb?'

'It looks,' the prime minister said, 'as if the French have managed to muzzle their media. So if they want to hush the thing up, who are we to make it hard for them?'

'But – '

'But nothing, Chaim. You will let the Quai d'Orsay know we know, and you will not make yourself unpleasant when they deny the whole thing, as they will in that inimitable bland manner of theirs. It will produce what is called a state of creative tension between us.' He wagged a finger at his colleagues. 'Can be useful if we live that long.'

'Simultaneously with any action we take here,' the foreign minister said, 'we must ask the Americans what technical help they can give. We will also raise the issue at the United Nations. I have no faith in an approach to the PLO or any of their friends. My understanding is that this Chatila gang is independent of all other Palestinian groups. Nevertheless, some approach should be made, if only for the record.'

'If, God forbid, one of the bombs should go off, what of our civil defence?' the prime minister asked.

'If a bomb is detonated,' the minister of the interior said slowly, 'things will be very simple. It will mean the end of our city, perhaps of our state. Who knows from civil defence?'

'Nevertheless, on such matters one cannot be defeatist. Also, the population will expect to receive advice.'

'We have our plans, as you know. We will put them into operation. Please God, no one will laugh in our faces.'

'I put to the cabinet,' the prime minister said, 'that we will prepare immediately for a search. As to the sub-committee, I will chair, and defence, interior and foreign affairs will attend, together with the mayor and the Memuneh. The first meeting will be immediately after we have finished here. Thank you, that is all, and may God protect us.'

The State Department having instructed him to see the Syrian minister for foreign affairs without delay, the US ambassador in Damascus tried to do just that. But the minister was incommunicado and the ambassador was shunted towards the deputy minister – an evasion on the part of the Syrians which the ambassador interpreted at once as a sign of Syrian complicity.

'My government,' he told the deputy minister, 'is deeply concerned at this latest manifestation of lawless terrorism in the area and would feel constrained to act if the matter is not speedily resolved.'

'With respect, your excellency, why is such a message delivered to us?' The deputy minister's face was a mask of bland and amiable surprise.

'Our understanding is that this Chatila gang operates from this city.'

'If so, it is unknown to us and completely unauthorized. If your excellency would be good enough to supply us with the evidence upon which this assertion is based we will naturally be happy to investigate.'

The ambassador ignored it. 'You realize, minister, the enormity of the thing. The possibility of an atomic explosion with the incalculable consequences for the peace of the region that would flow from it.'

'Of course we realize it.'

'I am to inform your government that the United States could not stand by.'

'If there were such an explosion?'

300

'If there appears to be a genuine risk of such an explosion. The importance of the distinction will not escape you.'

'Indeed. And might I ask what measures . . .' He allowed the question to trail off.

'I have no instructions on the point. But no doubt my government would consider among its options the use of the firmest measures, such as we have been obliged to take in the region in the past.'

He did not mention Libya. The deputy minister didn't need him to draw any maps.

'I will convey what you have said to my government,' the deputy minister said, rising to his feet to signal that he thought the conversation had gone on for long enough.

Back at the embassy, the ambassador drafted a report to the Middle East desk at the State Department which was an accurate enough account of what had been said, followed by a strongly worded appreciation to the effect that the Syrians were in this thing right up to their goddam necks.

Someone at state wrote 'Nonsense!' against this comment in the margin, but by the time the report reached the president's security adviser in the White House, the word had been erased and replaced with a pithy alternative: 'He's damn right, so what degree of force do we use here, bearing in mind that the Syrians have a non-agression pact with mutual aid clauses with the Soviets?'

'This business of the two weapons,' Ben Tov said. 'Are you sure it was two?'

'I am sure.'

'We hear rumours from Paris that it was only one, and minus the detonator.'

There was a short silence on the line as Baum collected his thoughts.

'If you were the military and such weapons were stolen from under your nose, would you not try to minimize what had happened?'

'The military would. I would not.'

'Very well. My investigation has convinced me that two weapons, complete with detonators, were taken.'

'May I quote you?'

'I am afraid not.'

'Why?'

There was another pause. 'Better men than I have been moved to the provinces. And in any case, it would be hotly denied.'

'I understand. But you realize my dilemma. Some of our people, including my boss, cling to the idea that the Chatila threat contains an element of bluff.'

'Please explain.'

'The official French rumour says one bomb. The ultimatum says two. These people prefer to believe the French since that somehow reduces the threat and makes them feel better. Also, they find it hard to credit a bunch of Arabs with the skill and imagination to hijack and transport two bombs. A second bomb isn't needed, they say. If the first bomb is detonated that is the end of the story anyway. If it is discovered and made safe, that will persuade the Israeli government that Chatila's second bomb also exists. And of course, we will be unable to find it since it isn't there, and we'll have to accept Chatila's demands for fear that it *is* there. *Ergo*, my friend, and in either case, a second bomb doesn't *need* to exist. Which, in turn, enables us to believe the French rumour, which we want to believe. It is partly subjective thinking, partly contempt for our opponents.'

'And you?'

'I think it is too complicated and therefore rubbish. We have psychologists and methods analysts and military-political theorists who make a living out of such nonsense.'

'You must leave this problem with me. I will see what can be done.'

'There is very little time. A few hours.'

'I understand.'

'Shalom.'

'Shalom.'

As he left the house in Abarbanel Street, Ben Tov glanced carefully in both directions. There was a parked van a short distance away, its driver sitting idly at the wheel. He shrugged and made his way back to the office. It would be like the Memuneh to get Section 2 to keep an eye on him

302

just to prove that a Memuneh could be neither incompetent nor stupid.

From 8 a.m. onwards in the United States, which was 15.00 hours Israeli time, people with relatives in Israel started phoning to see if all was well with them. What was the atomic scare? Was anything happening? By mid-afternoon those who understood Arabic were picking up garbled and exaggerated accounts from Egyptian and Syrian broadcasts. Then, at 18.00 hours the World Service news bulletin from the BBC in London drew together the American and Israeli ends of the story with a report of a statement by a commentator on Libyan radio that Israel was about to receive her punishment for years of misdeeds. Coming as it did in the measured and authoritative tones of the BBC newscaster, the story had greater impact on those who heard it than anything that had gone before. Crowds began to appear in the centre of the city. Strangers talked to each other. A collective emotion was taking hold. Those who knew members of parliament started telephoning, calling, demanding news.

In the cabinet committee, which had been in continuous session, the prime minister said: 'This is the beginning of the panic we feared.' The secretary to the cabinet was instructed to prepare the draft of a speech. The prime minister would go on television later in the evening. Meanwhile, what was the news?

'There is nothing yet,' the Memuneh said. 'We still believe their aim was to place a bomb here in Jerusalem but we have no evidence that they have succeeded. Our intelligence assessment is that the second bomb is probably a bluff.'

A working party of officials from Interior and Defence had produced a paper which the committee members had read. It was a forlorn attempt to foresee the consequences of two atomic explosions, forlorn because neither the location of the bombs, nor the conditions of detonation, nor the weather could be known. Whatever the parameters, the conclusion was always the same: the crowded country was an almost ideal target. Radioactive fallout would create massive contamination in inhabited areas. Even a bomb of low yield would make Jerusalem uninhabitable, regardless of the

303

location of ground zero. All that was known was that Plutons gave a fifteen-kiloton yield. Small as they were, they were more powerful than the Hiroshima and Nagasaki bombs. It was probable, the paper said, that it would be groundburst rather than airburst, since the bombs were presumably hidden at ground level. This would produce radioactive dust clouds which would contaminate the areas over which they were driven by the wind. About sixty per cent of the fallout would reach the ground within twenty-four hours, giving massive contamination. What happened to the balance was unpredictable. The paper then went on to paint a gloomy picture of the effects of the fireball and blast from a fifteen kiloton explosion.

The minister for foreign affairs had two reports. An official sent to Tunis to meet a representative of the PLO had received categorical assurances that they had no contact with Chatila. 'We believe it would be folly to set the Middle East alight in this way,' the PLO man said. From Washington, the ambassador reported that he had seen the president's security adviser. US naval units at present in the western Mediterranean were proceeding eastwards towards the Israeli coastline. A carefully phrased suggestion that Israel might threaten atomic retaliation against Syria had been met with horror by the Americans. 'In any case,' the minister told his colleagues, 'it wouldn't work. I don't believe the Syrians can control this genie they have let out of its bottle.'

The committee was divided on whether Jerusalem's population should be evacuated.

'It would be chaos. Where would we put them?' someone asked.

'If we don't do it, they'll simply get up and go. The chaos will be greater.'

'They are going already.'

It was true. By evening the exodus from Jerusalem had begun. As if by some collective instinct the population flocked on to the Tel Aviv highway, making for the coast. Cars, carts, bicycles, buses were reduced to a crawl by the thousands struggling coastwards on foot. The crowds were orderly, as if stunned and totally discouraged. No attempt was made to keep them in order and none appeared to be needed. There were appeals on radio and television for calm and discipline. The prime minister's speech was uncertain in tone. 'We will overcome this menace to our state as we overcame previous dangers. The government will not yield to blackmail, as previous governments did not yield. The Lord will not abandon his people. I call on all our citizens to remain calm and not to leave their homes·until the government can issue guidance.' But by then a majority of Jerusalem's population had already left their homes. The panic had spread to Tel Aviv and the other towns and villages of Israel.

The house-to-house search got under way as hundreds and then thousands of police and soldiers were deployed in Jerusalem. No one believed in the idea. At Kiryat Hayovel on the outskirts of the city a young soldier who had slipped away from his platoon, was caught and summarily executed. 'There has to be discipline,' the local commander said, and burst into tears.

Shortly before 22.00 hours the cabinet took their decisions. The army was instructed to send a team of engineers to the West Wall to install explosive charges. A detachment of armed police went with them. The Ministry of the Interior was to see that the mayors assembled on the following morning on the Syrian frontier in the area of Kuneitra. Preparations were made to empty the jails of Arab prisoners, of which there were over 300.

At 22.30 hours Israel radio made its first broadcast intended for Chatila. It announced on behalf of the government that it wished to negotiate and asked Chatila to respond.

An hour later a message was handed to the Italian news agency in Rome. There was nothing to negotiate; Chatila's demands had been made and were not negotiable.

Shortly afterwards the president of Syria stated in a broadcast that despite US warnings he would accept the mayors as hostages since that might ease the way to negotiations.

305

Chapter 32

'What you ask,' Vallat said, 'is politically impossible.'

The president's gaunt and impassive chef de cabinet gave Alfred Baum a look of bleak discouragement. Baum did not allow his own cheerful expression to fade from his face.

'Embarrassing, perhaps. But impossible?'

'Absolutely impossible. Consider the scenario, Monsieur Baum. The minister of defence has stated categorically: one Pluton without detonator. The minister, as you certainly know, is the president's close political ally in the coalition. It is therefore politically impossible to undermine his position. There would be a crisis of the greatest magnitude and we could well be driven to dissolution and a fresh election.'

'And that is so terrible?'

A wintry smile creased the corners of Vallat's thin mouth.

'No politician will endanger his tenure of office unless he has to. And the president is already saddled with a prime minister whose policy is unacceptable to him. And now you ask that it be admitted that two weapons are missing, thus destroying the credibility of the president's closest associate? The press would crucify the administration. The idea is absurd.'

'What if we were to notify the Israelis in confidence that there really are two bombs on their soil?'

'In the first place it would mean admitting that the bombs were French, which we have not done and cannot do. Added to that, the president would effectively have placed his political future in the hands of the Israelis, who would certainly milk the situation for all they were worth. They would only have to threaten a public declaration – the French have told us, and so on – and we would have to concede all manner of demands.'

Vallat allowed himself a stiff gesture of dismissal with his left hand. 'Impossible, Monsieur Baum. And, if I may say so, any leakage to the media now would necessarily lead one to believe that you and your colleagues . . .' He did not finish the sentence, feeling that no conclusion was necessary.

Baum lifted his bulk wearily from his chair.

'Thank you for your time, Monsieur Vallat.'

'Not at all. Please convey my respects to Georges Wavre.'

As Baum reached the door, the thin voice of Vallat reached him once more.

'I have not taken official cognizance of your opinion that two weapons were taken since we have no concrete evidence that Defence are mistaken on the matter. I trust that is understood.'

'We can't do it,' Alfred Baum said later to Ben Tov on the telephone. 'I have had the clearest signals from on high. It will be denied, heads will roll, and it would put paid to our own co-operation since I would no longer be here.'

'But you are absolutely sure . . . ?'

'Absolutely.'

'Two?'

'Two.'

'So how am I to persuade my people here that there must be a second bomb, now that they've seized on this story from Paris that there was only one?'

'The story is a plant.'

'All right. But I am having trouble with my boss. I said some unkind things, and now I am cut off from contact at ministerial level and no longer attend the relevant committee. Everything travels up through him and he has seized on the one-bomb theory. He likes it. It accords with his lack of imagination. How could the French government lie about such a thing? How could an Arab terrorist group manage to steal, transport and smuggle in *two* atomic bombs, for God's sake? If Ben Tov says two, why then it must be one. *I*, the

307

Memuneh, say it's one.' Ben Tov paused. 'Stuff like that. It drives me crazy.'

'Can't you reach someone intelligent on the sly?'

'I intend to.'

'You could also tell this intelligent person something else,' Baum said. 'There is unusually close contact between the man Savary and the Syrians. It could indicate Syrian complicity. Your people should know this.'

'Anything hard?'

'Only the fact of contact. I do not know what they talk about.'

Back in the office, Baum found on his desk the transcripts from the telephone bug in Tavernet's apartment. That morning Tavernet had had a conversation with his office. Among the innocuous material an exchange leapt at Baum from the page.

'You have the ticket?'

'Yes, monsieur. Saturday, the 09.30 flight from Orly to – '

'All right, all right. I didn't ask for details on the phone. What else is there?'

'Monsieur Caracci called again. He said, "Tell him he has until midday Saturday." That was all.'

Baum grunted, re-read the passage. It looks, he said to himself, as if our friend Caracci plus my boys' surveillance have finally got him on the run. Clearly, the man owes money. It is something to be explored.

Then he asked Mlle Pineau to call Orly to find out what was flying out at 9.30 a.m. on Saturday. When he had the answer before him he called Jo Leduc at the Brigade Criminel.

'Another favour, Jo.'

'Always a pleasure, but you're building up a lot of credit.'

'I take it you have a pipeline of some kind into Caracci's gang.'

'Correct.'

'I want you to make sure Caracci knows that Jaloux, *alias* Tavernet, is booked on the 9.30 a.m. flight from Orly to Santiago de Chile on Saturday.'

'That all?'

'Yes, can it be done within the next couple of hours?'

'No problem. Just a phone call.'

To Allembeau he issued firm instructions. 'Keep the lads on Tavernet's tail but if they find someone else is interested they are not to get in the way. I've tipped off Tavernet's creditors and if they decide to settle scores in their own way that's none of our business. If our masters won't let us do the job decently it will have to be done the other way.'

'Are you sure things will work out like that?'

'I am not, and so I want the man intercepted at Orly if he ever gets there. Talk to Giroux of the Police de l'Air and have him picked up after he passes through immigration. Then he should be brought back here.' Baum looked impassively at Allembeau. 'But all that is merely a precaution. I fancy our friend will not get that far. Debts or no debts, I would have thought the man is now a very great embarrassment to his friends over in the Avenue Mortier.'

'You must understand,' Ben Tov said to Mordechai Poran of the Prime Minister's office, 'that I am absolutely convinced the second bomb exists. This man Baum in Paris is an old friend. Also a very smart operator. He gives me his word that there were two bombs, complete with detonators. I do not pretend to understand the politics, but it appears impossible over there in Paris to extract an official admission about the second bomb. The army is covering its ass, as armies do.'

'Your Monsieur Baum,' Poran said, 'a Jew?'

'An Alsatian. Also a friend. He doesn't need to be a Jew in this.'

'It would help.'

'I have known some unhelpful Jews in my time.'

'True. But I interrupted.'

'Talking of unhelpful Jews, the Memuneh believes in one bomb. I do not know who believes what in the committee. All I want is that the prime minister should be a two-bomb man. This you must bring about.'

'The Old Man will get weary of your little private interventions.'

'I do not care.'

'Can I tell him what you have told me?'

309

'Yes, but tell him also that if he uses the information publicly it will put paid to the only fruitful contact we have left in the French intelligence community. My friend will lose his job.'

'The prime minister is not a fool,' Poran said.

'I never thought he was.'

Ben Tov then told Poran what he had heard about the Syrian contact in Paris.

While Ben Tov was talking to his friend Poran at the prime minister's office in Tel Aviv, in Paris the man on duty in the DST car in the Rue Spontini noticed two young men who climbed out of a car just ahead of them and entered No. 26. The DST man glanced at his watch: it was just after 17.00 hours. He made a mental note of the event. Perhaps this was the intervention of third parties that he had been told to ignore.

'Dirty work, no doubt,' he said to his companion. 'One of them looked like Mabert.'

'With luck it'll bring the whole damn exercise to an end. I've had a bellyful. Who's Mabert when he's at home?'

'A thug who works for Caracci.'

The two young men took the lift to the fourth floor. One of them rang the bell of the apartment on the left.

'Yes?' Tavernet's voice came from the far side of the door.

'Registered letter. I need your signature.'

There was the sound of bolts being drawn. Then the door opened. As it did so, the man who had rung the bell threw his full weight against it. Tavernet was thrown back as both men burst into the hallway. They had drawn revolvers.

'What is this?'

'We don't talk in the hall. Aren't you going to ask us to sit down?'

'Who are you?'

'We're from Monsieur Caracci.'

'Put those guns away, please. They are not necessary.'

'We'll see.'

Tavernet led the way into the salon.

'Sit there,' one of the young men said. He waved with his

gun towards a chair. Tavernet sat. The two men seated themselves in front of him.

'The money,' the senior of the two said. He wore reflecting dark glasses. With his eyes invisible it was impossible to discern his expression. The mouth was thin, the nose long and sharp. He had a bad complexion. The gun tapped gently against his thigh as he talked.

'I plan to pay by tomorrow as promised.'

'Tomorrow, Saturday?'

'That's right.'

'Monsieur Caracci wants to know at what time you'll be at his place with the money.'

'I will be there at midday. I told Caracci that when we spoke on the telephone a few days ago.'

The gun tapped against the young man's thigh. His companion hawked and, leaning forward, spat on the carpet just short of Tavernet's feet.

'What the hell is this?' Tavernet's words belied his expression. There was terror written across his pale face.

'We will have the money now,' the young man said. 'And Monsieur Caracci says what with the aggravation and delay there's interest to pay. Fifty per cent.'

'This is ridiculous. I don't keep cash here. I will collect a bank draft from my safe deposit in the morning on my way to Caracci.'

'We think you have no intention of paying.'

'Rubbish. I'd be mad to cross Caracci of all people.'

'That's our view too.'

'So why do you come bursting in here with your guns? It's an outrage. My business relations with Caracci are perfectly straightforward.'

The second man had risen from his chair and was wandering idly round the room. He came to a side table with a large Chinese vase standing on it. He picked up the vase, and with a sudden, brief show of violence, crashed it to the ground.

'I didn't like it,' he said.

Tavernet's eyes travelled from one to the other. There was sweat on his forehead. His hands clasped and unclasped spasmodically.

'I repeat, I do not keep money here.' His voice was weaker, carrying less conviction.

'We have reason to believe that on this occasion you are likely to have substantial sums.' Tap, tap of the revolver. 'In readiness for tomorrow morning.' The thin smile creased the edges of the mouth. 'For your journey.'

The other man had moved over to the glass case containing silver trophies. Holding his gun by the barrel, he brought the butt down hard on to the main sheet of glass, jumping back as lumps of glass crashed to the floor. Then he moved slowly round until he was standing behind Tavernet's chair.

'Shall I hit him?'

'I don't like violence,' his companion said. 'It may not be necessary.' Then, addressing Tavernet: 'Is it necessary?'

Tavernet shook his head. 'Wait, I will see what I can do.'

'We'll come with you.'

Tavernet led the way to a bedroom at the back of the apartment. With the two men standing behind him, he opened a cupboard. Inside, on the floor, stood a small safe. He bent down, manipulated the combination. After a moment a clicking of the mechanism was followed by the solid metallic sound of the bolts drawing back as Tavernet turned the safe's handle. As he did so one of the men dragged him back from the safe, thrust him to the floor and stood over him, the gun pointing at his head.

'All right, we'll do the rest.'

His companion advanced to the safe, rummaged inside.

'There's a gun here. Some papers.' He drew them out and passed them back. 'Not much else.' He straightened up. 'No cash. The little bastard was after the gun.'

'Dear, oh dear,' the other man said. 'Was that wise? I fancy not. So now we'll have to talk much plainer. Here's what we offer you. To save us the trouble of tearing the place apart, you will tell us where you keep the cash. If you do that, we won't hurt you. But if you don't, my friend here, who likes such things, will light a cigarette and simply burn you until you come clean.'

Tavernet was trembling, his eyes fixed on the gun waving gently above him.

'I can make a deal with you fellows,' he said. 'No doubt you'd like to make something for yourselves – something really substantial. Say a hundred thousand each?'

The second man laughed. 'We plan to make that sort of cash anyway. It's too late for you to do us any favours.'

'Now,' his companion said, 'the money.'

Tavernet got to his feet and took a suitcase from under the bed. He opened it on the bed and removed a pile of shirts and underwear. The suitcase had a false bottom. When he had opened it, neat piles of banknotes were revealed.

'Take what you want and leave me alone.'

The men upended the case and the notes fell in bundles on to the bed.

'Looks about right.'

'Maybe, but he's bound to have more. He'd be a fool to give us everything.'

'Stands to reason.'

The one whom the DST man had rightly identified as Mabert came round the bed and stood close to Tavernet, his weasel face inches away from his terrified victim. 'It's like this, monsieur. You see, Monsieur Caracci's instructions are plain, and we always follow instructions, my friend and me. "If he won't talk," Monsieur Caracci said to us, "hurt him until he does. But if he talks and you get the cash without too much trouble, you don't have to hurt him. Just lose him." So you see, monsieur, that is what we now have to do.' The thin smile appeared briefly. 'Lose you.'

The gun came up slowly and as it did so, Mabert seized Tavernet's necktie so that his head was held at half arm's length. Then he pressed the silenced gun to Tavernet's temple and the *phut* of the explosion coincided with the shriek which escaped, half strangled, from Tavernet's throat. He sank slowly to the ground as Mabert let go of his tie.

The two men spent a half-hour ransacking the apartment. Then they loaded what they had found into the suitcase and let themselves out.

'There they go,' the DST man said to his mate as they emerged from the building and walked back to their car. 'They've got some loot, too. I reckon I was right. That

313

was Mabert and it was the intervention we were told to ignore.'

'What intervention?' his mate said. 'I never saw anything.'

'Nor did I.'

Chapter 33

The next day was the Sabbath.

The exodus from Jerusalem, which had continued throughout the night, was different now. Those with energy and enterprise and those with money and resources had left the city. As the dawn light brightened beyond the Judean Hills it revealed a new scene on the roads out of the city. The cars had been replaced by carts and broken-down trucks. There were more people on foot. The city was coughing up its derelicts and incompetents, its simple people who had seen no cause for hurry and were leaving now because it seemed to be what everyone else was doing. Yet even now many of the inhabitants of Me'a She'arim stayed behind.

The mayor of the city had argued with leaders of the zealot groups, including the rabbis who led Neturei Karta.*

'Do you see what kind of madmen we are dealing with? In the name of God Almighty, come to your senses. Or do you prefer to be blown to pieces?'

'It is Shabbat,' the rabbis said doggedly.

'It is arguably the last shabbat you and I will live – the

---

*Certain ultra-Orthodox groups, of which the Neturei Karta is the best known and most intransigent, refuse to register as Israeli citizens, to pay taxes or do military service. They consider the state an 'abomination' since the scriptures say the Jewish state will be set up only after the Messiah comes. The Neturei Karta and similar sects have their main strength, leadership and source of funds in the USA. They speak Yiddish and refuse to speak Hebrew.

315

last Shabbat known in the state of Israel. Have you no interest in this catastrophe?'

'I do not seek a catastrophe,' a rabbi said. 'But nor will I anger the Lord and thus increase his wrath against us.'

'This is the wrath of a mad terrorist. What has that to do with the Lord?'

'Did not Ezekiel say after the destruction of the First Temple, "They will fall by the sword and be prey to wild animals and disease and the land will be left desolate"? And did not Ezekiel also tell us why? "Hashem has laid the land desolate because of their abominations." Is not that event in our history about to be repeated today and for the same reasons – the abominations of you Zionists, the misdeeds of the state, the desecration of the faith? What use, then, is it to take administrative measures, to anger the Lord still further, if this is His will as the holocaust too was His will? Our people are at prayer. It would have been better if you, too, had been at prayer. Instead, you and the politicians have angered the Lord, so that now He visits this disaster upon us.'

'We wish to search the quarter,' the mayor said.

'It is a desecration.'

'You realize, Rebbe, that we are also called upon to blow up the West Wall.'

'No Jew could bring himself to desecrate the Wall.'

'Perhaps we shall have to.'

'Our people will be ordered there, and if you blow it up you will have to blow them up at the same time. You will have it on your conscience.'

The time was close to 10 a.m. when an army unit passed through the Avodat Yisrael entrance to the quarter and reached the Neturei Karta synagogue and yeshiva.

'Zionist pigs!'

'Abominations in the sight of God! Servants of the devil!'

'Zionist swine!' The curses echoed down the narrow lanes. Boys stoned the soldiers as the struggling Neturei Karta youths in their strange garb, but hatless in the struggle, screamed and bit and flayed with their arms as they were pushed aside by the soldiers, who cursed and sweated, suffering bites and bruises, bespattered with spittle.

316

Nothing was found in Me'a She'arim.

'A hopeless task anyway in this rabbit warren,' the young officer in command of the unit said. He withdrew his men amid curses and shaking fists.

The cabinet committee had been in session all night, a line held open to Washington. By mid-morning no progress of any kind had been made and a further broadcast directed at Chatila remained without response. Also by mid-morning, the mayors had assembled near the frontier. A channel to the Syrians had been opened via the Italian embassy in Damascus. The Italians were also busy in Tripoli, where the ambassador had called on Gadafi, pleading with him to put a stop to the madness in Israel.

The meeting was short and stormy.

'You are here on behalf of the American imperialists, who are trying to save the necks of their puppets in Jerusalem,' Gadafi shouted.

'I am here, your excellency, on behalf of humanity,' the Italian replied. He had been shaken by the stormy reception.

'Talk humanity to the Zionists. They have lessons to learn.'

'I am instructed to ask you to intervene without fixing blame on anyone.'

'I have no influence,' Gadafi said. 'Your own intervention is unacceptable. Damnable!' His fist crashed down on the table before him.

The Italian wondered whether he had not gone too far. 'I am a messenger, excellency,' he said. 'We would not wish this unfortunate incident to damage in any way the cordial political and commercial relations between our two countries.'

'Then please keep out of this thing,' Gadafi said. 'And I repeat: I have no influence in the matter.' And he clapped his hands as a signal to his aide to show the visitor the way out.

The media correspondents who had reached Damascus, and were denied all access to ministers, were filing stories based not on what anyone had said but on who appeared to be calling on whom. It was observed that by midday the Soviet, French and Moroccan envoys had all called at the ministry of foreign affairs in Majlis el Nyaby Avenue. A

317

posse of correspondents and cameramen who had taken up positions at the entrance to the presidential palace in the north-west suburb of the city had to build their stories around the sight of a US embassy car which swept into the forecourt soon after 11 a.m. and left a half-hour later. The ministry of information issued a communiqué and refused to add to it:

'The government of Syria has no knowledge of a group calling itself Chatila. The government does not condone terror or the threatened use of atomic weapons and calls on Israel to meet all reasonable demands of the Palestinians for self-determination.'

Shortly before midday, the cabinet in Jerusalem reconvened and the ministers, dazed from lack of sleep, were presented with a motion by the minister of defence. Fighter-bombers would be readied at three air bases and armed with atomic air-to-ground missiles. A clear threat would be made to Damascus: get Chatila to reveal the location of the bomb or bombs or Syrian targets would be attacked by dusk.

The row in cabinet lasted for a full hour.

'Our moral position would be impossible,' the prime minister said. 'If we threaten to attack before the Chatila deadline and carry out the threat, what if Chatila were bluffing all along? What if the Syrians genuinely cannot control this thing, as I myself suspect? Or on the other hand, if we say we will attack after we have all been blown to pieces, what is the *point* of that? Also, Chaim has already been told three times in three different ways by the Americans that if we use our atomic capability the cause is lost for the future in congress and the nation. That I can believe.' He looked round at his colleagues. 'It is madness.'

In the end the prime minister's view prevailed by a small margin.

The cabinet decided on a response to the ultimatum. The mayors would be handed over at 23.00 hours – two hours before the threatened explosion. The West Wall would be blown up at the same time. Arab prisoners in jails around the country had already been assembled at an army camp in the Galilee. They would be bussed to the frontier and held there for transfer at 23.15 hours.

318

'This timing,' a minister said, 'it is Russian roulette. We leave only two hours to 1 a.m., but how do we know these people can respond in such a short period and in time for us to find the bomb and defuse it?'

'We must give way at the very last minute,' the prime minister said. 'Otherwise, it will be taken as a sign of weakness and their demands will escalate in respect of the second bomb.'

'If it exists,' Defence said.

'It exists,' the prime minister said. 'On that you can take my word.'

'You have information?'

'It exists. We will now discuss our response to the further demands — the ones tied to the second bomb.'

By early afternoon the government had lost control of the situation in the country. Vast crowds had congregated along the Mediterranean shore from Galilee in the north down into the Negev. Units of the US fleet arrived at Haifa and Tel Aviv, ready to take off US citizens, but the commander abandoned the attempt by mid-afternoon when the shore authorities warned him that it would cause riots as the crowds tried to scramble aboard the boats put out by the warships. At Haifa, where the ships were close inshore, hundreds swam out to them and were pulled aboard. The ships were withdrawn to a safer distance.

American TV crews and press correspondents flew in on the last flight from the US before Ben Gurion airport was closed down at 17.00 hours.

'Why hasn't she contacted us?'

Ben Tov asked the question for the tenth time.

'They may be preventing her.'

'So what do we do?'

Essat shrugged. 'Did you get any joy from the cartographers?'

Ben Tov snorted. 'They say there is nothing on the street plans which corresponds to your sketch. No doubt the work was skimped; they didn't believe in it. On the other hand, I put half a dozen of my own people on to the same task and they came up with the same answer.'

'Our only hope now is Rasmia.'

'Unless the search throws something up.'

The time was 21.00 hours.

It was fifteen minutes later that the phone rang.

'I have a call for someone called Essat,' the man on the switchboard said. 'We've nothing on that name in the internal directory.'

'Put it through.'

'I call on Rasmia's behalf,' a voice said.

'Who are you?'

'Who I am does not matter. Am I speaking to Essat?'

'No. Hold, please.'

Ben Tov passed the telephone to Essat, nodding, and picked up the extension.

'Yes?'

'Is this Essat?'

'It is.'

'I call on Rasmia's behalf. She cannot reach a telephone. Please note: at the corner of Sonnenfeld and Rokach in Me'a She'arim there is a synagogue. It is the one built in brick with a dome above. Go down Sonnenfeld and turn into the third lane to the right. On your left you will find a house with a green door. It is there, beneath the floorboards.'

'Who are you?'

'It is not relevant.'

'How do I know this is not a trick?'

'Ask your friend in Paris about Kovacs. You can say I am on the same side as Kovacs.'

'How can we contact you again?'

'You can not. Now hurry. I am told the timer is functioning.'

'One moment. What about the second bomb?'

'She does not know its location yet. We will contact you again when we know more.'

The line went dead. The accent had been that of a Jew from North Africa. It was nothing to go on.

Ben Tov banged his palm against his temple. 'I am a complete bloody fool – blinded by preconceptions. Your

320

sketch said a dome, and what do I do? Assume that an Arab bomb would be planted near a self-evidently Arab place – a mosque. I do not consider in my foolishness that some of our synagogues also have domes. I do not reckon, even after we have traced your Rasmia there, that Me'a She'arim might be the place. What, among all those holy Jews? Ridiculous! Yet, so it appears to be.'

He picked up the phone, dialled a number and spoke to an officer at the army engineers' barracks.

'We are leaving now. Have your men at the corner of Sonnenfeld and Rokach in Me'a She'arim as soon as you can. What? Yes, we think this is it, so send good men. And don't report it back to your ministry in case it's a false trail after all.'

They raced down the stairs and to the car park and drove through the deserted streets as if devils were after them.

By the time they reached the house with the green door, the army unit had caught up with them. A major was in charge. The military had taken Ben Tov's warning seriously.

'We go in hard,' the major said. 'Down with the door then fast through the house. For all we know it's not a timer but a detonator with a madman in attendance to activate it. Speed is what we need.'

The operation was over in little more than a minute. The house was deserted, save for a half-starved cat which cowered in a corner, its fur bristling, strange cries coming from its throat. The major's men began to lift the floorboards, delicately and with minimum force lest the vibration set off the detonating mechanism. Beneath the floor of a back room they found it.

'Not very big,' Essat said, peering at the sleek cylinder.

'It doesn't need to be,' the major said. 'Now the room will be cleared, save for myself and you two.' He designated two of his men. The others crowded out into the lane.

'What can you get on that radio?' Ben Tov asked a sergeant.

'Headquarters.'

'Get them to put me in touch with the prime minister's office. Can they do it?'

The man nodded, got to work. Moments later Ben Tov was speaking to Poran.

'We've found it. It's being defused now. Yes, by the army, who else? If annihilation descends ahead of time in the next half-hour or so you will know that a mistake has been made here. But before they are annihilated I would like the cabinet to know that Arab Affairs delivered after all.'

'All this will annoy the prime minister,' Poran said. 'You know he warned you to work through proper channels in future.'

'Enough joking. We have not yet found the second bomb.'

'Any leads?'

'No. But I am, as usual, hopeful.'

It was an hour later that a great shout went up inside the house. Then the major emerged, a wide grin on his face, sweat pouring down his neck.

'We fixed the little bastard. My men are just checking her over, but she's safe.'

He exchanged a bear hug with Ben Tov.

Chapter 34

The blazing row in the cabinet next morning was about the second bomb.

'We must stop our people moving back to Jerusalem. It is the most logical location for the second bomb,' the prime minister said.

The Memuneh had spent time with the minister of defence: both had concluded that there was no second bomb.

'The situation along the coast is desperate,' the minister said. 'Services have broken down, even with the help of the army. There is a major public health hazard. Also, there are reports of riots in the Tel Aviv area – looting and shouts against the government.'

'And you conclude that we should tell people to go home to Jerusalem?'

'I regard the risk as small. I do not believe in this second bomb of theirs.'

'And what if we send them back and there is a second bomb and it is, as I fear, in Jerusalem, and it goes off? What about shouts against the government then?'

'The Memuneh's intelligence appreciation is that it will not happen. I agree with that view.'

Two other ministers nodded.

'The world is littered with corpses created by faulty intelligence appreciations. Whoever recommended that man to run the Mossad has a lot to answer for.'

'I put it to cabinet: Jerusalem should be reoccupied.'

'So you're saying that we place the survival of the capital's population in the safe hands of the French, who say there's no second bomb missing, and these fanatics who say there is?' The prime minister snorted in a way that he had when driven beyond exasperation. 'I tell you, Eli, you are a fool. What is more, an irresponsible fool.'

The ensuing shouting match ended in a victory for the prime minister. A statement was broadcast that there were fears of a second bomb, possibly in Jerusalem, and that the population was advised to remain where they were until the army had found it, as they surely would, for had they not found the first one?

The cabinet took note of the fact that the thousands of people who had fled eastwards to the Jordanian frontier were being allowed to trickle over the Jordan river crossings at the Abdullah and Damya bridges, thanks to British intervention with the King. It was still considered unsafe for the US fleet to take off US nationals.

At the United Nations in New York a specially convened late-night meeting of the Security Council had passed a resolution condemning terrorism in general and the Chatila action in particular, and calling upon states in the region to lend all aid.

'*Most* helpful,' the Israeli prime minister said sourly.

At midday Chatila issued a statement:

The further atomic device on Israeli soil will be detonated at 19.00 hours. It is not timed. It will be detonated by heroic defenders of the Palestinian cause who yearn for eternal life in heaven and will achieve it today. Chatila will not communicate again unless and until the known conditions are fulfilled by the Zionists. They should be warned that leaving compliance to the last minute would be foolish and criminal, since instructions to Chatila forces now in Palestine may not reach them in time.

The message had been handed to reception at the Athens radio offices and was broadcast within fifteen minutes of reaching the news desk.

At 13.20 hours there was a call for Essat at the Mossad office.

'I spoke to you yesterday. You recognize who I am?'

'Yes.'

324

'There appears to be a problem.' The voice was calm, unhurried.

'What problem? What news from Rasmia?'

'Communication has been broken off. A call was expected. It is several hours overdue.'

'What conclusion do you draw?'

'We conclude that she has been prevented from making contact. It is possible.'

'Are you saying you have nothing, no clue, on the location of the other bomb?'

'I am saying that.' There was a pause. 'I am sorry. The situation is very grave.' There was still no emotion in the voice.

'I agree. You will call if anything changes?'

'I will.'

'Ask for Ben Tov's office. You can leave the message with whoever is here. I may be absent.'

'Very well.'

The caller rang off.

'Where is my bible?'

Baum looked up suddenly from the transcript of the first Chatila ultimatum. He had taken it home with him, had read it maybe a dozen times, had puzzled over the way the text shifted gear suddenly at the end to embark on a brief foray into biblical language.

All right, Professor Hanif was a scholar who knew his bible and was steeped in the history of Palestine. But was an atomic ultimatum the place to parade such knowledge? Maybe he reckoned that the way to move the Israelis to action was to thrust their own history and folk legends before them. But what history? 'The battle of the great day of God Almighty . . .' The words had a distinctly familiar ring. Baum was sure they were taken straight from the bible. Had he not pored over the texts, learned great slabs by heart in his two abortive years of study for the priesthood? Surely he could recall the context now.

'I'll get it,' his wife said.

She opened the glass-fronted bookcase and peered along the rows of books in their tooled bindings – books kept as valued objects but never read nowadays. On a high shelf she found the bible and lifted it down.

'It's a long time since you read that,' she said.

'I know, I know. Perhaps I'll be forgiven; I shall have to plead lack of opportunity.'

He started leafing through the pages, ignorant of where to look, getting the feel of the thing, waiting for inspiration. His wife returned to her knitting, looking up from time to time as he muttered to himself, shaking his head.

'Perhaps I can help. I, too, was raised on the bible.'

'Perhaps you can. It says here: "The battle of the great day of God Almighty when there fell upon men a great hail out of heaven." Assuming that comes from the bible, which I believe it does, where in heaven's name is it?'

'The Book of Revelation,' his wife said without looking up from her knitting.

'Are you sure?'

'Not sure, but it sounds to me like Revelation. I remember what a lot of bloodthirsty threats there were and how I thought God could not be that hard on us.'

Baum found Revelation and there was silence for five minutes as he read.

'Ha! Listen. This is chapter 16.' He strained to read the small print and his voice had an edge of excitement. ' " . . . For they are the spirits of devils, working miracles, which go forth unto the kings of the earth and of the whole world, to gather them to the battle of that great day of God Almighty." ' He looked up. 'There you are – the great day of God Almighty.' He returned to the text. ' "Behold I come as a thief. Blessed is he that watcheth and keepeth his garments, lest he walk naked and they see his shame. And he gathered them together into a place called in the Hebrew Armageddon. . . . And there were voices and thunder and lightnings: and there was a great earthquake such as was not since men were upon the earth, so mighty an earthquake and so great . . . And every island fled away and the mountains were not found. And there fell upon men a great hail out of heaven . . . " '

He looked up, snapping the book shut. 'This maniac knows the text. He hasn't been able to resist the symbolism,

326

the irony, the awful historical logic of the thing. Here he found an actual prophecy of what? An atomic explosion! Don't you see? Armageddon!'

'But Alfred, I don't know what you are talking about.'

'Quite right, my dear, nor you do. But your help has been invaluable. Absolutely invaluable, since I now believe I actually know what has to be done.' He smiled broadly, levered his bulk out of the easy chair and crossed to where his wife was sitting. Bending carefully, he planted a noisy kiss on her forehead. She laughed and pushed him gently away.

'I didn't know I was that clever.'

'I have never doubted it. And now I'm afraid I must go out to phone. I shall not be long.'

Installed in the phone box, he waited for the call to connect. The time was just before 13.40 hours.

'Yes?'

Ben Tov's voice sounded weary, exhausted.

'Any luck?'

'No. It seems the girl can no longer communicate.'

He described briefly the latest phone call.

'I believe I know where the second bomb might be. Listen carefully and on this occasion try not to interrupt.'

He took Ben Tov slowly through his reasoning. Then he read to him from chapter 16 of Revelation. After which he paused.

'So? We all know about Armageddon.' Ben Tov did not sound impressed.

'And presumably you as an Israeli also know that the ancient Hebrew name Armageddon is generally accepted as referring to Tel Megiddo.' There was silence as Baum paused again. 'I would not wish to send your men on a wild-goose chase at a moment like this, but I believe a most careful search of Megiddo and the Jezreel valley could be rewarding. My instinct tells me this, my dear friend, and I hope that this time I am being more helpful to you than in the recent past.'

At last Ben Tov spoke. 'The psychology,' he said. 'I believe the psychology is right. This highly intelligent man who is also a deeply arrogant man couldn't resist this small display

327

of knowledge.' He laughed briefly. 'This gratuitous act of rubbing our noses in our own culture. It adds up, my dear Baum.' He was laughing again, as if great tension had been relieved. 'If you are right, I make a vow.'

'What is it?'

'I will definitely give up smoking!' And he slammed the receiver down in a sudden access of aggressive joy.

Anyone close enough to the portly middle-aged man walking slowly back through the streets of Versailles could be forgiven for taking him for a lonely eccentric with nowhere to go. For Baum had reduced his speed to something less than a saunter and he was talking to himself.

'I don't like it. It smells wrong. Why has all her information come so late? Why does she know the location of one bomb but not of the other? Why do I, a mere outsider, know about Megiddo while she apparently doesn't? Or maybe what I think I know is wrong. Or again, maybe Kovacs and his friends have at last broken our rule never to lie to each other on these occasions and are using the myth of the KGB girl to feed me what they want me to believe – which has nothing to do with the truth.' He sighed and stopped walking for a moment. The day was close and humid. He loosened his shirt collar, took out a handkerchief and dabbed at his face. Then the slow shuffle forward again. 'One thing only has been consistent throughout this affair: I have been consistently wrong, consistently outmanoeuvred by the other side. Why, then, should I suddenly be right? My turn for a little success? Come now, God does not hand out his favours evenly like a teacher in the nursery class.' He stopped again, shook his head. 'Clearly, there was a risk that her associates would realize what she was and maybe catch her as she made contact. It is the logical thing – the likely thing.' He had reached home. He searched absently through a pocket for the keys. Perhaps he should call Kovacs and put his cards on the table. They would not make an impressive showing. Anyway, Kovacs was a messenger, nothing more. No good could come of it. Also, it would show weakness – not wise when dealing with these people.

Maybe these doubts were the paranoia to which security people were so susceptible. After all, the girl had led them to the Jerusalem bomb. Without her, would they have found it? Doubtful. Yet now he was condemning her because she hadn't delivered the other one. Maybe she was dead. Here was this courageous young woman risking her life while he, Alfred Baum, safe in Versailles, cast doubt on her. Security work did not foster generosity of spirit. Only deep, unrelenting suspicion. It was the kind of useless speculation one got up to on a hot and airless Sunday afternoon.

'You will set out at once for Megiddo,' Ben Tov told Essat. 'I will follow you as soon as I have spoken to the military and got some forces into the area to help. First I'll see that the engineers are on hand.'

He picked up the phone, signalling Essat to listen on the extension. But when the colonel answered he had his own story to tell.

'These atomic warheads of yours, there's something odd going on.'

'Explain, please.'

'We've taken a closer look at the bomb from Me'a She'arim. It had been tampered with, you know.'

'How could I know?'

'Someone who knew what he was doing had already rendered it safe.'

'You don't say.'

'I do. The electrical circuit had been broken. It couldn't be seen until we took the thing apart. We were using it as a learning device in case we had to defuse the second bomb. It was a dud.'

'Could that have been an accident, a fault?'

'Absolutely not. It had been sabotaged. I thought you ought to know.'

'Now let's talk sensibly,' Ben Tov said. He told the colonel what was needed at Megiddo. 'And fast, please. It is very likely that the second bomb is there somewhere. With a lot of luck my man may find something by the time your engineers reach the spot.'

'No problem,' the colonel said, and rang off.

'You heard what he said.' Ben Tov looked at Essat.

'I heard.'

329

'You will draw no conclusion as to the second bomb.'

'Very well.'

'Now go. It's nearly two; it should take you an hour and a half if you keep moving. That leaves you very little time before we blow up the West Wall and start delivering Arabs.'

'The roads are empty.'

'They need to be.' He came round the desk, seized Essat by both shoulders. 'You are as a son to me and now I speak to you as a father. Your life is not important here. Nor is mine. You will take whatever risks are necessary, but remember that the survival of our country is tied up with what you are able to achieve. So don't die stupidly in a car crash before you reach Megiddo. Also, no heroics, please. Now go, and God bless you. I will be with you as soon as possible.'

When Essat had left, taking the stairs two at a time and dashing for the car park, Ben Tov busied himself with calls to the Ministry of Defence, demanding that troops be transferred to the plain of Megiddo from the bases at Haifa and Beit She'an. Then he sat for a moment in thought. Could any conclusions about the state of the second bomb be drawn from the odd condition of the first? He grunted. The exercise was fruitless. Maybe yes, maybe no. On the one hand, on the other hand . . . 'I sound like a Talmud scholar when I ought to be on the Jenin road doing ninety.' He took his revolver from his desk, checked it, and like Essat took the stairs two at a time and ran out of the almost empty building. He had resisted the impulse to call Poran at the prime minister's office to tell him they thought the bomb was at Megiddo. They might believe him, delay the measures that had to be taken around 17.00 hours, and what if there were no bomb at Megiddo, and . . . ?

He put the thought out of his mind as he got into his car. 'One of these days I will shoot my mouth off once too often. It had better not be this time.'

Chapter 35

Tel Megiddo stands at the western edge of the Jezreel valley. Over a span of 6,000 years a series of fortified cities – twenty in all – have looked down on invading armies in the plain below and have sent out armies to meet them. For the city commands a key defile into the north of the country, sitting astride the great trunk route from Egypt to Mesopotamia. Here the great battles of antiquity were fought. Joshua defeated the king of Megiddo outside the walls of the city and Barak defeated Sisera. Excavations have revealed King Solomon's stables and King Ahab's chariot sheds. Judean Kings Ahaziah and Josiah were killed here. At Megiddo, says the New Testament, the final battle of all will take place. Armageddon! Today the ancient ruins offer hints of past greatness. King Solomon's city is a maze of crumbled walls and pavements. Watering troughs and tethering posts for the chariot horses stand where they have stood since Ahab ordered them placed there. The debris covers a mound of thirteen acres, a monument to the impermanence of regal might.

Har Megiddo. Armageddon! The battle of the great day of God Almighty . . .

It was 16.00 hours when Essat turned off the Jenin-Haifa highway on to the road leading out of the valley and up towards Megiddo. He knew the area. A few kilometres to the north the Arab village of Lajjun lay off the highway on the same side. At Megiddo itself the mound lay within the perimeter of a kibbutz. It seemed to him inconceivable that

Chatila could have found some kind of refuge within the kibbutz itself. When the first troops arrived he would get them to deploy in the surrounding countryside to search out a farm or house where Rasmia and her associates could have gone to ground. If they had somehow smuggled the bomb up on to the mound, among the remains of the ancient cities, they must surely have had a base from which to do so.

The main gate of the kibbutz was open and unattended. Within there was silence. The inhabitants had fled. The living quarters, workshops and public spaces echoed back at him when he called out. He raised his eyes to the ruins on their steep hilltop. There was no one to be seen. The sun beat down, throwing short shadows. Somewhere a dog was barking, abandoned by its owner. A search of the ruins seemed pointless. Better try to find their base. But maybe there was no base. He glanced at his watch. It was 16.40 The sound of truck engines reached him from the highway. The military were arriving.

The captain in command of the leading unit was intelligent, energetic.

'I want every building within, say, five kilometres to be searched. We are looking for a small armed group. Among them will be a girl. She is not to be harmed. It means taking them alive and only shooting when your men have no choice.'

The captain nodded. He had a map of the area. With it spread out before him, he prodded it with a finger.

'There are several buildings between here and the highway and what look like farm buildings on the other side, towards Hayogev. The Arab village is well outside your five-kilometre radius. Shall we cover it?'

'The nearer stuff is more important.'

'I have twenty men and two vehicles. I'll allocate targets.'

'Give me a couple of your men and I'll take the buildings on this side of the highway myself,' Essat said.

'Do we search the kibbutz and the mound?'

'Later, if we fail to find anything in the surrounding countryside.'

'Why do you do this?' Rasmia asked the young man. They sat on upturned crates opposite each other, the remains of a meal before them. 'After all, you are a Jew and we are fighting for the Palestinian cause.'

'The state of Israel is a defilement of the Jewish faith,' he said. 'Today we live in a condition of disgust between the holocaust in Europe and the coming of the Messiah. One of our rabbis has said: "Better that Israel cease; better that Israel perish than do evil." And I tell you, she does evil. Perhaps God has decided that she should perish.'

As he spoke she noticed that he wrung his hands. His death-pale face was contorted into a grin of anger and in his excitement he allowed little spurts of saliva to come from his mouth and fall on the floor before him.

'Then why did you come to Israel?'

'I am from Poland, the son of a survivor. Many of our people are from New York. Why are we here? We are here to teach the people the error of their ways and to bring them back to the way of the bible and the Torah. The holocaust was divine retribution for the sin of Zionism. The Torah says: "They have committed all the abominations and they want to inherit the land." In Deuteronomy you will read that the Ammonites and Moabites were not accepted into the community because they tried to entice the Jews to sin. I tell you, the effect of sin is so profound on the sinner that it continues even beyond the tenth generation. Thus, causing sin is far worse than he who kills. The holy writings tell us this.'

'It seems a harsh religion.'

'It is a harsh religion.' His eyes were blazing now, as if in sheer delight. 'Read the psalms. Read how Yahveh kicked in the heads of his enemies, how he split open their skulls and roared down in anger. "The tongues of your dogs lapped your enemies' blood." You can read it. And why is God angry with us? The Torah teaches that one must not rebel against nations, and the Jews have ignored the sacred teaching of the Torah and have rebelled. It teaches that the chosen people shall not be gathered in to the land of Israel until the Messiah comes. Has the Messiah come?' He paused, intoxicated. 'He has not. Every night we lay out our best clothes to be ready for his coming. And he has not yet come. And the Zionists are turning Jews into atheists and gathering

333

them in when we are told that only after the Messiah can they be gathered in.'

'So?'

'So this abomination must be purged. We are the instruments of the Lord and our duty is to visit a punishment on the state and those who support it. Isaiah said: "In time to come I will become as a torch to the nations of the world." On the 9th of Av, our day of mourning for the destruction of the temple, we pray: "Thou O Lord, didst consume her with fire, and with fire Thou will in future restore her." '

He had risen to his feet and was pacing back and forth in the bare storeroom, his feet crunching on the straw which covered the earth floor. 'We shall consume her with fire.' He was shouting at Rasmia now, transported to fury or ecstasy – she could not tell which – by his own rhetoric, the disjointed snatches of intoxicating language from the old texts. 'It is why we accept, why we welcome what you are doing against this satanic kingdom, controlled by Samael, prince of darkness. You want proof? It is simple. Was not the ancient Jewish kingdom of Bar Kochbar meticulously observant and righteous? It was. We know this from history. But it was nevertheless destroyed. Why was it destroyed? Because it had sinned. What was its sin? It attempted to hasten the redemption when the Messiah had not come. And it is happening again today.'

He stopped, triumph on his face, as if there could be no refuting his arguments.

'And you,' Rasmia said, 'you are prepared to sacrifice yourself, to be killed in an atomic explosion?'

'If that is God's will, yes.'

'Everything is God's will?'

'Of course.'

'Including the demands we are making?'

'What do I know of demands? All this is politics between nations. I have explained that the Torah forbids the Jews to stand against nations. The sole task of the Jews is to prepare for the coming of the Messiah. Without Him there is no virtue and no salvation. Without Him there is no role in the scheme of things for the Jews. Deny the Messiah and you have Auschwitz, you have atomic destruction. It is written.'

334

The sound of footsteps reached them from outside. The silhouette of a man appeared in the doorway. He was carrying a Kalashnikov.

'I don't like the activity down on the road. I heard diesels. Could be military.'

'There's nothing to lead them here,' Rasmia said. 'Don't get jumpy. Just keep a watch.'

'Perhaps we should move further from the highway.'

'We stay here.'

'If we're to detonate why not get on with it? I hate the waiting about.'

'You are under orders. Get outside and behave yourself. You were chosen, so show yourself worthy.'

The youth shrugged and his dark shadow left the narrow doorway. Outside, he concealed himself once more in a lean-to. Through the high window he had a clear view of the road a few hundred metres below in the valley. A car crossed his line of vision, travelling fast towards Haifa. A moment later a military truck came up from the south and stopped by the roadside. A soldier got out and made off in the direction of a farm further down the valley. He was joined by another man. The watcher by now was alarmed, torn between the instinct to follow orders and the desire to go back and report what he'd seen. He decided to stay where he was. He was barely seventeen and this was his first taste of action. He was honoured and he was also terrified. It was not death that frightened him, since he had volunteered to die and would surely not survive the action. But he had been told terrible things about what the Israelis did to their prisoners. Death was one thing; agonizing pain another.

A dog barked in the distance, up towards Megiddo. Without fear or favour, it was the dog that had barked for Essat and was barking again now for sufficient reasons of its own.

The youth strained to see what was happening on the road below. The truck had moved on. In the distance, across the valley towards Hayogev, he thought he could see movement. He wasn't sure. Then he distinctly heard new sounds from behind, up the hill. On that side there was no lookout. They had sent the others back to find their way across into

Lebanon if they could. It was Rasmia and this youth who had been chosen to die for Islam. Only the two of them and the crazy Jews in their fancy dress who weren't armed and didn't seem interested in the success of the mission. He wondered what motivated them. Surely Jews didn't conspire with Arabs against other Jews? He didn't understand, didn't bother his head about it.

He was frightened. He felt his bowels were not under control. Really, he would like to check on those noises higher up. He went back to the room.

'There are suspicious sounds coming from behind. I'll go to check.'

'Don't go far and don't be long,' Rasmia said. She had been tuning a short-wave radio, an army field set. She did not bother to look round at the youth as he withdrew from the doorway and turned westwards up the hill, into the sun. Soon he had disappeared into the surrounding trees and scrub.

Essat first saw the house from the roadway below. It was partly concealed by trees and he hadn't noticed it before.

One of the soldiers was still with him; the other had set out for a broken-down barn further along the road. 'I'll check that house among the trees,' Essat said. 'You catch your mate up and bring him back to the house when you've checked that the barn is clean.'

The man set out and Essat started to climb towards the house, moving carefully among the scrub to keep out of sight of the windows. It was when he was some twenty metres away that he heard the static from Rasmia's radio. He advanced, crawling on hands and knees behind a low wall. The sounds from the radio grew louder but he could distinguish nothing. It sounded as if someone was station hopping.

Between the end of the wall and the side door of the house was a distance of about five metres. He could take it at a run and hope the door was unlocked. That, or wait for his men to catch up with him. He decided that time was what mattered. He drew his revolver, released the safety catch, and gripping it in his right hand, dashed for the door.

As he thrust open the door he saw Rasmia. She was sitting

across the room, the radio on the ground before her. Next to her the Jewish youth sat with his elbows on his knees, his head thrust forward as if in meditation. As Rasmia looked up an expression of blank astonishment appeared on her face. For a brief second Essat thought he read furious anger there too. Then, as if a new thought had come to her, she switched off the power of the radio, rose to her feet and took the three steps to reach him.

Flinging her arms round him she buried her head on his shoulder, gasping at the relief of tension, clinging to him.

'I'm sorry. I don't usually give way like this. I should know better.'

With his free hand Essat stroked her hair. 'In your place I'd do it too.' It sounded as though she was sobbing.

'We thought they'd got you,' Essat said. 'We were waiting for a message but nothing happened.'

Rasmia seemed confused, hesitant. 'I couldn't reach my contact. I think the Chatila boys got suspicious. I wanted to let you know we were here but I was afraid.'

She glanced towards her companion, who was standing, a look of bewilderment on his face.

'Two of my men will be coming up the hill,' Essat told him. 'You will go out to meet them.' He turned to Rasmia: 'Will he behave himself?'

'Do as you're told,' she said to the young man.

'But – '

'But nothing. You will obey my orders.'

The youth shrugged and made off through the open door.

'You did a marvellous job for us on the Jerusalem bomb.'

Rasmia said nothing. Then: 'You know my – role?'

'Yes. I never guessed, of course. When we were advised to let you in I couldn't believe it.' He shook his head. 'Brilliant.'

She smiled as they stood looking at each other. Essat had put his revolver back in its holster.

'So the bomb is here? For Armageddon, eh?'

She nodded.

'Where is it?'

She did not answer.

'But you must know where it is.'

Still she said nothing. Slowly her expression, which had

seemed both afraid and puzzled, had been changing. Now the hardness that he knew so well had come back into her eyes. It was as if a mask had descended, hiding the girl behind the political automaton. Essat stood mesmerized, unable for a moment to act, as she pulled her gun free of her belt and brought it up. It was pointing at his heart.

'Put your hands up.'

Essat gaped at her and did not move.

'*Fast!*' She spat the word at him, prodding the air with her gun. 'Up, up! That's better.'

She stepped forward, circled behind him and extracted his gun from the holster. The thing was done expertly, with confidence. Then she returned to face him.

'I don't understand,' Essat said. It sounded weak, absurd.

'None of you understood. You, the Zionists, all of you have been stupid. Your arrogance prevents you recognizing the intelligence of your enemies. But all that is about to be wiped out anyway.'

'But you were working for the KGB.'

'I was working for my people, for the liberation cause and for no one and nothing else.'

'So the KGB thing – a fake?'

She smiled in the humourless way he had known back in Damascus.

'What is the word you use? A double agent. I was a double agent. It got me into Israel. It worked.'

'And Hanif, he knew?'

She shook her head. 'He is a man who has contempt for women. He would not have sanctioned something requiring so much nerve. Like you, he is a prisoner of his prejudices.'

'And the Russians?'

'Oh, they are as terrified of an atomic explosion as the rest of you. They support us but they like to lay down the rules. A little armed action here and there, why not? Public support for the Palestinian cause, certainly. But real action – the bomb – no, no. That would spoil their image, destroy the basis of big-power supremacy, the famous balance of terror. After all, without crime the police would have no jobs. Without oppressed minorities the great ideologists would have no insults to hurl at each other.'

338

'That's rubbish.'

'It is realism. The only ones with a true interest in an atomic explosion are the dispossessed since they have nothing to lose.'

'You cannot possibly get away from here. Even if you shoot me, my men will get you when you go outside.'

'I am not interested in getting away. My life has no importance. Only the cause is important. My only objective is to ensure that the bomb goes off, here in Megiddo – Armageddon. The greatest act of poetic justice in history.'

'So the bomb is up there on Megiddo?'

'I would not be so foolish as to give you hints, my poor Essat.'

As she spoke she reached with her left hand for what appeared to be a TV programme changer, save that a solitary red button was set in the centre of the black plastic casing.

'It was to be detonated from here if our conditions were not met.'

'And now?'

'Now, since you have found me, it will be detonated anyway.'

He tried again.

'So it's up in the ruins?'

'With such a device it makes no difference – here or a mile or so away, down in the plain. Either way it will destroy both of us. It will destroy the Zionist state.'

He stared at her. 'I think you must be mad.'

'If I am mad it is the injustices I see around me that have made me so.'

'Any minute now my men will come back.'

'I shall shoot whoever comes through the door.'

'You can't shoot them all. They'll capture you and make you talk. They do terrible things to make people talk. No one can resist these things. Perhaps I should tell you what they do.'

'I am not afraid of pain.' She was holding the device in such a way that a slender index finger rested delicately on the red button. 'You will realize that I am in control of the situation, for I have two advantages. I can and will detonate the bomb. And I am not afraid to die. Physically and psychologically I am beyond your reach.'

Essat cast around desperately for some opening which would offer a chance – he did not know what chance.

'The Jerusalem bomb had a broken circuit. Someone had cut wires – a deliberate act.'

For a moment a look of surprise came into her eyes. 'I don't believe it.'

'It's true.'

'You are telling me lies. That bomb was intended to go off if necessary. I led you to it without consultation with the professor. His plan was simple: two bombs would ensure that one at least would remain undiscovered. It was insurance. The plan was good but not good enough. The Jerusalem bomb had a timer. It gave you thirty-six hours to carry out the terms of the ultimatum. If, by hour thirty-five, you had obeyed his instructions that far he would have signalled you the location of the bomb and your engineers could have defused it. But we would still have the second bomb to ensure that the rest of the instructions about the West Bank and Israeli atomic weapons were obeyed. If not, the second bomb would be exploded. By then, of course, the first bomb would have convinced you that we meant business. It would have ensured the success of the rest of our programme. But I took a different view. The professor's scheme to get me into Israel on a false passport was naïf. The risk was too high. Also, we were lucky to get our first team ashore. We never expected it. We had two more teams ready to try. As for your airport security, I feared they had good pictures of me. The professor thought not. I was not prepared to risk the entire venture on that sort of hunch. And so I used my Soviet contacts. I reckoned they would tell you to let me through.'

'You were already working for them?'

She nodded. 'The professor has a fine intelligence, but it is too narrow. He sees the cause narrowly: Islam versus the Zionists. I have a broader view. I believed the Russians could be used. They are not stupid, but on the other hand they are no cleverer than a merchant's daughter from Tabriz. I first contacted them two years ago.'

340

'But you didn't have to lead us to the Jerusalem bomb before we had carried out all the terms of the ultimatum.'

'I did. I reckoned you would be tailing me. I had to get you off my tail, to persuade you that I really was working for the Russians. I had to be sure beyond a doubt that whatever happened in Jerusalem, *Armageddon would take place.*' She shrugged. 'I traded Jerusalem for this.' She waved her gun briefly. 'It is a better scenario. It is symbolic. And the fallout will make Jerusalem uninhabitable anyway. The Jews will have to leave their so-called capital city.'

'The fall of the Third Temple,' Essat said.

'The liberation of the oppressed.'

'You are mad,' Essat said. 'Quite mad. You have a just cause and you desecrate it with callous inhumanity.'

As he spoke the sound of footsteps on the gravel reached them.

'Tell them not to come in,' Rasmia snapped. 'It will save their lives.'

But as she spoke the door was pushed open by one of the soldiers.

The roar of Rasmia's gun was deafening in the small room. The shot was perfectly aimed, reached the man in the forehead almost exactly between the eyes. The impact of the bullet threw him back on his heels and he crashed against the doorpost before his legs gave way and his heavy frame heeled over, his head hitting the stone floor with a dull crack.

As Rasmia fired, Essat had leapt from his chair, lunging straight for the hand holding the gun. Before she had had a chance to turn it and aim at him he was grasping her wrist. And as he did so he saw distinctly, with shattering precision, the long finger press down hard on the button, the front of the device pointing in the direction of the doorway, the direction of Tel Megiddo.

It took Essat no time to wrest the gun from Rasmia's grasp. As he did so, the thought flashed through his mind: Why am I still alive? Why no explosion, no oblivion?

He wrestled Rasmia to the ground then pinned her there, her eyes blazing, her body coiled like a spring but unable to move under his weight. Men crowded into the room, seized her, pulled her upright and snapped handcuffs on to her wrists.

'There was no explosion!' Essat shouted. 'Where is your Armageddon? Or is there a time fuse?'

'We have been betrayed. There is no time fuse.' And her face crumpled suddenly and she choked as tears welled up in her eyes.

'Take her down to the road. Then get the metal detectors up to the ruins. You'll find the bomb there somewhere.'

One of the men prodded Rasmia with his gun. 'March!'

She turned towards the door without looking at Essat again, the soldier behind her. Outside, blinded for a moment by the sun which was sinking in orange glory behind Tel Megiddo, she stopped for a moment.

The chatter of automatic fire from the Kalashnikov was followed almost at once by the *splat splat* of bullets embedding themselves in the masonry close to the door. The thing was over in less than three seconds. Rasmia stood perfectly still for a moment after the burst of firing had ended, as if waiting for more shots. Then she slowly sank to her knees as the soldier next to her staggered sideways, clutching his shoulder. Rasmia's face was expressionless, her liquid brown eyes wide open as if in surprise as she died.

Essat seized the soldier's automatic and fired in the general direction from which the shots had come. But the thing was a mere gesture: the Chatila gunman was nowhere to be seen.

Other men were coming up from the road, among them Ben Tov. 'Deploy a few men,' Essat shouted. 'We'll soon pick him up.' Then, to himself: 'Perhaps he thought what we thought and decided to silence her. A big mistake among many mistakes.' He turned to Ben Tov. Then he went back into the house. 'It looks as if this one's going to be a dud, too. I don't understand it.' And then he told him about Rasmia.

In the place on Tel Megiddo called Ahab's chariot city the metal detectors found the second Pluton. It had been placed in a watering trough hewn out of solid limestone a thousand years before the birth of Christ. Where the chariot horses

342

had been watered the sleek metal cylinder lay now, covered with rubble.

An hour later the engineers announced it safe. It had been tampered with in precisely the same way as the Jerusalem bomb.

At 20.00 hours the radio announced that a second bomb had been found on Tel Megiddo and the army had defused it successfully. Terrorists had been killed, the bulletin said. The threat of destruction was over.

The government gave orders to remove the explosives from beneath the West Wall, where crowds were praying.

Shortly after the radio announcement, a call was received at the Ministry of Foreign Affairs. It was taken by the deputy minister.

'Cassagne here. I am calling from Paris to congratulate you on your news. I just heard it on our radio. Magnificent!'

'Thank you, minister. It is kind of you to call.'

'So you have found a second bomb?'

'That is so.'

'You will appreciate, this is a delicate matter for the relations between our countries.'

'I understand that. Particularly as we also understood you had lost only one bomb.'

'Before calling you I spoke briefly to the president. He is particularly anxious that relations should not be damaged by – what shall I say – a wave of popular feeling against France.' There was a silence. 'In view of the claim that the atomic devices are of French origin.' A longer silence. Jerusalem was in no mood to come to the aid of Paris. 'As you know, we deny such claims categorically. Nevertheless, we understand the position your government would find itself in when asked to identify the devices.'

'And, if I may say so minister, the position you too would find yourself in.'

'Quite.'

'Quite.'

'The president, by the way, has been informed of your interest in a licensing deal for certain Dassault Breguet planes. This is an opportunity, he feels, to let you know that the government would take a positive view of such a development.'

'It is very good of the president.'

'Also, we would like to meet with you soon to discuss other possible forms of collaboration in the economic field. We have some ideas.'

'We would welcome it.' Jerusalem did not sound as if it were in a mood to welcome anything from Paris.

The voice from Paris faltered. It was unlike the French foreign minister, but this was a peculiarly difficult conversation.

'Such collaboration, of course, could be impeded – badly impeded – by public opinion in both our countries if it were officially claimed in Jerusalem that the devices were indeed French.'

'Possibly.'

'Could I perhaps have your assurance on this notable day that this will be avoided by your government?'

'I will put it to my colleagues. Meanwhile, I think I can promise you that nothing will be said publicly until your views have been considered.'

And the conversation came to a close.

Later that evening an army photographer was sent to take pictures of the bomb as it lay among the ruins of Megiddo. A selection of pictures was released to the world press after the negatives of those which could identify the device as a French Pluton had been removed and placed in a safe at Foreign Affairs. 'You never know,' the minister said. 'Policy is something which can always change.'

Chapter 36

'I had your assurance,' the head of the DGSE said, 'that these Chatila people were not bunglers.'

'It was not bungling,' Savary said.

'What then?'

'Luck plays a part in these matters.'

'I am not impressed by the argument.'

Savary was in the director's office, seated erect in a chair as if he would have preferred to stand at attention.

'These complex schemes,' the director said. 'I do not like them. Simplicity is what the work requires: ever more simplicity.'

Savary resisted the temptation to say that the scheme had received the approval of the director when it had first been put to him. Suddenly, it struck him that he had never been asked for progress reports. The director had been keeping his nose as clean as his initial approval permitted. And now – disengagement.

'There was never any risk of explosions,' Savary said.

'So you promised.'

'I had two of my men aboard the vessel which took the weapons to Israel. They were technicians. They rendered the weapons safe. It was all what one might call a blackmailing bluff.'

'So you promised.'

'If it had succeeded, Israel would have made political and territorial concessions which she would have been unable to go back on later.'

345

'I know, I know. Very neat and clever. Only the plan failed.'

'We had no way of knowing that Chatila had an Israeli agent in its leadership.'

'It also seems to me that they had a friend here.'

'At the DST,' Savary said.

The director grunted.

'This harebrained scheme of yours will reflect discredit on the department. The minister will have something to say about it.' Savary remained silent. 'Who might talk to the press?'

'No one knows anything.'

'Was there not some kind of intermediary between you and this Chatila group – a cut-out?'

'Certainly.'

'So?'

Savary's face was expressionless.

'The witness,' he said, clipping his words as if he were reporting the outcome of a patrol behind enemy lines, 'has been eliminated.' He paused, seeking a detail that would add credibility to the assertion. 'Yesterday evening it appears that a gunman of some kind entered his apartment in the Rue Spontini and shot him through the head. The police are investigating.' He allowed a moment to elapse and decided to venture a shade further towards the facts of the case. 'I do not believe, *monsieur le directeur*, that they are likely to trace the assassin.'

General Badran, head of the General Intelligence Directorate in Damascus, having seen his minister and received clear instructions, was in conference with the head of his special operations unit.

'This man Hanif,' the general said. 'We know all about him.'

The head of special operations, who was a colonel, nodded.

'A dangerous man.'

'Dedicated, general.'

'Dedication without discretion. Dangerous. It is something we must now deal with.'

346

'Definitively?'

'Definitively. Both the Russians and the Americans . . . pressure, you understand.' He waved a hand. 'My instructions from higher up are clear. It is to be done promptly, cleanly and without publicity. Also, you had better run in his immediate followers. We want no nonsense from them. No shoot-out, you understand? And nothing – embarrassing left behind. Is that clear?'

'Yes, general.'

'Personally,' General Badran said, 'I regard Hanif as an outstanding realist, but realism is not in vogue. The politicians . . .' He spread his hands in a gesture of disenchantment. Then he directed a wave of dismissal at the colonel.

'Get on with it,' he said.

The congratulations of the Memuneh seemed to Ben Tov to have been extruded from somewhere inside him like a highly viscous fluid. As he talked, the Memuneh looked hard at his blotter. The procedure was causing him discomfort. But he appeared to cheer up when he came to the message from the minister of defence.

'The minister has heard somewhere that this woman who was killed in Megiddo was your Rasmia Burnawi. Is this so?'

'Oh, yes,' Ben Tov said, smiling.

'How did she get into the country?'

'I have no idea.'

'Did she lead you to the bomb?'

'Yes.'

'Please explain.'

'There was a phone call about the Jerusalem bomb and another about the bomb in Megiddo. Two calls, since there were after all two bombs.'

'It would be damaging to the department,' the Memuneh said, 'if it were to be known more widely that we had to rely on such a tainted source.'

'If you say so.'

'I do. I order that nothing shall be said.'

'No problem,' Ben Tov said. 'Any rumour that an Arab

347

terrorist who was also a KGB agent was deliberately let into the country is deniable.' He paused and bestowed another wintry smile on the Memuneh. 'Plausibly,' he added, and took his departure.